Helen Choate Pratt Prince

A Transatlantic Chatelaine

A novel

Helen Choate Pratt Prince

A Transatlantic Chatelaine
A novel

ISBN/EAN: 9783337000325

Printed in Europe, USA, Canada, Australia, Japan

Cover: Foto ©Andreas Hilbeck / pixelio.de

More available books at **www.hansebooks.com**

BY

HELEN CHOATE PRINCE

BOSTON AND NEW YORK
HOUGHTON, MIFFLIN AND COMPANY
The Riverside Press, Cambridge
1897

The Riverside Press, Cambridge, Mass., U. S. A.
Electrotyped and Printed by H. O. Houghton and Company.

A TRANSATLANTIC CHATELAINE.

CHAPTER I.

SOME people are so persistently and consistently followed by misfortune that it is difficult for the most tender-hearted to restrain an expression of annoyance at each new blow given to the unlucky one. It is hard to believe that the victim has not himself to thank sometimes for his reverses. To this class of unfortunates belonged Gilbert Edwards. Born in the early twenties of this century, the traditional golden spoon shone in his mouth during his youth. His parents were of a solid, wealthy, Boston family, drawing their ample means from the East India trade. He was an only child, gifted with beauty of person and brilliancy of intellect.

Great things were prophesied of him when he went to Harvard College, and yet he graduated low in his class, outrun by many a tortoise whom he had scorned. His admirers (he had hundreds) darkly hinted at jealousy of his unequaled genius which had influenced his judges;

his friend (he had but one deserving the name, Richard Huntington) bluntly stated that Gilbert was lazy.

He felt himself too much above the common herd to trouble his mind as to which was the correct view, and announced to his admiring and compassionating father and mother, soon after his graduation, that his ambition was to be an artist, and to attain this end he intended studying art in Paris. His decision was reluctantly agreed to, and before he left his home he fell in love with and married a young woman, an orphan, the child of a clergyman who had left her penniless.

The passion felt by Gilbert for his young, beautiful wife was an absorbing one. He took her to France, where they lived an enchanted life. It was in that country that their little girl Sylvia, their only child and our heroine, was born. Her baby eyes opened on a landscape that Corot might have loved, and perhaps saw, as the great artist did, wreaths of shadowy dancers where the others, with world-worn senses, saw but the mist rising from the river.

To the young parents, caring only for each other, the baby was somewhat of an interruption, and they were eased of a burden of responsibility by their country doctor, who brought them as a nurse a French woman, of good

farmer stock, whose mind had been almost un-
hinged by the losses of husband and child following close on each other. She came with a
stolid indifference to nurse the little stranger,
but gradually her apathy departed. At first
she imagined, then she grew to believe, that the
soul of her own baby had entered into the small,
warm body that she held to her breast, and her
solemn, cavernous eyes became bright once more
with the light of devotion.

Mr. and Mrs. Edwards saw her love for Sylvia with a selfish gratitude, and devoted themselves more than ever to each other. Then
from the cloudless blue of their skies fell the
shadow of Death's hand as he beckoned the wife
to follow him, and out of that shadow Gilbert
Edwards never came into the sunshine again.

Sylvia was six at the time of her mother's
death, and felt her loss but lightly. If her faithful Justine had not made the sacrifice of leaving
home and fatherland to follow her darling, it
would have been a far more grievous sorrow to
the child; for Gilbert, crushed and helpless in
his grief, turned his face homewards for comfort, but found none. His mother had died a
short time before his wife's last illness; he expected to find his father in great sorrow, but
was not prepared for his loss of mind, which
blow fell heavy on him.

Added to these misfortunes his friend Huntington met him with the news of yet another. Old Mr. Edwards had been ruined by a dishonest partner, and his fortune reduced from its former generous proportions to a small sum, which Huntington, himself a successful business man, had been able to rescue from the wreck, and invest prudently. He agreed promptly to Gilbert's request that he keep the management of this sum in his own hands.

The town house had been sold, but an old-fashioned country house was still theirs, and here Sylvia was taken on her arrival in the new world. Her grandfather died soon after, and her first recollections were of a brisk, sharp-tongued, sharp-nosed woman, with red corkscrew curls, called Deborah ; of Richard Huntington's regular Saturday to Monday visits, and of a brook that ran through the place.

This impudent, romping little stream was her only playmate ; it was a relief to escape from the hushed house, where papa was always writing, and dabble in its clear waters. There was something remarkable about it, that made it unlike other places, and to Sylvia it was the home of a fairy, a being of many moods, who sometimes laughed as the miniature cascades chased each other over the pebbles, and who sometimes told endless stories in a murmuring

flow of elfin words : and there were rare moments when she jeered and mocked the little
maid, filling her with an elusive terror, only to
be banished by feeling Justine's kind arms about
her.

Presently, after the first acute anguish of his
grief had been somewhat dulled, Gilbert became
interested in renewing his intercourse with the
companions of early days. He flung aside his
brush, for with his wife his inspiration had disappeared, and he took up his clever, facile pen
in its place; before long his articles on con-
temporary art drew notice upon him from the
literary world. Men of note sought him out,
and Huntington saw with satisfaction that his
friend, for whom he cared so truly, might redeem himself yet in the eyes of his townspeople,
who had called his career up to that time by
unflattering names.

But, alas, his hopes were dashed to the ground,
for Gilbert, in a spirit that deserves admiration
rather than blame, threw himself heart and soul
into the abolitionist movement, simply from his
conviction that it was the only course open to
one who felt as he did. In those heated days
there was no middle course, no compromise;
the dividing line was sharply drawn, and Gilbert's action cast him adrift from his old associ-
ates. Sylvia was too young when he first took

this step to understand it; she only knew that no longer men drove out from Boston to talk and smoke in the white parlor with him, — a room fast losing its right to the name as its wainscoted walls became hidden by books. She noticed, too, that her father stayed at home more and seemed more melancholy, yet busier than ever with his pen. He had never called forth her love by any show of tenderness; he was a vain man, believing in his own genius, and convinced that he was the toy of a fate which delighted in frustrating all his efforts. Sylvia was a burden, something to be fed and clothed suitably; as for getting any pleasure from her during the first ten years of her life, that was something which never occurred to him, and she grew up with much more warmth in her heart for " Uncle Dick," as she called Huntington, and Justine than for her father.

About Deborah, her feelings were doubtful; she liked her jams and plum cake, she enjoyed the severe cleanliness of her room, which was sometimes made into a nursery on rainy afternoons, and a button-box, filled with wonders from bygone days, lent as a plaything; on the other hand she indignantly resented the old servant's manner of washing her face, to which she was sometimes obliged to submit during a temporary absence of Justine, nor did it reconcile her to be told that her father had undergone the same indignities in his youth. But worse even than having her nose rubbed inexorably the wrong way and her eyes filled with soapsuds, was being taken every Sunday to the village meeting-house by the brisk and "orthodox" Deborah. There was a double grief involved in this course: first, it was Uncle Dick's one day in the week with them, and he was always so good and kind to her, bringing a fresh, north-wind sort of atmosphere into the silent house; his cheery laugh sounding through the hall, the very noise he made with his heavy boots stamping round, and the unconcerned manner in which he slammed doors, causing the little girl to feel that he was n't so very grown-up after all.

The second grief caused by the churchgoing was a deeper and farther reaching one; the minister was a good man and just, according to his lights, but narrow, his world embracing a very small plot of ground. There was no elasticity to his opinions. He believed that he was traveling Zionward with a select band of the chosen, and the only point where he betrayed any imagination was the limitless extent of those uncomfortable lower regions, to which he complacently consigned more than ninety-nine hundredths of his fellow beings.

Sylvia, whose silent, companionless life had

developed in her a faculty for vividly seizing
hold of ideas generally far in advance of her
age, had to listen to his denunciations Sunday
after Sunday.   Thanks to him her belief in the
efficacy of Justine's blue-and-white plaster Virgin faded away, also the dim, deliciously agitating idea of the naiad in the brook : but although
the well-meaning Mr. Andrews drove away these
fancies, he did not provide her with any affir-
mation to fill up the space created by the nega-
tion.   The child swelled with indignation when
he prayed pointedly, as he believed it was his
duty to do, " for all those who bend the knee
to images of wood and stone ; for all those
who turn from the Lord's house " (this meant
Mr. Andrews's meeting-house) " and spend the
Sabbath in vain worldliness ; may they turn
from their errors before " — and then would follow a description of the torments being prepared
for " papa, Uncle Dick, and Justine," as Sylvia
thought, that made her tremble with fury against
him.

Gilbert's active, intellectual life made him
absent-minded when with his little girl ; he had
no love for puppies or kittens — why, then, for
other undeveloped animals ? She had felt the
sting inflicted by an indifferent answer to some
question of vital importance to her, as only a
highly strung sensitive child can, and it drove

her into herself, forming at that early age the habit of reserve which grew with her growth. Huntington was the one person to whom she spoke freely of her little interests; he was always ready to listen and never snubbed her, even when he could not quite understand. It was to him that Sylvia owed the first important change in her monotonous life.

One winter twilight, Gilbert having disappeared for a time, the two friends, the little girl and her dear Uncle Dick, were sitting by the fire while the shadows clustered in the skeleton-like elm without, and the ceiling grew red and glowing within. Sylvia had been chatting about a hundred things, but for a few moments she had been silent, watching her companion's kind, strong face in the dim light; he puffed away at his cigar, waiting for more confidences, while a gentle melancholy stole over him, regrets for something that had gone out of his life for ever. Suddenly she spoke : —

"Uncle Dick, do you think it very wicked to say the Lord's Prayer in French?"

He looked at her with a quizzical yet kindly expression.

"No; do you say it in French?"

"Yes."

"Why isn't English good enough?"

"Oh, it isn't that — listen — let me tell you."

She came close to him, and he felt that she was shaking with nervous excitement. " It is because ' for ever and ever, Amen ' is so very terrible — I have to hold on in the dark to keep from whizzing off. Eternity is so awful. Do you think everything Mr. Andrews says is true? It all frightens me so."

Then Dick threw his cigar into the fire, and taking Sylvia on his knee he tried to tell her in halting words of the love enfolding the world. She listened, gradually calmed and soothed; the main comfort to her was that she need not believe in the bad part — the rest did not matter so much.

That night, when she had fallen peacefully asleep, no " eternity feelings " having disturbed her, thanks to Huntington, he had a serious talk about her with Gilbert. He urged a good school, where she would be among other children, but her father would not hear of it. He argued, with truth, that for many years to come her life must be apart. " I am too well known now, Dick, to expect that my daughter could meet with any decent treatment. I am obliged to sign an assumed name when I want payment for any article unconnected with my cause as it is. I am a marked man," he ended with a sigh.

Capricious, intolerant, vain he might have been, but Gilbert Edwards had in him some of the elements that go to make up enthusiasts. In spite of his absorption he yet listened to his friend's account of Sylvia's mental state with some interest, and announced his intention of forbidding any more churchgoing, and of taking her education into his own hands. Huntington shrugged his shoulders a trifle skeptically at the thoroughness with which the new broom swept neglected corners, but as month succeeded month, year followed year, and still father and daughter pursued their studies with eager interest, his incredulity gave way to admiration.

To Sylvia, her lessons were not unalloyed bliss by any means; she found in her father a severe, fastidious master, but one who had the power of arousing ambition. He found in her an intelligent, in some ways a brilliant pupil: he rarely praised her, showing approval only by absence of blame, so that she felt a glow of pride if she escaped during the lesson-hour one of his sarcastic sneers, — barbed words bearing more poison in their points than he suspected, poison that stung and rankled long after they had been spoken. The very admiration that Sylvia felt for her father's intellect added weight to his opinion. She was in constant fear, not of him, but of what he might say to hurt her.

As she grew older he treated her more as his equal. He spoke to her of his intense interest in the unpopular, nay, detested cause that he had espoused; and she, with the mantle of reserve folded about her from long habit, answered suitably and intelligently to his eloquent bursts. But he never dreamed that the self-contained little maiden often left him trembling with agony at the horror his words had called up to her, and spent hours of vain imaginings of what she fain would do.

Even Huntington did not suspect the intensity of her feelings on this subject, for she was often a silent listener during long discussions between him and her father, and she knew that with all his humanity, Uncle Dick was not one of *them.* She noticed, too, that her father met with scanty respect from the villagers, who did not favor the abolition movement in the beginning. Gilbert's tactless enthusiasm drove them to a scarcely-veiled hostility towards him and the cause. As the struggle grew fiercer between the various political factions, certain tradesmen refused to fill his simple orders. Gilbert was secretly proud of this feeble attempt to persecute him, but Sylvia quivered with indignation.

If we except an occasional call from good Mr. Andrews, who kept up a friendship for the son which he had formerly felt for the father, Huntington was now their sole link with the outside world. Although his sisters saw with much

loudly expressed concern his intimacy with a
man whom they characterized as an "atheist, a
Bohemian, and very French in his views," he continued to feel the same warm, loyal admiration
for his friend, and he never missed his Sunday
visit until Sylvia was nearly sixteen ; then some
important business called him to England.

Before going he handed over to Gilbert his
own property, which had grown to fairly comfortable proportions during his stewardship, ad-
vising him to alter none of the existing arrangements.

Sylvia hardly knew what a satisfying element
dear Uncle Dick had been in her life until the
ocean rolled between them, and there was nothing to mark the passing of the weeks, no sound
of rapid hoofs on the turnpike-road to listen for,
no interesting little package to open, no cosy
twilight confidences. Like a child waiting for
the holidays she kept a calendar in her room,
and each morning marked off a day. During
his friend's absence Gilbert went often to Boston, pleading business as an excuse; he fre-
quently stayed for three or four days at a time,
leaving Sylvia to wander at will among his
books, a method fraught with some danger for
a young girl.

The hours dragged heavily, but all things
come to an end at last, even that dark solitary

winter of '60 and '61 ; and the March winds blew
Huntington back to a land seething and writh-
ing with internal strife. The Sundays were
taken up with long, excited talks between the
two men, Richard still holding his more conservative ground, and refusing to believe in the
shameful rumors of those agitating times.

Sylvia listened, her heart beating and her eyes
glowing, but all her feelings hidden as she sat in
her corner, her hands quietly folded in her lap.
Beneath this cool exterior, however, ardent and
inspiring thoughts and emotions were seething
and bubbling, much as the brown waters of her
old playfellow the brook swirled under the thin
films of ice, still lingering one April morning in
the shadow cast by the little foot-bridge span-
ning the stream. Sylvia stood looking down at
it in the clear sunshine; it was swollen by the
melted snows and rushed on with mimic fury.

" I used to be afraid of the brook when I was
little," she said to herself : " I thought that a
fairy lived there who laughed at me sometimes.
I wonder if I *did* hear anything then I 've lost
the sound of now ? "

She walked slowly back to the house, stooping now and then to pick a golden crocus for
the breakfast-table. Her slender figure was as
straight as a river-reed ; her dark-brown rippling
hair was brushed away from her low, broad fore-

head, and fell down her back in a heavy braid,
tied with a black ribbon ; her gray woolen dress
was made with conventual simplicity, only re·
lieved by the white collar and cuffs which gave
her an air of dainty precision. Her features
were delicately chiseled, her color fresh, and
her eyes deep gray, edged with black lashes —
but there are hundreds of other girls who might
be described in these words, and yet give no
idea of our heroine. The difference lay in a
suggestion of latent force, a reserve that belongs
by rights to people double the child's age, and
in a lack of that careless happiness which we
connect with youth, scarcely realizing what a
distinctive feature it is until we miss it.

On this fresh dewy morning the caws from
a flock of crows taking their heavy way over
the treetops were the only sounds of life in
the serene country calm, and yet at that very
moment hundreds of thousands of hearts were
beating fast with excitement, for north and
south, east and west, flashed the news that the
flag had been fired on.

But Sylvia, all unconscious of the tumult,
went into the house out of the sunshine to arrange her flowers. She had just set her bowl in
the middle of the table, when her father's step
was heard in the hall, and as he entered the
room, she glanced through the window, exclaim-

ing, "Why, papa! look! there is the station-wagon coming in by the upper gate! Who can it be?"

Forgetful of her usual dignity, she ran to the window.

"It is Uncle Dick! what can he want?"

Gilbert's pale face grew a shade paler.

"You are too old to be such a tomboy, Sylvia," he said testily; "you are sixteen and Huntington is still a young man. For God's sake don't lose your womanliness."

The slightly disdainful look habitual to her crept into the girl's face, and she stood still instead of running out to welcome her friend. He jumped hastily from the flimsy vehicle, and in another moment was in the room. There was an unfamiliar expression of excitement and exaltation on his manly face, and some emotion seemed to be silencing him, for he laid his hand on Gilbert's shoulder, and stood looking at him without a word. Sylvia thought how big and broad he appeared beside the slight boyish figure of her father, whose face had a curious drawn, shrinking look, as he fixed his dark, burning eyes on Richard.

At last, "Come!" said Dick, almost with a shout, his lips trembling. For a moment his excitement seemed to reach Gilbert, who half rose, and stretched out his hand, while a wave

of feeling rushed across his face with the evanescent rapidity of lightning; then with a groan
he sank back into his chair, covering his eyes
with his hand.

"I cannot," he said; "God help me, I cannot."

"Gilbert!"

There was an incredulous protest in the exclamation, but it was unanswered. Sylvia could
remain passive no longer.

"Where do you want him to go, Uncle Dick?"
she said, coming forward. Huntington looked
at her vaguely as if she had been a stranger.

"I don't understand; he knew it was coming,
a call to arms, and this morning the President's
Proclamation is issued. We have talked it over
so often, and he was always the eager one; why,
he has laughed at me, and said I was tied to my
money-bags, and now he — I don't understand,"
he reiterated in a helpless fashion.

Gilbert moved impatiently.

"It is my destiny," he said, his voice sounding hollow and muffled under his hand which
still covered his face.

"Destiny be hanged, Gilbert," said Huntington roughly; "this is no time for phrase-mak-
ing. There are two hours before the train goes
back to Boston, and let us have the glory of
being among the first of old Massachusetts' sons
to enlist."

"I cannot go; I must not leave Sylvia."

"Your country has more right to you even than your child; for God's sake don't disappoint me in this; show yourself a man! Throw off this shell of indifference and stand to your guns! Think of all you have said in answer to my lukewarm arguments about law and property. Property! I thought I cared for mine until I read this morning's paper, and now I feel it is nothing, *nothing*, compared with my country. Why, Gilbert," he added with a half-embarrassed laugh. "I believe I am crazed with patriotism, and you must catch it from me."

A stifled groan was the only reply. The glow of enthusiasm died slowly out of Richard's face as he stood looking down on the bowed head, and his voice was cold when he said, "Do you mean to let me go alone, Gilbert?"

"Yes — I must. Don't you — can't you, understand me? I *must* stay at home."

Huntington was baffled by the repeated refusals: he drew his hand over his eyes and choked down an angry rejoinder; he had considered the whole matter deeply and anxiously during the past year, and now, when he had buried doubts and uncertainties, and his heart leapt responsive to his country's call, the friend on whose ardent coöperation he had counted failed him. That there was some grave reason underlying and accounting for Gilbert's attitude, he was sure, and it was a keen disappointment to him, for he had gloried in the prospect of seeing his friend's gallant and chivalrous nature bring him the commanding position that he felt sure he deserved, and of which only circumstances, according to his belief, had deprived him. Not for a moment did any unworthy doubt creep into his loyal thoughts.

But Sylvia, standing unnoticed with her eyes flashing scorn, and her breath coming quick and hard, could not endure the sight of Richard giving up the struggle ; she came swiftly across the room and shook her father's shoulder.

"Look up, papa ! I'm only a girl, but rather than sit at home and think that no one of our family is fighting to defend my country, *I* will follow the army ! I will be a nurse for the wounded ! I will do my share and yours too ! Let me go with Uncle Dick in your place."

There was scornful command rather than entreaty in her voice ; her father did not reply with words, but raised his head and looked at her with an expression of such haggard suffering, that she exclaimed, "Oh, forgive me ! I did not mean " —

"No, no ! you are both right in thinking me a coward ; I am one, but not in the way you believe. Dick, while you were in England I speculated and lost every cent of my money, — it was not for myself, God knows ; it was to help a little in the cause, — but I failed as I do in everything, and now my poor scribblings are all that stand between Sylvia and starvation. Now you know why I must stay at home."

Huntington felt an impulse of angry impatience, but Sylvia was overcome by remorse that she had been guilty of thinking him wanting in bravery ; she put her arms about his neck.

"Poor papa, never mind me ; I can do very well here alone, and I can live on milk and eggs, which cost nothing. Go, dear papa, and when you come home a conqueror, I shall feel I have helped you, and shared a little in your sufferings."

"You are a brave girl : you are like your mother, Sylvia," he said gently ; "but it cannot be. I have sinned, and I must bear my punishment. 'They also serve who only stand and wait,' you know."

"No, no ! it is unjust that you should have to give up every chance, only because you lost your money. Uncle Dick, dear Uncle Dick, tell him how nicely I can live on nothing. I will earn money for myself."

But Huntington was standing at the window staring out into the sunshine, and did not answer. Gilbert looked at him with a wistful appeal in his eyes that was very pitiful. There was a feeling of suspense in the silence which Sylvia dared not break; she gave a little start when Richard turned round abruptly and strode across the room to her side.

He took her hands in his and looked deep into her eyes, his own full of a resolute light.

"Sylvia," he said, and his voice stirred some chord in her heart that vibrated in response — "Sylvia, you are a brave girl, and I am going to ask you to make a great sacrifice for your country and your father. If you were a boy I should not hesitate to ask you to risk your life, and now I do not hesitate to ask you if you will give up all dreams of a young, happy marriage, and take me, battered old fellow that I am, for your husband."

All sorts of visions of personal bravery and exposure had floated through her mind as he began to speak. Her throat had felt as if a hand clutched at it, so high rose her enthusiasm, and the surprise of the ending came like an anti-climax. To her mortification she gave a quick, nervous laugh. "Why, Uncle Dick, I love you dearly; it is nothing you ask me to do; give me something hard."

The determined lines in his face softened a little.

"You do not know what you say, dear. You

may love me as you would an uncle or a grandfather, and I love you as dearly as if you were
my own child; but I lost my heart years ago,
and you have never found yours. No, let us be
frank; it is only that I shall be able to provide
for you, and in case of my death make you my
heir without interference, that I ask you to marry
me. And if you accept, it is because you are
willing to lay your youth and happiness on your
country's altar."

Gilbert, who had been listening as one in a
dream, sprang up.

"No! no! you must not make this sacrifice
for me, Dick! I am not worthy of it; I will
leave Sylvia to starve before accepting it."

"It is not I who make the sacrifice, it is your
daughter. I gain the prospect of a happy home,
and a wife whom I love dearly, if I am spared
to come back; she loses all those dreams of love
which are sacred to any one who has ever had
them. You of all men should appreciate her
generosity."

"Papa — Uncle Dick — don't talk in this way,
please. I am ready to thank God that He has
given me a chance to do something noble. All
my life I have longed to show how I could die
like Marie Antoinette or Jeanne d'Arc, and if
they asked to burn me, so that the slaves might
be free, I would laugh with joy, and go to the

stake singing. I only wish there was something hard, *hard* for me, instead of marrying my dear old Uncle Dick."

Gilbert stared at her in surprise. He had never suspected the enthusiastic love of romance and heroism underlying her quiet manner; but the excitement of the moment stirred her, and self was forgotten. The brilliant color glowed in her cheeks, her deep gray eyes seemed full of violet fire, and her slight, willowy figure assumed an air of dignity.

"Then it is decided; you will marry me, and at once?" said Huntington.

Sylvia smiled proudly as she laid her slender hand in his. "Yes," was all she said, but her voice was full of resolute loyalty.

"If I come back alive I will be a kind husband to you, little girl, and try to make you forget all you have given up. But time is short," he added, looking at his watch; "we ought to be married at once, for I do not know when I shall be free again."

"Run upstairs, Sylvia, and tell Justine to put some things in my valise for me; then wait till I call you," said her father, suddenly rousing to energy.

She gave the bare order to the French woman, neither explaining the reason of his departure, nor telling of the great event in her own life;

she was so unused to sympathy, so accustomed to lock her feelings in her own heart, allowing no one to pry at them, that reserve and silence had become a second nature to her.

She went to her own room and sat by the window waiting. No nun about to take the veil ever had her heart filled with higher, purer thoughts; no hint of self entered into that sanctuary. Sylvia was unconscious that her attitude was one of worship, for she thought neither of the avenging Jehovah of whom Mr. Andrews thundered, nor of the blue-and-white Virgin in Justine's room, and these were the only deities she knew; but as man is made to adore, her whole being was prostrate before the abstract virtues of patriotism, bravery, and self-sacrifice.

She looked about the room, eloquent in its appointments of Huntington's tender thoughtfulness of her, that had followed her ever since she had known him. The engravings on the wall, the knickknacks on her dressing-table, everything she called hers, had been given by him, except the few books in the hanging shelves; those had been some of her father's infrequent gifts. As she looked, her eye fell on an ivory prayer-book — her mother's. She took it from its place and turned to the marriage service. "Till death us do part," she read to herself, and the thought of dear, kind, generous Uncle Dick being taken from her brought tears to her eyes. He was the only person in the world she really loved, and even to him it was a vague, luke-warm affection she gave. Never in her life had she known the hot, eager rush of love that chokes with sobs and blinds with tears, called forth by the mother bound to her child by a higher, holier tie than that we speak of as instinct. Sylvia was ignorant of any stronger emotion than that roused in her by the history of a noble deed, or a brave act; but whatever she had of tenderness to bestow was Richard Huntington's.

While she sat absorbed in her thoughts she heard wheels, and saw Mr. Andrews driving up in the station wagon, which had been sent for him. Her heart beat faster, but her voice was steady as she answered her father's call, and her step light and calm as she went down the turn-ing stairs, a child in years, a woman in high courage and purpose.

Her father took her by the hand and led her into the white parlor, where Mr. Andrews stood solemnly with bowed head behind a small table. Justine and Deborah were in a corner, each showing her deep feelings characteristically, the French woman telling her beads inaudibly, her streaming eyes lifted to Heaven; the New Englander holding herself rigidly, and scorning to use the handkerchief for which her loud sniffs called.

Huntington was standing staring into the newly lighted fire, and seemed startled when Gilbert touched him on the shoulder; he had seen the face of his first and only love in the blue, hurrying smoke as she looked mockingly forth, and he was wondering if things did even up in the end, if he could ever feel his life complete, full as it had been of all that men prize, and now inspired by the dream of a glorious future; and as he pondered, he could have found it in him to envy his friend Gilbert, poor in everything except the memory of a few imperishable years, filled with an ardent, undying love.

The girl he took by the hand, promising to love and to cherish, had but a small share of his thoughts.

Mr. Andrews had rather reluctantly agreed to use the Episcopal form of service, urged on him by Gilbert, who pleaded lack of time for a longer ceremony, really dreading an interminable prayer.

Almost before she realized what she was doing, Sylvia felt Richard's warm, hearty kiss on her forehead, and heard his voice say, with a natural ring that in part took off the dream-like effect of the scene, "God bless you, my wife."

There was a touch of amusement, too, in his tone, and his eyes had a friendly twinkle that dried the tears in them. Sylvia put her arms round his neck, and hid her face on his shoulder; she was not touched, but shy, and wished that stupid old Mr. Andrews would go away. To her delight she heard her father tell him that they would drive him home as they went to the station, bidding him hurry; then he kissed Sylvia with a tenderness she did not recognize, and said that he would try and come to see her again if possible; if not, he would write, and Dick's lawyer would tell her what arrangements were to be made for her during the coming months. Huntington himself took her in his strong arms, and kissed her as unceremoniously as if she were still the child he had first known, telling her that his sisters should call on her at once, and if she liked she should visit them. But she said, "Oh, no; don't let them ask me," in such a disdainful tone that he laughed and said she should not be troubled by any invitation. Then Gilbert called out anxiously that they had only just time, but he had mislaid his watch; there was a rush to look for it; Mr. Andrews, already in the carriage, kept urging the need for haste, joined by the driver; Huntington confounded his friend's carelessness, and so with much bustle and some laughter they drove away, softer thoughts banished for the time.

After the first hour, when the house seemed very silent, and she found it hard to settle to her usual routine, Sylvia slipped back into her old habits, and by bedtime had been so engrossed in " Les Trois Mousquetaires " that she started with surprise at Deborah's playful address, " Mis' Huntington, it 's time to put out the lamp."

CHAPTER II.

THE next day the whole affair seemed like a
dream to Sylvia; she had not even a wedding-
ring, properly speaking, for Huntington had
replaced on her finger one that she habitually
wore, and which had belonged to her grandmother. When, according to the promise made,
a grave, civil-spoken lawyer called on her, and
informed her with much respect of the generous
allowance that her husband had ordered to be
placed to her credit at his bank, and instructed
her in the mystery of drawing a cheque, she
had the impression that she was taking part
in private theatricals. But she filled her rôle
with a dignity rather pathetic in one so young,
and when alone set herself to consider what she
should do with this overwhelming wealth.

She had a strong conviction that it would not
be becoming in her to give any of it to aid the
cause she and her father had so much at heart,
for she knew that Richard was not one of them;
as for herself, what did she want? It would be
absurd to get gay, rich clothes; her own simple,
well-made dresses were much more fitting for

her. Her father being away, she had the use of his saddle-horse, and that was a delight to her, for the pony, a present of long ago from Huntington, had grown too old, and she herself too tall, to make him of much use, except to drag his little cart.

Some books she did want, and Deborah should have a silk gown and Justine a gold watch. She sent Mr. Andrews a handsome sum for village charities, and after her one trip to Boston, guarded by both her handmaidens, to make her few purchases, she settled back into the old life.

There came one break in it, the day that her sisters-in-law made the visit that their brother had ordered — there is no milder term to use. Sylvia realized that her father's attitude in regard to abolition had made him conspicuous, and she also knew that he had been treated harshly on account of his beliefs, and gloried in picturing him to herself as a martyr ; but she had no idea of the horror he inspired in her conventional, narrow-minded sisters-in-law, or of the indignation which they felt at their brother's *wickedness* in marrying his daughter. Besides the social wrong that he had committed in their eyes, they both felt aggrieved, because, regarding him as a settled old bachelor, they had counted on their children being his heirs, and it was hard to be forced to receive a little chit of sixteen into their

family, who would bring with her ideas harmful
to all ranks of society.

The visit, therefore, was not a success; neither
lady would eat a crumb of the cake that Deborah
had prepared with fluttering care, nor drink a
drop of the old Madeira for which the Edwards
family had long been famous. They sat with
their eyes fixed on the clock, horribly afraid of
losing the return train to town, and explained
elaborately why they were unable to invite Sylvia
to make them a visit: they were shutting their
houses for the summer, preparatory to going to
the mountains or the seashore. She listened
with her grave air, treating them with all possible deference, and no one could have suspected
how amused she was at their transparent subter-
fuges, and clumsy attempts to patronize her. If
Sylvia had been older, more versed in the ways
of the world, she would have been decidedly depressed by her new relations; but in her wise
inexperience she took a "short view of life,"
looked upon the episode as something extremely
ludicrous, wished that she had some one to sym-
pathize with her amusement over the anxiety
displayed by the worthy dames to impress on
her their grandeur and importance, and forgot
the whole affair during a twilight canter.

Not so Deborah, who had not been above hov-
ering about the hall while the ladies were there,

and had gathered enough of the general aspect
of things to rouse her wrath. She brought the
untouched tray with the heavy cut-glass de-
canter of an old-fashioned shape, and the jin-
gling glasses, out to the " clock-room," where
Justine sat at her work in the western sunshine.

"Such as them to scorn Miss Sylvia," she
burst out, having carefully set her burden on the
table. " *I* can remember the day when they was
only too glad to be asked to sip a drop of that
wine when it was a good many years younger,
and would nibble any crumbs old Mis' Edwards
would throw 'em, and now they feel too fine to
break bread in this house! They was always
flattering and coaxing Mis' Edwards, and encouraging their brother to be friends with Mr.
Gilbert. Their impudence beats me."

Justine's eyes flashed with a dangerous light.
" Did they trouble my lamb? " she asked, fold-
ing her arms dramatically.

" Oh, they ain't worth our bothering over them,
Joosteen," returned Deborah, recovering her
serenity under the healing effects of sympathy,
and having, besides, a wholesome fear of the
French woman's temper, which, joined to mutual
respect, produced a peaceful combination.

" I guess they didn't mean to set my back
up the wrong way they did, and Miss Sylvia 's
worth ten of 'em anyway."

" Mademoiselle is fit to be a duchess," said Justine warmly: " I have seen fine ladies in my time, but not one more beautiful, more worthy than my lamb."

" Yes, you 'll not find a smarter girl under the canopy," assented Deborah, and calm reigned once more.

And the calm continued to reign in the solitary house, the only ripples of excitement being caused by occasional letters from Edwards and Huntington, who were engrossed in their work of organization, previous to leading their regiments to the seat of war — real war now, in grim earnest. Sylvia read the papers eagerly, and followed every step of the gathering forces. She burned to have her two soldiers begin their work, and chafed at the necessary delay.

Then one day came a letter, bidding her to go to Boston to look her farewells on husband and father. She obeyed the directions, taking Deborah with her. A young man sent by Huntington met them in the city and conducted them to a room in a business street, through which the regiment was to march. Every window was crowded with faces, and Sylvia scanned them with interest. Some of the women wept; others, still more pathetic, talked and laughed; there were boys chafing at the youth which kept them at home, and old men who regarded sons and grandsons with envy.

At last, a dry sound, the tramp of feet was heard; many a wife and mother fluttered her handkerchief gayly as her brave boy in blue marched steadily by, and then, when he had passed and her courage was not needed to cheer him, pressed it to her eyes.

"Why do they cry?" Sylvia asked herself with a sort of scorn; "*I* feel like singing a battle-hymn."

"Here comes your pa — may God bless and keep him," said Deborah in a shrill voice that broke in a sob. Sylvia saw him, the sunlight falling on his face, glad and confident as he looked up at her window. "That's the way he used to look as a boy — bless him, bless him! Oh, if his mother could see him now — Perhaps she does," said the faithful servant, twisting her fingers together as her emotion burst through the shell of her New England self-consciousness. Sylvia leaned over the sill, and sent him glad look for glad look; they were both proud and exalted; they were strung up to an heroic pitch. Then, when Gilbert had disappeared, down the street came Richard, his broad shoulders and manly air giving her a thrill of possessive pride. She leaned out, her fresh lips parted, her cheeks glowing, a brilliant image of enthusiasm, a very goddess spurring him on to victory she seemed, in the dingy frame of the stone window-casing.

Their eyes met in one long, farewell look; the light faded from hers, as she read in his a simple courage, and a wistful pity for her in her young ignorance of life. The pomp of war vanished, and in its place remained duty in all its nakedness. She saw the yearning in his face, and her heart went out in a rush of tenderness to him. "I know now why they cry," she thought as she drew back into the room, the tears rolling down her cheeks.

From that moment he lost his identity with the Uncle Dick of her childhood; he was a hero, and his life was a solemn drama to her — a tragedy moving with inexorable, fatelike steps to the last act, when they brought him, shot through the heart, back to old Massachusetts.

His sisters were frigidly kind to her. She went to them for a short visit, and came back to her quiet home bewildered at the views they had given her of human nature, — views in which the importance of crêpe and bombazine were curiously mingled with texts from Scripture appropriate to their affliction, but where a thin although sincere grief reconciled the incongruous elements of the mass; the kinder they were to her, however, the more absolutely apart from them did she feel, and she left them with the sensation that she was going back to find

Richard, and to mourn undisturbed for his untimely end.

It was an untimely end, but better his lot than that of poor Gilbert, who had set out in the "glad, confident morning," hope and ambition gilding his attitude of self-sacrifice; for humanity he was willing, nay, eager, to give all. But sometimes all is simpler to give than half. One gray, rainy evening, when the wind wailed in the chimney, he crept back to his hearth, wounded, broken in body and mind. His career on the battlefield had been but a repetition of his whole life, — he had never found an opportunity to distinguish himself; he had not been a favorite with his men; his real gallantry had never been given a chance until the battle where he had been wounded so severely that his life was despaired of at first.

Disappointed, his only friend gloriously dead, his small fortune melted away, what was left for him? Nothing but to drag out his remaining years a pensioner on his daughter's charity. He did not face this fact; he was not a man to face anything disagreeable; but it was forced on him.

Sylvia during their three years' separation had grown from a child to a woman; her simple black dress, her grave bearing, the high nobility of her thoughts, her best companions, which shone seriously out of her eyes, made her seem

older than she really was. At first she cared for
her father, humored his whims, bore his caprices
with Spartan patience. Nevertheless, the sudden
change in her life was a severe test, and she
was but a very human creature after all. For
these last years she had been as a queen in her
tiny realm : she had given money and energy to
organize a Sanitary Commission in the village,
where her youth, her generosity, and her solitude
made the country-folk forget her father's unpop-
ularity, and remember only her husband's gallantry. Never contradicted, her simple material
wants supplied by the ever watchful Justine and
Deborah, loved and praised by the inferiors surrounding her, her character had sent out vigorous shoots in one direction, but there was nothing
to stimulate a balancing growth until her father's
return.

Then came the rub.

At first he was too shattered to rouse any sentiment save that of pity ; but as he grew bodily
stronger, Sylvia began to realize the fact that
she was the possessor of a very quick temper,
which was daily severely tried by his bitter,
sneering words. It mattered little whether they
were directed against her or not; they invaria-
bly produced a tempest of indignation, only to
be calmed by a long, solitary ride. The various
physicians and surgeons whom she called in to

aid him all agreed in saying that his wound had
affected Gilbert's heart, and that any contradic-
tion or undue excitement might end fatally, so
that self-restraint on her part was imperative.
His society, too, destroyed for her the unconscious content she had felt in her quiet life;
his stories of the people he had known and the
things he had seen gave her new light, and
opened her eyes to the fact that she was young
and fair, that the world was vast and filled with
allurements. Suddenly she began to long for
companionship, for gayeties and amusements,
turning with distaste from her books, from the
brook's song and the perfume of the flowers.
She neglected her work on the Sanitary Commission, giving as an excuse her anxiety to be
with her father, and then spent long hours in
vague discontent, none the less poignant that
she could give her wishes no name. It was but
the natural reaction against the unnatural solitude and gravity of her upbringing. She begged
her father to move to Boston, so that they might
break the monotony of their existence by going
to concerts and theatres, but he shrank from the
ordeal. He dreaded to have the cold eye of the
world scan the broken failure of his life. Traveling was forbidden, and at any rate they were
both too much bound up in their country's weal
or woe to willingly leave her.

There were days when Gilbert rallied and grew young again ; once when Lincoln emancipated the slaves, and again when the decisive news came that the North was victorious.

That day was a festival ; to please him, Sylvia gave up her heavy black, and sat opposite to him at dinner in fresh white with a bunch of violets at her belt.

" I think I can make a new start now," he said gayly : " I am no longer a moral leper — I will begin my writing again ; I have a thousand plans in my head."

She sympathized, trying to believe that he was able to keep his word, but the next day he was very ill ; the slight excitement had been too much for him, and Deborah, whom he had called in the night, had thought that he was dying. He rallied, however, and the doctor said that there was no cause for further fear at present, so the old routine began once more.

It was April again, and one morning, a few days later, Sylvia woke early. The birds were rioting outside, but through their singing came a sullen clang : it was the bell tolling in the village. She could not sleep ; a heavy depression enveloped her ; a loathing for her occupations, her lack of living interests, her powerlessness.

She dressed and went down into the hall. It was earlier than she had thought, she said to herself, for the morning paper had not come ; it was always left on the hall-table, and she took it to her father with his breakfast tray.

She stepped out into the crisp air. It was four years since her wedding-day, and in that time nothing had changed. The elm-tree was a little fuller, the house had had a fresh coat of paint, the crocuses were more plentiful — that was all.

" Will nothing ever change? " she thought with a rush of impatience.

" Is it my fault? am I wanting in energy, or am I paralyzed? Oh, that bell, that bell, it will drive me mad."

She went round to the other side of the house. Deborah was standing in the kitchen porch, looking after the retreating form of the postman, an expression of horror in her face.

" What is it? " asked Sylvia ; the woman's rigid attitude told her clearly that some blow had fallen.

" They 've killed the President," answered Deborah, with rapid conciseness.

" Oh, no — it 's impossible — it can't be true."

" It *is* true. Listen." Clang over the tree-tops came the plaint of the persistent bell. " There, that 's for *him*."

As she spoke she flung her apron over her face, and turned away, dumb with sorrow and anger. Sylvia was stunned by the tidings for a moment, and then her thoughts flew to her father.

" We must keep it from papa. Where is the paper, Deborah ? "

" I left it on the hall-table nearly an hour ago. Sam Morris has been here all this time, just saying nothing."

Sylvia went back into the house : no, the paper was not there. With a sudden fear shaking her, she went swiftly to Gilbert's door and knocked : there was no answer. She spoke; all was still. Then, summoning all her courage, she turned the handle and entered.

He was sitting beside the table, with his head fallen on to his outstretched arm ; one hand clutched the paper crumpled in its grasp, the other hung heavy by his side. He did not stir when his daughter came to him, nor did he answer when she called his name. She put her hand gently on his shoulder, and then a solemn awe came upon her, for she knew that he had reached the end of his journey, that no longer would he stumble on his uncongenial way ; that betwixt him and her spread the mystery of mysteries. Through the open window came the measured tolling of the bell and the unconcerned jubilees of the birds. Fifteen minutes before, she had complained that nothing ever changed, and had chafed at her life ; now to her vision, cleared and enlarged by death's presence, her murmurs seemed petty and childish.

Had she loved him more, she would have missed him more, but she would have been spared the anguish of remorse. The memory of a thousand trifles tormented her in the weeks and months following that eventful morning — words unspoken, that might have cheered him ; her frequent lack of sympathy expressed by an eloquent silence ; her hidden, but sharply felt impatience at his strictures and criticisms.

"If I had only known how soon I was to be free, I would have been more patient," she cried in her bitter self-reproach.

There were very few letters or other mementos of her parents' life together ; in their seven years of bliss they had seldom been parted ; but the rare fragments she found showed Sylvia a new phase of the dead man's nature, which was expressed in tender, self-abnegating words to the woman who had made his life black when she withdrew from him the radiance of her presence.

In the long summer days Sylvia pondered over this strange passion, this love, sung by poets, deified by men ; and the more she thought of it, the more she grew to regard it as a madness. She saw from her own experience how it had ruined her father's life, and deep in her heart she made a promise to herself that she would so mould her life as to avoid its enchanting poison.

Richard Huntington's death and burial had taken place but a short time before Gilbert's sad return to his home, and Mr. Belknap, Sylvia's lawyer, had duly presented her late husband's will for probate. According to its terms she was to enjoy the use of the income of the property until she was twenty-one, when the entire fortune, barring a few bequests, was to be put into her hands. It had now become her duty to make her own will, and this, in her isolated condition, was no easy task. She could not consult her father, for any kindred subject agitated him sorely, so she must settle all for herself.

She had decided on nothing in her own mind, except the fact that half of all that came to her was to go back to Richard's family (his sisters were both wealthy women, but she felt that this was only an act of justice), when one afternoon Mr. Belknap's card was brought to her as she sat in her father's room reading aloud to him; it was one of his bad days, and he had not ventured downstairs. She found the lawyer waiting for her in the white parlor ; he was a middle-aged man, of rigid integrity, with a profound reverence for money; in person he was small, and his manner was dry and cool. He seated himself to his satisfaction, after greeting his client, inquired for her father, expressed his concern at the bad report she gave him, and spoke casually of the weather, before introducing the real reason of his visit.

"I am afraid there is going to be a contest over the will, Mrs. Huntington," he said at length, looking at her with his sharp little eyes to see how she would take his announcement.

"What's the trouble? was n't it drawn right?" she returned.

He was a little stung at her remark. "Drawn right — yes; there's never any trouble about *my* wills. That is not the point the other side will bring up."

"Who is the other side?"

"Your late husband's sisters, Mrs. Townsend and Mrs. Adams."

"And what do they want?"

"They want everything," he said with a short laugh. "I will explain matters to you. I suppose I can't see your father about it?"

"Oh, no," she answered hastily, "it is out of the question."

"That's bad — that's unfortunate; but we will do our best without him. The other side base their claim on a charge of undue influence brought to bear on your husband to induce him to leave his entire fortune to you."

" Whose undue influence ? "

Her eyes were so truthful, bearing no trace of suspicion in their limpid depths as she asked this question, that Mr. Belknap hesitated a little. " Well," he said at length, stroking his chin, " I presume they intend to suggest yours and your father's."

" How wicked of them! how false! Why, Richard begged and entreated me to make the sacrifice," she burst out.

" That 's good — very good ; now, my dear young lady, tell me all about it." She repeated the events of her wedding-day, simply, and in a manner that told she spoke the truth. At the end of her story Mr. Belknap seemed plunged in thought ; then he said, " Well, well, who would have thought that Huntington could be so romantic. It shows how little we know our clients. Now," he added in a brisker tone, " we 'll prepare for the fight. I 'd better have Henley on our side ; he 's a very clever advocate, and they have a dangerous fellow to represent them. I wish that Huntington had consulted me first — there was really no need for so much haste ; but there 's no use crying over spilt milk."

"Let me ask you one or two questions now. I may be very dull, but I can't even yet see why they think they can get all this money. Did n't Uncle — Mr. Huntington mean me to have it?"

"Certainly; that was his wish."

"And was the money his to do what he pleased with?"

"Of course it was; he and his sisters inherited equally from their father; Richard increased his property by his business talent, they increased theirs by making rich marriages. It is a family where money seems to pour in."

"Then why do they attack me?"

The man of law gave an indulgent chuckle at the display of so much innocence.

"Because, my dear young lady, they covet still more; they want to see their cups running over, and their granaries bursting with wealth. Good-afternoon; you may count on me to keep you informed."

His last answer had roused Sylvia's indignation. What baseness, what hypocrisy was theirs! So little while ago they had seemed all kindness and tenderness for her at Richard's funeral, and even then perhaps they had been plotting against her. It was cowardly to strike in that way at a young, unprotected woman, — a stab in the back. "If they had asked me, I would have given them half, but now" — This mood

continued, so that when she received a line from
Mr. Belknap, saying that the other side seemed
inclined to draw in their horns, and had whispered the word " compromise," she wrote back,
" *No ;* I will not compromise for a dollar. That
would put me in the wrong, and make me feel
that I had no right to the share left me. I will
fight it with your help."

She might have decided differently had she
foreseen the endless trials and complications to
which her answer pledged her. There was the
necessity of keeping her father in the dark
regarding her frequent trips to Boston ; there
were tedious hours of waiting in Mr. Belknap's
or Mr. Henley's office, for interviews with those
busy gentlemen ; there was the humiliation of
learning how low the estimate was of human
nature, as shown by the carefully prepared questions that Mr. Henley put to her.

He, by the way, was the one bright spot in
this dreary time ; he had known her grand-
parents, had been in love, he assured her, with
her grandmother, and showed her a kindly good
will that touched and warmed her. He was a
man of the world, too, the great outside world,
who spent every season in London, and knew
everybody ; she felt more at home with him
than she did with fussy little Mr. Belknap, and
he became interested in his young client.

At last the day for the hearing came; Sylvia had braced herself up for the torture-rack, and after all it seemed rather a tame performance to her. When the testimony that her father was too ill to appear was stated, there was in one or two questions an implied sneer that brought the angry blood to her cheeks, but she controlled herself, and presently, to her relief, it seemed to be all over. Before she could congratulate herself, however, Mr. Henley whispered, "These are but preliminaries, you know; they are merely feeling their way; they want to see our strength. The real struggle will come before a jury."

He rubbed his hands with a pleased look as he said this; he was great in a jury trial, and he knew it. Her face fell. "When do you suppose that will be?" she asked in a discouraged manner.

"You can never tell; in six months perhaps, or, again, not for a year," he answered.

So it dragged on uncertainly, and then came her father's death. While she was still feeling the sharp remorse and the new tenderness caused by it, she was summoned, with Deborah and Justine, to Boston for the trial. Mr. Belknap engaged rooms for them in a dreary, respectable hotel, where she had the prospect of a graveyard from one window, and a narrow gray court filled with lawyers' offices from another, to amuse her;

there she waited until the day of her trial, as it indeed proved, arrived.

The opening by the advocate on the other side, " the dangerous fellow," filled her with angry humiliation. He painted in crude, vulgar colors the innocent, noble friendship which existed between Huntington and the inmates of the old white house, — the disappointed, struggling man and his little girl. He portrayed Sylvia at the age of ten with all the clever wiles of a Becky Sharp, and no one in history or fiction ever approached Gilbert for cunning duplicity. That opening argument crushed her so that her mind scarcely took in what followed, and she was in a confused state until the time came for her cross-examination. Then she rallied, and answered the questions put to her with so much clearness and dignity that her womanly personality evidently impressed the jury as much as did her fearless, honest eyes, dark with feeling. She looked very young and pathetic as she stood alone, her black dress and veil accentuating the slender lines of her figure, and the delicate color coming and going in her face. Mr. Henley and Mr. Belknap felt that they had won when their practiced eyes noted the favorable impression made by their client, and whispered encouraging words to her as she took her seat once more by her faithful servants. But at that time nothing could comfort her; she was overwhelmed by the horror of it all, and felt that no number of fortunes, piled one upon the other, could repay her for the agony of hearing the judge's voice ring through the court-room in his charge to the jury. The mere naming of such suspicions was an insult to the dead and to the living. She drew her heavy veil across her face; she could bear no eye to look upon her.

When the jury left the room, she, too, rose and went to her hotel. Nothing seemed of any consequence now, not even the appearance of Mr. Henley in an incredibly short time, who bore the tidings that the jury had brought in a verdict in her favor. " And a pretty bill of costs the other side will have to pay," he ended with a chuckle.

He advised her to stay yet another night in town, as there would be business matters for her to settle the following day, and left her, his kind old face beaming at her gentle thanks, and at the successful issue. When he had gone, she sent Justine and Deborah home, rejoicing, and then sat down alone in her dreary little sitting-room.

The victory was hers — but what a barren triumph. All this humiliation and angry suffering merely to keep her own. And now that it had been proved hers beyond all doubt, what

pleasure did it bring to any one? She turned
from her own thoughts with a sigh, and glanced
at some newspapers left by Mr. Henley on the
table. A rough woodcut caught her eye, — a
bold, ordinary looking woman, with an exaggerated crêpe veil hanging in stiff folds from
her bonnet; underneath were the words, "The
Widow Huntington fighting for her millions."

It was so bad, so beyond caricature, that if
any friend had been with her, Sylvia would have
laughed; as it was, she cried instead, not merely
on account of the picture, but because of her
sudden realization of her loneliness.

"I can never show my face in Boston again,"
she thought, with a yearning to be at home in
her quiet house. She shrank behind the window
curtains so as not to be seen by the tired, dusty-
looking men, most of them carrying green bags,
who came out of the dingy houses across the
way, going, bat-like, to their homes in the gray
dusk. A hand-organ ground out a dismal tune;
over the graves came the sound of traffic from
a busy street on the other side; a lean cat stole
stealthily along the iron fence of the burial-
ground. It was all ugly, sordid, and Sylvia felt
stifled. "I want to go home," she repeated like
a child.

But the next day, when she had left the dull
town behind, she found that home had nothing

to say to her. Deborah and Justine welcomed her with joy; but she could not tell them of her thoughts. She sat solitary at the little feast that they had prepared to celebrate her victory. The good souls had been busy all day about it, and had been eager to leave the city so as to have plenty of time; flowers and candles decked the table; Deborah beamed through the pantry door, watching Justine serve their young mistress, who sat alone, pretending to be pleased, and forcing herself to smile and taste and praise, but her heart was heavy within her, and it was a relief when Justine left the room, and she was free to go into the white parlor.

There she found the same sense of loneliness and unnaturalness. It seemed unlike the room she had always lived in, and bore an aspect of frigid, unused cleanliness. Not a stray book lay about, but they all stood in serried lines dusted by careful hands, staring at her from their shelves; her writing-table was arranged in immaculate order; her work-basket had been put away; every chair stood in a formal attitude and the atmosphere of home was banished. Truth to tell, it had given Deborah untold joy to put the room " to rights," and she had been at work since the first faint glimmer of light to accomplish her task.

The evening was too warm for a fire, too cool

to have the windows open ; Sylvia did not know what chair to take, or what book to read. All her old pursuits seemed to have lost their interest, and she had not even been to the stable since her return to see the pony and her saddle-horse. A sudden panic seized her, a fear of the solitude ; the brook's babble sounded through the evening quiet, and she felt afraid, as she used to when a child. She rang for Justine.

The woman entered, her heavy tread falling noiselessly, her square face at first stolid and impassive ; after Sylvia had spoken, however, the stolidity vanished and her deep-set eyes glowed with the intensity of her feelings.

"I want you to talk to me, Justine dear," Sylvia began. " I don't like being here alone ; sit down, please."

Justine obeyed. " I know," she said, taking a lowly place on a footstool, — " I know how my lamb has suffered. Deborah thinks only of the money, but I think of the cruel words, the insults. I would like to kill mademoiselle's enemies ! "

"Oh, no, Justine, it is not quite as bad as that," said Sylvia with a faint smile.

" If I had my way I would kill every one who hurt my little mistress. I would carry her in my arms away from this cold, hard land, where gold is the cry ; I would take her to my country, where she would be as a queen, — where she and not her money would be worshiped."

"Why, Justine, I have never heard you talk like this; why have you always been so silent with me?"

"There are times for all things, mademoiselle; I was silent when words were useless."

"Tell me, my old dear, were you sad when you first came here from France?"

A quiver shook the muscles of her square face as Justine replied: "Mademoiselle may well say sad; my heart was well-nigh broken within me. Many and many a time I was on my way to monsieur to tell him it was stronger than I, the longing for my country, when a caress, a word, a laugh, or a sob from my lamb stopped me. I reflected that it was she who made my sunshine; of what use is it to have a warm body, if the heart is cold? so I stayed. Time arranges most things, and I have been content."

"Oh, Justine, you have always loved me; my money is nothing to you, I am all. How can I ever pay you for such love?"

"Mademoiselle has paid me over and over again. I never would have spoken before, but now she is free. Oh, come to my beautiful France! Leave this cold land, come to my country, where the nobles wait for a king to follow, and hold aloft the white lilies."

" Ah, that is past, dear Justine ; the emperor has brought peace and plenty to France ; perhaps that is better for the people than the days of romance, though I would dearly have loved to live in those times."

" Mademoiselle, I am of a humble family, but we have our traditions as well as the great ones ; my great-grandfather fought with the Vendéens when they mowed down the Blues like so much withered grass ; our seigneur was a powerful noble, and I know what I say. Come away with me! Come where the sun is more kindly, where the earth is more generous ; where the saints seem close to you in the great cathedrals, and touch you with their blessings as the light streams on you through the colored windows. Leave this cold country, where they would rob you and insult you ! "

The woman had risen, and stood glowing with a still, inward excitement, her hands folded on her broad bosom, which rose and fell with her quick-coming breath. Sylvia seemed to see a new personality in her old nurse, whose enthusiasm caught her in its rush.

" We will go, Justine, you and I ! We will go back to the land of our birth, to sunny France ! "

CHAPTER III.

WHEN Sylvia, accompanied by her faithful Justine, began her journey through the Old World, her character was a curious mixture. In certain ways she was advanced beyond her years; in others, more ignorant than many a child. Her wide knowledge of books gave her a singular sense of familiarity with the places she visited, whilst personages of history and fiction produced a fascinating confusion of ideas. At Venice she felt that Shylock had as truly trodden above the springing arch of the Rialto, as that the Ten had whispered their deadly secrets in the Doges' Palace. In Spain, Don Quixote's adventures were as real to her as the fact that Columbus had set forth from Granada with the queen's promise of aid. Her imagination, always vivid, was stimulated by the new scenes about her, and for a year she followed her hero or heroine of the moment, taking unnecessary journeys, retracing many a step, and enjoying her life in a way that she had hitherto thought impossible. All this time she lived in the lives of those shades, who made up to her for friends

and family. The chance acquaintance of travel
were to her the misty ones, and she herself only
a mirror reflecting days and emotions that were
past. She took pleasure in buying and wearing
dainty apparel, because it seemed to her right
to respect herself, and her instinctive good taste
was an inheritance from her mother. But at
first, beyond this natural love of beautiful surroundings, she paid very little attention to herself, or the effect she produced on others. The
years had brought her many gifts, and she was
a woman whose grace and charm impressed
themselves on the beholder before he had had
time to discover how delicate were the lines of
nose and mouth, how classic the shape of the
well-poised head; that the dark thick hair grew
just low enough on the broad, fair brow, and
over the small ear; and that when one looked
closely, the deep-set, gray eyes, fringed with
black lashes, had gleams of violet in them that
flashed into brilliancy at any excitement. All
these observations, however, came gradually; at
the first sight Sylvia's real but unobtrusive
beauty was less noticed than her harmonious
movements and subtle air of refinement and
breeding.

At first, in her ignorance of the world of to-
day, with all its seething intensity, she was well
content to live dreamily in the past; but this

could not last always. There came a time when
she looked wistfully at two sisters discussing a
painting, and even envied a share in the little
quarrels and bickerings she saw going on among
families spending their vacation in traveling.
She began to want companionship, to need some
one who could understand her enthusiasms: but
she knew no one. She always had her private
apartment at the hotels, and her evenings were
as solitary as in the old days, for she did not
care to take Justine with her to the theatre or
opera, the servant feeling out of place. This
sentiment of loneliness had come upon her
strongly at one of the Italian lakes. She had
been standing on her balcony, watching a party
of English people coming home after a day's
excursion. In spite of tumbled hair and dusty
dresses, they had looked so amused and interested, had laughed so heartily as they entered
the hotel, that Sylvia longed to ask them to tell
her, and let her laugh too. As they disappeared
beneath the portico, two young men came into
sight, swinging along with that easy walk which
looks like play, but means business. They were
talking earnestly; suddenly one turned, and
something in the landscape caught his attention; he pointed, and the other, after looking,
gave his companion a glance of sympathy. They
walked on more slowly, and in silence, but Syl-

via felt that they understood each other; that
to them the blue mountains and glittering lake
gave a pleasure unknown to her. She turned
away with a sigh, and entered the salon where
Justine was arranging some flowers.

"Tell me a little of your country," she said.
"We have only seen Paris in France, and I think
I want to go back there." The woman stood
upright, dropping her flowers on the table. Her
square, ordinarily stolid face became animated.
"It is long since I have been in my country, but
it is always the same, though all my people are
dead. We are waiting for the old glories again,
madame. It is all very fine now, but we who
were born in La Vendée know that it is not the
real thing. We want no emperors; we are waiting for our king — and he will come! Oh, if
madame could only see some of the *vraie noblesse*
of my country. They are brave and gallant;
they always pray for the king's return. It is so
different from the people we have seen, — these
pigs of Germans and Italians, English and Span-
iards. If madame would only go to France, she
would see true gentle people."

Sylvia laughed a little sadly. "I should see
the outsides of their chateaux, Justine — that's
all. I am getting tired of seeing only exteriors;
I would so like to get inside."

Justine stood looking at her mistress help-

lessly. It seemed to her that no one in all the
world was so beautiful, so noble, as the child
she had brought up. She was sure that if once
the door could be opened into that life she longed
for, all would bow before her; but in her ignorance she saw no chance.

"I always think madame was meant for a
duchess or a princess," she said loyally.

"Go down, Justine dear, and arrange for a
place at table d'hôte for me. I must speak to
some one — I must do something different."

When she was left alone she sat musing, thinking of herself, a most unusual thing. It came
to her that there was no one in the world, with
the exception of two servants, who loved her;
and no one whom she loved. Richard had cared
for her in a way for her father's sake, but not
as he had loved the woman he told her about.
Her father had given her a grudging affection,
more because she was her mother's child than
because she was his. What a strange havoc-
working malady was this love of men and women.
It never seemed to work well for its victims
except in novels; it was truly a malady. She
had given it a good name, and would always
avoid it; she knew its dangers, and would alone
be to blame if it was ever allowed to influence
her. But companionship was different. What
she longed for was cool, sympathetic, reasonable

friendship — how could she ever find it? At this period Sylvia's character was like a half-ripened peach, — her intellect, which had been over developed by her severe training, was like the ruddy, downy hemisphere of the fruit, kissed into perfection by the sun's heat; but the side towards the wall as hard and untouched as was Sylvia's heart. Her impulses were all kindly, but lacked enthusiasm. Some instinct within urged her to help the distressed, to be gentle and courteous to all in her path; but there was no comradeship in her rare relations with the outer world; she went her way like one apart, until a glance, a silence between two men, strangers to her, made her understand what a friend can be. As she sat, wondering in a vague way, how it would feel to have some one near enough to her to praise, to find fault, to criticise, even to quarrel with her, the door opened, and Justine, her face all aglow with interest, came in. "What is it?" asked Sylvia, "you look as though something had happened."

"Madame is right; something has happened that will please her. Who should I see coming up from the boat but Monsieur Henley, the good, the amiable? I told him we were here, and he is to call for madame, and take her down to dinner with him."

Sylvia was interested and pleased; it was a

link with her past, slight enough, but pathetically important to her.

When, prompt as the dinner-gong, her old friend made his appearance, she greeted him with a cordiality that flattered him, coming as it did from a young woman of such pronounced distinction of appearance. He took her hand as if he had been her uncle, and patted it gently as he said : " This is a great pleasure — a great pleasure — and it would have been a surprise to see your good serving-woman, had I not already heard of your being here."

" How did you know, dear Mr. Henley ? "

" From an English woman, Mrs. Lee-Blair, an old friend of mine. She is staying in the hotel and had been on a day's excursion, and I met her on the boat. I told her that I hoped the place was not overrun with American tourists, and she said that there was one countrywoman of mine here, who looked charming, but was very exclusive. I asked the name, and she said Huntington ; still I should not have known it was you but for her description."

" What did she say about me ? " asked Sylvia.

Mr. Henley chuckled.

" She said that you held your head so that one looked for the tiara, and had a smile that seemed to say you saw and knew things that no one else did."

"Your friend must be a close observer," answered Sylvia. She was partly amused, and partly annoyed by the description. "Shall we go down now?" she added; "and you will let me prove to your friend that I am not as supercilious as she would make me out. Her description is like a combination of a race horse and the Mona Lisa."

"She is a clever woman, nevertheless, and I mean to introduce you; she will sit by me at dinner."

So Sylvia found herself suddenly launched into the little world of the hotel. It was chiefly filled with those birds of passage whose sole business in life seems to be to flutter after the best climate. Winter finds them on the Riviera, spring in Paris or Venice, summer at the Italian lakes or French watering-places, and autumn, migrating southward in a leisurely manner to begin the round once more. One wonders if any one of this restless tribe ever longs for a nest of his own? If they never weary of beating down hotel bills, of trying to become intimate with other birds whose gayer plumage and crested heads proclaim them of a nobler birth, and of pecking spitefully at the meeker, dingier songsters, who are perhaps engaged in that most desolate and despairing game of hide-and-seek with health: a game where the poor little bird

is always " it," as the children say, and catches
but rare, tantalizing glimpses of health's rosy
mocking face as he beckons them on.

Mr. Henley's friend, Mrs. Lee-Blair, did not
strictly belong to any of these of whom I have
spoken. She came of a good family, being, as
Mr. Henley informed Sylvia, the daughter of a
baronet, but with so little money that she was
forced to live economically on the continent. Her
late husband had left her a bare pittance, and,
the old gentleman added, it was extremely cred-
itable that she managed to make such a good appearance. Flora Lee-Blair was no longer young,
but she gave no effect of age ; a modern artist
would probably have fainted had he heard her
figure praised, but in her eyes and in those
of her admirers it was her strongest point, with
broad shoulders, large bust, and a waist whose
size gave striking evidence of a patient martyrdom that would have been called heroism in a
better cause. Her rather large, beak-like nose
and prominent chin gave her at first sight an
eager, rapacious air, which the full-lipped, good-
humored mouth, and small, merry black eyes
contradicted. Her thick, dark hair was elaborately dressed, and her toilettes were usually in
fairly good taste, with the exception that she
rejoiced in an astounding quantity of turquoise
which she wore bravely on all occasions. Her

voice was rich and low, making the listener feel
that it was almost vulgar to sound final *g's* and
pronounce *ow* as one syllable, so charmingly did
her accent strike on the ear. She could write a
daintily expressed note in a dashing hand that
left the reader unsure as to the exact spelling,
so cleverly she made one letter look like another.
It is doubtful if she ever read anything but
society papers, and her prayer-book; but her
want of education was atoned for by great social
knowledge, and a limited amount of tact sup-
plemented by a really warm heart. There was
no pretense about the woman; she honestly
acknowledged her deficiencies in a way that
disarmed criticism. Had she been enabled to
spend her life in the manner she had been
brought up to expect, with no lack of those
things we consider necessary until we lose them,
she would have been as good, straightforward,
kindly a creature as could be found; but years
of trying to make a pound do the work of a
guinea, always a little behindhand with her bills,
occasionally compelled to submit to rude insolence from unpaid inferiors, had developed in
her a strain of hardness generally characteristic
of an adventuress. Gradually she had lost her
former rather fine sense, and had come to the
point where she congratulated herself gleefully,
with no touch of remorse, when she had success-

fully lowered a just bill by threats of what her influence could do, or quitted a place a week in advance of the time she had previously named, leaving no trace by which the despoiled and bewildered tradesmen could follow her. She kept these little transactions very quiet, and eased her conscience by ardently recommending her unpaid tailors, milliners and dressmakers to all her rich, aristocratic friends, thus more than making up to them for their losses. Some lingering habit from her early, methodical days made her keep a strict account of all she owed, and the receipted bills were filed no more carefully than their less fortunate brothers. In spite of this bad streak in her character, which was not natural to it, being caused more or less by her circumstances, she was a lovable woman, and also an extremely amusing companion. Partly because she found Sylvia attractive, partly because of a judicious hint from Mr. Henley, she was very kind to the young stranger, and introduced her to all the grandees of the place.

Sylvia soon became a personage among them; her dignity, and the air of indifference it gave her, made them credit her with a hauteur that raised her immensely in their opinion; and a woman young, beautiful, independent, and wealthy is always interesting to her fellow

beings. She was delighted with the new atmosphere surrounding her; the give and take
of conversation, although not always clever,
amused her; even the all-day picnics, which
brought forth groans and abuse from those most
ardent in organizing them, gave her pleasure.
She regretted that it could not last; but Mr.
Henley always disposed ahead of all his time,
so he could not linger, and Flora Lee-Blair had
told her that she must be moving on at the
end of another week. She was frankly sorry,
and in a talk with Mr. Henley told him so; he
threw out a hint; Sylvia caught at it eagerly,
and before the night closed in she had made
an agreement with Mrs. Lee-Blair that the latter
should become her companion.

She liked her, found her kindly and entertaining, and for the time she was willing to ignore
that the older woman was absolutely incapable
of sympathizing with the deeper interests of
life. Flora was so elated over her prospects that
she became emotional, — something very rare
for her, — and refused to dwell on the thought
that she had sunk to the level of a governess;
it haunted her a little, but she banished it resolutely, and went to her room in a mood of sincere gratitude. Half her first year's income
would enable her to pay the more pressing of
her debts, and in twelve months she would be a

free woman, — always supposing Mrs. Huntington chose to remain Mrs. Huntington. Well,
part of her task would be to discover her charge's
tendencies, and a word here, a look there, can
work wonders with a woman over twenty — girls
are the only absolutely unmanageable creatures
in the world.

She sat down at her writing table, and opening her prayer-book, elaborate in its purple
velvet binding, read the General Thanksgiving
with enthusiasm. It is probable that she gave
to the word "preservation" therein contained the
meaning of preservation from unpaid accounts,
insolent shopkeepers, and all the ills attendant
on a small income, but there is no doubt that
her impulses at this time were good, and her
intentions praiseworthy.

Having shut the book, she took from a large
brass-bound oaken box two formidable packs
of requests for immediate payment. They were
neatly arranged in order, and the oldest were
dated years before. She began making calculations, — cheering ones, to judge by her expression
at the beginning of her task, but as the lines of
figures grew longer, so did her face. She had
resolved to pay every penny she owed, make a
fresh start, and be economical : but when she
had resolved this she had not realized how ap-
pallingly large the sum of her debts was. A

year's income pay them off? No, nor two, nor
three years, generous as the offered salary was.
She thought despondingly how unlikely it was
that a woman like Sylvia should remain unmar-
ried — do what she might to prevent such a
catastrophe. Then it occurred to her that she
had not troubled herself much about her indebt-
edness before; why should she now? She took
all those prayers for payment over a year old,
and sitting by the fireplace began to burn them.

As they curled and shriveled, sending a pleasant aromatic odor into the room, she caught
sight of the various items. Three hundred
francs for that old blue silk; how ridiculous
to think of paying it now, when the dress had
been in rags for longer than she could remember. That leghorn bonnet with the roses —
what a price she had paid for it, or no, rather,
what a price the milliner had asked — it was
pure robbery, and the roses had faded, too;
then that turquoise bracelet she had got dirt
cheap at Genoa; but one of the stones had
turned green almost immediately. Tradespeo-
ple were nothing but brigands and cheats, she
decided with righteous indignation, as the last
paper rose with a dying protest against her judgment, and fell exhausted on the black, crackling
heap.

"Now, if I am to live with a swell I must
have something decent to wear."

So saying she wrote an order to her Parisian dressmaker for some new creations, and inclosing a cheque for her previous bill, she rang and sent it downstairs for the early post. When she laid her head on her pillow, it was with a clear sensation of comfort: if all her debts were not exactly paid, one of them at least was, and the greater part were burned, therefore forgotten.

The next morning her maid was made happy and astonished by the payment of her wages to date and the present of a very presentable frock : so she approved of the new order of things quite as much as her mistress.

Sylvia had already felt a thrill of pleasure by being able to use the pronoun " we " instead of " I," and the only person who felt a doubt about the suitability of the arrangement was Justine. An instinct, perhaps born of jealousy, made her suspicious of this English woman, with her showy presence. She even wondered if the Mr. Henley, whom she had sincerely admired until now, was not in a plot against her darling.

" You don't look pleased, Justine." said Sylvia, a little severely, as she told her news that same evening.

" Madame will never see France now ; she will go to that cold, foggy England," retorted the servant, her eyes dark with wounded feelings. " Madame will be obliged to have a new maid."

" Why, Justine, you foolish old sheep! Part
with you, my dear, dear nurse? Never! And
if you please, my lady, since when have you become so formal with me? For shame, Justine.
You have no right to doubt my love and gratitude for you, — you, who have been almost a
mother to me. What would have become of me
when I was little, without you?"

" You would have had Deborah," mumbled
Justine, a little appeased, and allowing her jealousy to take another turn.

" You are too unreasonable to listen to me to-
night," said her mistress; " but you must understand one thing: we are going almost directly
to France, to Trouville, where Mrs. Lee-Blair
knows many people. Now are you satisfied —
old grumbler?"

" Trouville is not really France, it is only a
watering-place for Parisians and strangers; but
it is better than nothing."

CHAPTER IV.

TROUVILLE nearly thirty years ago, — Trouville under the second empire! In modern times was there ever such a seething maelstrom of extravagance, false taste, fierce excitement, and romance, both real and fictitious? Is it the distance lending enchantment that makes us feel that women were more beautiful, men more redoubtable and fascinating in those days? Did hearts beat with more fervor and less self-control under lace fichus then than they do now under a stiff mannish shirt front? As comradeship between the two sexes has increased, has sentiment diminished? Perhaps the many interests that have come into the lives of women of later years have made them less susceptible to love; the great gain has been attended, it may be, by some little loss. To read a novel of that period makes one think so, at all events, and it was into this emotional whirl, this concentrated imitation of Paris in her heyday of dissipation, that Sylvia made her first acquaintance with the world, the flesh and the devil. They were all very rampant, and some women would have been confused and

bouleversée by the novelty of the situation. Sylvia, however, kept her head admirably. She was
so familiar with the fabulous splendors of history, which lost nothing pictured to her by her
vivid imagination, that realities fell short of her
mind pictures. Who among this showy crowd
could boast of a retinue to equal that of Car-
dinal Wolsey? What jewels shine like those of
Anne of Austria? It was all very gay and very
brilliant, but it seemed thin to her, — as thin
as the walls of the spacious, luxurious, over-
furnished villa that Flora had secured for her.
Everything had a transient air; it was a mushroom growth.

In spite of her unexpressed disappointment
she took keen pleasure in her first plunge into
the society of the place. Mrs. Lee-Blair was a
very pointer in her social nature, and had an
unequaled eye for the "best" people, — those
who would be of use. She was charmed to find
that Sylvia bade fair to be a success; a woman
of her nature adores success, and she congratulated herself twenty times a day on her discern-
ment. At the end of ten days Sylvia became
the fashion. It had taken her very little time to
adjust herself to her surroundings. With the
facility common to her countrywomen she learnt
in a flash the ways of thought and the terms
of speech of those about her. Those who were

not clever enough to perceive her real brilliancy took it for granted from the lips of the more discerning; and all the Trouville world found it easy to admire, without being told to, her charm and distinction, her good looks and exquisite clothes, her irreproachable turnouts and excellent dinners.

At first Sylvia entered into it all with the zest of a child; the compliments pleased her, her popularity so easily gained delighted her. Then came the trail of the serpent; the thought that it was her fortune, not herself, that put her where she was. The morning papers that Justine, beaming with pride, brought her with her early cup of tea, rubbed in the disagreeable truth. She was called "the witty and wealthy Madame Huntington," "the beautiful millionaire," in the florid accounts of balls and races. She grew to have a sensitive loathing of the mere sound of money; it began to have a vulgar jingle in her ears. Who would have discovered her wit, her fascination, her beauty, if she had come unheralded among this butterfly throng? Before the first three weeks were over, she had become cynical; behind the smiles of her flatterers she fancied that she could see greed and avarice barely hidden by an assumed mask. She used to tell herself daily that Justine had been right; the ideal France must be different, and she would

ply her old nurse with questions about her country. In spite of the frivolous life about her, the
frothy vice, the constant repetitions of scandals
that made her soul feel withered and worldly,
she kept her belief that somewhere, hidden in
the green interior, still existed romantic, gallant
hearts, and she resolved to find them for herself, to see the reality. Moving in the midst of
frivolity, seeming to an observer merely on the
surface, a charming embodiment of worldliness,
Sylvia still kept hidden in her heart a store of
romantic faith. Most people need imperatively
something to worship, an idol of stone, or an
abstract virtue, for lack of anything better. She
had her belief in heroism and self-sacrifice to
dream over. No other belief had been presented to her in a manner that appealed to her.
The lurid doctrine that she had listened to during her youthful days had only inspired revolt
and skepticism ; the unreasoning devotion to
signs and symbols taught her by Justine had in
their turn led her to a spirit of mockery ; but
bravery for and devotion to a noble cause meant
God to her, and her dearest, closest wish was to
be identified with such a cause.

Thus she lived her life of gayety and amusement, surrounded by all outward signs of success
and luxury, simultaneously with an inward, hidden life, the only signs of which were the sudden

glow of warmth in her serious eyes, and the inexplicable, subtle smile on her lips, brought there by some chance word, some vague association of ideas, at the most unexpected moments.

But she was always searching for some embodiment of her ideal ; every new presentation might mean that she had found at last the right path : but one disappointment followed another.

"Are these the best people?" she asked Flora one day ; "they all seem so commonplace and *banal* to me."

"I don't know what more you could wish," retorted Mrs. Lee-Blair, somewhat offended. "We began with a baronne, and yesterday a duchesse invited you to dinner ; I am sure I can do nothing more."

"We are not talking exactly of the same thing," said Sylvia, puzzled to know how to express herself ; and then the incongruousness of it all struck her with rather a dismal amusement. She caught sight of herself in her mirror, dressed to perfection, the incarnation of worldly grace and beauty ; her horses were stamping impatiently at the gate, where her victoria waited for her ; her footman stood respectfully holding her wrap and her card-case, in which was a list of the calls that she and Flora were about to make, — a list which seemed to glisten with high-sounding titles : and she stood dreaming of a chance for heroic deeds, longing for a cause worth dying for. Little wonder that her unconscious smile gave her a sphinx-like touch of mystery.

Just as she had decided that Trouville bored her, and had begun to wonder if it would be unkind to drag Flora away from its distractions, a newcomer appeared on the scene, and Sylvia found that he made life more interesting; he was a fresh type, and he stimulated her. Mrs. Lee-Blair, who by dint of confidential talks just before bedtime thought that she had found the key of Sylvia's ambition, namely, a title, — for what else did her rare words about nobility and greatness mean ? — bent all her energies to the task of blackening the character of any count or baron who was in the least devoted to her charge ; and in passing, be it said, that her task was not a difficult one. But she paid little attention to the newcomer already mentioned, — a young cavalry officer, Captain Maurice Regnier, not even possessing a *de* before his name. To her mind Sylvia was so cold and immovable that the fact that Regnier was handsome, well built, and brilliant was of no importance. To Sylvia herself, however, this fact did convey something. What this something was she did not analyze ; but she knew that the very first time they met their conversation plunged from the conventionalities of an introduction immediately into the heart of things: that almost without realizing it she had permitted him to join her in her morning rides; that a dinner without him, even with all the table between them, became an intolerable bore. She took it for granted that it was their mutual tastes which brought them together: they both loved horses and riding with enthusiasm: they met on the common ground of literature, for she found to her delight that he knew as much of English authors as she did of French, although he spoke only his own tongue. But it was something deeper and wider than mutual tastes which made her when with him find salt in the world she had called insipid. She did not suspect what the real charm was underlying his beauty of face and form, his boyishly gay manner, and his high spirits; she did not feel that Maurice Regnier's nature had just the tenderness, the enthusiasm, for the soft lovable things of this world that she had missed all her life. He spoke of his feelings with the unconscious naturalness of a child, and liked to tell this gracious woman about himself, watching her grave eyes brighten and glow until the gray turned to violet. He even confided to her the secret of his life, that he wrote poetry, although he confessed that his brother officers would never give him a moment's peace, were

they to know that he was the author of a volume
of poems which had been praised by the Revues
and had become the fashion in Paris. Sylvia
found herself feeling young and careless when
with him ; there was a breeziness in his atmosphere, a sudden shifting from grave to gay, a
possibility of an outbreak of his hot but forgiv-
ing temper, that gave a variety and fascination
to his companionship. Imperceptibly the heat
of the sun was turning to pink the hard side of
the peach ; little by little Sylvia's temperament
was waking from its profound slumber. It is
the old fairy story again, the sleeping beauty
and the prince. But alas, life is not all a fairy
story : heroes and heroines do not always " marry
and live happily forever after."

" How beautiful it all is ; how I love your
France !" exclaimed Sylvia, standing at the open
window and drinking in the fresh breeze. The
day was drawing to a close, and over the hori-
zon a soft grayish pink haze had begun to settle ;
the low rays of the sun striking the dancing
waves were reflected on the ceiling of the gay,
over-furnished salon ; from the casino on the
beach floated up the music of a waltz, and the
confused sounds of laughter and talk. Sylvia
had just returned from a drive, and Maurice,
being by some strange chance at the gate, had
followed her into the house. Turning from the

window she seated herself in a low chair, and began drawing off her gloves, while her eyes still lingered on the expanse of sea and sky.

"My France!" said Maurice, echoing her last words energetically. "This is not France, this hurly-burly, this mushroom growth of villas springing up in a night and insulting the rocks and the ocean. Please do not call it by that name: it jars on a man who really loves his country, as much as if you thought his mother was one of those painted, bedizened old creations of this second empire, who toss their heads with pride, because the mountebank now in power labels them princesses or duchesses."

Sylvia listened earnestly. She might learn something of that higher, finer life she felt sure existed out of sight, hidden by the rush and glitter of the world of fashion. "Tell me about your real France, and your real nobility, there," she said.

"I would give a year of my life to be able to have the right to show you my home and my people," he answered, a little tremble in his voice, showing the sincerity of his words.

"Tell me about them," again said Sylvia, dreamily resting her head against the back of her chair, and looking at him with half-closed eyes. At her request Regnier started from his chair and took two or three turns up and down the room.

" I don't know how to begin," he said at last.
" I am bound to it by such strong, and at the
same time such fragile, ties that I am afraid the
spell might disappear if I spoke of it, and yet
there is no one in the world I would rather tell
all my dearest thoughts to than you."

" I know that curious flitting-away effect
some ideas have," said Sylvia, ignoring his last
remark. " You cannot always call them by
name, they seem to need different words to express them."

" Yes, that's it — they are always just ahead
of us. And I suppose that is what genius can
do — fix them either on canvas, in words, or in
marble, and make them permanent. I am no
genius, but I want you to see through my eyes
for the moment. You may think that I am wild,"
he went on, blushing in a delightfully youthful
way that he had, " but if I may take your emerald ring and look at it, I believe I can describe
better."

Sylvia did not smile as she handed it to him ;
she knew a little what he meant.

He laid it on the table before him, folded his
arms and leant forward, looking at it intently.
Sylvia watched him, thinking how handsome he
was : how well his crisp brown hair grew behind
his ears and on his muscular neck ; how sweetness and strength were combined in the curves

of his lips, and how nice it would be to see him
in his full uniform : but not a suspicion of any
warmer feeling than friendly admiration made
her pulse beat faster, or her eye gleam brighter.
Presently he spoke, and his voice sounded as
though he were telling a fairy story to a child.
" Once upon a time," he began, " nearly nine
hundred years ago, there lived in Touraine a man
of force and courage, not always used by him
for the best causes. His name was Foulques
Nerra, and the legend runs that he loved a beautiful woman, not his wife, and that he built
a castle for her which he called La Roche, and
gave her the title of Countess de La Roche.
There she lived in grandeur, and there he often
came, until a feeling of remorse for some of his
brutalities prompted him to leave France on a
crusade. He rode away, and during his absence
she bore him a son ; but the time was long, and
before he came back she had died, and was
buried in the chapel tunneled into the rock beneath the castle, and there she lies to this day.
Her son, who inherited both title and fortune,
grew strong and brave, like the roving Foulques,
and the time came when he in his turn went
to the Holy Land. On his return he had with
him the cone of a cedar of Lebanon, which he
planted on the terrace, and he had these words
cut in old French on a stone shield in the chapel :

' When the green turns brown, shall crumble the stone.' He gave orders that when his time came he should be buried beneath the carving. The old cedar, or perhaps its offspring, still lives, and it was under its branches I learned to love all things that are beautiful and strong as it is. Your emerald has not its bluish-green color, but it is like the century-old moss on its bark, which shines like a jewel when the sun strikes it."

He paused for a moment, but Sylvia remained silent; she was touching at last the things of which she had only seen the shadows before.

" There are only three existing reminders of those days," he went on; " the old cedar, the square dove-cote tower standing a little apart from the chateau, and the chapel in the rock. The three greatest truths in the world symbolized : the cedar standing for nature, the dust of the past generation in the chapel for death, and the home of those gentle domestic birds for love."

" Love, always love," thought Sylvia impatiently. but she said : " Tell me more ; how does it all look to-day, and who lives there ? "

Maurice leant back in his chair and resumed in a more commonplace tone. " The mother of the present count lives there now. Her husband, who had all the good, and none of the bad qualities of his ancestors, died about six years ago. He was my hero; brave, loyal to the lilies of France, and ready to die for them : but when he found that was a hopeless dream he took up his life at home, cheerful, kindly, generous to every one. The only thing that made him lose his temper was to hear the emperor praised, and the only thing that saddened him was one of his rare visits to Paris, where he could not help seeing the changes."

"But how did you come there, in his chateau?" asked Sylvia.

"My father was not only his agent, but his very dear friend : he managed the estate for many years, and lived in the old wing ; my sister and I were both born there, and my mother died there when we were children. The young Count Philippe and I are about the same age, and we were educated together for St. Cyr. When his father died he left mine a legacy that made him independent, so the dear old man bought a property that belonged formerly to his grandfather, not far from La Roche, and there he lives among his vines and his books with my sister and her children."

"Weren't you sorry to go away from your old home?" asked Sylvia.

Maurice's lips tightened, as if to suppress a quiver. "Yes," he said ; "I cannot quite under-

stand why it was such a terrible wrench for
me. Even to-day I am made gloomy for a week
after a call on the countess. I felt as though I
had been banished, and I still have a sensation
of rage that it is not mine. But I never spoke
of this to any one else, because I would not
trouble my dear old father for the world, and
he is a thousand times happier now than he ever
was before. He and the countess are very fond
of each other; she consults him on business
arrangements, and often comes to see him, but
he very rarely goes to the chateau."

"Describe a little more, please; I do so love
to hear all this," said Sylvia.

"Stop me if you get tired, won't you?"

"I am never tired when I am interested — it
is only when I am bored: so go on — you interest me."

He looked his happy thanks, and continued.

"The chateau stands on a slight rise looking
down on the Loire, and consists of two wings
facing each other; they are connected on the
side farthest from the river by a low line of
buildings in the centre of which is the gateway
under a stone arch; you enter the court-yard
through this arch, and opposite you, forming
the fourth side of a quadrangle, is a wall, from
which descends a broad flight of steps leading
to the terrace where the cedar stands; below

that again are the gardens stretching nearly to the river."

" I can see it all," exclaimed Sylvia ; " and now, on which side of the entrance was your wing ? "

"On the right," answered Maurice, pleased and stimulated by her eagerness. " It is supposed to date from the time of Louis XI. In the time of François I. it comprised the whole chateau, and in it lived the head of the family. He was a great favorite with the king, who sometimes visited him, and La Roche is one of the few properties which received its grant immediately from the Crown. The counts have always held themselves above every one but the royal family ; they acknowledge no superior among the nobility. In spite, however, of their lofty bearing, this count I am telling you of, the friend of François, was very poor. He was a born gambler, and little by little everything had gone. Ruin stared him in the face, and he became desperate. The legend runs that he played dice with the devil : the stakes, his soul against a fortune. How true the story is I cannot say, but the fact remains that he divorced his wife, and married a lady of great beauty. With the money she brought him he built the new wing after the fashion of the day. The lady's ancestry was never discovered. A portrait destroyed in 1793 pictured her with auburn hair, and very fair skin, if old tales can be believed. Her very name is a mystery, and it is said she never spoke a word of French, which points to her being a foreigner. At first her husband was infatuated with her; but in a few years he grew tired of her, and, after the fashion set by Henry of England, did his best to shake her off, too. He failed in his attempt. The rest of their lives is unknown; but it is easy to fancy what it was. Nothing is so unbearable as the ashes of a burnt-out love."

"And yet," said Sylvia, a little scornfully, "just now you put Love with Nature and Death. Why? What right has it there?"

"What right?" he echoed vehemently. "Are you in earnest when you ask a question like that?"

"In earnest, yes, — dead, grim earnest. I am afraid of love; I dread its power, that seems like a poison. My scheme of life shuts it completely out from me."

"But you are wicked to say such a thing! you are worse than wicked, — you are unnatural!"

"No," answered Sylvia, "it is only that I see things as they are. I have seen my father's whole life embittered and brought to an empty end, because he loved my mother so exclusively that when she died he lost interest in everything. I have been persecuted and nearly beggared by the very people who should have protected me."

" You have had a hard experience : but you should not allow it to color your life. Believe me, there are still *many*, *many* people in the world full of romance and disinterested feelings."

" Perhaps — but it is a mercenary age," she said, with a dreary fall to her voice. " I may misjudge it — it may be that my education was in fault. Still, in spite of his failures, my father never lost his ideals, and I grew up caring nothing for money, but building an altar to patriotism and nobility of character, where I worshiped."

" It is an altar worthy of a hero's devotion ; but for you, — a woman, — is n't it rather a cold, hard place ? Does it satisfy you ?"

" No," she said frankly ; " it does not. Nothing has ever satisfied me in all my life, except the feeling I had the day when I saw my husband and my father marching at the head of their men, all going to risk their lives, some to lose them, for the sake of their flag. I had made my little sacrifice in the same spirit that they were making their large ones. Then, and then only, I felt that I was a part of a whole ; not an insignificant atom, tossed here and there,

but of importance, because I had done my share
as well as they. I try to remember papa as he
looked that day, the sunshine falling on him,
his face young and glad and proud. Justine
said it was always so when my mother was alive.
Her death crushed his vitality, his joy in living, his sense of duty to me, out of him. Only
patriotism had the power to bring back his own
nature. And without judging him, I have pondered ever since what a selfish, narrowing force
this passion is that we call love : it is a remnant
of the dark ages. We should rise above it, and
I mean to try in my small way to do so."

"You can't," said young Regnier; "it is
stronger than you ; it is nature ; it is woman's
religion."

She shook her head. "No ; it is an idol worship, adopted more as an excuse than anything
else."

"I wish you would not say such shocking
things ! I hate to hear you," he said with a
flash of temper that amused his hearer, and as
he spoke he rose, and stood at the window
against the glitter of the sunlit sea. Sylvia
could see his well-poised, Greek head, his col-
umn-like throat, full as an athlete's, and his tall
figure ; but his face was in darkness, owing to
the dazzle without.

"Sit down where I can see you," she said

with a gentle imperiousness. " That is right. Now I can tell just how angry I dare to make you."

In spite of his twenty-seven years Captain Regnier's face showed his feelings like that of a child. Just now his dark brown eyes, set wide apart, were black with momentary heat, and his short upper lip curled with an expression far from peaceful. His was a face full of possibilities for good or bad. A student of such signs might have foretold that his actions in one direction or the other would be guided by his vehement, enthusiastic nature, which was a little too credulous perhaps, too prone to jump at conclusions ; whilst the firm, square chin gave promise of a latent power of self-command, to be roused to action, or not, as circumstances arose.

" Before you judge me," Sylvia continued, " let me ask you one question, and answer me fairly. Here am I, a young, independent, wealthy woman. Which course is the nobler one for me to follow : to marry a man who tells me he adores me, who may seem to me as being attractive and fascinating, to spend one or two years — perhaps a quarter of my life even — in a supreme selfishness *à deux ;* to lose him in the end either because he dies, or is tired of me, or because I die, or am tired of him. No, let me finish," she insisted, as he began an interruption.

"There is one side; here is the other: I take my fortune and give it freely, together with my hand, to some nobleman, the last of a great family which is dying out for lack of means. I sink myself in the case, only caring to see an illustrious name shine out again, bringing credit to all connected with it. Which is the more unselfish, the more noble?"

Maurice did not answer her question, but turned catechizer in his turn.

"If you have these high ideals of self-immolation," he asked severely, "why did you come over the seas; why did you not stay at home, and marry one of those mercenary relations you just complained of?"

"How dull men are, even Frenchmen!" she exclaimed. "That is just it! I don't want to be married for my money, but for what my money can accomplish. Besides," she added with a swift, charmingly illogical twist of her ideas, "I love great names, great families, titles, and if I give up everything, why have n't I a right to please myself in the giving?"

She herself saw the weakness of her argument, and smiled at him. He forgot her words for a moment in the joy of looking at her; then he said, recalling himself a little sharply, "Who has put these ideas into your head? Is it Mrs. Lee-Blair?"

Sylvia resented his tone. "No, monsieur, I am woman enough to think out my own plan of action. But why do you dislike poor Flora? you never say anything good of her."

"I never said anything bad of her," he answered evasively.

"Then let us be friends," she returned, quickly dropping the touch of displeasure in her voice, "and don't scold me because I own that I care for some of those things for which half the world is struggling."

"I have no right to *scold* you, madame," he answered, a little puzzled at her remark.

Perhaps one of the reasons why she fascinated him was her originality; her careless friendliness of speech was mingled with such gentle dignity of manner, and such purity of mind, that he bowed before her even when he understood her the least. It would have been impossible to be on the same terms with a French woman.

It may have been this peculiarity that led the people of the gay world at Trouville to regard Mrs. Huntington as a new variety of the human race, and led to much discussion of her character; she was an iceberg — she was an intrigante — she was unusually stupid — she was excessively clever, and so on, according to the bias of mind of those discussing her. In short, she was one of the first American women to rouse French curiosity. Then, as to-day, feminine morality was called frigidity, and ease of manner the flower of coquetry.

" I am not presuming to find fault," Regnier went on, " but if you had seen as much of these fine sounding families as I have, I think that you would consider very gravely any step such as you propose."

" Tell me a little about them," she said eagerly. " You seem so different from these people here ; they make me feel that they are hired to go inside the villas, and that they will be stored with the satin furniture when autumn comes."

He laughed a little, and then returned to his charge.

" Please tell me that you were in fun just now ; you did not mean what you said about love ? "

" Yes, yes ; I meant every word ; it is something to be avoided, and the mere thought of it frightens me."

" Then you do not know the true meaning of love, if you are frightened by it. You are talking in ignorance ; some day you will feel differently."

His words were insignificant, but his manner and the brilliancy of his eyes that seemed to imperiously compel hers to meet their glance embarrassed Sylvia. She looked at him for a moment that seemed an hour to her, and then her lids drooped. She could not understand why she felt confused, and why her blood seemed to be racing tumultuously through her veins; it was a new experience, as it is to every man and woman when first that elemental feeling, underlying all the refinements and concealments of modern times, makes itself apparent. But to Sylvia it was only a vague trouble that stirred her, roused by the passion ready to spring into force that was swaying Maurice. He knew that it was not yet time for him, and with an effort which drove the color from his face, he walked again to the window and stood there, willing himself to calmness. The silence grew unbearable, and Sylvia broke it.

"Let us avoid personalities," she said in her coldest tone; "they only annoy me: besides, I want to hear more of La Roche: tell me a little about the present count; is he like his father?"

"In looks, yes," answered Maurice shortly.

"Do you care for him? Is he brave as well as handsome?"

"I cannot tell; we are not making history today; we have no chance to be heroic."

Maurice still stood staring out of the window, and his voice told Sylvia that she had hurt him.

Collected enough, now that his eyes were not burning deep into her soul, she tried to cure the wound.

" I found a new road this afternoon," she said tentatively. He made no reply. " It was too rough for the carriage, but it would be delicious to ride through." Still silence. " I hate to explore with Jenkins, he grumbles so if the briars scratch his beautiful hat ; but I do want to go down that lane. Shall you be too busy, Monsieur le Capitaine, to ride with me to-morrow ? "

One of Sylvia's charms was her voice, — rather low pitched, it had at times the effect of a caress, so velvet soft was it. Maurice felt his sensation of injury stealing away, bewitched by her words. He knew that for the time he was as wax in her hands, but he did not resent the knowledge.

" Too busy ? No ; you know that nothing short of duty would keep me from a ride with you. Of course I will be here at any time that you say."

" Let us start early then, in the cool of the morning. Is half past seven too soon ? "

" Not a second too soon for me."

" Then it is settled," said Sylvia. " And now please tell me a little more, or I shall think that you are angry with me."

He leant over the table again, looking into the

emerald's depths. "I can only see the old cedar," he said: "it is to me the spirit of the whole place. I can remember all my old dreams as I used to lie beneath it, watching the glimpses of deep blue sky with the puffs of clouds drifting over it. The wind tossing among its hundred branches sang songs of the seas it had swept over on its way to its friend, and I used to listen and long to be on some gallant ship, plunging through furrowed waves to far-off lands. I lived in the old crusader's past, and followed him to the holy sepulchre ; I felt it all in *me* somehow ; I was a part of it, in spite of my being only an outsider, the son of almost the servant of the count. I cared more for it, a hundred times, than Philippe ever did. It is his in name, but it is really mine, by right of the love I have for it. He never stood with his cheek against its bark trying to learn its secrets. He never felt as though he were in some great dim cathedral when the sun set behind it, and every cone, every needle, made a tracery against the pulsing, quivering colors in the sky more beautiful than any stained glass window, and listened, straining every nerve to hear but one echo of the choir invisible chanting somewhere."

"You are a poet," said Sylvia softly.

After he left her, through the evening and far into the night, she thought of what he had

told her; his words had appealed to her imagination, and the picture of the old chateau and
the older cedar rose vividly before her. Mingled
with all the scenes she painted to herself was
the hope that some time she should see and
know the owner of this wonderful place, a man
with the blood of kings in his veins. Even in
sleep she dreamed of him, the unknown, and had
scarcely a memory to give to Maurice, who found
the hours all too long that kept him from the
woman he loved.

The next morning he was at her gate punc-
tually at the appointed time, where her English
coachman stood holding her horse, while her
groom, in all the glory of the last fashion in
livery, controlled his own mount. He had not
long to wait; a light step on the path, and Sylvia
was coming towards him, dawn's rosy touch on
her cheek. There are few times when a young
and pretty woman looks more entirely charming
than in the early morning, and Sylvia had never
captivated Maurice more than now. Her color
was glowing, her eyes had the dewy look that
tells of past child-like sleep, and her whole appearance was one of freshness and sweetness.
Her habit made her seem slighter and more girlish than her usual dress, and the simple round
hat gave her a very youthful look.

She greeted Maurice cordially, and after

stroking her horse's shining neck, and giving a knowing glance at her saddle and stirrup, put her little foot in his hand and rose like a bird to its perch.

"You need not go this morning, Jenkins," she said to her groom as he prepared to follow.

"Very good, madam," answered that worthy, and he stood by his superior, watching the riders disappear, and wondering by what trick a "Frenchy" managed to look as though he were a good horseman. It never occurred to either British brain that Monsieur Regnier was really as much at home on a horse as any fox-hunter in the United Kingdom; indeed, they had once wisely remarked to each other after having seen him win a bet by putting a balky horse over a four-barred gate, mounted on a saddle with neither strap nor stirrup: "'T ain't nothin' but a bloody balancing trick he's got, any'ow."

But Sylvia, not sharing her servants' race prejudice, admired Maurice's skill and tact with horses, and she spoke of it this morning as they slowly passed the sleepy-looking villas, before they gained the open country.

"Who taught you to ride? You have not only ease, but such knowledge. I am always wondering at it."

"The Count de La Roche put Philippe and me on ponies when our legs were so short that they stuck straight out, and we could not have used stirrups if they had been allowed."

" Then the young count rides as well as you ? "

" Exactly," answered Maurice.

Before long the road led them over one of those wide stretches of plain so characteristic of Normandy. The larks were mounting into the blue sky, leaving a wake of ecstatic melody behind them ; the breeze came brisk and fresh from the sea ; it was a day made by the Lord to rejoice and be glad in. Both Maurice and Sylvia were happy for different reasons, and in different ways. She was spontaneously, unconsciously merry, because everything was beautiful, her horse suited her, health and strength made mere breathing delightful, and for the time life was a pleasure. He, on the contrary, felt that his present bliss was too lightly held to give more than a tremulous joy that was half pain. He was laying his all at her feet; would she stoop and take it, or spurn it?

They had been trotting briskly over an open field, and presently the track they had followed dipped into a sudden lane, and the horses fell into a walk as they descended the slope. "There, isn't this lovely ? This is the road I told you of," said Sylvia, looking into Maurice's eyes.

She was not troubled by them to-day, though

they had lost none of their intensity. She felt
free on horseback, for it would be so easy to cut
short an embarrassing remark by a change of
gait; she reflected sagely that no one could
attempt love-making in the course of a sharp
trot. But her very sense of security was her
danger, and as they plunged yet deeper into the
shady, stony lane she found herself forced to
listen to those words of love, strong when sincere, with a strength almost divine.

"Sylvia," said Maurice, bending that he
might better see her, "do you not know how it
is with me? Surely you have guessed a little of
the love I have for you; but no one can tell it
all. I am yours; take me or leave me, body and
soul. To me you mean everything that is holy
and beautiful and noble. Tell me, Sylvia, that
there is hope for me!"

His voice trembled, and his face was white
with the power of his passion. Sylvia was
touched by its force; she, too, became pale.
For one moment she felt a fleeting regret that
love was not for her; that she had resolved to
renounce it; her voice shook as she answered:

"Please do not say such things: we are so
happy as we are, why do you spoil it all?"

"Heaven knows I don't want to spoil it — I
want to perfect it. You have no idea what real
love means; let me teach you, Sylvia."

Her head drooped a little. She would have liked to play with the new sensation sweeping over her, — a sensation as of being borne on an irresistible tide ; but she was too innately honorable to deceive even for a second. " I owe you truthfulness," she said ; "and since you have shown me your heart, I will show you mine : love is not for me ; I do not wish it ; I shrink from it. Maurice, I shall never marry any man who cannot put me among the really great of this world ; my ambition is high, and I am cold as ice to everything else. I like you better than any one I have ever known, but even you cannot stir me, for what could you give me in return for the sacrifice I should have to make to marry you ? Nothing, nothing."

" I could give you a stainless name, and a love an empress might envy," he retorted haughtily, " and you call them nothing. You are a child, Sylvia, and you do not know what you have decided to renounce. Is it nothing to know that there is in this cold, careless world one heart that is yours for weal or woe ? one person to whom old age would only draw you closer ? Is it nothing to you, my darling, that I am ready to die for you ? Oh, if I only had the power to make you understand how I worship you. Everything else fades beside you, my pearl among women. I cannot believe you

will send me from you. Tell me, Sylvia, must
I go?"

His voice had grown soft and pleading.
Against her will and judgment she felt herself
stirred and uncertain; nature was beginning to
awaken the heart that had slept its cold sleep
unstirred until now. Maurice's hand was on
her pommel, his face close to hers; he was
strong and beautiful, like a young Greek;
woman-like she temporized.

"But you must not go away just because I
will not love you?"

"Yes, by the Lord who made me, I must.
Do you think I am not flesh and blood? Do
you suppose I could endure to dangle about you,
fetch and carry like your dog. and see some
other man win you with his title? I am not
made of the stuff to bear such a strain. Tell
me there is no hope for me, and I will never
willingly let my eyes rest on you again; whisper
one word to me, and I am your slave."

Nature was busy at her work; the sleeping
heart stirred and throbbed. Sylvia blushed
divinely.

"Maurice," she murmured, and then stopped.

"Yes, yes, my darling — what is it?" he
answered eagerly.

"You hurry me so I am confused; let me
have a week, or a month, and then — perhaps
— there will be something to tell you."

" Oh, Sylvia, Sylvia, God bless you for that promise."

" It is not a promise," she said hastily ; " it is only a suggestion or perhaps a hope of what may never be."

" I will give you a week, but don't be too cruel, don't make it longer. Shan't I see you all that time ? " he added disconsolately.

" No," she answered, growing more mistress of herself.

" But I shall be near you," he broke in ; " I cannot leave Trouville ; even you would not be cruel enough to insist on that."

" I cannot dictate to you where to go — only I must have time to think it all out. I have told you, Maurice, my soul's thoughts this morning. I could not have believed it possible that I could speak to any one of what is almost my religion — my desire to be high and noble and powerful ; to lead a winning, or if it must be a lost cause ; but at all events to give myself up to great things. If I abandoned my ambition it is because you have really roused me to love you. Just now I feel that I do, but I do not trust myself. I will take my week for thought, and whichever way I decide, believe me, dear Maurice, it will be done honestly."

Her lip quivered, and two tears welled up into her eyes : she had lost her nerve, and she did not understand the sensation. Maurice had not gained all he hoped for, but neither was he left hopeless; his heart was on his face as he leaned closer to her.

"Just one kiss, my darling, my pearl, before this parting." he pleaded. She swayed towards him, and then drew back.

"No, Maurice, no," she answered. "It seems like binding myself, and I must be free."

"Oh, if you knew how mad with love I am, you would pity me," he exclaimed. "It is such a little thing I ask, but it means heaven to me."

"Listen." she said, "I promise you a kiss the next time we meet after the week. Either it will mean good-by forever, or it will tell you I love you as entirely as you do me."

As she spoke she gathered up her reins that had been pulled through her unheeding fingers by her horse's efforts to nibble the grass by the roadside, and the animal, feeling her touch, lifted his head and started forward. Maurice followed, but half satisfied, and almost without another word they trotted rapidly back.

Flora Lee-Blair was in her room, overlooking the entrance, when she heard the beat of the horses' hoofs, and leaving her cup of tea, she went towards the window. She was in her most becoming wrapper, and had no intention of spying without being seen, but neither of the two at the gate gave her a glance. She saw Maurice swing himself to the ground, and throwing his bridle reins to the waiting groom, go to Sylvia's side. She saw her turn in her saddle, place her hands on his shoulder, and let him lift her down. If they spoke she could not have heard, being too far off, but what she saw told her much. Sylvia had never run away from saying goodby before, with her face held down as if she were trying to hide her blushes, leaving her horse without the carrot with which she generally rewarded him, and parting from her companion without a touch of the hand or a word. For a moment Flora hoped it was the result of a quarrel, a refusal perhaps, but one glance at Maurice's face, as he stood gazing towards the house, robbed her of this comforting theory.

Her life had made it necessary for her to use her wits, and she had become used to studying faces, manners, and expressions, to see if by some chance gain might come to her through a side door. Her long experience in knocking about the world had taught her much that her own quickness of mind easily assimilated. Among other secrets, it had told her how to know the signs of a true love, — signs which had never failed her. She cast her mind back unconsciously, recalling how she had helped an influential woman to hoodwink her husband, by boldly taking a prominent part in a family comedy that, but for her, would have turned into a tragedy, her only authority being her reading of the wife's bearing and looks. That would have meant continual patronage for poor Flora, but for the unfortunate event of the blissfully ignorant husband's death, after which his widow had promptly married the man whom she had loved for years, and given a very cold shoulder to her late ally.

She had never so far been mistaken in her diagnosis of the tender passion, and her heart sank at the memory of the two faces at the gate. She was a woman of action ; she must probe the affair as deep as possible, and at once ; so she stepped on to the landing of the stairs, just in time to meet Sylvia as she ran up to her room.

" Well, early bird, did you enjoy your ride ? " she asked with fictitious gayety.

" Yes, thanks," said Sylvia, her hand on her own door-handle. " I adore to be out in the air before all the world is up, and can claim their share in it. Are there any engagements for to-day ? I want to know what dress to tell Justine about."

It was very well done, thought Flora, this indifferent attitude, this calm bravado which acted

as if there were nothing to hide ; but there was
an inward light shining through Sylvia's eyes,
as if a pure white flame had been lighted in her
heart that no amount of acting could quench.
That she was in love was sure ; so Flora decided
dolefully, once more in her own room. In a case
like this, love meant marriage ; there was nothing to prevent it ; Sylvia could do as she
liked ; the young cavalry officer was handsome,
clever, and would attract nine women out of ten.
He knew every one worth knowing, although
he seemed very indifferent regarding the world
of society. He was terribly honest too ; he had
allowed Mrs. Lee-Blair to see that he did not
like her, that her powder, her black curls, her
little coquetries were all the reverse of attractive to him, and in return she had shown a
marked disposition to snub him, and to make
him see how little she valued his opinion. She
had been deceived in Sylvia ; that was it. She
had fancied that the words she at times let fall
about nobility, and high-standing, meant the desire to marry a titled man ; it seemed that it
only meant the stupid, abstract qualities, and
the girl was fool enough to think that Maurice
Regnier represented these things, just because
he had a reputation for bravery. If these horrible suspicions proved true, Flora was hopelessly
ruined financially. She cast a frightened glance

at her toilet-table, which was strewn with her last purchase, a set of apparently numberless brushes and combs and boxes of ivory, with solid gold monograms inlaid on their backs; a circle of diamonds was on her wrist; her wardrobes were filled to overflowing with expensive dresses: over the foot of the bed hung a night-dress, — and the money for the valenciennes ruffles which trimmed it, and its twenty-three companions, would have formerly dressed her for two years.

And she owed for almost everything!

Her first association with large sums of money had gone to her head; intoxicated by the novelty of her increased income, she had blindly ordered anything that struck her fancy, rushing into debt on all sides, and soothing any uneasiness by reminding herself how infinitely less she spent than Sylvia. Now a moment's glimpse of two faces had affected her like a cataract of water falling on her; she was stunned and frightened.

"Something must be done — something must be done," she said over and over to herself. But what was this potent something?

It was like a nightmare to picture going back to the old life of shifts and shabby economies. She could not, once having known the full extent of luxury, and how much it meant to her. Besides, those horrible debts! Could they imprison her for them? she wondered. Anything but that; she would never be able to bear the disgrace of it; but what could she do?

Her hand trembled, her head swam; she unscrewed a silver-mounted flask, poured out a stiff dose of its contents, and swallowed it without winking; it warmed her and gave her courage.

"Cheer up," she said to herself. "All's not lost yet. Let's see if for once the British brain cannot accomplish something, in spite of their jeers at our obtuseness."

CHAPTER V.

When Maurice entered the hotel after having left Sylvia, his first idea was to write and beg her to reconsider her decision, which seemed to him at that moment unbearable; but he was not able to carry out this most undiplomatic plan, for in his salon, waiting to see him, sat the Count de La Roche.

They had scarcely met for six years, and Maurice felt the glad color rush to his face as he greeted the man whose name meant so much to him. The lapse of time erased the memory of boyish disagreements and uncongenial characteristics; he only saw before him the son of his father's benefactor, and of his own hero; also the head of a house which he revered and loved. Here was the Philippe whom he had envied in his generous way, and looked up to with that respect only given by one boy to another who is a little his senior. Philippe had been the straightest rider, the surest shot, and the champion in all athletic games; and as Maurice gave him a frank, hearty welcome he still felt the old sensation of the other's superiority.

Although only two years younger, Maurice had still at twenty-seven the unrestrained enthusiasm of youth; he might equal the other now in all outside accomplishments, but Philippe always kept ahead. His manner made Maurice conscious of a certain rawness in himself, as he accepted the welcome so warmly proffered with the greatest ease and charm, but with a slight restraint.

Without being exactly handsome, Philippe de La Roche was one of those men who attract attention by that harmony of details, that welding together of the whole, which bestows the mark of birth upon the possessor. Not as tall as Maurice, although of good height, he was finely proportioned; his physical condition was perfect, and his powerful muscles were visible, to an eye trained to look for such things, under his light summer suit. His thick, close-cut hair had a rich chestnut tinge, and his heavy moustache was decidedly red; it overshadowed his well-shaped, full, curving lips, and rendered inconspicuous his large gleaming teeth until he laughed; then they were easily seen. His forehead was rather low, and square; his eyes of a brown topaz color, a curious shade, that caught the rays of light and seemed to hold them in restless discontent. In spite of a superabundant look of robustness, the air of race was clearly visible, accentuated by the fine lines of his nostrils, and his well-formed hands and feet. With nothing of the exquisite or dandy about him, he was perfectly appointed : after the observer had perceived his virility and breeding, he noticed the delicate finish of every detail of his dress.

He answered all of Maurice's inquiries in a courteous but absent-minded way as if waiting for the right moment to introduce some particular subject. His voice, which was one of his chief attractions, rich, low pitched, and with a quality that at times thrilled his listener, seemed veiled ; but the only sign that he gave of any lack of ease was the nervous haste with which he smoked one cigarette after another in rapid succession. His movements were as a rule deliberate : he had none of the vivacity common to his countrymen, his eyes being the only restless thing about him, suggesting that his quiet manner might be assumed.

As he tossed away the end of a cigarette, he broke in, almost interrupting a remark of his companion, " Maurice, I am in trouble."

His voice and manner gave added weight to his words.

" I have come to you — for help if you can give it, for advice at all events."

" I will do my best for you," said Maurice, suddenly grave. " What is it — money ? or honor ? "

" Both," answered Philippe. " I mean that unless I can get the money I am ruined."

" How much must you have ? "

Philippe drew his hand down over his moustache, and held it there, concealing his mouth ; no one looking at him, however closely, could have seen if the hidden lips quivered ; no one would have divined any deep emotion from hearing the level tones of his musical voice as he replied, " A hundred thousand francs, and at once."

" The devil ! " exclaimed Maurice with a long whistle.

" I know, I know it all," burst out the count with unexpected vehemence. " It is a fearful sum to hold out your hand for like a beggar. But what can I do ? Think of my name. Every generation has added to its age and nobility. Can I bear myself like a de La Roche on my miserable income ? What is open to me ? I will not serve in the army under a government headed by a canaille. Trade, commerce, every profession is forbidden me. How can I be expected to live as my father lived, on half the money ? Forgive me, Maurice," he interrupted himself : " I am beside myself with anxiety. I should never have alluded to that — forget it."

Maurice flushed ; for the first time his father's inheritance seemed a burden. Until now he had gloried in the friendly generosity of the former count, but Philippe's words made him feel like a pensioner, and galled him with a sense of dependence.

"You meant nothing, of course," he said a trifle awkwardly.

Philippe continued : "I would do anything to make money enough to support the old place. I can't give that up — my God, Maurice, I can't!"

"You must not think of such a possibility."

"No, rather than that I will go to another country, sink the name, work like a slave, and only come home to die where my father died. How he loved you, Maurice."

The voice broke now ; he bent his head on his folded arms.

There was as much fascination about him in this hour of abandonment as in his usual attitude of superiority ; perhaps even more so to Maurice, whose quick sympathies and lively imagination filled in the lines sketched by the count's words. A picture of Philippe as a little fellow flashed into his mind : he saw him perched on the back of a pony, his yellow curls bobbing under his wide hat, his chubby, vigorous legs clinging to his charger's sides as it cantered over a broad green field ; he saw the light in the old count's face as he watched him ; he heard the tenderness and pride in his voice as he said to

Monsieur Regnier, who stood beside him, "That's a boy worth living for, eh, Armand?"

And here sat his son, bowed under the burden of a threatened disgrace. Maurice drew his hand across his eyes.

"That must not be even thought of," he said. "Now let us be practical. Have you no one who can help you out?"

"No," returned Philippe, raising his head; "no one. The only person I might turn to is out of the question."

"You mean my father?"

"Yes; I will never ask a favor of a man who might feel bound to grant it."

"Then let me ask it for you."

"No, no, Maurice, my dear boy, that is too much for you to do."

"And why? Don't we owe everything to your father? are we not bound to your family by a hundred ties?"

A strange gleam, almost of amusement, and inexplicable to Maurice, flashed across Philippe's face before he answered. "No, your father would refuse. In his quiet life he cannot realize my obligations; he will never do it."

"He will if I ask him; he has never refused me anything!" answered Maurice hotly.

"He will this."

"I pledge you my word that he shall not."

As he spoke he held out his hand: the count took it in his firm clasp.

"I know what that means. I can sleep to-night. You are just what I expected to find you, a true friend," he added simply.

"You say you must have the money directly?" asked Maurice, his thoughts reverting to Sylvia. Good-by to all the sadly sweet alleviations he had promised himself durihg this week of banishment from her presence; good-by to the hours he had dreamed of spending under her window, rewarded by a gleam of her candle behind the curtains; good-by to the contraband glimpses he might have caught of her, to the doubtful joy of hearing her spoken of by others: duty, friendship, gratitude, and the honor of the name he loved called him away, and at once.

"Yes, or it may be too late," answered Philippe. "Ah, my boy, it seems a very simple thing at first not to get into money complications; your father will doubtless call me extravagant and reckless; but you know, as he in his quiet life cannot, how impossible it is for me to refuse to meet the men of my set at play. Can I allow a fellow like de Sainville to say I dare not give him his revenge? And if I begin to lose, I can't call the game off. Ah, these days are not like those when he and my father were young; now a louis does half what it did then.

and double is required of a man in my position."

Maurice, with the sympathy of youth for
youth, agreed heartily. Although he kept within
the limits of his own ample allowance, having
been educated with a horror of debt, he knew
that the count would consider this but a bourgeois virtue, and he had seen enough of the
world to be aware of the large demands on a
man in Philippe's set, one of the fastest and
most extravagant in that age of dissipation and
extravagance. In his eyes this last member of
the de La Roche family was most royal. If he
had vices, as doubtless he had, were they not
the outcome of his inheritance? It would have
seemed ignoble to bind down to dry rules a man
in whose lusty veins the blood of the old An-
gevin counts ran riot. "But," said Maurice,
referring to Philippe's last words, " we live to-
day, and must make the best of it."

The count rose and moved about the room.

" How I hate these modern bonds and
shackles! " he exclaimed. " I was not meant to
be tied down to conventionalities. What would
my old ancestors have done in my place? They,
lucky dogs, would have attacked a neighboring
baron, sacked a monastery, taken a walled town;
and then they would have enjoyed the fruits of
a glorious warfare. What am I told to do?

Fight, conquer, work even ? — and I would, God knows, if I had the chance, — no, all these doors are shut, and the only one open is that of marriage. A rich wife well dowered has grown to be a regular parrot-cry with my mother. Pshaw ! the idea is disgusting."

To Maurice, in the fresh dawn of his love for Sylvia, it seemed a profanation. " It is degrading." he agreed warmly. " Don't marry a woman you can't love, Philippe."

" I don't intend to marry at all if I can live without it," said the count dryly. He perceived from Maurice's tone that they were not looking at the question in the same way.

Maurice took out his watch. " I must be making my arrangements," he said, " for my train leaves at three. I have some notes to write," he added : for he felt that he must be alone so as to send a message of farewell to Sylvia.

" Then I will go to my rooms." said Philippe. " You will breakfast with me, of course ? "

" Thanks."

De La Roche put his hands on Maurice's shoulder, and for a second his roving eyes settled on the other's face.

" You have done for me more than I can acknowledge," he began.

Maurice interrupted him. " Please leave all

that alone. I understand you, and, Philippe, I thank you for your frankness and friendliness to me."

The count's heavy lids drooped under Regnier's warm, open glance, and he turned abruptly away.

When he reached his own apartment, he called for his valet, " Marcel ! " almost before he had closed the door. There was no answer. He looked into his bedroom and dressing-room, finding them empty. There came into his face a shade of worry, quickly replaced by a look of triumph. He went to the fireplace, and, leaning his elbows on the mantelpiece, gazed fixedly at himself in the glass. He smiled as if in con- gratulation at his image, and there was a foxy expression of cunning as his lips raised slightly at the corners.

" I don't look like a man who has been up all night," he thought, marking the clearness of his eyes, and the fresh glow of health on his cheek. " Still, I am not quite as I used to be. I don't sleep as well ; I am getting nervous. This sort of thing must stop, by Jove ! It 's growing monotonous, and it will end by making me old."

He left the mirror, and sat down at his writing-table, carefully arranged by the absent Marcel with regard to comfort. Philippe loved thoroughness, and paid minute attention to de-

tail. It was a pleasure to him to write a letter
in his bold, clear hand, on suitable paper; to
fold it accurately, and to seal the envelope with
nicety. He used his well-shaped hands dex-
terously, with no hesitation, no fumbling. He
always knew what he wanted and where to find
it, with the one exception of money — he did not
always know where that was to be found. With
a different education this man might have made
a mark in the world; he had more than the
average quantity and quality of brains; he possessed a determined will. Had he been taught
to exercise this will in conquering these impulses
of his lower nature, he would have built up a
strong character, dominant for good; but all the
influences brought to bear on him had been of
a kind to stimulate a love of false excitement,
and an aptitude for cunning. Like the mass of
French boys he was never permitted the least
freedom, always being accompanied by his parents, his tutor or an abbé, and his impetuosity
resenting the restraint, he began at an early age
to circumvent those in authority over him. Thus
sinning, not only in obtaining his liberty through
deceit, but in misusing it, at a time when the
conscience is most tender, he eagerly caught at
the doctrine of confession and absolution. The
imposed penances were not severe, and what
could be more delightful for a young fellow than

to have all the excitement and amusement of
eating forbidden fruit, sure of a mild panacea
against the pangs usually caused by this pursuit?
He thought, at that time, that this belief in his
church was sincere, but as he became less of a
sentient, and more of a reasoning creature, his
restless intellect pushed him into a course of
serious reading, during which he wandered far
afield among unorthodox writers. With his
mind already ripe for revolt, he confessed his
forbidden researches, and received a severe reprimand besides a heavy penance; when he re-
monstrated, citing his former mild punishments
for what seemed to him graver offenses, his
father confessor replied, "My son, your sins
until now were against the flesh, therefore lighter
than this, which is against the spirit."

Then and there Philippe shook off all religious
shackles; the spirit of skepticism pervaded him,
and when, at his father's death, he became his
own master, he revered neither God nor man.
From that day, nearly six years before we first
see him, his course had been a brilliant, rapid
downward rush; and at the moment he applied
for help to Maurice he realized that the speed
was getting too breathless; he must put on a
brake. The question as to where this brake was
to be found absorbed him after he had written
his letter. He sat almost motionless, only his

eyes showing him to be awake in their constant
restlessness, revolving plans for the future. He
was sure of the hundred thousand francs now;
but what were they? — a mere stop-gap for the
moment. He must have money, and he did not
see his way clear. "What on earth is there for
me to do?" he asked himself. "My mother
would say 'marry a fortune,' but neither she
nor I can discover this fortune in the right
hands. All the legitimists I know are poor. I
have not sunk low enough, thank God, to take
a wife from the Imperialists. No, I would
rather marry a bourgeoise than that. But I
don't want to marry at all, and what else is
there for me in France?"

As he pondered, his hands plunged deep in
his trousers pockets, his legs thrust out in front
of him, a dark cloud on his low brow, the door
opened, and Marcel came noiselessly in.

"Well," said Philippe, and there was a sharp
note of anxiety in the word.

"It is all right, Monsieur le comte, for the
moment," answered the man; "I have put the
Jew off the track for two days at least. Has
Monsieur le comte got the money?"

"Yes, Marcel," said Philippe; "I landed my
fish so easily that there was not much fun in
the game."

"Thank God," responded the servant. He

was an ignoble copy of his master when out of his presence, trying to imitate the air of superiority which in him became insolent swagger; but he was invaluable as a valet, and did not confine his usefulness to his legitimate duties.

" I should have been here sooner, but I thought it would take Monsieur le comte longer to attend to his business. I tricked the Jew finely," he chuckled.

" How did you do it?"

" I saw him from the window of the hotel, watching. I knew his game, so I looked up the *rapide* for Paris; it left at 10.40. I took the valise, umbrella, and one or two things of my own in my hand, and went out; the minute I appeared Master Jew slipped round the corner out of sight. It was then only half past nine, and I went straight to a restaurant I know, where there are little partitions round the tables, with curtains to draw when people want to be private. I know the lady in charge there, and at an hour like that she wasn't very busy. I stood chaffing her, with my eyes on a mirror behind her, and pretty soon I saw my man's ugly nose come round the outside door. Then I invited her to keep me company while I took a snap to stay my stomach. I ordered a good breakfast for me, and a syrup for her, and we sat down in one of the pens, with the curtains drawn. I was no sooner settled than I heard the door open and shut, and some one ordered a bock; then a chair scraped in the pen next mine."

" Give me an absinthe before you go on," said Philippe.

The man obeyed, and then continued. He looked very tired, and rested first on one dusty foot, then on the other ; but the count was not a master to encourage familiarity, although intimate enough with him, and never would have dreamt of bidding Marcel sit down, while he told how well he had served him. Strangely enough, this very mark of a brutal superiority made him more fascinating to his inferiors.

" I saw," said the valet, "that the beggar had fallen into my net; so says I, ' Well, now, I suppose you think it 's odd, madame, to see me eating at this hour, and all ready for a journey when I have just arrived.' ' Indeed I do,' says she. ' What game are you up to now ? ' ' It 's not my game,' says I : ' It 's my master's, bad luck to him, whose mind changes with every turn of the wind. Just here, when something scares him, so we are off to Paris by the 10.40 *rapide*.' After that we only had some joking, and pretty soon I heard old jewsharp go out mighty quiet, so I jumped up, paid my reckoning, loaded up and started for the station.   I kept my man in sight, and saw him go into the post, to telegraph, I suppose."

" Yes, without doubt," said Philippe. "Well, go on."

" I kept on steady but slow to the station, never looking round. There was a crowd at the ticket office, and I stood a little sideways to watch. Sure enough ; there came my beauty, his hat down low. I never seemed to see him at all, but when my turn came I sang out, 'One first, one second to Paris,' paid down the money, and came away. He was pretty close behind me, and I knew he was on my heels when I went to the train. I put your valise in a first-class carriage, and my own duds in a second. I saw him go ahead, and get into a second, near the engine. Then I went out as if to meet Monsieur. I waited until the last moment. Then I came running down the station, and held open Monsieur's carriage door. I saw the Jew's beak out of his window, but, the door of our carriage being open, he could not see beyond it. I made as if Monsieur had entered, shut and locked the door ; and when I looked again, the beak had gone. Then I came down the platform and had a good laugh when I saw the train take Monsieur Heins to Paris, where he and the officer he telegraphed for will find an empty valise and an umbrella."

Philippe threw back his head, and burst into a laugh, which showed all his strong glistening teeth. In no way did he differ more from Maurice than in his laugh. Even if you had failed to see the joke, the young captain's fresh contagious peals constrained you to join in his mirth, so honest and hearty was it. The count's had a wolfish sound ; few laughed with him.

" Well done, Marcel," he exclaimed. " You are the very pearl of valets ; now that he is disposed of for twenty-four hours at least, we will try to make it longer. I don't believe Captain Maurice can raise the money for five or six days, so to keep my good friend Heins away, do you send word to three or four Paris society papers the important fact that the Count de La Roche is at Trouville. Then buy the papers, mark the paragraphs and send them to Heins. He will then go anywhere but here to look me up. Do you understand ? "

" Perfectly, Monsieur le comte."

" Now, then, where have you been since your train went, Marcel ? It is nearly twelve ? "

" Yes, Monsieur le comte, I know, but I have been to see my aunt Justine, who has turned up after twenty years. She is the maid of a very rich American widow. I was extremely glad to see her again — especially since my losses at the Grand Prix," he added thoughtfully.

" You are a dutiful nephew, Marcel. Well, did the old lady help you out when you told her of your reverses ? "

" Oh, Monsieur le comte, I did not mention such a thing to her. I saw at once that she was dévote, so I gave her a few holy sentiments, and she gave me ten louis d'or."

He chinked the coin in his pocket, and grinned.

" She is a veritable gold mine," he continued, " or her mistress is, which is the same thing. Oh, if Monsieur had but a tenth of her money all this weary work would be over."

The man sighed. He was worn out with his morning's exertions after a sleepless night. The excitement of his escape was gone, only the fatigue remaining.

" Did you see the mistress ? " asked Philippe.

" No, Monsieur le comte, but I hear that she is young and pretty. My aunt told me that she stood as high in her country as Monsieur stands here. And what an old woman for family my aunt is ! Holy Virgin, she nearly went on her knees when she heard whose servant I was. She has all the old names of France at the tip of her tongue."

" And you say her mistress is rich ? "

" Enormously. I understand that she is going to marry Monsieur le Capitaine Regnier."

" Who told you that, Marcel? No hints, no gossip now. What do you know?"

" To tell the simple truth, Monsieur le comte, I know nothing; but with the little I got out of the captain's man, that dumb dog Jean, and my aunt's anxiety to know what I could tell her about him, I put two and two together."

" What did you tell her?"

" Only this, Monsieur le comte."

Marcel raised his shoulders, spread his hands, and thrust out his under lip; his appearance was a whole family history. Philippe laughed again.

" You are discreet, as always, Marcel; here is another louis to go with your aunt's gift. Now you may go."

Alone, Philippe's mind began again its task of solving the problem of his future. Marcel's adroitness had amused him in the telling, but stripped of its outside cleverness, it showed a contemptible condition of affairs. He who should be able to hold his head as high as any noble in France, saved from open disgrace by the cunning of a servant! It was degrading. He felt that something must be done, and done quickly. Outwardly as sound as ever, he alone was conscious of internal tremors and commotions, and recognized that his self control was less iron in its firmness. Once more his mind reverted to a rich marriage. " Maurice going to marry millions?

I don't believe it; he would n't have gone away for me so willingly if it were true. A foreign wife would be better than one either from the bourgeoisie or the Imperialists. My mother could not make much of a row, for I have a precedent to go by, — my sainted ancestor who sold his soul for a rich wife. Probably the story about the devil grew because he got a divorce. That is priestlore. I will take a look at this Yankee widow at all events, and, by Jove, if she is like my ancestress in not being able to talk French, I 'll marry her with her consent or without it. A wife whose scolding you could n't understand would be the mare for my money."

CHAPTER VI.

PHILIPPE'S first idea, after having said good-by to Maurice, was to find out more about this tempting American widow of whom Marcel spoke with such enthusiasm. For this purpose he went to the club, and there found the very man who could give him all the information he wanted. Monsieur de Belfort, small, dark, Parisian to the tips of his long supple fingers, was so elated at being singled out by the famous de La Roche for a tête-à-tête, that he would have assumed much knowledge on the subject the count questioned him about, even if he had not possessed it ; but being by nature and habit a tuft-hunter, he had by heart all the private affairs of all the frequenters of Trouville, and eagerly set himself to satisfy his questioner.

Putting on an air of vast importance, he led Philippe to a corner of the room, ostentatiously placing himself in an attitude that implied much intimacy.

"You ask me what I can tell about the rich, the charming Madame Huntington, the belle of this season? Much. First, that she is undoubtedly the possessor of a large fortune ; ten million francs."

" And that is certain ? "

" Certain. De Beaucorps wanted to marry her ; he made her an offer, which she refused, by the way, and before doing so he found out about her property. It is well invested, in her own right, and she is quite alone in the world, with neither children nor parents to interfere. Oh, my dear friend, I assure you that she is a rare prize. I have regretted my state often and often this summer. If I had no wife, who knows ? "

The little man waved his hand with a conquering air as he spoke, giving the impression that it was alone his unfortunate wife who had prevented Sylvia from succumbing to his charms.

Philippe leant forward, and put his hand on his companion's arm ; he knew very well that this touch of familiarity would do much for him ; few things done by him were unstudied when he had an object in view.

" My dear fellow, I am making you my confidant ; you must keep my secret, for you are the only one I trust with it."

" The grave is less safe than I, when friendship is involved."

" Well, then, I am not at all disinclined to run for this prize myself. Now can you give me any pointers, as to her likes and dislikes, her character, and above all if there is any one who has an influence over her ? "

" She is rather exclusive : that will work well for you. She is fond of horses; Regnier can tell you about that. By the way, he is a great deal with her ; did you know it ? "

" No, I know nothing ; Regnier left Trouville an hour ago, so I have seen him only for a few minutes. Go on."

" As for influence, there I am in the dark. They say that her companion, an English woman, Madame Lee - Blair, has an enormous deal of tact, and can persuade her to a good many things ; but of that I can assert but little."

" Thank you, my dear boy, for what you have told me. Now we 'll go to the casino, and see if my beauty shows up."

How de Belfort longed for stilts as he strolled along by Philippe's side, his eyebrows raised, his manner expressing confidential importance ! He talked steadily to his companion, who swayed insolently along, quite aware of de Belfort's flutter of excitement, and secretly amused by it.

Suddenly the little Parisian grasped his arm, and exclaimed, " There she is ! " at the same time raising his hat with an exaggerated politeness to two ladies, flashing by in a victoria. Philippe only caught sight of a fresh summer toilet, and the graceful bend of a slender figure; but his quick eye, accustomed to note such details, had taken in the quiet elegance of the turnout, the good taste of the liveries, the perfect grooming of the horses.

" Your widow knows a horse, if she picked out those cobs," he said carelessly.

" Yes, she's a great horse-woman. As I said before, you have only to ask Regnier about his rides with her," said de Belfort with a chuckle.

Philippe disliked these allusions to Maurice; he preferred to know nothing of his affairs at the present moment. So he made no answer, and they walked on in silence. Some people require tangible proofs before they realize anything forcibly, and the mere sight of Sylvia's horses and carriage had made Philippe believe in her fortune more than any amount of figures could have done.

" Shall I introduce you? " asked de Belfort as they stood near the entrance of the casino.

" To Madame Lee-Blair, if you please."

" Ah, diplomat! You look ahead," exclaimed de Belfort, leading the way through the groups of gayly dressed women and well-appointed men, wishing that all the world were seeing him.

Flora was sitting listening to the music of the orchestra with a worried expression; for the moment she was alone, an unusual thing for her,

as she was a general favorite, and all her anx-
ieties were very present to her. Sylvia the wife
of Regnier, a man who disliked her, as she felt
instinctively, what would become of her? The
figures of the money she owed danced before her
like spectres at the feast. She was idly wondering if it sounded more alarming in francs, or in
pounds, shillings, and pence, when a voice murmured a request in her ear, and in another moment Philippe was bowing before her.

What is the subtle aroma called by us fascination? It is apart from beauty, it seems to
have little or nothing to do with intellect; but
that it is as positive a force as gravitation, or
capillary attraction, is certain. Some of these
days a new kind of X-ray will be turned on it,
and the scientists will give us a formula of its
component parts, but they will not alter its mysterious powers. I have seen a man enter a room
filled with women, most of them young, pretty,
and attractive; if one of those beings possessing
fascination is present, he knows it as soon as if
she wore a placard on her breast announcing the
fact. Often she has none of the exterior charms
of her companions, but in nine cases out of ten
the man will say to his hostess, " I should like
to know the little woman in gray."

And what is true of one sex is equally true
of the other.

Philippe de La Roche was the owner of this quality; he would have possessed a power over his fellow beings had he been in the most humble position, but his name and high standing added their weight. Flora had not spoken a dozen words to him before she felt his charm. He had begun the conversation with the ease of an old friend, and the stimulating interest of a new acquaintance.

Sylvia, surrounded as usual by a little court of admirers, saw Flora and the count laughing and talking with much animation; she had heard his name spoken when he entered as if his advent was an event of some importance, and she was interested to see the man of whose home and surroundings she knew so much. She had already invested him with a halo of romance, and she was not disappointed when she saw the original of the portrait painted for her by Maurice. His easy bearing, his air of superiority, his manly physique were as she had imagined them; and the attitude of the leaders of the Trouville world towards him, yielding him at once the most important place, had its effect on her.

She had noticed how quietly, and yet how decidedly, he withdrew himself from those who had tried to attract him on his entrance; she noted that the very people whom Flora pronounced most worthy to be courted paid him marked deference. The wish flashed into her mind that Maurice might command a kindred position, and she sighed involuntarily.

Meantime Philippe was making headway with Flora. " I am a great reader of character," he said, smiling; " I can tell you much about yourself."

" If it's complimentary, I should like to hear it; if not, we 'll change the subject."

" It's true, I think; therefore it must be pleasant for you to hear. You have, I should judge, a most self-denying nature."

This did not strike Flora as a piquant remark; she would have preferred something more flattering, but she smiled nevertheless, and asked why he thought so.

" Because you have chosen glare and distance from the music. You can't find your seat an agreeable one, and yet you sit there contentedly."

" Now that you speak of it, the glare is disagreeable, but I fancy that you are a late comer if you imagine any one listens to the band here. No, we only use our ears in this Garden of Eden to find out what the serpent really said, and what Eve told Adam he said."

" How delightfully refreshing to come to a place where there are such natural objects as serpents. We don't allow them in Paris. But

is your place so beguiling that you won't take a
stroll with me? You don't give me your undi-
vided attention, and as I am a monopolist of all
good things, I dislike to see you bowing to this
one, and smiling at that one."

He rose as he spoke, and she followed his
example with alacrity; it was a good adver-
tisement to be seen engrossing the attention of
a man like de La Roche, who seldom wasted his
time with women of the whole world. So she
sauntered along the sands, wondering how soon
he would tell why he wanted her society so much,
for Flora was shrewd enough to know that he
had some motive. It soon appeared, just as she
had expected.

" Your friend Madame Huntington looks very
charming," he said, throwing a side glance at
Sylvia, as they passed the group of which she
was the centre.

" Yes, she is charming, charming," answered
Flora.

" Of course you have had innumerable offers
for her ? "

" Oh, of course ; one does not find an heiress
who is so presentable every day in the week."

" You must be very clever to have kept her to
yourself so long."

He looked full at his companion when he
made this advance. He was feeling his way,

and he must not make a false step in the beginning.

Flora drew herself up a little. " Your remark might be taken in a bad sense, Monsieur," she replied with some hauteur.

" It might," he answered composedly, " by a woman who did not belong to the world of which you and I are conspicuous inmates."

It was not unpleasing to Flora to be tacitly received by the count as one of his own sort; her voice was more genial when she said : —

" Well, take it for granted that I have been clever. I call it lucky, but the result is the same."

" And it is not hard to foretell that the result will continue to be the same, until you choose to pull the other set of wires, and your puppet nods her head, instead of shaking it."

Who does not enjoy the reputation of power? The inference that she was influential in guiding Sylvia flattered Flora extremely, although she knew how untrue it was.

" What sort of a person is Madame Huntington ? Is she easily handled ? "

" *Mon dieu*, no !   It requires the utmost tact to make her see things with your eyes."

" A positive nature, then ? "

" Very positive, for all she looks so soft and yielding."

Flora thought with a pang of Maurice as she spoke ; was Sylvia going to prove obstinate about him ? The count continued his catechism.

" Is she generous ? "

" With her money, no one could be more so, but with her affection she is a perfect miser."

" Ah, cold. I inferred as much when I heard that she was from New England ; those women are all icebergs. Then it is probably untrue what I was told at the club, that she is dead in love with Captain Regnier."

Flora's heart gave a quick, agitating leap ; others had noticed the affair, then, as well as she. " I don't know," she said, in a depressed tone. " It has been troubling me dreadfully. Do you know Regnier ? "

" Know him ? I should think so ! He was brought up in my chateau ; he has just gone down to Touraine to do an errand for me. He 's a — a — Well, if you know his position, you will understand me when I say that he is a sort of hanger-on of our house."

Flora did not know what the position was to which de La Roche alluded, and his expression. did not seem to fit the dashing, rather haughty young officer ; she could not somehow fancy Maurice being sent on an errand, but the phrase gave her a gleam of hope.

While the words faltered on his tongue, Philippe had been assailed by a fierce temptation. Up to that moment he had had no intention of playing Maurice false, more than was implied in trying to take his place with the young widow. But suddenly his active mind saw a move to be made, so simple that a whisper could accomplish it, and which, once successful, would give him an undoubted advantage. They turned unconsciously, and moved nearer the crowd and the music again. Mephistopheles was busy at his old game of temptation, making suggestions with infernal ingenuity, and as he generally busies himself about a soul of which he is almost sure in advance, his work received a final touch when he brought in his Marguerite to play her part. Sylvia was listening to the men surrounding her with an air of attention and interest that was one of her chief charms. At first her air of distinction eclipsed even her grace and beauty. Perfectly at her ease, she turned her flower-like head first to one, then to another. There was an unusual beauty in her face to-day — perhaps caused by a softened expression — and a luminous glow in her eyes. With her world at her feet, courted, flattered by all, she would have been the first to smile in derision at the idea that she was pathetic, infinitely pathetic, in her young ignorance. She thought at that moment that life was a very simple affair: she

fancied that she knew all the baseness of the
world, and was prepared to meet it, because
some of the more conspicuous scandals had been
repeated to her; she felt herself as wise in her
new experience as if she knew it all. And if
she had been told that she was but a quarry, to
be hunted down and claimed by the most skillful
huntsman, she would have mocked her informer,
and said that her future was in her own hands,
and she could make it what she chose. What
could she know or guess, in her New World
guilelessness, of the atmosphere of diplomacy
and finesse which is native air to the people of
the oldest European civilization?

As Philippe gave a swift glance that took in
each detail, an animal light flashed into his
eyes.

"She is very pretty," he said, in an indifferent
tone, turning to Flora, — "a little unripe for
my taste; she will be improved by a year or
two more."

Mrs. Lee-Blair felt the implied compliment;
it was very soothing to her racked nerves to be
with the count.

Once again they strolled over the sands.
Flora had not taken so much exercise for years,
but it did not seem to fatigue her. Philippe
kept up a perfunctory conversation, having abruptly changed the subject, and all the time his

brain was working, working. It was absurd to think of Maurice with all that money; what could *he* do with it? He had no estate to keep up, like La Roche; he was not a gambler; his tastes were not expensive. It was wicked to think of him weighed down by what would only be to him a responsibility, whilst to Philippe it meant restored honor, delight for his mother, comfort for all those dependent on him. Was it not his duty to think of the greatest good for the greatest number? A young fellow like Maurice had no right to wish to monopolize so large a fortune. The thought was preposterous. Besides, he deserved some punishment for being so confoundedly secretive; had not Philippe told him of all his troubles? Why, then, had he been hiding his own affairs?

Philippe and Flora were again at the point farthest from the casino, the very spot where Philippe had before alluded to Maurice's position. Her mind took up the remark there, just as they had dropped it; she was thirsting to know what he meant, and wondered if she might introduce the subject again. She *must* find out; it was her duty to Sylvia. So she said with a little sigh : —

"You mentioned young Regnier's position just now. It is an anomalous one for him to be in ; so young, too."

She prided herself immensely on the word "anomalous." She was n't quite sure what it meant, and so considered it delightfully noncommittal. Philippe was amused in a grim way to see how the bait had attracted his fish. He knew that she had not the least idea to what he had alluded, as indeed how could she? But this attitude of hers was just what he wanted, so he replied, —

"Of course it's hard for him; he's a good fellow, and I 'm fond of him. But I come in for my share of pity too. You can understand that it 's not any too pleasant for me."

Flora was on pins and needles, as the saying is. What was this extraordinary complication, of which she, — she who prided herself on her general knowledge of family affairs, — knew nothing? Should she be honest, and confess her ignorance? or should she grope her way, thus perhaps learning more in the end? She decided on the latter course, and with another sigh said, "Oh, no, of course not. In what way do you feel it most?"

"Why, to be honest, I think that being deprived of, at the least, half my income is the shoe that pinches in the most disagreeable way; but added to that is the feeling that Maurice's mere existence is an insult to my poor mother, the best of women; and she worries continually to think that I, who have the name to keep up, and the estate to maintain, should be hampered by my insufficient means."

" That must be fearful for you." Flora made this remark with true sympathy. That was a subject of which she knew much by experience.

" It is hard," he rejoined frankly. " For with about the same fortune, I am a poor, while Regnier is a rich man. You see before you, madame, a living illustration of the saying, ' The sins of the fathers shall be visited on the children.' "

He smiled as he spoke; but it was a sad smile, which she felt to be very touching. Her mind had enough to keep it busy for a moment. She could see but one solution to his remarks : what else could he mean? So she took another experimental step along her path of discovery, quite ignorant of the force behind her, impelling her on her way.

" You look on these affairs so differently in France to what we do. Now in England young Regnier would be placed in a haberdasher's shop, and that would be the end of him as far as the family were concerned. Here, on the contrary, I fancy he could marry, with his money, about as he pleased."

" Oh, no ; oh, no !" said Philippe with emphasis. " His one chance will be to find some foreigner, either ignorant or careless of his origin.

Unless a wife of that sort turns up for him, he will have to marry into the bourgeoisie. From the gossip I have heard, I imagine that Madame Huntington is willing to overlook any small irregularity in his family matters, eh ? "

" And *I* imagine that she is quite ignorant of any such irregularity."

Philippe stopped, and fixed her with a severe look.

" You will pardon me if I seem to be interfering with you, but as a gentleman I think it my duty to tell you that you should be careful regarding the antecedents of a man who has made your charge as conspicuous as Maurice has Madame Huntington."

" I see now how careless I have been. But everybody nice seemed to receive him."

" The position of the de La Roche family is high enough to give any one connected with them a place of respectability in the world. I wonder that you have heard nothing of this matter, and my advice to you is to conceal your ignorance about it. To speak frankly, I think that you would be rather severely blamed for letting things drift."

" But I must tell Sylvia — Madame Huntington — what you have said," she replied. She was beginning to feel jubilant: all was not hopeless. If she could gain time, only a year, she would retrieve the past, pay her debts, and turn over a new leaf. The count's intelligence gave her courage.

"Remember, I don't ask you to take anything on my authority. I am too new a — may I say friend? — to take the liberty of dictating to you. All that I dare venture on is a little advice. Don't let things go any farther without demanding Maurice Regnier's family papers. As to telling Madame Huntington, perhaps she would not care about his birth. Those Americans have rather crude ideas."

"Ah, but not Sylvia! No, no; she is full of all kinds of notions about nobility, descent, and that sort of thing. It has surprised me that she encouraged this Regnier, even not knowing the stain on his birth, because he holds no high station."

"How strangely things turn out," he said in another tone, as if that subject were ended. "Here I asked you to walk on the beach with me, simply because I thought you would prove a delightful companion, and we have at once plunged into the heart of things."

"Life is full of such surprises. I came with you for the same reason that you say you asked me, and here am I indebted to you for a very great service."

"Let us hope that it is but the beginning of

many mutual good turns," he replied with his quick smile. " Here we are at the casino once more. Will you introduce me to your charge?"

He had time but for a few words with Sylvia, for the sun was sinking, and the hour conse- crated to the toilet was at hand. So he was compelled to cut short his conversation. After helping her into her carriage, and standing with lifted hat as she was driven away, he went back to his hotel, evading the intrusive de Belfort, who had served his brief turn, and fell again into his position of a bore.

As Philippe walked swiftly along, his head bent, his brows gathered in a thoughtful frown, he was congratulating himself on having done a clever stroke of work, and at the same time laying plans for the future.

" I told no lie, strictly speaking. I told her how to get proofs, that 's all. Now Marcel must be posted in regard to his aunt, the maid. And as for the English woman, I must find her price. Maurice is such a fool that I doubt if it occurred to him to buy her services. She 's not too stu- pid, and she 'll never give up her fat place with the rich widow without a fight. If a fellow has the prospect of the income from ten million francs, he can make some tempting offers."

When Flora had introduced the Count de La Roche to Sylvia, the mere mention of his name brought to her suggestions of romance, chivalry, and beauty. She was frankly interested in the owner of the castle by the river, with its Old World histories. He seemed to belong to an older, more enduring class than the habitués of Trouville, who fluttered in and out of their villas with the evanescent air of butterflies. She had scarcely spoken a dozen words to him, and yet he had impressed his personality strongly upon her.

She left Flora as soon as she entered the house, and ran to her own room murmuring something about being late for dinner. She wanted to be alone for a while, for she did not trust herself since the morning, and feared that she might say something to betray her secret. As she closed her door she noticed an odor of roses, and there, on her dressing-table, lay a mass of long-stemmed, white, half-opened buds. She took them up, and an envelope fell from them. In it was Maurice's card with these words: "Farewell. I obey you, and shall be gone for an eternity,—a whole week,—but I love you, I love you. Until you see me again let every breeze that blows, every star that shines, tell you of my love. M. R."

She read his message twice, and then she buried her face in the roses. Even with herself she was shy to acknowledge that her lifelong enemy was vanquishing her. She stood with her eyes fixed on the sea, and wondered at her own state of mind. Did she really love Maurice? It was impossible for her to decide. She tried honestly and fairly to picture a whole life with him, and only him, but it was difficult to realize such a state of things. She knew that she felt a new excitement and interest, that she seemed to have grown years younger since the morning; but she did not know that the cause of this was not so much in Maurice as in herself. The inevitable hour had come when the love for which she had inherited a marked capacity asserted its power. She was swayed by the attribute, but not by the individual as yet, and after all, what was there in the young cavalry officer besides his manly presence, and the flattery caused by his love of her, to make her renounce the dominating determination of her life? Other men were as good horsemen, as clever poets, as bold wooers as he; but then the other men were not by her side who would have had an equal chance on these grounds, and Sylvia had still to learn the loyalty and strength of his nature.

As she thought over the events of the day she wanted to believe she loved Maurice, and yet she shrunk from having the belief confirmed; she liked to feel her heart beat more quickly as she pictured his eyes plunging their burning glances into hers; she delighted in the blushes that ran over her face as she recalled the pressure of his arms when he lifted her from her horse. And yet — and yet she did not know him. She had told herself for years that love made slaves. She had never wanted to come to this pass — and here she was.

For the first time in her life she longed for her mother, who in this crisis would have helped and advised her. A little water-color sketch that Gilbert had made of his bride hung in its simple frame by Sylvia's bed, and she stood looking at it entreatingly, and invoked the spirit of motherhood to help her in her confusion of mind. All in vain. No light broke in on her darkness. When she joined Flora at their tête-à-tête dinner, the older woman felt that there was something new at work. Sylvia talked rather more gayly and easily than usual, but there was an aloofness about her, too delicate to be described. It was as if she spoke and listened without understanding. As they went into the drawing-room, however, the little mist was dispelled by a word.

"Young Regnier was not at the casino this afternoon," observed Flora, pluming herself before a mirror.

"No, he has gone away for a week," returned Sylvia. There was no lack of vividness now in her tone.

"I am not sorry, dear," said Flora gravely, seating herself so that she could see Sylvia's face. "People have begun to talk about you and this young bourgeois. You know that even your nationality cannot excuse everything. And these morning rides " —

"They mean nothing," interrupted Sylvia. "What a backbiting, scandalous world this is! Has it already begun to gossip about you and your new acquaintance, Monsieur de La Roche? Tell me if you really found him as engrossing as you seemed to."

She bent her face so that the fragrance of the rose in her berthe reached her. It was one of Maurice's roses, and as she breathed in its perfume she listened to Flora's enthusiastic praises of the young count. After a while she went out on to the terrace, into the moist, starlit air. The far-off hum of the town reached her; the roll of carriages mingled with the regular cadence of the waves. She tried to call up Maurice's image. She wondered where he had gone, and if he would disobey her and write to her during this week. She must make up her mind, for he was not a man to be played with. She loved his impetuosity. Then she began to resolutely turn her mind to the future ; did she love him enough to give up all her dreams for him? He had told her he could offer a stainless name, but that was not quite enough for her ambition. A famous name, even with a stain of some tragic sin, some glorious failure, seemed less insipid to her. Flora had spoken of him as a *bourgeois.* Why was the term so utterly crushing? Could she be contented as a *bourgeoise?* Then her thoughts slipped away to the chateau by the river; she pictured the spreading cedar, the storied building; but the most vivid impression on her mind was the memory of the few unimportant words spoken by Philippe de La Roche as he had put her into her carriage; the strange sensation she had felt of his authority; she could not account for it. Maurice, all unknowing, had painted a background with such magic that it made the figure to which it belonged that of a hero.

When she went to her room for the night she found Justine in a flutter of excitement.

" I trust Madame did not miss me when she dressed for dinner. I had to go away and pray; I owed it to the saints. After all these years, Madame, I have found one of my own family, my brother's son. Oh, he is almost a gentleman ; and how could he help being, placed, as he is, in one of our noblest families? He is valet to Monsieur le Comte de La Roche."

" Why, Justine, you chatter like a girl. I am glad you are pleased."

"It is enough to make any one pleased; I would rather have my nephew a servant at La Roche than secretary to the emperor."

"How the name haunts me," thought Sylvia, looking at her image, soft in the light of the candles by the mirror. Her eyes had an expectant look. From one of the white roses, more fully blown than the others, a petal dropped softly. She looked at it tenderly. Justine, standing just behind her, spoke in a muffled voice.

"Madame knows how I love her — that in spite of her grandeur and beauty, she is always to me my baby that I followed over the ocean. She will not be angry if I say something that lies heavy on my heart?"

"No, dear Justine, never angry with you. What is it?"

Sylvia turned to face her, suddenly pale with a vague fear.

"You will promise your old nurse not to marry this Captain Regnier until you know all about him? The Count de La Roche could tell you everything. Marcel could tell me if I pressed him."

"I cannot see why you think of such a thing, Justine. I certainly will marry no one in ignorance of his position. That is all I need. Good-night."

The woman crept sullenly away, all her joy in her nephew's appearance spoiled by the displeasure in her mistress's tone. And the sweet elusive melody that had sung in Sylvia's heart was jarred into discord by the suspicions aroused by Justine. She asked herself, why had Maurice suddenly left Trouville after swearing in the morning that nothing should take him away from her? Had it anything to do with the arrival of the count, who, as Justine said, knew all about him?

CHAPTER VII.

THE next three days were filled, for Sylvia, with a strange glamour, bringing new sensations, reviving old ambitions. Nothing seemed real. The savage, treacherous ocean stretched itself out like a stage background ; the sun set in scenic magnificence, and she was like an actress in the midst, who had to wait for her cue before recalling her part. Each morning a cluster of fresh roses, nowhere sweeter, more regal than at Trouville, brought to her the memory of Maurice ; but he was absent, and Philippe was always near her, — and roses fade.

There was a succession of dainty, luxurious breakfasts and dinners, to which she was invited by the leaders of the " swim," almost on their knees, for the lion of the moment, the irresistible de La Roche, refused to go anywhere without the promise of meeting the lovely American. She was the queen of these entertainments, and felt the stimulus that comes with adulation. Hour by hour she grew more interested in the count. He spoke to her of France and his hopes and fears. He was graver, more restrained in his

language than Maurice, and Sylvia, imbued with
the true Anglo - Saxon distrust of enthusiasm,
deemed him more sincere, and invested him with
depths of patriotism and devotion. He paid her
the compliment of remembering opinions expressed by her, and discussing them afterwards
with wit and skill.

At this time Sylvia's self was like a fair for-
tress : two opposing forces were battling for it.
On Maurice's side were those qualities, barely
awake after their long sleep, of whose overwhelming power she was ignorant, — those qualities which give the ardent love of a pure woman
a force closely allied to the divine. On Philippe's side were ranged her lifelong idols, fame
and honor ; and also the strength of her temperament, which stirred her tumultuously. The intellectual and the physical fighting the spiritual,
and no voice to teach which was the path for
her to take.

She was not unhappy, but restless and excited
during these days. At night her dreams were
agitating, and she never lost in slumber the
monotonous sound of the waves. She felt that
a crisis was approaching, and she longed for
Maurice to come back and help her to a decision. She was free as air, and yet she saw his
brown eyes everywhere, heavy with reproach.
Where was he? What had Justine meant by

her hints ? Why, *why* was she so weak as to
be haunted by Flora's derisive term *bourgeois ?*
Her old nurse spoke continually of the count ;
her nephew was often with her and his stories
of his master's gallantry and importance lost
nothing in the telling.

One afternoon Sylvia felt that she must give
herself an hour for thought, for decision, and
she refused to go to the casino with Flora.
Alone on a balcony outside of her own room, she
set herself resolutely to think ; but her eyes wandered to the beach, and she found herself idly
watching some nursery-maids and their charges
digging in the sands. The gay world was hidden from her by the roofs of neighboring villas ;
but the wearying, never ending strains of the
strident music floated above these obstacles.

Suddenly two figures, a man and a woman,
came within the field of her vision, from behind
some rocks at the end farthest away from the
casino. Even at this distance she noticed their
absorption of manner, their heads bent towards
each other as they moved slowly along. As she
watched with awakening interest she saw them
stop abruptly, and strike their hands together as
two men might in concluding a bargain ; then
they resumed their walk, more rapidly, and were
soon lost from sight behind the villas. Maurice
was forgotten in the wonder as to what Flora

and the count were plotting together. She was
alive with curiosity, and determined to ask her
friend ; but when Mrs. Lee-Blair arrived, shortly
after, her first words banished all former thoughts.
She came directly to Sylvia's room, and joined
her on the balcony ; her eyes were sparkling, her
whole manner breathed triumph.

"Sylvia, my darling, darling child," she said
effusively, and then sat down close beside her,
kissed her, patted her hand, all the time casting
significant glances.

"You have something to tell me, Flora?" asked
Sylvia, roused to a sudden determination by these
demonstrations.

"Yes, my sweetest child : the best thing in
the whole world has come to you, and I am happy
and grateful to be the bearer of the good tidings.
Sylvia, dearest, the Count de La Roche wishes
to marry you."

It was here, this crisis towards which the play
had been moving, and still with a sense of unreality, Sylvia found the words of her part as if
already learned.

"I am profoundly grateful, but, Flora dear,
don't be disappointed : I cannot marry Monsieur
de La Roche."

Mrs. Lee - Blair's face blanched suddenly.
"You cannot mean that : you know nothing
against him?"

"Oh, no, nothing, nothing; that is not the reason."

"Tell me then, Sylvia, your real reason. I am older than you, dear; I am in a way responsible for you. Tell me why you refuse one of the highest titles in France?"

All the effect of a woman of the world slipped from Sylvia; the outside dignity fell from her like a discarded garment, leaving her shining with the innate dignity of youth and love; her face flushed divinely, and her eyes glowed in their violet depths. Her head drooped a little as she said, "Because, Flora dear, I am beginning to know what love means, and to believe that I owe it to the man I marry. I don't love Monsieur de La Roche."

"Is that all?"

"Not quite all."

"Is there any serious obstacle, Sylvia? Do not speak without thought; this is a graver matter than you think."

There was a pause. Sylvia found herself with no words. "What is a serious obstacle?" she pondered, and her position became undefined in her estimation as she tried to see it clearly. At last she said in a doubtful tone, "No, I cannot say that there is anything really settled."

"Thank God," breathed Flora, leaning back in her chair. The moment had come for her to strike. She shrank from giving pain, and had hoped that the count's offer would be accepted without delay, and that she might thus avoid a duty that seemed very hard to her; but it was not to be; she must speak. "Thank God," she repeated still more fervently; "I had hoped, my dear, that I should not be forced to tell you something exceedingly disagreeable, but which would have been absolute agony if you were bound to young Regnier."

The same distrust, but sharper, now came to Sylvia as when Justine had first spoken.

"What is it you have against him? Tell me at once — quick!"

"He is not in a position to ask you to marry him; he has been most culpable in making you conspicuous, in almost compromising you by his attentions. De La Roche is so in love with you that he is willing to overlook it. Besides, he knows Regnier well enough to see how things were managed by him."

"Tell me what there is against him," interrupted Sylvia, maddened by the delay.

"He is the count's illegitimate brother."

As she spoke, Flora experienced a horrible sense of guilt. She felt that Sylvia was entitled to know what Philippe had told her; but the fact that she herself would benefit by her words, gave her a feeling that she was doing something shabby. It seemed brutal to put things so plainly, and yet it was her duty.

It appeared a long time to her before Sylvia answered, and when she spoke her voice was muffled.

" I do not believe it," she said slowly.

" It is dreadful, but it is true, my dear child. The former count went so far as to divide the property between the two sons. La Roche is very nice speaking of it, but he can't help feeling it."

Sylvia rose and entered her room through the long window. She spoke over her shoulder, so that Flora did not see her face.

" We dine at home to-night, don't we? Do give a look at the table and see if all is right." Mrs. Lee-Blair rose at once, accepting her dismissal. She could not judge how Sylvia was affected by her communication; she only knew that the count's offer was refused, and the stain on Regnier's birth denied. As she went downstairs a panic seized her regarding her future. If Sylvia really loved the young captain, and persisted in marrying him, her case was worse than ever. Vague fears of being thrown into prison for debt shook her; she had cut herself off entirely from her charge, by her endeavors to help her. She knew that no woman ever forgives interference such as hers, if it is ineffectual.

She entered the dining-room half dazed, and saw Justine through the open door in the passage beyond. She called and beckoned her to follow to the drawing-room. Justine obeyed with her heavy, noiseless tread, and stood respectfully on the threshold.

"Come here, come closer," said Mrs. Lee-Blair half hysterically, sinking into a chair.

"Justine, oh, Justine," she murmured. "you must go at once to your mistress, and tell her what Marcel, the count's valet, has told you about Captain Regnier. I am afraid she will marry him in spite of all I can do."

Justine's square face and stolid features did not change, but her deep-sunk eyes gave a sudden wild gleam.

"She shall *not*," she said, her voice low and guttural. "She was not made to marry such as *he ;* and when she knows all, she will not want to."

Sylvia had not moved since Flora had left her. She stood, one hand resting on the back of a chair, her head bent, her eyes fixed, thinking, thinking. After the first shock a great sorrow had come into her heart for Maurice. She pitied him, for a spirit like his must be terribly galled by his position. Then the thought came unbidden, "And yet he has tried to bring me into it too."

Fast on the heels of this first doubt crowded others, and then the memory of his words, " I can offer you a stainless name," flashed across her.

" I do not want to believe him false, I will not," she moaned ; " I could love him if he were true."

There was a faint sound, and the door opened.

" I do not need you yet, Justine," said Sylvia, very gently. She did not wish any eye to rest on her in this hour of doubt and grief ; but the old woman came steadily towards her.

" You may turn me away to starve," she began abruptly, " but I did not bring you up from your cradle to see you throw yourself away now. You, fit to be a duchess, a queen, — you must not marry this captain."

There was a tone of assurance about her that impressed Sylvia; she did not silence her as before.

" Then you, too, believe that this story is true about Monsieur Regnier's birth ? " she asked.

" I know it is true. The moment I heard the name of the Comte de La Roche I remembered something I had known long ago. I have been so much away that I forget things sometimes. I confused it at first with something else, but my nephew Marcel knew all, and he told me. He said " —

"Stop," said Sylvia imperiously. "I will hear no more. Leave me."

Her head drooped no more; her eyes were no longer soft with sorrow, but a dry, angry light burned in them. She heard Justine creep out, and then she went across the room towards her dressing - table with almost a tigerish sweep; there stood the roses. Maurice's gift, fresh that morning, innocent of offense. She caught them up, and with a swift, fierce movement threw them from the window. The action seemed to calm her a little. "I can breathe now," she said.

It seemed to her impossible to remain still. Up and down the room she went, still with the suggestion of the tiger in her quick, gliding steps, her head turning restlessly from side to side. Thoughts, memories, fancies thronged her brain. He had made her conspicuous, almost compromised her. He had lied to her. If his love had been real, how could he have sought to tie her to him? No, it was her money, not she, that had attracted him, and he had been willing to put her in such a position that the very servants had felt justified in gossiping about her. This mortification maddened her. Oh, if she were a man she would punish him, but what could a poor, helpless woman do? Suddenly she stopped in her frantic, aimless walk : she could

do something, and she would. She would be
Countess de La Roche. That was to be Maurice's punishment.

The count dined with them that night, and
neither he nor the other guests had ever seen
la belle Américaine so beautiful or so gay.
Flora, too, was in high spirits, for a few words
from Sylvia just before dinner had raised her
from her despondent mood, and colored her
future once more with golden tints. Oh, yes,
it was all very brilliant, no doubt. The table,
gleaming with its burden of fruit, flowers, and
sparkling glass under the rose-shaded candles;
the women with their snowy shoulders and shining jewels, the soft silks shimmering in billows
about them. The sound of laughter, the easy
ripple of talk, and underneath the warning dash
of the waves on the beach below, which seemed
intrusive with its daring intimation of nature.

To Sylvia it brought the memory of some play
she had seen long ago, where the music and
merriment of a feast are heard behind the scenes,
while the tragedy of a life unfolds before the
spectator's eyes; only here it was the tragedy
which was hidden.

She did not realize that any decisive steps had
been taken until the guests rose to say good-
night, when, as Philippe bent low over her
hand, he raised his eyes to hers, and whispered,

"Thank you." Then she knew that Flora had found time to speak, and that her freedom was gone.

She kept her air of gayety until she was alone once more, but she had not been able to speak of her future even to Justine, although she knew the ecstasy in store for the faithful creature. When at last her door closed, and she was again face to face with her bitter anger, the light died from her eyes, and her lips met tight in a rigid line. She could not sleep, and throwing open her blinds she lay staring at the square of sky. There was the Great Bear, slanting across the northern heavens. She well remembered standing with Dick, her childhood's friend, on the piazza, as he taught her how to find it. The square white house still stood tenantless save for the careful Deborah, and she had spoken the words which pledged her to make her home in a new land, on new soil. Her country was hers no more ; the hour had passed, never to return, when she had owned the right to suffer for it. Had happy, tender memories played about her youth, her regrets now had been of a softer nature, but there was only a severe renunciation in her heart as she recalled the years behind her. She had always been unconsciously searching for some object on which to lavish her love and enthusiasm. Her father had repressed any demonstration of affection, although so little tenderness on his part would have repaid her doubly. The only time she had ever felt a reason for the thrill of feeling was when her eyes met those of Richard Huntington, as he raised them to hers for the last time, on his steady, resolute way, to die for his flag. In a few hours those stars would be shining on the summer fields about her old home, as unconcerned and indifferent there as here. What did they care for human agitations and distractions?

Under their cold light Sylvia became more passive. Happiness, after all, was more a question of temperament than surroundings, she reflected, and resolved to give to the country of her choice all the ardent enthusiasm she had felt formerly for her own fatherland.

She would find her ideal in her future husband; he was brave, noble, and loyal. Their mutual aims should not be merely a selfish gratification of love; they would look higher. She resolutely put Maurice out of her mind. One more meeting, and then that episode belonged to the dead past. The stars grew pale, and a breeze came with the dawn, blowing the muslin curtains into the room. Sylvia turned her face to the wall, closed her hot eyes, and slept at last.

CHAPTER VIII.

It is not often given to one of us poor feeble mortals to feel the serene satisfaction in the result of our well-doing which made Flora Lee-Blair walk as if on air during the days following Sylvia's acceptance of Philippe. He too was glowing with gratification at his own good luck, although his spirits were a trifle subdued by a condition his future bride had insisted on making; namely, that when she had been recognized as such, and suitably welcomed by his mother, she would telegraph for her man of business and consider herself formally engaged, but not before. He had a clear idea of the difficulties before him. Not only would Sylvia's nationality be an awkward obstacle, but her religion might prove an impassable barrier with the countess. Very carefully, with infinite skill and tact, he opened the latter subject, treating it with all the delicacy which he had imbibed from the priests in his conversations with them. Sylvia learned that behind the music and incense, the shrines and saints, lay a beautiful belief of which they were the symbols ; she reverenced Philippe for

the reverence he showed in speaking of them,
and felt stirred by his well-chosen words. He
spoke always dispassionately to her, as if subdu-
ing his deeper feelings for her sake. She told
him frankly that he was influencing her, but
would promise nothing as yet. An unsuspected
loyalty to the faith of her fathers stirred within
her. Was it not enough to renounce everything
else ? She would cling to that until convinced
of something better.

Philippe saw the strength beneath the yielding
exterior, and concluded not to press matters.
After all, there were many arguments he could
bring up against those of his mother; and if
Maurice succeeded in getting the money from
his father things might be delayed a little without danger. The more he saw of Sylvia in the
few days following her conditional surrender the
surer he felt of her, especially as Mrs. Lee-Blair
was no half-hearted ally.

"Oh, my child," she would exclaim, "you
are very, very fortunate ! Philippe is a prize.
Fancy having a husband like him, so noble, so
good-looking. I can quite imagine him going to
the guillotine, like Marie Antoinette and that
'resurrection and the life' man in 'Tale of Two
Cities,' he is so calm and strong. Then think of
being able to have coronets embroidered on all
your linen. A count's coronet may not be quite

as distinguished as a marquis's, but then it has seven points, and one in diamonds with the points tipped with rubies would be too awfully lovely. Oh, Sylvia, God has been very, very good to you."

Then the kindly, frivolous creature would wipe away a genuine tear very carefully, so that it might not interfere with her complexion, and flutter off, grateful for the part that she had been allowed to play in this great scheme.

Justine received the news of her mistress's future plans with a joy almost unnatural in its quiet ecstasy.

" I have prayed for everything good for my child, and the saints hear ; praise be to Mary. I felt that she would be great and noble when I first took her in my arms, only a baby, but with the seal on her forehead. Now I know why it was that I was sent to those desolate shores to watch over her, to bring her here for great things."

Three days more slipped by, no definite step being taken. Philippe intended to wait for Maurice's return before going to see his mother, and excused himself to Sylvia for his delay by pleading the distress it caused him to think of leaving her. She accepted his flattering apology with her usual graciousness, which had always a touch of aloofness in it. She felt that until she

saw Maurice it would be impossible for her to
adjust her mind to her future life ; that dreaded
interview with him must be behind her ere she
could feel settled and content. Regarding Philippe she was satisfied that her choice was a prudent one. He suited her taste from every point
of view. He never jarred on her, never showed
himself as opposed to her in any way, making
even the delicate question of their religions easy.
She did not reflect that when he was absent it was
of his name, his castle, and his position that she
dreamed, not of him ; for when they were together
his dominant virility exercised a strong influence,
and she mistook for symptoms of love what were
in fact but natural impulses. His relations with
Flora puzzled her a little. When they were all
three together he and Mrs. Lee-Blair preserved
a cold formality of manner which was contradicted by the familiar attitude into which they
seemed to fall naturally when alone, and in which
Sylvia had once or twice surprised them. But
she was not apt to be suspicious, and did not
dwell on this subject.

One evening he announced his intention of leaving Trouville the following day, for Touraine ;
he said that he felt like a coward in having post-
poned it for so long, but did not add that he had
received a telegram from Maurice announcing
his return that same night.

Yet this arrival meant an important moment in three lives.

For the first time Maurice had chafed at being under his father's roof, and had found the hours drag heavily. He had determined to keep his own counsel regarding his hopes and fears, but the last night at home, a fleeting look of disappointment or wounded feelings on the face he loved and honored so deeply broke down his reserve, and, withholding her name and nationality, he told his father of his passionate love for Sylvia, and how it hung in the balance. The older man was deeply moved, and seemed shaken by the communication, but he gave his sympathy and good wishes generously. When they parted the next morning he only asked wistfully that Maurice would telegraph him his success, — "for I am sure no one can resist you, my boy," he said with rather a tremulous laugh.

Not twenty-four hours later came the message, "Have failed; shall try to get exchanged into African regiment. — M." That was all, and the sender, blinded by his own grief and disappointment, gave little heed to the pain the words bore. Perhaps it is as well that children are selfish sometimes : if they knew the pain their sorrows cause, it would double them, and like two mirrors reflecting one another, woes would continue multiplying until the whole world became one vast moan.

Maurice, cheered by his father's confidence in his success with Sylvia, came back to Trouville full of exultant hopes, so overflowing with them that there was no room for fear or doubt to creep in. His love for Sylvia was so intense, so vital, that it seemed an impossibility it should not have an overpowering effect on her. She must return it! It was too clearly heaven-sent not to be irresistible. To-morrow, to-morrow! sang the wheels of the train that bore him back to her. To-morrow! to-morrow! whispered the night wind creeping in from the sea, as he stood, late as it was, before her villa, so as to slip under the door with his own hand a note to tell her of his return, and of his wish to see her in the morning. He stood in the dark gazing up at her window; behind the closed blinds perhaps she slept and dreamt of him. Or better still, she woke, and thought of him. Ah, it is good to be young and love with passion ; it broadens and ennobles, even if Sorrow follows, blotting out the rapturous memories with her tears.

But there was no hint that anything but joy was in store for him to disturb Maurice as he at last turned away from the magic spot, and went back to his hotel. He thought over every detail of her appearance as he had last seen her. How young and approachable she had seemed in her riding-habit and round hat ; how freshly the

color came and went in her cheeks; what a soft
sheen was on her dark hair, closely coiled in her
neck.

He had forgotten Philippe, his errand, everything but Sylvia for the moment, when the sight
of the sleepy night-clerk, handing him his candle,
woke him up from his visions. " No," the man
replied to his question, " Monsieur le Comte de
La Roche was not yet in : did Monsieur le Capitaine desire to leave any message for him ?" So
Maurice left word that he had returned, and
would be with him in the morning, and went to
sleep, breathing the one name in all the world
to him.

He had been moderately successful in his
quest, for his father had advanced Philippe about
half the sum he had called for ; but he had made
it plain to his son that although this was not the
first drain that the young count had made on his
purse, it should be the last.

" I have already given him back, franc for
franc, nearly the entire sum left me by his father,
which helped me to build up my fortune. His
mother knows that he has applied to me for help,
and I have promised her that I would give him
nothing more. I should be firm now, had you
not pledged your word, my boy ; but if either
break faith, I prefer to be the one."

He followed up these words with a short ac-

count of Philippe's life of reckless self-indul-
gence, softening nothing, for he wished to impress Maurice with his own disgust that the
name which should stand so high was thus dab-
bled in the mud of the gutter.

Any tales of ordinary extravagance and excess
would have found excuses in Maurice's heart;
youth generally obeys the esprit de corps which
bids it take the part opposed to age. But Maurice had a nature which recoiled from degrading
details, and the deliberate statements made by
his father destroyed once and for all the hero-
worship he had felt for Philippe.

It was with the feeling that he was the superior, not the count, that he followed Marcel
the next morning to his master's room. His
mind was too much occupied in thinking of his
coming interview with Sylvia to notice the change
of attitude assumed by Philippe: a week ago he
had come humbly for him, to ask a favor; to-day
he sent as to a tradesman to know the result.
Perhaps Maurice would not have been struck by
this at any other time, for he was only suspicious
on rare and obvious occasions; but his eyes having been opened by his father, he could not help
shrugging his shoulders slightly when he entered
the count's bedroom, at the luxurious surroundings of a man half ruined financially.

Philippe was still in bed. On a table by his

side was a silver tray on which stood his early cup of coffee ; every detail of the service was in Louis XVI. silver, delicately wrought with garlands and bow-knots. He himself was gorgeous in pale blue silk, and his toilet articles, just arranged by Marcel, were in ebony and gold. His morning's mail was scattered about the bed, and he kept his eyes on a letter he held, even while he said : " Ah, Maurice, glad that you are back at last. You may go, Marcel. Open the other window first ; it is infernally hot to-day."

As he finished, he read the last word of the letter, returned it to its envelope, and waited until Marcel had left the room ; then his tone took on a touch more of eagerness as he said, " Well, any luck ? "

" More than I expected, less than you hoped for."

" How much ? "

" Forty thousand."

Philippe gave a low whistle. " I suppose I can worry along with that ; it 's deuced little, though."

His words implied disappointment, but he took it very coolly. Maurice looked at him keenly for a moment ; he wondered if he meant to accept the loan, made by his father at some inconvenience, without a word of gratitude to the old man.

Philippe resumed : " Have you the money here ? "

" Yes."

" In notes or a cheque ? "

" In notes ; I cashed my father's cheque in Paris yesterday. You will have the kindness to sign a receipt for them."

" Oh, of course ; hand me that writing-case there, will you ? — thanks. Have you a form made out ? "

" No," answered Maurice, irritated by the other's manner and marked callousness. " You ought to know how to word it well enough."

" Yes," drawled Philippe, as his pen flew over the paper, " I 've had plenty of experience in this sort of thing. There, it 's signed and dated. Does it suit you ? "

" Yes," returned Maurice as shortly as before, when he had read what Philippe had written. " Now be good enough to count these bills."

He flung a heavy roll on to the bed ; the count went through them once methodically, then a second time. " They 're all right."

" Good-morning, then."

" Are you going ? Can't you stop a little ? "

" No, I 'm in a hurry," answered Maurice, his hand on the door-handle.

" Good-by, then ; and oh, I say, wait a bit. Present my most respectful thanks to your father when you write, and tell him how grateful I am," called Philippe, but he received no answer, and was doubtful if his tardy thanks were ever heard.

Chafing at the insolence and ingratitude with which he had been met, Maurice left the hotel as rapidly as possible, and going on to the sands, deserted at this hour, lounged there until it would not be too unconventionally early to seek Sylvia. The morning was very hot; already the heated air rose from the rocks, making the objects behind it glimmer and shimmer; the ocean lay heaving slightly, untouched by a breath of wind, and seemed too exhausted to do more than break in languid little waves on the sand.

For the twentieth time Maurice looked at his watch, and at last decided that he might climb the cliff and enter the villa at which he had been staring. There was a slight land breeze higher up, and the interior of the house felt cool and refreshing as the butler ushered him through the hall and, throwing open the salon door, announced him.

The room was darkened, and at first he was conscious only of a scent of flowers and a faint light in one corner. Then as his dazzled eyes grew used to the obscurity, he saw that the light came from Sylvia's white dress, and that she was looking at him intently.

"I did not see you at first: I was blinded!"
he exclaimed, going towards her. As he drew
near, her long dark lashes drooped on her
cheeks, and when he raised her hand to his
lips, she murmured a scarcely audible word of
greeting. He sat for a while without speaking,
looking at her ardently, hungrily, and withal
humbly. He wondered at his own fortitude in
deliberately banishing himself for a week. She
sat impassive under his gaze, her eyes still
veiled. He saw now every detail of her delicate
beauty, and noticed the ivory-like gleam of her
rounded arms showing through the loose drapery
of her muslin dress; the arch of her instep in
its openwork stocking; the beautiful lines in
which the hair grew on her temples and just
over her dainty ear. He was mad with longing
and doubt, while she sat as motionless as a statue,
a bunch of white carnations on her bosom barely
stirring with her breath. How was he to know
the passion of resentment and anger under this
cool exterior? The only movement that betrayed
agitation was the tremulous action of her hands
as she opened and shut a tortoise-shell fan.

She had steeled herself for this interview, and
until she saw Maurice had thought that she could
control all signs of emotion. She had decided
to give no explanation of the reasons which had
led her to refuse him : she would be cold and

firm. But when she saw him all her soul was in a tumult; she dreaded the mere sound of his voice. She did not wish to be shaken, to be tempted. She believed him false, and any tender feeling coming now into her heart would make her false to herself. He should not have that power at least. But she hated him, to think that in spite of all resolves some power was his; that she dared not fully meet his glance; that merely his presence shook her before he had spoken; and that his voice, in speaking the simple words of greeting, had made her shiver. This man, who might have meant so much to her, had deceived her, had humbled her in her own eyes and had almost succeeded in making her a jest for the world.

Maurice spoke at last. How should he know that this reserve meant hidden fury? He thought that it expressed her readiness to hear him tell his love, if not to respond to it.

" Sylvia," he said, " have you no welcome for me, no word? Do you know what this week has meant to me? a very purgatory, and now I come to you to tell me if heaven or hell lies beyond."

" I consented to see you, Monsieur, because your letters made me think that you attach more importance to a few words I spoke last week than they deserve. I was carried away by the beauty of the morning, the quick ride, — how

can I tell what? — and perhaps a little infected
by your enthusiasm. But really that is an episode that is passed, and should leave no trace."

She paused, and clattered the sticks of her
fan against each other.

Maurice sat silent for a moment, a look of
incredulity and wounded feeling in his eyes.

" Then, Sylvia," he said, " you are ungenerous
to play with me like this. If you could know
what you are to me — how I adore you — what
you mean in my life — you would be merciful,
and drop this trifling. It is unworthy of you."

" How shall I express myself, then ? " she
asked, always looking down. " In plain words,
I find that I do not care for you — that I am
incapable of loving you."

For the first time he began to feel the fear of
losing her.

" For God's sake don't say that. You could
love me — you could not resist my love — if you
would only try."

" Perhaps. But why should I try ? "

There was almost a sneer in her voice now.

" Why! you ask me why ? Are my feelings
nothing to you ? is my love nothing ? " he demanded.

" Nothing," she answered composedly.

" What has changed you in this short time ?
A week ago you were nearly yielding — you did

love me last Thursday, by Heaven you did!
Give me some reason for this alteration. I demand it!"

"You are not entitled to demand anything,
Monsieur Regnier. If I was foolish enough to
give way last week to the influence of a delightful morning, and a most eloquent companion, I
should be blamed for what I did then, not for
what I am doing to-day when I am trying to
repair my fault."

He drew a deep breath, and leaning his elbow
on a table near him, covered his eyes with his
hand. Under all her anger, Sylvia's womanly
heart could not repress a throb of sympathy at
this sound of suffering. She raised her eyes
and looked at him furtively, ready to avert her
gaze at his least movement. How forlorn he
looked, and how young, poor boy.

Impulsively she spoke again. "Don't feel so
badly, Maurice; I'm not worth it. I am not
even ice, for that can be melted. I am granite,
like my native hills. Now go away, forget me,
and some day you will thank Heaven I saved
you from myself."

As he listened his heart beat high with hope.
She had spoken in gentler accents, she had
called him by his name. Raising his head he
made one final effort, and he believed that it
would be successful.

" Hear me a moment. Sylvia," he began :
" think before you sacrifice my love for your
ambition. It is true that I cannot give you
high position ; but my name is honorable, and
oh, my darling, I love you so truly, so deeply,
that no woman on earth ever had such devotion
laid at her feet before."

The old feelings, but intensified, returned as
she heard his words. He dared try again to
deceive her. She shivered internally, endeavor-
ing to maintain the calm dignity she had assumed, so as not to betray her crushed, bleeding
pride. Maurice saw her grow a shade paler,
and the long lashes quiver on her cheek. He
thought she hesitated, and his courage grew.

" Listen to me a moment. Do not send me
away until I have given you a little glimpse of
what love, true, Heaven-sent love — love like
mine for you — means. It is many sided : I have
had this long week to look at it in all its phases.
I love you with the ardor of a lover, and with the
purity of a worshiper. I give you the admiration your beauty, your daintiness, call forth ; but
no dull detail of every-day life could dim your
radiance in my eyes. My love is strong ; loss of
youth, of grace, cannot weaken it. Sylvia, I am
not offering you only the passion of a few years,
I am laying at your feet the devotion of a lifetime.
Before you say no to me, think what it is to know

that for one person in the world you can do
no wrong, can never lose your charm, will stand
first in his heart through time and eternity."

She was sorely shaken. Her intellect, her
pride, and her god ambition drew her from him.
Her heart pleaded for him; it beat tumultuously
while she spoke; it told her that his words rang
true. But the ugly fact remained that he had
been false in one respect — why not in all?
Should she give up all her lifelong dreams of
greatness for a reality more unsubstantial than
a dream? And under these dominant thoughts
lay a fear of the capabilities in herself.

"I have listened to you patiently, Monsieur;
you must now listen to me. Love is a myth,
very pretty, but not for me. You are wasting
your time here, — as I have just said, I am
hard. For a moment your words stirred my
superficial emotions; but I am immovable. You
must understand my life plan before you can go
away satisfied: my heart is with the high ones
in this world. I want to be identified with a
cause, and if I ever marry, it will be some one
who can give me a great name, and can open
great possibilities to me. Love and I have nothing in common."

"You would sell yourself for a title, then?"
said Maurice bitterly.

"Yes; I always fancied that a handkerchief

with a coronet on it would dry my tears before
they could fall."

She spoke lightly, hoping to bring the interview to a calm ending. She thought she might
turn him off ; but she was mistaken. He felt
that this would be his only opportunity, and determined to leave no stone unturned. So, con-
trolling himself with difficulty, he spoke in a
more commonplace manner.

" I should be less urgent if I thought that you
had the least idea of what you are talking about.
What are the great names in France to-day, and
what do they mean ? Almost nothing. Your
own country has taught us a lesson."

" If the great names mean nothing," interrupted Sylvia, " I suppose the little names mean
less." She wished that he would leave her. She
had forced herself to speak gently to him, but
he would not take her dismissal, and was driving
her wild with his persistency, backed as it was by
the voice of her deepest nature, crying to her in
words she could not, or would not, understand.

" No," said Maurice to her last remark, —
" no ; to-day our country gives us all a chance
to make a name, even if we have not inherited
one. Oh, Sylvia, think what I could do with
your help. Would you not feel proud to hear
me spoken of as one of the poets of France, if I
were your husband ? I have no coronet to offer

you ; but if I were crowned with the bays of the Immortals " —

" This is folly, and worse," she broke in. " I have been patient ; but you have no pity on me. Is it so impossible for you to understand that my mind is fixed ? "

She rose as she spoke, and faced him for the first time. She felt that her emotions were getting the upper hand. She was losing her self-control, and the interview must come to an end. Maurice looked at her, the mad longing in his heart growing stronger. There was a haughty poise to her head that seemed the refinement of provocation. He was desperate now : it was lose all or gain all. He had a dim idea that if once he could hold her in his arms, once cover her face with kisses, crush it savagely almost, against his own, that his love would win. She could not resist its contagion. He stood before her, the memory of her words in the sunken lane ringing in his ears : " I promise you a kiss the next time we meet — either it will be one of good-by forever, or it will tell you that I love you as entirely as you do me." Would she remember her promise, too ? There was a sense of compelling her to do so as he stood there silent and grim in his uncertainty.

The echo of that promise came to her also. She had remembered it in fear all through the

interview, hoping, almost praying, that he would
not recall it. But now his waiting attitude told
her plainly that it was as vivid to him as to her.
She had been pale, but now the blood rushed to
her cheek, crimsoning it, her eyelids quivered
and fell, and her hand tightened about her fan.

" Ungenerous," she whispered, but he did not
hear her. He only saw signs of relenting in her
confusion, and in another moment his arms were
round her.

She shrank from him, a look in her face that
he could not read. If she had blushed a moment
ago she was white now, the color leaving even
her lips, which scarcely opened to let the word
" Coward!" slip through, while, hardly knowing what she did, driven to a frenzy, she struck
his face with her fan. Maurice dropped his
arms to his side, drew himself up, and before she
turned swiftly away, she saw him whiten under
his brown skin, only a pale red streak showing
where her blow had fallen. She swept down
the room, but as she reached the door she heard
his voice : " Stop, Madame! there is one word
you must take back before we part. Call me
anything you like, but not — coward."

" The word is spoken," she retorted, looking
over her shoulder.

" If you will not recall it now, by Heaven
you shall before either of us dies," said Maurice,

and as he spoke he pushed open the long blind opening on to the terrace, and stepped out into the dazzling heat of the sun.

Sylvia moved vaguely forward, and then sank on to the nearest chair. All her self-control had been but surface deep. She could subdue her voice, choose her words, veil the anger of her eyes, but she was powerless over the turbulent riot of her heart. She hated Maurice with an intensity which frightened her. She could have killed him in her excitement. Her whole body felt alive with physical suffering; tremors attacked each nerve, and she could hear the quick beats of her heart, throbbing in her ears. For a time she remained very still outwardly, but as her agitation abated she became more conscious of her surroundings, and noticed that her hand was grasping something so tightly that it hurt her. Looking down she saw the fan. A wave of shame, of fear, swept over her. The thought that if it had been a dagger she would have killed him overpowered her: she threw it from her, and sat trembling and cold at the reaction. Maurice dead, and by her hand — yet in her heart she had willed his death. She felt weak and faint. Dreading interruption, she yet managed to stumble to her former seat, her back to the open blind, and to speak intelligibly to Flora, who came bustling in.

CHAPTER IX

PHILIPPE DE LA ROCHE reached his home the following day. The sun was pouring its softened radiance on the lovely and lovable Touraine landscape. The influence of autumn was apparent, enveloping even the near distance in a haze. The double row of tall poplars on the main road were shedding their golden leaves, which fluttered slowly through the blue radiance. The "stately Loire," as Wordsworth calls it, kept ever on its way with a placid, dignified indifference to all that is hurried, unclean, unbeautiful on its shores, reflecting only the clear heavens and the white clouds. It was the vintage season, and among the reddish purple vines covering the hillsides the peasants were busy at their work, filling with the ripe grapes the baskets slung on their backs.

As the carriage turned aside from the main route, the gray, weather-beaten towers of the chateau were visible for a moment through an opening in the trees; they were then hidden again as the horses trotted up the gentle incline of the avenue, and were next seen from the other side, where the moat had to be crossed before entering under the fine, old archway into the court of honor. La Roche was in reality two buildings facing each other, and connected by a low towerless wing with the arch in the centre. The side opposite this was bounded by a low, ivy-covered wall, and was open to the broad expanse of green meadows with the river flowing through them; stately trees clustered there in groups, and in the foreground on the terrace, close beneath the wall, stood a noble cedar of Lebanon. The east wing was clearly older than its opposite neighbor, the absence of carvings and embellishments proclaiming its origin in the grim times when dwellings were built not only for purposes of living, but required strength for defense against enemies. The west wing had evidently been built in happier days, and was richly decorated with carved stone in the forms of grotesque beasts and distorted gargoyles. The upper row of windows, finished with a wreath of intricate openwork stone tracery, looked like lace against the brilliant sky. Both wings ended in round towers, and the iron weathercocks, with their strangely fashioned standards cut like an animal's head, turned as the wind blew, just as they had turned when the massive cedar, or even the cedar's ancestor, was but a slip whose slender trunk could

have been clasped by the strong, rude hand of
Foulques Nerra's descendant.

It was a home to be proud of; to make a
man's heart beat high with the resolve that he
would leave it richer in its annals of noble deeds
for his life; to bring unconsciously a wish for
children, to whom he could hand down an un-
stained name and a love for the old place. But
Philippe was not a man given to thoughts of
this sort. When he recalled his ancestry, which
was seldom, it was to laugh with a touch of
scorn at the unsanctioned loves of the old crusader who had founded the family, and to speak
of the doubtful transactions which had brought
wealth to it. When his mother would do her
best to urge him to other ambitions, another
train of life, he would jestingly turn the matter
aside and ask her what she could expect of a
descendant of an unholy alliance. If his lazy,
disused conscience awoke after some ruder shock
than usual, he could always soothe it by reminding himself that his faults at any rate had the
quality of kingliness. And so this delicious,
golden, mellow September afternoon, his only
feeling was one of impatience as he entered the
west wing, having told the coachman that his
horses were a disgrace to a gentleman's stable,
and asking him if he had ever been taught the
use of a currycomb. As the old man, who had

served his father many years, turned away, hurt and angry, the count entered the door held open by another lifelong servant, the butler.

"Madame la comtesse will receive Monsieur le comte in the oak salon," he said, his eager, wistful expression showing plainly how he longed for a word of greeting from the master whom he had seen christened; but beyond a careless "Thanks," as he handed him his hat and cane, Philippe said nothing. He was glad his mother had noticed the last time he was there how much he disliked having her at the station or even at the door to meet him. It was much better form to keep family scenes quiet. As he followed the butler across the enormous hall he shivered.

"Why the deuce don't you have a fire here?" he asked abruptly; "this is like stepping into a tomb after the outside air." The room where he found his mother was a trifle warmer, for the hot sun had been trying to work its way through the narrow, small-paned windows sunk four feet in the thick walls; but even here there was a touch of chill. The walls were hung with Flanders tapestries of great age, and brilliant colors that made one think of Chinese embroideries. The ceiling gave its name to the room, being of oak, and unlike the majority of old ceilings the beams were not painted, but the natural wood

was elaborately carved. Although this was one
of the smallest apartments the chateau boasted,
it was large enough to make an enormous stone
fireplace seem in exact proportion. The furniture was old and heavy, and the few unavoidable
modern touches were lost sight of in the general
aspect of ripened age.

The Countess de La Roche was sitting in a
high gothic armchair, her face turned towards
the window looking beyond the cedar to the
river. For the last hour she had sat in the same
attitude, her hands folded on her lap, only the
quick changes of expression sweeping across her
face showing she was in truth a living being,
and not a phantom chased from the gay tapestry
behind her, for that her sombre garb struck too
discordant a note in their bright symphony of
color. She was a woman who had been handsome. The gray-streaked hair was brushed simply away from a low beautiful brow; the finely
cut features were still perfect in outline; but the
eyes were sunken and dimmed, with heavy lines
about them; and the mouth when in repose had
almost a cruel look, so rigidly it closed. She
wore her usual heavy mourning, although it was
nearly six years since her husband had died, and
the thin golden thread of her wedding ring was
her only ornament. Quiet and unassuming in
her manners, she yet impressed every one with

whom she came in contact as a woman to be respected and revered. Every one? Hardly; for her son was the exception to be found to every rule.

As he entered the low carved oak door she rose, and a look of apprehension came to her eyes; Philippe saw it, and his vanity was touched by it. Had it come to this, that she only connected bad news with his appearance? She should find out her mistake. He raised her hand to his lips with an exaggerated formality, and then submitted to her kisses on each cheek, — long, tremulous kisses, as of one hardly daring to hope.

"Are you tired, my dear? Shall I ring for wine, or something to refresh you?"

"No, thank you, mamma. I stopped over a train in Tours and breakfasted there, knowing your tyrants do not care to be disturbed by extra meals."

"You know they would do anything for you." This was said in a reproachful tone, and he moved uneasily: he loathed reproaches, and he had had so many in his life.

"Do you know that the house is beastly cold? You ought to have fires even if it is against all the canons of the church. I will light this one now, and you can ask the curé to absolve you for over-luxuriousness after I am warm."

He drew an enameled match-box from his pocket, and touched a taper to the well-laid logs; the flames went roaring up the great chimney, and after giving it a careful look, he turned his back to it, set his feet wide apart, and said genially, —

" You should have me down here once in a while to show you how to be comfortable. I really believe women like to make martyrs of themselves ; there is no other way to account for a lot of things in this world." As his mother made no answer he hummed softly an opera bouffe air, and let his gaze wander over the well-known room. Although affecting ease he dreaded what was coming, and longed to have it over. As he thought of it he heartily wished that he were twenty-four hours older, and the coming interview a thing of the past; but, realizing that wishes are very inadequate aids, he brought his tune carefully to a finish, and twisting his moustache plunged in.

" I suppose you know Maurice came to see his father last week ? "

" Yes," answered the countess shortly.

" And you know why he came ? "

" I fancy I know, though I could not make him tell me. Oh, Philippe, Philippe — why do you bring such shame to me ? "

" Well, don't worry, mamma, dear ; I think I

see my way out of all my troubles if you will help me."

" I suppose you mean that you are going to marry."

" That is just it — what a clever creature you are. Yes, I have met a charming well-bred woman, an American with an enormous fortune in her own right, — and — and — Why, what 's the matter now ? Why do you look at me so ? "

" An American ! you, a de La Roche, marrying a creature of yesterday ! Have you no pride? Do you never think of your duty to your house ? "

" My pride takes another form, you know ; and I prefer a mésalliance to any other that offers."

" Is there no other way ? Must we fall to this ? "

He fixed his eyes on her working, agitated face. There was something oppressive in his steady gaze, for it seemed as if he were making an effort to control his habitual restlessness, and that this effort cost him dear.

" Yes, there is another way ; but as you have told me never to ask you again to do that we may as well ignore it."

" Philippe, you insult me when you ask me to sell an acre of the property your father left me to hold for you. Never — never will I do it. Besides, of what use would it be ? No sum that

I can raise for you will ever keep you out of
debt. You come here complaining of this, that,
and the other thing. Do you know why the
chateau is cold? It is because I have sold every
available bit of timber to have money enough
to live through another year. I anticipated my
income when you last came to me with one of
your shameful stories, begging for more money.
I have now only four house servants, for I cannot afford more, — I, with an income so large it
could easily pay for three establishments like
this. Will you never grow old? Will you
never cease to be a thoughtless, careless boy?
At twenty actions like yours are excusable; at
thirty they are revolting."

"Can you give me seventy-five thousand francs
in a week?"

"You know I cannot."

"Then will you consent to my marriage with
the lady I have spoken of?"

"My consent? What need is there for such
a farce? You are of age; marry whom you
will, and ignore me."

"But Madame Huntington, — that is her
name, — makes it a condition that she shall be
made welcome by my family."

"A widow, too, is she? — oh, no, even you
would have stopped at that — She is not a
Protestant?"

"Dear mamma, the world to-day is not the same place you left thirty odd years ago when my father brought you here to rusticate; if a woman is well-bred, rich, and virtuous, her religion is taken for granted."

Madame de La Roche covered her face with her hands. She did not speak; she could not. All her soul was in revolt at the prospect before her. As she looked at the matter, the family she had belonged to for so long, of which she was so passionately proud, would be disgraced by her son's proposed marriage.

"A rich American widow, a Protestant." The words seemed to glow in scarlet letters before her closed eyes. To her, Americans were well enough in their way, but, oh, how far apart that way had always been from hers! and Protestantism meant to her not only a backsliding from the true faith, but something connected with vulgarity, hypocrisy, and obtrusiveness. Both her religious and social susceptibilities were hurt by the thought. If any personal sacrifice could save — not her son, but the name — from this loss of position she would make it; but, short of selling some of her land, she saw no way: and that she had solemnly promised her husband should never be done.

"Starve first," he had said jestingly: and she repeated, "Yes, starve first."

One of the blazing logs parted in the middle
with a crash. Philippe rearranged the fire, and
then said in a would-be cheerful tone, " Well,
will you give your consent ? "

" You mean, will I accept my martyrdom ?
I must."

" Don't be too sure this is a bad thing. Sylvia
is a very presentable woman. She is handsome
too, and young, only about twenty-five, I think.
Her husband left her at the church door to join
his regiment, and was shot in their civil war.
He left her ten million francs in her own right.
There is not a breath of suspicion against her
character, and barring her nationality, which
she can't help, she is about all I could expect.
As for her religion, she is not very firmly rooted.
Anyway, the queen of England has the same
faith as Sylvia, so at all events she travels in
good company towards the promised land. Besides, what a chance for you to convert her, eh,
mamma ? "

He had seated himself beside her, taken one
of her hands in his, and was playing with it;
she drew it quietly away. While he had been
speaking, a great pity for this unknown, dreaded
daughter-in-law had crept into her mind — so
young, of perfect reputation, and what was before her ? A marriage with a man already old
in dissipation. caring only for the doubtful ex-

citements that gambling and the demi-monde could give him, who had captured his prey simply for her fortune.

"Oh, another thing in her favor I forgot — she is an orphan with absolutely no near relations."

"Poor child, may God help her."

"Well, you are hardly complimentary to me. If that remark means she'll need such extraordinary help on account of her being my wife — But I'll forgive your plain speaking if it means you are still, what you always have been, the very dearest, most adorable mother in the world and will smooth my way for me."

"What do you want me to do?"

Her voice was level and expressionless and she did not look at him.

"Write her a nice letter, such as you are famous for, and ask her to make you a visit. You need n't say a word about our being engaged, for she made it a condition that she should not be bound; and you had better tell her to bring along an English woman, her companion or something, a Mrs. Lee - Blair — hold on, I'll spell it for you."

Thankful for something to do, he bustled about looking for a bit of paper. He opened the countess's desk, took a sheet of her note-paper, and unfastening a heavy gold pencil crusted with rubies from his watch-chain, scrawled the name over it. She looked on, with the bitter memory in her mind of all the sordid little economies she had practiced for his sake ; all the self-denials that he had made useless, and her heart swelled within her as she thought, " Rather that a thousand times, than that he should sell his birthright."

They parted when the dressing-bell rang, and when they met again she handed him an unsealed envelope.

" If that does not suit you, perhaps you will tell me where it can be improved."

He pulled the letter out and ran his eye down the sheet.

" Perfect, absolutely perfect. Mamma, no one knows better than you how to do a thing of this sort gracefully."

All through the elaborately served dinner he showed his gratitude by his rattling good nature, ignoring many small omissions in the butler's service that he mentally noticed and resolved to change before Sylvia's arrival. He discussed with his mother what rooms should be made ready for their guests, showed himself a master of all the details of modern luxury, and even volunteered to procure an extra number of servants for the time of the visit. Madame de La Roche listened with cold attention, assenting to all his plans with no pretense at enthusiasm. Although his spirits were high in proportion to the dread with which he had looked forward to this evening, he was relieved when she rose and bade him good-night. He closed the door behind her, put some fresh logs on the smouldering fire, lighted a cigarette, and throwing himself into an armchair, gave himself up to self-congratulations and a few calculations of a cheering nature.

His mother went slowly to her room. She soon dismissed her maid, and then wrapping a heavy fur cloak about her, opened a door hidden beneath the tapestry on the wall. Her glass-shaded candle showed a small turning staircase built in the stonework of the chateau. Cautiously, and yet with the tread of one accustomed to the difficult descent, down, down she went. When the last step was reached she took a heavy key from her chatelaine and opened a door, closing it behind her. Her candle threw its feeble gleam about her, showing glimpses of a chapel hewn out of the side of the rock upon which the chateau was built, and from which it took its name. This was not only a chapel, but the burial-place of the family, and the floor was inlaid with slabs of stone or marble with the names of the dead and gone cut into them. Against the walls were ranged carved effigies,

most of them gray with age, and touched roughly
by the hand of time, but among them one shone
white and fresh : a recumbent figure, with dra-
peries flowing in majestic folds, and a faithful
hound at its feet. Here the countess paused for
a moment, the thought coming to her, " Was it
because I loved you more than my child, more
than my country, more than my God, that this
burden is so heavy upon me ? Must I expiate
by a life of woe the years of golden happiness
I spent with you, my love, my husband ? So be
it ; I am ready. I have had all that life can
give of joy. Now let me bear what it has in
store for me."

She moved forward through the gloom towards a glimmer of light coming from a taper
that burned day and night before an altar of
the Virgin ; and there at the feet of the divine
mother the mortal mother knelt. At first only
black, despairing bitterness filled her heart ;
then the quiet, the associations of the place also,
perhaps a blessed human inability to bear more
than a certain amount of suffering, touched her
healingly, and she found herself praying.

" O Holy Virgin, help me to bear my cross ;
send me thy comfort. Have mercy on me. Take
from me the sense of shame and guilt I sink beneath. Thou Blessed Mother, have pity on me
who have drunk of a bitterer cup of sorrow than

fell to thy lot, for I can only blush for my son,
I can only feel the bitter agony of shame for
him. Forgive me, forgive, if I am bringing a
young, pure life under the shadow of my grief.
Help me to do what is right; but, O Holy Mary,
Mother Mary, hear my prayers, and save my
son : save him from worse than death. Redeem
him before it is too late. For the sake of thy
blessed son, to whom nothing is impossible, save
my wayward, erring child ! "

Prostrate before the altar, the faint light
touching her long black garments, the countess
stayed until her low-burning candle warned her
to depart. And so Philippe won his first move
in the new game, and his mother lost.

CHAPTER X.

SYLVIA received the cordial invitation from Madame de La Roche with a feeling of approval, but hardly of surprise. It had occurred to her that there might be some coldness in her welcome into Philippe's family, and for that reason she had insisted on a proper reception assured beforehand; but the extent of prejudice felt against her by his mother had never entered her head. She answered graciously and gracefully, naming a date the following week for her arrival at La Roche, but limiting the length of her visit to three days. Flora was much excited at being included in the invitation, although she did her best to hide her exaltation.

"You know it is very seldom a foreigner gets a chance to see one of the regular, swell old families at home, Sylvia. We must not be too fine in our clothes; you can see by the seal that she is in mourning, so there won't be much gayety, I fancy; one large trunk apiece ought to be enough, don't you think?"

Sylvia did think, and showed herself a true woman in the discussion of frocks that followed;

it was a relief to turn to every-day details, for just now there was a feeling of unreality in her life that was almost painful.

This sensation was by no means dispelled when she reached the little railway station about five miles from La Roche, and was met by the family carriage. She and Mrs. Lee-Blair left their maids to follow with the luggage, and drove almost in silence along the river-road. As they came to an opening in the trees the coachman turned, and pointing with his whip, said proudly, " The chateau ! "

Sylvia caught a glimpse of her future home. She felt frightened vaguely as though she would like to jump from the carriage and run away; she put out her hand and took Flora's, clasping it convulsively.

" Poor girl, I know just how you feel; but don't be scared. You will be welcomed with open arms, see if you 're not; and if they do snub you, all you have to do is to turn your back on them."

Sylvia smiled faintly and took her hand away; sometimes it is rather comforting to be misunderstood in a nice, commonplace way, and she felt that she was silly to let the ghost of the future shake her nerves.

The skies were overcast, and seemed to accord with the east wing in its feudal severity, making a fitting background for the grim building.

Philippe stood at the open door, and nothing could have been more appropriate than his warm, respectful greeting.

" I will take you at once to my mother," he said, showing them across the vast hall, through the stone corridor, and at last reaching the oak salon.

There was no chill in the air to-day ; great flames rushed roaring upwards in every chimney, and made one forget the lack of sunshine.

The countess rose as the door opened, and holding out both hands came towards Sylvia. The two women looked each other full in the face ; each felt that this was no time for empty compliment ; there was a look of inquiry in their eyes as they met : they seemed to be asking mutely, " Do we meet in peace or war ? "

" You are welcome at La Roche, madame."

" I am very happy to be here," answered Sylvia simply.

They were both strangely agitated, and Philippe and Mrs. Lee-Blair worked valiantly during the next ten minutes to give the interview an every-day aspect.

At last it was suggested that if Sylvia were not too tired she might like to see a part of the chateau, saving the gardens for a sunny day, and all were relieved to be able to move and speak naturally.

They walked through the rooms rich with memory and legend. Philippe knew all the romances of the place, and told them well, giving vivid touches that made the past live. Flora was deeply impressed by all that she saw and heard, and took the burden of conversation on herself, to Sylvia's relief, for she felt unable to do more than walk in dreamland, her eyes seeking those of Madame de La Roche in a wistful fashion. The older woman appealed to some unsuspected chord in her nature; her voice, her walk, her deeply sad expression, touched her sympathy.

To the countess it was a trying ordeal. To see this young, fresh woman, moving in an atmosphere of gay prosperity, yet with a subtle indication of something deeper, of capacities for joy or suffering as yet unwakened, was to feel two distinct sets of emotions. Her well - appointed beauty, her dainty feet treading over the stone floors where crusaders' feet had trod, the rich silk of her dress rustling where formerly the clang of mailed armor had rung — all these signs of a new race, new wealth coming to these mellowed old walls, stirred something like indignation in the countess's heart. Would this product of a new, raw civilization be able to feel the least stir of the veneration which to her made the chateau sacred?

Then a look from Sylvia's deep eyes, the sound of her soft voice, turned her to a new view of the matter. Did this girl know what was before her? Did she know the man she was going to marry? If not, then God help her.

The two women were a little behind the others, when Madame de La Roche said, " I will take you to the chapel; I prefer to be alone there with you; my son may show it later to your friend."

She led Sylvia down the narrow stairs in the wall, and through the heavy door. The pale afternoon light crept reluctantly in at the narrow stained-glass windows set in the side of the rock, and for a moment it was difficult to distinguish the carved statues; but gradually their eyes grew accustomed to the twilight, and Sylvia followed her guide, deeply moved as she listened to her level, unemphatic voice repeating the names and deeds of the dead beneath their feet. At last they came to the white statue, and the countess stood there without speaking for a moment's space; then she said, " This is where my husband, Philippe's father, lies. He was worthy of his race; he was brave and true as every de La Roche has been; up to the present no man bearing the name has dimmed it. Look to it that you are ready to bear a great responsibility in marrying into this family. New ways have arisen, new manners, new morals. If my son is not what his father was, may I bear all the blame. Think well, my child, before you take this step."

Her voice broke, and she turned her head aside, covering her eyes with a gesture at once mournful and dignified.

" I have thought well," answered Sylvia ; " my courage is equal to what lies before me ; far from thinking lightly of the noble name your son bears, it is from my admiration of it that I have consented to marry him. I tell you this frankly. I am not a young romantic girl whose fancy is easily gained : but I am a woman with a passionate love for all that is great and honorable, and I can promise you that you will find in me a loyalty to this house equal to yours."

"Then you will find in me a true mother."

They clasped hands as two men might have done, and standing before the tomb each prayed silently. The countess felt a burden lifted from her heart.

" I have warned the child ; I have done my best : now in Thy hands I leave the future."

Sylvia for the first time in her life longed for a clear faith ; the words in her heart were sincere, but they seemed to echo drearily back, meeting with no response. " Help me to live worthily ; to do faithfully my part ; to fail in nothing that I have undertaken."

As they stood there a loud laugh sounded outside the door. The countess closed her eyes with
a look of pain as if it jarred upon her, but she
assumed her calm dignity of manner when Philippe showed Mrs. Lee-Blair in ; he subdued his
voice when he saw his mother, and the tour was
made almost in silence.

The following days were full of intense interest to Sylvia : she was seeing with her own eyes
the home she had chosen for her future ; she
was learning to know and reverence her future
mother-in-law as she had never reverenced any
woman in her life. The simple austerity surrounding the countess, her business capacity as
shown in her directing her farms and vineyards,
her unceasing efforts to help the peasants in the
small village clustered at her gates — all this
opened the younger woman's eyes to a new type
of existence, and in her present state of exaltation she found it admirable and enviable. To
her friend Flora, however, time dragged heavily.
There were no gayeties. As Madame de La
Roche explained, she did not entertain generally,
and the relations whom she would have liked to
invite to meet Mrs. Huntington lived too far
away to come at such short notice, whilst her
dear friend and neighbor Monsieur Regnier was
unfortunately away from home at this moment.

They were sauntering through the garden to-

212 A TRANSATLANTIC CHATELAINE.

wards the house when this explanation was given,
and Sylvia felt an angry blush rise to her face
at the sound of Regnier's name. Then she wondered a little at his being Madame de La Roche's
friend, considering what she knew about Maurice;
and then the whole subject distressed and puzzled her so that she dismissed it from her mind.
On reaching the court she said that she had letters to write, and left the others talking together :
but she had not been long in her own room when
Flora entered, and stretching herself on a sofa
yawned dismally.

"Can't you speak to me, Sylvia? Won't you
be kind enough to say some English words? I
don't care what they are — anything in a row,
just to hear the dear sound. Say *hog* if you
will; they tell me it is not a pretty word, but oh,
the good, broad open sound it has, — hog! hog!
I love it. My lips are worn out squeezing themselves up to fit these detestable French prunes
and prisms. Stop laughing, child — talk."

"You don't share the fastidiousness of your
countrywomen, the Cranford ladies, who were
so dreadfully distressed because the village doctor's name was Hoggins, and used to wonder if
it would do to ask him to change it to Piggins,"
said Sylvia, pushing her writing-desk away and
leaning back in her chair.

"Cranford? No, I was never there; how
silly of them."

" I am afraid, dear Flora, you are not amused here."

" Amused? I have grown ten years older since day before yesterday, and we don't leave here until to-morrow at half past one; that makes — let me see — four o'clock now — thirteen, fourteen " —

" Oh, for Heaven's sake do your sums in your head," interrupted Sylvia. " I am happy here, and I do not want to be reminded how soon it is to end."

" Twenty-one hours and a half," exclaimed Flora, who had continued her count. " Can I stand it? Two more meals of seventeen courses, a mouthful to a course; all this evening to keep up such an inane conversation as is possible, with you expressing heart-felt interest in the new vintage, and looking quite mad with grief when you hear the noble hens of La Roche don't lay more than one egg apiece a day. Can't you think of some game of cards for this evening to keep me from losing my senses? Heavens, can this be I, actually craving a merry round game, a thing I have always avoided? "

" Poor Flora, I am glad you are showing me yourself in your true colors ; now I shall know enough never to invite you here unless every room is filled with the nobility of France."

" Well, your eyes are opened to the advantages and disadvantages of such a marriage. This is certainly a very distinguished family, and the most beautiful estate I ever saw; but they are evidently as poor as church mice. Still to you that makes no difference."

She paused, sighed, and looked pensively into the fire; then, with a sudden change of tone, she began again: "What rooms shall you take for your own? and shall you make any changes?"

"I do not know, I can make no plans. The minute I begin to arrange details I lose all my identity and feel powerless. Now go and dress for dinner, and I will suggest a merry round game for your evening's amusement."

But in spite of her promise Sylvia forgot all about her friend's amusement, for after dinner, on their way to the salon, Philippe contrived to get her alone with him in the billiard-room. He looked very determined, and handsome in his robust way, as he stood facing her, and she felt a new, not unpleasing excitement gain possession of her. He began abruptly: —

"I am no phrase-maker, and I have only two words to say: first, I love you more than ever, and it has been a torment not to tell you so these last days: second, are you still of the same mind? Will you let my mother speak seriously with you to-morrow morning about our marriage?"

" You never seem to care whether I love you;
all you ask is that you may love me and marry
me. Are you really as indifferent to my feelings as you seem? "

He let his eyes wander over the room, and
then settle for a moment on her face before he
answered.

" Nine men out of ten would lie to you, but I
am going to begin at any rate by telling you the
brutal truth. I have been brought up to regard
marriage as a business transaction, and to look
out for a wife with money or birth, or both if
possible: and it was in that state of mind I
began to try and win you. But, by Heavens!
Sylvia, you have made me forget your fortune,
everything but yourself; for you are a sorceress,
and have used your power to such an end that I
am in that condition I have always said made a
man look like an ass, — in love with the woman
he wants to marry. Still, a fellow can't learn
everything all over again at my age, and I am
so sure you will love me when we are once married that as long as you consent to that I am
contented enough as it is."

She gave a little laugh, that stopped short
half way.

" You are far from being an ideal lover, Monsieur le comte, but then I am far, I am afraid,
from being the ideal wife you imagine; so, as

long as we start fair, we may surely hope that
life will not be so very bad."

"And you will see my mother to-morrow and
talk it all over?"

"Yes."

"Thank you, thank you," he exclaimed, putting one arm round her waist, and kissing her.
She blushed and left the room.

Philippe de La Roche had spoken a momentary truth when he told Sylvia that he was in
love with her, for he had a habit of being in
love with the nearest available woman as long as
she continued a novelty; indeed this softness of
heart was one of the reasons he was always in
money difficulties. His susceptibilities had responded easily to encouragement, and it had not
been difficult for him to get up a genuine passion for the charming woman he hoped to marry;
even that prosaic consideration failed to cool his
ardor, and he congratulated himself on the fact
that Sylvia's figure, walk, voice and face were
quite as alluring for the time being as those of
any of the facile ladies who had hitherto shared
the honor of his admiration and gifts.

He was a very Jack Horner. His plum was
big, and his virtue in being in love with his
future wife undoubted. As he strolled across
the hall to the oak salon it even occurred to him
that he might shut down on a certain small but

expensive apartment in Paris, whose occupant
had a fatal way of emptying his purse ; but he
considered that it was never wise to burn one's
bridges behind one, and that was a painful duty
which could easily wait a little.

The next morning, according to agreement,
Madame de La Roche and Sylvia had their business talk. Sylvia insisted on settling her entire
income on her husband, in spite of his mother's
advice to the contrary, for she said that she believed it would be an impossible relation for him
to ask her for money, and quite natural and easy
for her to ask him. The countess, however, carried her point in making Sylvia promise to keep
the control of the principal in her own hands. It
was agreed that any children that might be born
to them should be brought up in the religion of
the family. This was acceded to readily by the
younger woman, who felt her own faith too frail
and insufficient to induce her to do battle for it.

Madame de La Roche undertook to obtain the
necessary dispensation for the marriage ceremony.

During the whole conversation there had been
no appearance of excitement, embarrassment, or
any emotion. Both women made it as much a
matter of business as possible, and it was only
after consulting a slip of paper she held in her
hand and assuring herself that every point had

been covered, that the countess leaned across the small table which separated them, and, taking Sylvia's hand, said, —

" My child, it is time for me to take a personal part in this matter, and I promise you from this day on a loyal friendship that shall never waver. You will have trials, — God help you, we all do. But while I live you may come to me in sorrow or in joy, and you will always find true sympathy."

Sylvia's eyes filled with tears. She was touched deeply, and for a moment her voice failed her; then she said : —

" I know myself too little to promise much : but you have made me love and admire you more than I ever loved or admired any one before. My life has been a very barren affair as far as affection goes ; and if I make anything out of the years before me, it will be because you will be my help and inspiration."

CHAPTER XI

Love (?) affairs move rapidly in France,
and even with the necessary delays caused by
the waiting for Sylvia's man of business, who
brought innumerable papers to be signed, and
the dispensation from Rome, the marriage took
place early in January. The months that went
before had been so filled with a hundred and
one things that Sylvia had seen Philippe but at
long intervals. Had she been the most design-
ing of women, she could not have found a better
way to increase the love he thought he felt for
her. It piqued him to have her put him off
from day to day, to say that she had no time to
receive him, and to seem absorbed in a multi-
tude of interests, — so that the dawn of his wedding-day really found him an impatient lover.

Sylvia, in this interval, set herself to learn the
lesson of forgetfulness, with such determination
that at times the past, that past connected with
Maurice Regnier, grew dim. But again there
were hours, sleepless hours, perhaps at night,
when he seemed to stand before her, with spectral, reproachful eyes, his stern lips repeating

the word "Coward!" Had she been mistaken? Had she been cruel? That she had yielded to a burst of passion amounting to frenzy she had acknowledged; but she could find excuses for an emotion which had swept her along, taking all powers of self-determination from her. She was shocked, ashamed, when she thought of her violence; but her deepest self-reproach was caused by the questions that she put over and over to herself: had she been hasty in believing the account of his birth? Had her underlying, selfish ambition pushed her to accept what she was told without sufficient investigation? Would she jump at a conclusion regarding Philippe with the same impetuosity? Her feelings were too subtle for her to analyze them with precision. The idea that Philippe could deceive her brought no maddening contraction of the heart, such as she felt when she recalled Maurice's attempts to blind her to his position. Often she would lie awake the long night, in her apartment in Paris, and know that morning had come by the muffled sounds without, telling of a new day. And the reflection that no matter what she felt, or what she thought, Time was always moving on with his measured tread, gave her a fatalistic philosophy, and she would sleep, soothed by the inevitability of events, as by a melancholy slumber song.

These dread hours of self-revelation made deep impresses on her character; but they were overlaid by the events and excitements that lay uppermost, and during the days, filled with a fresh charm, she could ignore them. She was elated by the thought that at last she was to be some one. It was not what she owned that brought her the new respect in the voices addressing her: it was what she was. No thought of her loneliness, her lack of friends and family, dimmed the glitter of her triumph. It was with a proud heart that she became Philippe's wife, the Countess de La Roche.

The first weeks of her married life passed in a turbulent joy. She had not considered love as an important element in the bargain she had made, and, lo! love, or its counterfeit presentment, was hers.

In her ignorance of life beneath the surface, she took Philippe's passion for genuine affection, and her strong, ardent temperament responded to it.

They went to a villa near Nice, within a drive of Monte Carlo, and at first the days seemed too short for the enjoyment of all the pleasure offered to her. Philippe was a man who had read much, and could talk well and brilliantly of his own thoughts, and the thoughts of others. His experience of life was extended, and he showed

Sylvia a new existence : one which repelled even while it fascinated her. Vice in itself is revolting to a pure mind. Vice described in an alluring way, with subtle reticence, may be made attractive. Sylvia felt that all her former convictions and theories were useless in this new adjustment of life. She had played like a child on the brink of hell, never seeing the abyss by which she had danced. Now that her eyes were opened, it lay with her to accept the inevitable, or to shrink away and deny its existence. It is so much easier to shrug one's shoulders, and say that you don't believe half the bad things that you hear, than to investigate, know the grievous truth, and then take your stand according to your convictions. At the very first, while under the power of her husband's strong charm. Sylvia temporized. But her nature was too fine to allow her to pretend to be led blindfold, when she saw the way before her. As long as they could be by themselves, it was a simple matter to let things drift ; but when the neighboring villas began to be filled by friends and connections of Philippe's, she saw that she must struggle, either with her new environment, or her own convictions.

Philippe had often amused himself by telling her what he knew or had been told about the various occupants of the country - places about them ; so that she knew by name almost all her new neighbors, and had a clear idea of whom she was to meet when the necessary round of visits came to be made. Philippe was making a list of names on a sheet of paper, while she looked over his shoulder, showing her good memory by her remarks as he wrote one after another. At one she put her hand down on his, —

" Philippe! Not that woman? You are not going to take me to see *her?* "

He looked up at her with surprise.

" Why not? She is a cousin of my mother's, and no one is better known."

" But is n't she the one you told me that story about? — that disgraceful affair? You know what I mean."

" Yes; but what has that to do with your calling on her? "

" Everything. I don't care to know a person of that sort, and I refuse to call on her."

" Well, upon my word, you 'll find it hard to know many people at that rate; you were n't so particular about your dear Madame Lee-Blair."

" Flora is not in the least like this creature. According to you, there is n't a good woman in the world."

" Oh, yes, there is : and she 's not only good, but fascinating and beautiful. I love her so much that she won't refuse me this first favor that I ask of her. It would hurt my mother, too."

Sylvia was puzzled and troubled by this. She was no prude, but her standards were high, and it hurt her to lower them an inch; but she reflected that after all she was bound to do as Philippe bid her; that she was very ignorant of the social code of the world she had entered, and in the end she reluctantly yielded to his entreaties.

From that day their continual tête-à-tête was over. Invitation followed invitation, and Sylvia found herself in the midst of people whose mere names suggested all that she had cared most for. The small coterie into whose midst she was admitted were the descendants of men who had made the history of Europe. For the first time in her life she was treated as an equal by the people about her; she received neither the exaggerated adulation that had been hers at Trouville, nor the snubs and slights which had belonged to her girlhood. Here she took her place naturally; she was no more lovely to look upon than some of the women ; her fortune did not seem colossal beside those belonging to some of the men. She was thrown upon her own resources to hold her own among them, and began to regard herself with humility. She lost the tinge of self-assertiveness that had been hers, re-

sulting perhaps naturally from her former life,
and accepting the lesson with much sweetness,
and not a trace of bitterness, her native charm
became more vivid than ever.

But in spite of the varied amusements of her
days, she was beginning to be uneasy. She
began to mentally criticise her husband's attitude regarding her. If he would only shield her
more from contact with people whom he did not
respect! If he would only look at things from
a more dignified standpoint! But once having
decided that her duty was to obey him in matters
about which he was supposed to know vastly
more than she, it made all simple. After all,
contact with imperfections would do her no
harm personally : she must try the more strenu-
ously to keep her own mind high and pure, and
look on life with a larger vision.

With some characters this régime would have
failed, but with Sylvia it succeeded ; she gained
in force and depth, while apparently living in a
giddy round of pleasure ; she was unaware of
having any influence on those about her, and
doubtless they were also ignorant of any such
unlikely occurrence. But it is certain that a
subtle air of discretion pervaded the conversation when she was present, and a delicate note as
of higher, cleaner motives changed in a slight
degree the atmosphere.

As for Philippe's state of mind, that too had undergone some variations since his wedding-day. At first Sylvia's very innocence had for him a certain piquancy, and her views of the life about them, although he considered them narrow and puritanical, seemed to fit her with a bewitching precision. The sensation that the more pressing of his debts were paid, and that he still had money in his pocket, gave him for a time supreme satisfaction ; but we are unfortunately so constructed that we grow accustomed to agreeable sensations, and they lose the power to stimulate us ; so it happened that gradually the feeling grew on him that he was caged, a prisoner ; the very respectability of his surroundings smothered him ; he longed fiercely for an hour of the old liberty. But the conventions of his present life hemmed him in, and he had only a round of engagements among his neighbors to divert his mind. Not an hour's drive away glittered Monte Carlo, that meretricious jewel in the midst of the pure gems bordering the Mediterranean, and his thoughts recurred to it again and again. It represented at that time all that he most cared for, all that had formerly filled his life with change and excitement. He had taken Sylvia there soon after their arrival, and she had enjoyed the drive along that most perfect shore ; she had been amused at the gay sur-

roundings in the café, where they had breakfasted : but the gaming-rooms had filled her
with a dreary sadness. The air oppressed her,
and the people depressed her. She was thankful
to be rolling towards home, violet mountains on
her right, a violet sea on her left. Since then
they had been too much occupied to think of
going again, and Philippe found himself planning how to break away, if only for a day, and
forget that his debts had been paid, that his life
had been changed, and that he, in short, had become respectable !

He was thinking of this one evening as they
returned from an unusually long ride, just in
time to dress for a dinner at a chateau some
miles away. As they entered the hall, the butler handed a note to Sylvia, which she read with
a little exclamation of annoyance, and then explained to her husband that it was from their
hostess, asking them to postpone the dinner on
account of illness in the family.

His chance had come !

" It may be just as well, Sylvia ; you must be
tired to death after such a ride, and you can put
your feet up by the fire, and rest."

" And you ? " she asked with a little playful
nod ; it was pleasant to have him so thoughtful
of her comfort.

" Oh, I will take the carriage, and drive over

to Monte Carlo ; they couldn't get me anything
fit to eat at such short notice at home. It's a
pity that you are too tired to go with me."

" But I'm not tired at all! I'd love to go.
We'll have the victoria, it is such a delicious
night, and I will fly to dress."

In less than an hour they were bowling over
the hard road behind a pair of fresh horses ;
the salt, pleasantly chill air blew fresh in their
faces, making Sylvia nestle among her furs,
as she gave herself up to the pleasure of the
moment. She was unaware that Philippe had
not spoken since they started ; she had no idea
of the angry tempest gathering force in his
breast, as he sat so quietly by her side. He
had been childishly disappointed when she had
offered to accompany him, but it had been impossible for him to tell her that he did not want
her. They were still in the honeymoon, and she
was young and fair, even if she were his wife.
But at the moment of starting, she had unconsciously given him an excuse to show her his
displeasure ; and he resolved to benefit by it.
The coachman had respectfully suggested that
it would be safer to start for home fairly early,
as the moon set at eleven, and he did not like
to drive on that road in the dark.

Before Philippe could answer, Sylvia, accustomed for many years to give her orders without

reference to any one but herself, assured the man that they would be ready to leave Monte Carlo by nine ; as soon, in fact, as they had finished their dinner.

It was tactless on her part, but after all it was a trifle, and her husband's silence gave her no hint of his indignation. The real essence of love was so utterly wanting between them that they had never had one of those intimate disputes which an indifferent person seldom provokes ; their views on almost all deep subjects varied widely, but they never discussed them with any warmth, only with a good-tempered tolerance which proved how little either valued the opinion of the other ; therefore like a growl of thunder from a cloudless sky came to Sylvia's ears her husband's angry voice, saying : —

" Is it too much to demand that I shall be treated, at least in the presence of the servants, as though I were a person of some small consequence ? "

She turned quickly towards him, half-suspecting a hidden joke in his words, but even in the dim light she saw his expression. Her voice was genuinely concerned as she said : —

" Why, Philippe, I do not know what you mean, but if I have offended you I am very sorry."

" It is not a question of being offended," he

returned in a surly growl; "it is a question of teaching you not to answer my servant when he speaks to me, and giving him orders that I shall countermand."

Sylvia was far from being a meek woman; although her father's training had not subdued her spirit, it had taught her self-control, therefore her voice was if anything sweeter and softer than usual when she said slowly: "I hardly think you see how brutal and ungentlemanly a remark that is. I have never been spoken to so before, and I am willing for this time to forget that you have insulted me."

"Well, if you call it an insult I am sorry for you, for it is a method of treatment most women put up with, and I fancy you are no more an exception than I am. What people do in your country I don't know or care, but let me tell you that here the husband is master."

She was dumb with fury: and trying to keep from bursting into a storm of angry tears, leant back in her corner without a word.

At first her silence stirred Philippe to further surliness, but as it continued unbroken, and the gray night settled round them, he felt that he had had his blow-out, and began to wonder why he had been so infernally out of temper. There was also a feeling of relief that he had said his say, for up to this time he had had a lurking fear of what his wife might really be; he had never seen the depths troubled, and he had dreaded the first experiment; now, thank Heaven, he had made the plunge, and to his comfortable surprise he found, as he imagined, no depths, only shallows. Hugging his new knowledge of her character he thought: "By Jove, I am lucky. Most women would have stormed back or cried; but she's been well trained, and takes it like a man."

So consoling had his reflection been that his voice had regained its usual affability when he said: —

"That effect of the moon rising is pretty over there, Sylvia, — no, on your right, dear; you don't see."

She neither answered nor turned her head; her anger had not abated, but only cooled from the red-hot molten state into the hardness of iron. He peered at her through the soft gray light, but could only see the fine lines of her profile dark against the pale sky; her silence surprised him, although it did not daunt him; tears or a fierce outburst of temper would have annoyed him, but he would have known how to deal with them: this attitude puzzled him.

He put out his hand and drew one of hers from her muff, pressing it affectionately: his pressure was not returned, and for a few mo-

ments it lay passively in his; then it was with-
drawn gently.

" Would you mind my smoking a cigarette,
darling ? "

" Not at all."

" Oh, you have spoken at last; why would n't
you answer me before ? "

He laughed as he said this, and put his arm
round her shoulders; her voice was still low and
unshaken as she replied : —

" I did not notice you had asked me any question."

" But you are angry with me because I blew
out at you ? "

" Oh, no — hardly that; I have not the right
to be angry."

" What do you mean by that ? "

" I fancy you would not understand if I told
you. I hope you will not think me rude if I do
not speak any more ; the air is too fresh for my
throat."

He drew his arm sulkily away, and she settled
herself again among her furs ; he began to be
sorry that he had been pleasant so soon. It
never did any good to let a woman see that you
were too ready to kiss and be friends again.
Not another word was spoken until they arrived
at the café where they intended dining, and then
as Philippe carefully helped his wife out of the
carriage he said to the coachman : —

" Be here at eleven, and be sure the hot-water tin is filled for Madame la comtesse."

The man looked puzzled and said, —

" Monsieur le comte said eleven ? "

" Yes," returned Philippe sharply; and offering his arm to Sylvia, added, " You see how you have already given the impression that you are the one to take orders from, and, by the Lord, I won't stand it."

As they sat in the brightly lighted room, filled with groups of gay people, the women in their prettiest frocks, the men well groomed and full of animation, Sylvia felt as if she were in a jail. She played with the food placed before her, and answered her husband's remarks mechanically, —" yes," " no," hardly," — she could have repeated every word he said to her, but the meaning did not penetrate, only the sound reached her ; and all the time her mind was working.

" I have no right to complain ; I married him, not for himself, but for what he represented ; I told Maurice I wanted a coronet on my handkerchief — well, I have more coronets than I can count. I am beginning to hate the sight of them. Are there no men, then, in the world to be trusted? I don't say love, that means so little, and goes so soon ; a word kills it. These people do not know they are sitting in the room with a murderer, but if love can be all poets tell us it is, it is more real than anything in the world, and mine has just been killed."

"Drink some champagne, Sylvia, you look pale : you were too tired to come after such a deuce of a ride as we took."

She obediently lifted her glass to her lips, but set it down again without tasting it ; her throat seemed to be closed, and it was impossible to swallow.

Philippe felt her change of manner, but it was difficult to challenge, so impalpable was it; he relapsed into an offended silence, and began to mentally justify his conduct. He most uncharacteristically growled at the bill when the garçon brought it, but the man was used to daily remarks of a like nature, and would have felt a sense of something being wrong if he had missed them.

In the same sullen manner he offered Sylvia his arm and they crossed the brilliant little *place* and entered the casino : her quiet passiveness annoyed him more by this time than any outbreak could have done. He found her a seat at a table, and gave her a handful of gold : then he watched his chance, and at last secured a place at the same table nearly opposite her, and settled to play with almost a ferocious eagerness.

The air was heavy, bringing the hot blood to Sylvia's cheeks, and making her temples throb

with pain ; she knew that she could not sit long
where she was unless she played, so at intervals
she pushed a napoleon on to some place ; once
or twice she gained, but generally the gold piece
was raked away from her. It was nine when
they entered, and every now and then she looked
at the jeweled watch hanging from her chatelaine ; slowly, slowly the hands moved round
to ten. Could she bear it another hour? She
glanced at Philippe : he was playing steadily with
apparent indifference, but she noticed, in spite
of his careless manner, that his nostrils were
dilated, and that there was a glitter of excitement in his roving, restless eyes. Heavier
and denser grew the air ; the women in their
gems and paint and meretricious clothing moved
quietly through the rooms, their real business
hidden beneath the cloak of an occasional stake
won or lost. As Sylvia looked at them, and de-
tected the greed and lust lurking in their faces,
she shuddered ; then she grew cold and tense as
she thought : "Can I blame them ? Did I not
sell myself for a price as surely as they are selling themselves? I am more to blame than the
worst creature in this place ; no want drove me
— only a caprice." The memory of Ethel New-
come's words about the advisability of ticketing
the engaged young ladies with the word SOLD
in large letters came to her, and with a bitter

self-scorn she thought, "How trite I am; only a repetition of a species without end. I have not even the consolation of being original. I have not even the excuse of ignorance."

She felt stifled morally as well as physically; there was a fierce revolt going on in her. The reaction to her short-lived excitement and satisfaction had come, and with it all loss of common sense, of the proportion of things for the time being.

Doré has painted a picture called The Novice. Among a group of old, time-benumbed monks who sit mumbling over their beads, a young man has just realized that he is hopelessly, irretrievably bound; either he must become like his companions, or go mad, and one can see the dawn of insanity in his agonized eyes that look out from the white face, his whole attitude reminding one of a dog straining dumbly at his leash. It is a picture that haunts and sickens you, that you cannot forget. Years afterwards Sylvia saw it, and she said, "He must have seen my soul that night at the gaming-table, and then painted this."

It did her no good to remember that she had been warned, or to reflect on her own courage and determination to shape her future to her own ends; she had lost both courage and resolve; she felt **frightened** for the first time in

her life, for she had seen a glimpse of a brutality
that had descended through countless generations, hidden by modern refinements, forgotten,
perhaps, during whole lifetimes, but always there,
ingrained in the very nature of a race which had
acknowledged one master only, the lawful King
of France.

For the time mental distress had made her
forget her physical discomfort; then some one
jarred her chair, — the chain of thought was
broken, and she realized that her head was
aching violently, and that the room was swimming and swaying about her; she moved away
from the table, and steadying herself by holding on to the backs of the players' chairs, for
the hour was late, and few people were standing
about, she reached Philippe.

As she stood behind him she looked once
more at her watch, and saw that it was five minutes of eleven.

" It is time to leave," she said. He shook
his head impatiently, but did not answer; for a
moment she waited, until she saw the heap of
gold before him raked away, and as he placed
another on a square she said: " I am going
now; if you do not care to drive home with me
you can probably find some way of following."

Her anger had given her strength, and she
walked steadily towards the entrance hall, but

before she had reached the outer lobby her husband was by her side.

He did not swear; well-bred Frenchmen seldom do, but his expression and the tone of his voice were oaths in themselves.

"You changed the luck; it is the last time you shall come to Monte Carlo with me."

"Yes, it is the last time," she acquiesced, holding her head high, but white to the very lips.

When a woman bears an insult in silence and stifles her fury, she is more to be feared, also more to be pitied, than one who is able to rave and cry, and lose sight of the mental in the physical.

During the long, dark drive towards their villa there was time for thought, and the hopeless questions, "But what can I do? — how can I help it?" again and again asked themselves, always answered by, "Nothing — I cannot help it."

They entered the house in silence, and without a word Sylvia went upstairs. Justine was in her room, and began to help her mistress as usual to undress; she had taken the fur cloak from her shoulders and was laying it over a chair when Philippe walked in without knocking.

"You may go, Justine, — good-night," he said abruptly, and stood looking at her until she left the room; then he went close up to Sylvia, who had seated herself in a low chair by the fire. She was bitterly cold, and felt stunned; his words roused her.

" Now, then, what is it ? — answer me ; are you going to make a scene every time I find fault ? "

" I did not think I had made any scene," she answered slowly.

" I don't care what you think, Sylvia, but you have made me very uncomfortable and miserable to-night; you know I love you, my darling, you know that anything that disturbed our happiness together would be unbearable."

He had seated himself on the broad arm of her chair, had put his arm over her shoulder and drawn her, almost crushed her, against him ; his familiarity, his appropriation of her, revolted her ; but she did not draw away, she remained passive.

" Why don't you speak to me, chérie ? " he said tenderly, bending and kissing her on the smooth nape of her neck ; a thrill of horror ran through her, but still gently she rose and stood facing him.

" I am very tired to-night, and hardly able to talk ; I may look at things to-morrow in a different light, but now I would like to be alone," she said.

He eyed her narrowly for a moment, half inclined to push matters further : then he saw her marble whiteness and decided to believe her words; it was more politic.

"Very well then, mignonne, have your own way; kiss me good-night, and let Justine give you something to drink and take care of you."

She submitted to his embrace, and then stood as he had left her until he went through the door between their rooms; very quietly she moved towards it, closed it, and turned the key. As she did this a look of momentary relief swept over her face.

"There are always keys," she said; then for one moment her self-control gave way. She flung herself on her bed, and sobbed with the outspoken grief of solitude.

"O my God, to be free again, only to be free," she said over and over.

Without the door, her square face pressed against it, stood the old servant, hearing every moan, every bitter word. She did not move; she scarcely breathed, but her eyes gleamed with the savage light of a wild beast whose cubs are killed before her. A hatred against Philippe leaped into life in her undisciplined breast, and from that hour on became a part of her very being. At length the sobs within the room ceased, silence fell on the darkness, and hoping that her idol slept, Justine stole away.

But Sylvia had only worn out the wrappings

of her grief; when she became calm again she
rose, drew her furs about her, put some fresh logs
on the fire, and spread out her hands in the
warmth; she knew that this was a crisis in her
life, and felt that she must use all her powers
to reason with her anger and disappointment;
nothing must be done hurriedly or without reflection.

At first her only thought was how to escape
open scandal, and yet never, never live the life
again of the past five weeks. Wild plans of disgusting her husband with her, of making him
fall in love with some other woman, came to her,
and absorbed her in a sort of story-book way
for a moment, but she dismissed these fancies,
and tried to lay out a definite and defensible
course of action. Suddenly she saw as in a
vision the chapel at La Roche, the recumbent
figures, the tempered light; she remembered her
promise to Philippe's mother.

Was she planning to keep it? Had she foreseen any love in her married life?

" Oh," she moaned, " the make-believe love I
have thought real has made it so much harder
to bear."

Then the thought faced her, stern, relentless:
" I am no longer free to live for myself alone.
I have, with open eyes and warnings in my ears,
bound myself to an important family: I have

no right to think of my own pleasures or sorrows; I have knowingly assumed a great responsibility. Am I to allow the name of La Roche to die out because I have fallen out of love — with my husband? I may not; I must do my duty fairly, — I must accept the life I have chosen, God helping me." But though she spoke the words, it was with a dreary consciousness that God's help was not for her, that she did not believe in it when it was needed, and a terror fell upon her at the utter helplessness of her condition. She repeated over and over to herself mechanically: " I have a husband who is brave and faithful, true to his Church and his country. I must not ask for more."

The flame of the lamp sputtered, flared up and then died down, leaving the reddened, smoking wick; the gray morning light showed between the drawn curtains. There is the "jocund day that stands tiptoe on the misty mountain-tops," gilding the fair world bathed in the dew of night, and bringing light and joy in its train. There also is the cold dawn that shows life as it is.

Sylvia looked about her with hot, aching eyes; her crumpled gloves were on the sofa, where she had tossed them the night before; the roses she had worn at her breast lay drooping and faded on a table; the wood was burned out, and the ashes were heaped soulless on the hearth ; the smoking lamp had filled the room with its odor, and as she opened the window to let in some fresh air she shivered ; a light fog hid the sea ; a half-used cigarette lay on the unraked path ; over everything was an exaggerated aspect of the commonplace, the unbeautiful.

"It is like life without love," Sylvia thought, as she moved towards her bed, stiff with fatigue, unconscious that as the last red spark of passion faded out, the faint, glimmering belief in love as love was kindled.

CHAPTER XII.

WE all know how easy it is to form plans, and how difficult it is to carry them out; and Sylvia found herself much tried at first in her new relations to her husband.

He had slept off his anger and his headache. The many gold pieces he had won served to make him forget the few lost at the end of the evening, and he generously, as he thought, decided to overlook Sylvia's outburst of temper; consequently he met her with his usual affectionate manner, and she found herself wavering during the following week between a feeling of aversion and a stinging self-reproach at her own revolt against him. She had, however, a stubborn will, and she forced herself to play adequately her new part. She was always dignified, acquiescent, and cold, receiving but never returning his caresses. If this had been the state of things immediately after their marriage, the chances are that Philippe would have been piqued, and would have set himself resolutely to win her love ; but now it was a little late in the day for that. He had done all the wooing he intended to. For the future he proposed to please himself. If his wife did not care for him, then there were those who did, and he smiled insolently as he thought of the little Parisian apartment still occupied.

At this juncture Sylvia sent for Flora, who gladly obeyed the summons. She arrived one blue, dazzling afternoon towards the end of February, and was an animated question mark for an hour afterwards.

" Dearest Sylvia, are you well? you look pale, but very handsome. Who made you that gray poplin? Who are your neighbors? Do you find this enchanting house comfortable? Are your servants satisfactory? Is your husband — well — is he " —

" Is he satisfactory, too? don't hesitate to use the same expression for him and the servants, dear. They say that brides always boast that their husbands are perfect, and illustrate it by saying they button up their boots. Don't be shocked if I tell you that Philippe has never even offered to button mine."

Sylvia's voice betrayed nothing to her friend's quick ears, but there was a new look about her eyes that would have struck even a less observant person than Flora Lee-Blair. She had never been so lovely or so womanly. The slight touch of self-assertion of former days had gone, and

her low, thrilling voice was seldom heard now
saying sharp things. Always graceful and rather
quick in her movements, in repose she gave an
effect of absolute quiet, and impressed one as a
person who required a luxurious setting. Flora
looked at her admiringly, as she leaned back
in her low chair, the fire touching with rosy reflections the silver gray of her dress, one small
slipper resting on the white fur rug.

"You always make a picture, whatever you
do, and I don't understand it," she said almost
complainingly.

"Oh, how nice it is to hear you say kind
things to me again, you dear old Flora," said
Sylvia, with a little break in her voice. She
had not known how she longed for a bit of love
until now.

Mrs. Lee-Blair was as affectionate as her
rather hard life allowed her to be, but it was
seldom that she showed it. Now for some
strange reason the memory of her little girl, the
only child she had ever had, who died when she
was eight, came to her, and the tears rushed to
her eyes.

"Sylvia, dear, I have no child — and you have
no mother, — and — well, let's be awfully good
to each other," she ended rather lamely, rubbing
her face violently with her handkerchief.

"Thank you, Flora. Every one must live his

own life, but a little love goes a long way towards making it bearable."

When Mrs. Lee-Blair was alone in her own
room she dabbed a little powder round her eyes,
and over her nose, wondering at her sudden
emotion.

" Yes, — my black satin," she said over her
shoulder to her maid ; and then went on to herself, " It was the look in her eyes, poor girl. It
is enough to make any one cry ; and a bride of
six weeks to speak of life being bearable. Dear,
my eyes are all red again, and that tear has
made a paste with the powder. What a fool I
am : yesterday I should have said I did n't care
a tuppenny for her except as a convenience, and
to-day I feel fond of her. Ah, but you see it is
not the same person."

That Flora had been largely instrumental in
making this marriage ; that the power over Sylvia, flatteringly suggested as belonging to her
by Philippe, had become hers in reality, thanks
to the poisoned dagger with which he had armed
her ; that she had benefited by the affair from a
mercenary point of view, — all these propositions
were true. It was in vain that she told herself
it was the best thing possible for Sylvia, a little
nobody, to have become the wife of one of the
best known nobles in France. It was in vain
that she repeated over and over that she had

done only what hundreds of other people did, in accepting a handsome commission from the count, or at least the promise of it. Up to the present moment her bank account was very agreeable reading; but if Philippe kept his word it would become an every-day affair to have money enough to supply her wants. He had told her that she should own enough to live comfortably on the income. But in spite of these complacent musings, the first sight of Sylvia as a bride had been very distressing to her. She could not shake off the impression that if the young wife were unhappy, it was owing to her meddling. Justine, too, had an exasperating habit of looking at her with reproachful eyes, never speaking, but conveying a mute accusation.

There were days when she was tempted to take herself off, she was so uneasy; but calm reflection restrained her. Sylvia knew an extremely smart set of people, and Flora liked going to dinners and breakfasts with them. She enjoyed the soft delights of the daily life; besides, as she argued honestly enough, she could make things happier, more cheerful for Sylvia if she stayed. So the days went on, and she grew used to the want of spontaneous happiness in the household. There were no disputes, no sharp words, and in time she began to tell herself that she had been over-sensitive in the beginning.

Philippe found it a great convenience to have some one to whom Sylvia thought it necessary to devote herself, and when she was with her friend it was easy enough for him to reach Monte Carlo. His old passion for gaming, which seems ingrained in the French nature, shook itself after its short rest, and showed renewed vigor. There were other things, too, that were attractive in the small kingdom between the sea and the mountains, and friends running down from Paris for a day or two of change found him quite as ready to join them as before his marriage.

Mrs. Lee-Blair used to sigh and lift her eyebrows at him when they met after one of his absences, during which she and Sylvia had dined tête-à-tête, and spent a long evening alone together. Sometimes he would laugh sheepishly and look quite ready for a flattering, playful scolding; sometimes he would pay no attention to her little efforts to reform him. March was drawing towards its close, and the three months' lease of the villa was nearly exhausted. People were beginning to go to Paris for Easter, and one day Philippe announced that he thought they had better be starting for La Roche.

For weeks Sylvia had been longing for this.

She felt that she could learn her life's lesson more easily if she were in her future home, could harden herself to its rigors, and shape herself to its needs. Therefore she acceded willingly enough to her husband's wish, and gladly left the blue Mediterranean behind her. Their way took them through Paris, and there they lingered for Easter, for summer outfits, and also to leave Sylvia's apartment, as Flora was going with them to Touraine for a while. She had made the best use of her wits and time at Nice, and was rewarded by numerous invitations to the country places of her new friends, which quite filled up her summer and autumn.

These delays made it well into May before Sylvia and Philippe started for La Roche, leaving Flora to follow them in a few days. They took an afternoon train, and reached the station late in the evening. The primrose sunset light still lingered in the west, and a full moon poured its silver wealth over the warm, resting earth. Every fresh leaf glittered in the brilliancy as they drove along, the river shone with reflected splendor, and the tall poplars threw black shadows on the broad peaceful meadows. It was a night almost oppressive in its beauty. Sylvia felt unequal to it, her body hampered her; she remembered having told Maurice Regnier once that all her enthusiasm was for things,

not people ; but to-night she could not rise to
enjoyment. A sadness that had nothing to do
with the difficulties of her life possessed her.
There was a sense of something just beyond her
grasp which was escaping her forever, and with
it all a feeling of familiarity, as if in some other
life she had been bathed in a glory akin to this.

Under the massive horse-chestnuts that bordered the avenue in a double row, holding their
rose and white pyramids to be kissed by the
moonbeams, it was dark ; but when they had
driven through the archway into the court, a
brilliancy was over all. The main tower was
covered with a wistaria vine, and the delicate
violet of the blossoms, hanging in masses, was
plainly seen. This tower, which contained the
principal staircase, was pierced at unequal dis-
tances by narrow, quaintly leaded windows,
through which the yellow welcoming lamp light
shone, contrasting strangely with the frosty,
gleaming decoration of the vine. The soft,
warm air was filled with the perfume of honey-
suckle, and lilies of the valley, and syringa.
Against the tender, indefinite sky the great
cedar stood, not sharply outlined, but melting
into its background at its edges, and massing
its dark strength in the centre. It seemed to
be the presiding genius of the stately chateau,
and as Sylvia looked she remembered Maurice's

voice telling her of his boyish dreams beneath its shade. " Will his words always haunt me ? " she asked herself impatiently, turning to follow Philippe, who was just inside the door, giving some orders to his servant. But as she moved, a nightingale in the thicket below burst into song, and like one in a dream she went to the low, ivy-covered wall running along this side of the court, and leaning over it, drank in the beauty eagerly, ecstatically.

" I will enjoy it," she said to herself. " Ah, people do not know France who have only seen Paris and *les bains de mer ;* he was right when he said so."

She was still hearing the echoes of Maurice's voice, and this time she let them pass unchallenged.

A little, fleecy cloud blew across the moon, and the shadows lost their intensity : the nightingale ended his song.

" Where the deuce are you hiding, Sylvia ? My mother is waiting for you," called her husband impatiently. And recognizing the fact that he was her husband, therefore her master, she followed.

Philippe was in high spirits at this home-coming. For the first time he felt himself master of the situation, and able to come and go without the dread of reproachful questions from his mother. The supper that was prepared for them was eaten amidst much gay laughter, and the talk still went on in a merry strain as they seated themselves in the oak salon.

Philippe genially smoked his cigarette, as he stood with his back to the flameless fireplace, his feet firmly planted, and wide apart, one well-shaped hand stroking down his moustache. A faint color had come into his mother's face, as she listened to his account of Sylvia's triumphs among people whose names were familiar to her, and brought memories of her own happy youth. Sylvia smiled and listened ; but at her heart she felt a quick shock, as she realized how her opinion of Philippe had changed since they were last together in this room. The physical attraction was gone ; God grant that repulsion shall not take its place ! She felt rebellious towards him. This was what she had married him for : to be his countess, to be the chatelaine of his chateau ; to take her place in his family. Well, all this was just what she had planned, and yet she was not content.

Her eyes wandered over the room. All the beauty of tapestry and carving that she had so admired before took on a different look, now that she had her right to them. She thought with a passionate wave of loyalty of the white parlor at home. It was so humble compared to

this lordly dwelling, and yet she recognized that
in the small room there were treasures that the
chateau could not boast. Those simple, white-
paneled walls were bounded neither by space
nor time.. The books that covered them, and
the intellectual stimulus given there, made its
own enduring architecture.

As yet Sylvia had seen no books worth men-
tioning in the chateau. There was a magnifi-
cent hall called the library, but literature played
an insignificant part in its furnishing. She
wondered what the countess did with herself in
her many leisure hours. Sylvia was beginning
to feel dimly the rigidity of French country life;
to recognize how deep the line of tradition is
cut, stretching back to the dim past, — deep but
narrow, and going always on its beaten track,
straight as an arrow, swerving neither to left
nor right.

Her thoughts were recalled by Philippe's voice,
more animated than usual as he told his mother
his plans for improving the property.

" We should have that mill to bring water to
the farms more easily; and I mean to get it.
Then the coverts must be enlarged. There's
nothing now worth shooting."

The countess listened, her face all aglow; it
seemed to her that it was a bewildering, happy
vision. The old place, that she had struggled

so hard to keep intact, was almost sacred to her, and now her past efforts were being rewarded; the one who used to threaten it was now planning to add to its importance. She listened eagerly, suggesting ideas of her own, — ideas·that had been idle day-dreams with her in the past, now by the stroke of a fairy wand coming true.

Sylvia felt left out of this conversation; she did not know the names of the farms of which they spoke, and she did not feel impressed by the importance of having good shooting. It suddenly occurred to her that it was owing to her that all these plans could be made, and yet that she was neither consulted nor noticed.

Some subtle thought-transference must have suggested to the countess the trend of the younger woman's sensations, for she put her hand out with a kind gesture and said : —

" All this must seem very dry and stupid to you, my dear; but you need not trouble yourself about details. I know that the old place is a sombre home for you, but you must remember that it is your home, to come to when you want quiet. There will always be a welcome here for you."

Sylvia restrained the little start of surprise; *she* to be made welcome to La Roche ! She had understood that it was hers ! She had planned to make her mother-in-law feel that she must stay there, keeping her old place, as long as she lived: she had intended to usurp no authority, to give way in everything: and here were the tables turned with a vengeance.

She made a formal little bow to the countess, and murmured some words about her kindness. Philippe was watching his wife anxiously; he had not set her right when she had spoken casually to him of what they should do when she was mistress of the chateau: he had not felt called upon to explain his father's will to her. His wish was that the two women should live pleasantly together, and he did not want any misunderstanding between them this first evening. He broke in.

"You are like a couple of snow-capped mountains making pretty speeches to one another. Sylvia, the *madame* goes from this minute; do you understand? You are mother and daughter, eh? Is n't it better so?"

He laughed as he spoke, and pulling a lily of the valley from a bowl on the table he tossed it at his wife. He meant to be pleasant, and was doing his best to end rather an awkward situation, but Sylvia was not in the mood for pleasantries: the flower hit her on the neck with its wet stem, and she felt an angry flush mount to her cheeks: she knew it was childish to take it seriously, and said: —

" A good beginning, — buried in flowers."

She tried to speak naturally, but her laugh was forced, and her voice trembled.

A sudden unreasonable antipathy towards her husband overwhelmed her; just as the love between man and woman is more intense, more savagely natural than any other affection, so is the hatred between them, and as Sylvia glanced up she met her husband's cold scrutiny; their eyes flashed hatred for a second, then he turned away and rolled a cigarette. Almost any strong emotion is contagious, and just then he detested the graceful, lovely woman before him.

Sometimes it is enough to make one blush and cringe for shame to think how we are padded and enveloped by education, civilization, Christianity, and yet how the old Adam still lives in us, always ready to awake and drive us to the extremes of brutality. The spirit of their own unsubdued, untamed souls flashed, and shocked against each other in that look, and both the husband and the wife quailed at the lifting of the veil. Sylvia's disappointment was none the less keen that there was no one to blame for it, and no one to whom she could mention it; she was sure that Philippe had given her the impression that she was to be the future mistress of La Roche, and yet she could remember no definite promise.

There are always compensations, however, in

every trial, and the love and friendship shown by Madame de La Roche to her daughter-in-law proved a bright spot.

During the days following Sylvia's arrival, she showed herself in her truest, sweetest light. All through the dark winter she had prayed fervently to forget herself, to bury her doubts and fears, and to open her heart to her son's wife.

The prayers were answered, and she found it almost easy to admit this young woman with the smiling mouth and wistful eyes to her confidence.

They were walking in the garden with its exuberance of bloom one morning, when she said : —

" I want to drive you over to La Source this afternoon if you have nothing better to do. It is Monsieur Regnier's place, and you will love him when you know him, as I do : and I hope that you will find him as good and true a friend as I have."

" Who is Monsieur Regnier?" asked Sylvia abruptly. She longed yet dreaded to hear the version that Madame de La Roche would give of Maurice's reputed father.

" Has not Philippe told you? Ah, it is a sad story, but it is a thing of the past. Let us sit under the cedar, and I will tell you."

So leaning back in a low chair, looking up

through the gray-green branches of the old tree, and hearing them murmur faint tales of the ocean, Sylvia listened, every word sinking in and scoring deep the man she had married.

" My father-in-law," began the countess, "was only nineteen at the beginning of the revolution ; he was a headstrong boy, and had insisted on becoming engaged to a young girl of great beauty, the daughter of a gentleman who owned La Source. Her father was wealthy, but his family was of no consequence, and at first the match was bitterly opposed, but the young count was very fascinating, and won over his mother to his side ; she could do anything with her husband, and just before the outbreak consent was given. Both families were intensely loyal, and their names were well known in Paris, so it was no great surprise when La Source was attacked by some of the fiends possessing power, and Amélie (that was the girl's name) alone escaped imprisonment by her mother's ingenuity and devotion. She came at once to La Roche, and the countess received her kindly, soothing her fears about her parents, and promising that she should be married as soon as possible. But in those days a marriage was not easily managed, as the priests were in such terror that they hid, and were hard to find for anything but to administer extreme unction. While they were waiting and hoping the young people forgot all the terrors of the time in the joy of being together in unrestrained liberty, for the countess felt that it was not an occasion to insist on etiquette, and they were allowed to wander at will in the park and gardens. One day they were together by the hill, at the other side of the meadow there — you see where I mean — it is tunneled with caves."

Sylvia looked, and nodded.

"They were just outside one of them when a peasant thrust them violently in, his face white with fear, and pointing to a heap of brushwood, said, 'Hide — they are in the chateau — but I will save you — stay here until I come again.' The wretches who had been sent down to arrest the family failed through clumsiness, for the count and countess had just time to escape, almost wild with grief at leaving their son behind, but there was no help for it. Their pursuers, however, liked the comforts of the chateau, and stayed here nearly a week, defacing many of the portraits and carvings. When they left they lighted a fire round the east wing, but the lurking peasants put it out. All this time my father-in-law and Amélie had been in the cave, fed by the devoted man who had warned them, and it would take a harder heart than mine to blame the poor children for after events, although they brought much suffering to them and others. When it was considered safe they went back to the chateau, but some one betrayed them, and in less than two months they were arrested and separated. The young count was taken to Paris and thrown into the Bastile, whence he was liberated by some unexpected turn. His first thought was to find Amélie; he dared not search openly, but all he could do was useless. The poor boy was nearly wild with grief and anxiety, for he knew that she had more than herself to save, and the thought of their child being born, and dying, perhaps, in a jail, maddened him. There was no stone left unturned by him, and his reason was despaired of, so terrible was his suffering. But time brings healing, and after nearly ten years of waiting he consented to marry a distant cousin, who was in every way a suitable wife. My husband, the oldest child, was five, when a tradesman appeared, bringing with him letters and undoubted proofs that the missing child was under his roof."

" And the child was " — interrupted Sylvia. " Who? — what is he called now? "

" He is my dear friend Monsieur Regnier," answered the countess.

" And his son — Maurice? "

" Oh, Maurice's mother was a pretty, but

rather insignificant little woman, who died soon after his birth. She was never the equal of her husband."

" Her husband ? "

" Why, yes," answered Madame de La Roche, rather impatiently ; "don't you understand ? "

" Yes, yes, go on."

" There is no more to tell. Poor little Amélie had been confined after a long imprisonment in a country jail, and, weakened by hardships and suffering, died. She had become friendly with her jailer's wife, and confided to her care letters explaining her child's position. The woman, a kindly soul, apparently, would have brought the baby directly to La Roche, but her husband was suspected of helping aristocrats, and their only safety was to sail directly for America, taking the baby with them. When he was brought back he was a big boy of fifteen. My poor father-in-law could not make him legitimate on account of his son, but he brought him up in the chateau, and there was no one in the world my husband loved better than his half-brother. He left him as much money as he could, and during his lifetime made him nominally his agent, really his other self. They lived always in the old wing until my husband died, and then Monsieur Regnier bought La Source, formerly his mother's home."

" Is he made bitter by his life ? " asked Sylvia.

" Ah, no, his nature is too sweet ; he has been saddened by it, nothing more. His only betrayal of how he has felt it was shown by his command that his children should never know his story."

" So Maurice knows nothing ? "

" Absolutely nothing. Have you ever met Maurice, Sylvia ? "

" Yes, I knew him very well once ; but it was a lifetime ago."

She sat still for a moment not quite realizing what she felt, then seeing that the countess was waiting for some comment on her story, she said : " It was sad ; I feel as though La Roche must be haunted, so many things have happened here."

" I hope it will only be haunted by good and true spirits, dear, as long as you live here."

As she spoke she rested her hand lingeringly on Sylvia's shoulder, and then walked away towards the broad, moss-covered stone steps leading up to the court.

Alone, Sylvia covered her eyes with her hand. She was frightened by the tumult of her feelings. Was it anger, or grief, or an exultant joy she felt? It was joy ; she still had the right to believe in the man she had wholly trusted, almost loved ; life could not be the treadmill she had lately fancied it if Maurice were still true ; the world was not all bad while there were men — while there was one man — who dared to be noble and chivalrous, and who believed in great deeds still to be done. She threw a thought of scorn and anger to Philippe, and she shrank coweringly before the memory of the wrongs and insults she had heaped upon Maurice; then she gave herself up to happy, improbable dreams. She was to be free once more, and she would make him forget the past in the joy and rapture of her love.

The midday hush fell upon the garden; the birds were silent, and even the bees seemed absent: still leaning back and looking up to the brilliant sky, Sylvia thought of Maurice as he had told her of his boyhood, seeing visions of loyalty and bravery and love under the shade of this cedar.

CHAPTER XIII

"Oh, how charming — how English!" exclaimed Sylvia, as they drove through the billowy
park of La Source, which was cut in two by a
merry brawling baby river, or grown-up brook,
and the house came in sight; it was square and
low, only one broad step leading to the hospit-
ably opened door, and a wealth of ivy hid the
material of which it was built. The windows
cut in this wall of living green were daintily cur-
tained, and there were many gayly striped awnings giving touches of color.

Under a tree near the house was a table, and
by it sat a gentleman holding a child on his knee,
and showing him pictures. When he heard the
carriage he put the boy on his fat, sturdy bare
legs, planted well apart, and came towards his
guests, both hands held out in welcome. Madame
de La Roche was nearest him, and as he lifted
her hand to his lips she said: —

"This is my daughter, Armand; you must
promise to be to her what you always have been
to all of us, a true friend."

Sylvia put her hand into his, and at once felt

that mysterious bond of sympathy, rare but unmistakable to any one who has ever experienced it. Monsieur Regnier was very tall, as tall as his son, but so well proportioned that it was only noticeable when he stood by some other man. His skin was colored a deep rich hue by exposure to sun and wind; his finely cut features and dignified bearing gave him a reputation for being a handsome man, but his brown, deep-set eyes were his greatest charm. Although at times they were lighted into twinkling brilliancy by some jest, or softened to a happy glow as they rested on his grandchildren, they had generally a mystical, far-away expression that suggested a victory won, a struggle past and over. He said nothing in answer to the countess's words, but he smiled as Sylvia looked into his face, and the smile told more than words.

Out of the open door rustled a young woman, who greeted Madame de La Roche with overdone enthusiasm, and was then introduced as monsieur's daughter, Madame Lefevre. The solid little boy was called to take his share in the general presentations, and obeyed unwillingly enough, kicking the gravel as he drew near the group.

"Don't scuff, Maurice." said his mother, jerking him to her. "Do you think he looks like me?" she asked, turning her head artlessly, as a bird does.

Sylvia took his broad dimpled hand in hers, and said : " Maurice, perhaps your mamma will bring you to see me some day, and when we are great friends I can tell better whom you look like."

" Thank madame, Maurice, and tell her you would love to come."

He worked his small, stubby shoe into the walk for a moment; then in a low, awed tone he said : —

" Have you got a donkey at your place ? "

" Yes."

" Then I 'll come, for I think you look all right, not as if you were really a savage like " —

" Maurice," said his mother desperately, " run in and ring the bell as you go. We are going to have something to eat out here," she went on hurriedly, to Sylvia's great amusement.

" My father is never happy under a roof when the sun shines, so we — Oh, there is the butler. Here, Jacques, on this table," she rattled on, bustling about to move a chair here, or a footstool there, for her guests.

" Where is Maurice ? " asked Monsieur Regnier, as his daughter began to hand round a galette. Sylvia's heart beat violently, and she unconsciously kept her hostess waiting, so intently did she listen.

" Oh, I sent him into the house, papa. You

know I never allow him to eat sweets at this hour."

Sylvia took the proffered dainty. It was only the little boy they meant.

Madame Lefevre drew a basket-chair close beside her, and began to talk volubly.

" You know I am here all alone the greater part of the year with papa, for my husband is with his regiment in Algiers, and my brother is with his at Fontainebleau, so we see very little of them."

" Is little Maurice your only child ? "

" Oh, dear me, no." Here the little woman leaned back in her chair and laughed heartily at such a show of ignorance. " I have three boys at Notre Dame in Blois, and two girls at the convent in Tours."

" How can you send them away from you ? " asked Sylvia, thinking how she would treasure and watch over a life confided to her care. Madame Lefevre assumed an expression of obstinacy such as only a weak, insignificant person is capable of, and said, —

" I feel it my duty to bring them up under the influence of the Holy Church. Louis, my husband, and papa would like them always here ; but I say, ' Louis, my father is doubtless a good man, and you do well to speak highly of his influence, but can any man or woman of the world pretend to come anywhere near those who are dedicated to lives of sanctity?' Of course there is nothing to answer to that," she ended complacently.

"It must be a great trial to you," observed Sylvia.

"Oh, it is ; but I have help to bear it. My second little girl is dedicated to the Virgin: when she was three months old she was very ill, so I made a vow that she should be a child of Mary if she recovered. She got better from that day, and now she only wears white and blue, and I feel that it is a mark of heavenly favor that she has a high color like me, so blue is becoming to her, for my oldest child is sallow, and would have looked a fright."

Sylvia did not know whether she ought to laugh at this remark ; but as Madame Lefevre's face was serious, she only said very gravely, "How extremely fortunate."

Madame de La Roche smiled across the table from her seat, where she had been talking with unwonted animation to her friend. "Monsieur Regnier wants to show you the place, Sylvia, and I am sure Berthe and I can amuse ourselves very well while you two are away."

Sylvia rose, glad to think that she was at last to know Maurice's father. His sister was so unlike him in every way that she could not remember the relationship, but the likeness was strong to his son in the handsome, courtly old man.

They sauntered together over the dry, smooth shaven lawn, towards the stables and farm yards, and as they went they fell into talk strangely intimate for such new acquaintance.

"My books are my chief interest now," Monsieur Regnier said to her, when she asked him how he occupied himself. "My boy Maurice, who will soon be going to Algiers, with his regiment, filled every crevice in my life until his profession took him from me. Now I seldom see him," he ended with a sigh.

She looked at him sympathetically. "I should so like you to show me your books," she said gently. "All my young days they were my companions, and it would be delightful to find we had some mutual friends."

He smiled at her with the peculiar soul-touching expression some rare individuals possess. Whether it is caused by past sorrows, or innate humaneness, one cannot tell: but one may see it, and never in the face of him who has not battled nobly with life, and come out the braver and kinder from the struggle.

"It is possible we may have many," he answered; "although I have lost the pronunciation, I still read English as easily as I do French:

and I love the literature although not the people of that self-sufficient little island."

He had led her back to the house while speaking, and she found herself in a long, rather low-studded room, fairly lined with books. It took her at a bound back to the white parlor; she was at home again.

Delightedly she gazed at the titles.

"Ah, I know that edition of Thackeray — ours is like it. And here is dear, funny old Pepys; how lovely the binding is! Why, you have everything, down to Browning."

" Ah, but he is too hard for me. I like a word here, and a word there, but I am too dull to quite get at him."

"Many feel as you do," answered Sylvia, and as she spoke she reached for the volume of " Paracelsus," and opened it. A touch of roguishness, not often seen there, came into her face, as she found the line she wanted.

" I think you must be a magician, Monsieur," she said half shyly, " for I never paid a compliment in my life before that I can remember. But this is the way you look to me," and she handed him the book. He read the words, —
" That look! as if where'er you gazed there stood a star," — and a pleased light came into his eyes.

" Keep your compliments for old fellows like

me and they'll do no harm," he said " but —
you will pardon me for giving you a little advice." He paused, until she had assented.

"You are young, and a foreigner," he went
on. "It is unreasonable to expect you to even
guess at many complications in our life, that come
to us as natural things, but which will strike
you, when you find them out, as strange. You
may be frightened when you get below the surface, for we are radically unlike you Americans ;
there is something simple, wholesome, and truthful about you that we miss, — qualities that many
of us do not even suspect. I am always deeply
interested in all that concerns my dear friend
the countess ; and since I have seen you I am
interested in you personally. Now let me ask
you a favor : if you are worried and troubled by
any incidents in your new life, come to me, and
tell me frankly of them. Will you promise ?"

Sylvia thought of the trouble at her heart that
very moment, — of the deceit that had doubly
cheated her : of her inability to ever breathe one
word that would throw such blame on her husband.

" I do not think I can promise," she said re-
gretfully. " I should like to, — the idea tempts
me, — for I could trust you. But I am afraid
I must bear in silence."

She grew white to her lips as she spoke, and

he looked at her. Had it come so soon? he asked himself, and then, tenderly, tactfully he led her thoughts from her own life to those of others. He spoke of what his books taught him, and his words grew eloquent. She listened, exhilarated to be in touch with some one really sympathetic again.

" Sometimes," she said, half in jest and half in earnest, " I long to die so as to see the authors who have meant so much to me, and thank them."

Monsieur Regnier threw back his head with a gesture which recalled Maurice.

" And do you ever think," he asked, " of the terrible responsibility those men have assumed? If we could meet our ancestors in the flesh you can easily imagine how one would say, ' He has my eyes,' and another, ' He takes his coloring from me,' and these intellectual progenitors would see the effect their written words have had on the minds and souls they have helped to form. Think of the enormous influence Goethe and Byron have had in this century. It is overwhelming."

" Everything is overwhelming," replied Sylvia. " Until lately I never knew that I had a New England conscience. Now that I do realize it everything I do frightens me, for no act seems final, the results go on and on; it is terrible."

He smiled serenely. " You are young," he

said; "all those feelings right themselves with age." Then he told her how he had found his powers of happiness increase with his years. "Never be afraid of old age," he said impressively. "One of the few things I do care for in Browning are these words."

He opened a book on his table, and she saw that it was filled with writing.

"I copy everything here I particularly care for," he explained, running over the leaves. "Here it is: read those words to me in English," he concluded, handing her the book.

Her voice trembled a little as she began; she knew the lines well. They had been favorites of her father, but had never appealed to her until to-day. Now, the unbidden, vain, wrong thought came to her, "What if it were Maurice listening to me? Oh, if it were not too late, too late." Monsieur Regnier watched her as he heard the words, familiar in sense, strange with the new accent.

> "Grow old along with me,
>   The best is yet to be,
> The last of life, for which the first was made.
>   Our times are in His hand,
>   Who saith, ' A whole I planned;
> Youth shows but half; trust God; see all; nor be afraid.' "

"There is a great lesson there," he said when she had ended. "It has taken me nearly seventy years to learn it. Please Heaven it will come to you sooner. The last is the best: we are nearer Him. All the small worries that seem too hard to be borne when the blood runs fast and the heart beats quick, grow insignificant. Old people learn true sympathy — or, at least, they should learn it. Don't dread old age, Madame. It will pay you double for all your losses if you accept your experiences as lessons, and do not try to get rid of them by considering yourself peculiarly ill used when things go wrong. But here am I," he broke off with a laugh, " boasting of my slowly earned sympathy, and keeping you here chained by my prosing."

Sylvia looked at him gravely. " You have helped me. Will you come and see me, and talk to me some more ? " she asked.

He shook his head a little sadly. " I am always here, and often alone. The chateau has too many memories for me to be able to go there readily. Come to me, my dear, and you will always find a welcome."

As she moved towards the door he stopped her. " One more treasure to show you," he said, and then led her to his writing table. There, in a velvet case, lay a miniature of Maurice.

" It is my boy," he told her as he put it in her hand, an expression of pride mingled with a wistful appeal for her admiration in his eyes.

Sylvia took it, and looked into the ardent young face. The artist had caught the Greek touch of beauty, as well as the true likeness of character: there were the eyes, full of enthusiasm and truth — she had doubted them ; there was the generous curve of the lips — she had believed they lied basely ; and there on the cheek had a blow fallen from her hand. She dared not remember. She must speak and drown memory.

" I have met your son. He is handsomer even than his portrait, and as delightful as he is handsome," she said, still holding the miniature, although she no longer looked at it.

Her words were complimentary ; but they carried no conviction, and the father was dimly disappointed. They joined the others on the lawn, and Sylvia found her mother-in-law more than ready to start for home. An hour's talk with Berthe Lefevre was generally enough to make most mortals long for any change from her trivialities, and the countess was no exception. The little woman talked and fussed until they were in the carriage, and even after the horses had started, she ran over the lawn to intercept them, and called out. " I shall surely remember the *reposoir,* and will pray for good weather ! "

Madame de La Roche smiled and waved her hand, then settled back with a sigh. " This is

the eighth time she has told me that," she said.
" She is a good little creature, but not at all
like her father. Maurice is more like him.
Berthe was in a convent until she married,
while her brother was brought up with Philippe.
I suppose it is partly the home training which
makes him so much her superior — and yet I
don't know," she added, her voice falling drearily. Perhaps she thought of her own son, and
the result of his education.

" What did she mean by reposoir ? " asked
Sylvia.

" Oh, don't you know? It is the feast of
Corpus Christi, and before many houses altars
are erected in the open air. The curé marches
through the village at the head of a little procession, and holds a service at each altar. It is
very pretty, and we always have one in the court
of honor."

Sylvia promised to lend her aid in arranging
the next reposoir, and was thankful to have
some subject for conversation on their drive
home. Once there, she found that it was time
to dress for dinner, and not until the family
had parted for the night was she free to think
over the events of the day. Justine dismissed,
she lay down on her sofa drawn before the fire,
— for the nights were chilly, — and then her
mind ran riot. Under all, over all, through all,

rang the triumphant refrain. "Maurice was true, God is good." In some way she joined the two thoughts. Then came the blasting knowledge that the man who was true must be nothing to her, and the man who was false was her husband. At this idea she clenched her hands and moaned; then she walked up and down restlessly. At last she went to her window, and opening it, leant out. Philippe's room was next to hers, and she could see the light in it shining across the vivid green of the young leaves. For a moment she thought of going to him and confronting him with his deception. It seemed to her that she should suffocate if she did not let him know how she scorned and despised him. Then the impulse died away, its angry impetuosity quieted by the memory of a vague sweet hope, — a hope too tremulous and unformed even to dwell on, for a breath might blow it away. So faint was it that Sylvia pressed both hands on her heart to still its quickened throbs for fear of too much joy. And yet, feeble as it was, it had the strength to give her power to keep silence. If it were as she hoped, Philippe had found an innocent defender: as her child's father, he was secured from any outbreak on her part. "He is faithful to his church, and brave for his country. Let me only remember that."

That same night Monsieur Regnier wrote to
his son about the new countess : " She struck
me at first as very beautiful and exquisitely
high-bred in appearance. I say at first, because
when I had talked with her, and learnt a little
of the real woman, I lost sight of the dainty exterior, and thought only of the soul beneath it.
She is not happy, I am sure. Who could be, as
the wife of Philippe ? No one ; that is, no one
of any fineness or delicacy of character, and I
think she has both. She said she knew you ;
but either you never told me of her, or the cir-
cumstance slipped my memory. Poor child, my
heart goes out to her. If I had the power I
would forbid international marriages.

" I can hear you laugh, you rogue, at your
old father when you read these words. ' That
time - honored hobby - horse trotted out again,'
you say. I know all the arguments in favor of
them by heart : new blood improves the race,
etc. Yes, yes, you are right, no doubt, scientifi-
cally ; but I don't care for science at all, and
not much for the race, compared with the individual who is sacrificed. It *is* a sacrifice to give
up family, home, and country for a foreigner.
And all these sweet, gentle young girls who
come so freely to strange lands — what do they
suspect of the nature of the men they marry ?

" Nothing, absolutely nothing, I tell you ; it

is their ancestors who are unlearnable, and who look through ordinary eyes with untranslatable looks. Take the new countess, who looks, by the way, as nobly born as any daughter of kings, — well, why not? She has as many grandfathers as a duchess, I suppose, only one of them happened to sail the ocean; the land is new, but the blood is ancient, — take her for an example: she is like the cedar of Lebanon when it was first brought here from the Holy Land; atmosphere, past, background, all stripped from her. Imagine yourself among people to whom you could never say, ' Do you remember?'

" Half life's charm has gone. Well, well, it is after midnight, so I will have mercy on you and stop. Madame Philippe has gone to my head like strong tea, — if I were forty years younger it would have been heart instead of head. My dear old friend seems very happy with her daughter-in-law: God grant she may live out the rest of her life in peace. Ah, my boy, it is good to be able to make a friend of your son: let us be tender towards those who have not this comfort. I live for your letters. Good night. — Thy loving FATHER.

" P. S. Berthe has already begun to plan how best to convert the newcomer."

This letter brought to Maurice a renewal of the restless feelings that he had believed stifled since he had heard of Sylvia's marriage. For months he had been in bitter revolt against fate, — a revolt that would have led many a man into a life of reckless rebellion ; but he had a strong anchor in his father's love, and under the first adverse circumstances of his life he learned with pain and faltering to curb the enthusiastic violence of his character, and to come, through suffering, to strength. One may doubt if even he realized how much the encouraging, admiring words written by the old man helped him in his struggle.

What is more beautiful than the trusting, blind, heartfelt adoration given by parents to their children. The tender, indulgent appreciation never injures, for even the weakest, most shallow natures can see the affection prompting it. What boy has not been helped and cheered on to his first scholastic efforts by the memory of his mother's wonder at his cleverness in Latin, and his father's encouraging praise of his mathematics ? What girl has not had the triumph of her first ball heightened, or perhaps, alas, the mortification of an evening among the wallflowers softened, by the knowledge that at home she was considered to be without a rival for grace and beauty ? Happy, thrice happy, are those who have received and appreciated this home love and admiration before it is too late ; and let us who have had the ideal stimulus to spur us to our best, be very lenient to those who have never known it.

Maurice not only realized what he was to his father, but he felt a warm glow of gratitude for it. Sylvia had never stood securely, confidently sure in any heart but the one she had rejected.

CHAPTER XIV.

SYLVIA threw herself into the preparations for the reposoir with almost an exaggerated enthusiasm, so thankful was she to occupy her mind with outside interests. Over and over again she repeated to herself that Philippe's religion was deep and real to him, and forced herself to a sympathy with the symbols of it. She delighted the countess by her help and taste, and under the directions of the two chatelaines, the altar was erected in the court. The Sunday dawned clear and fresh, and by afternoon the last touches were put to the decorations, and the family assembled to greet the curé and villagers. Philippe and his wife stood by the entering arch to give the welcomes. This was the first time that Madame de La Roche had openly given precedence to her daughter-in-law, and she felt it a fitting time to step aside and let the little world clustered at her gates see that a new queen was to reign. There was no feeling of bitterness in her heart; only the natural melancholy which comes to us all when we realize the inevitability of years.

As Sylvia looked along the straggling street

of the little village which ran at right angles to
the avenue, ending abruptly at a gate in the high
walls, she saw the procession advancing: first
the women, tidy in their black dresses and snowy
caps, some of them with babies in their arms ;
then the men, awkward and slouching in the
unaccustomed finery of best clothes, and missing their ordinary garb of blouse and sabots ;
after them scudded a host of children, their
faces shining with recently administered soap
and water, their hair plastered to the sides of
their heads.   As they reached the archway, the
sounds of the village fanfare burst forth, herald-
ing the approach of the curé.

Before him came a group of young girls clustered about one who carried a banner ; their
white dresses and floating blue ribbons became
their sweet serious faces : they were still near
enough to childhood to feel the touch of Heaven
upon them.   Then, walking slowly and with dignity under a canopy surmounted by white plumes,
the curé advanced.   The sun glittered on his
gold-embroidered robes, and touched with silver
his white hair.   As he passed under the arch he
paused a moment, stretched out his hand in a
silent blessing, and then proceeded to the altar.
It stood facing him as he entered, towering up
until the gilded dome sheltering a statue of the
Virgin seemed almost to touch the piled-up

masses of snow-gleaming clouds, that sailed slowly through the deep blue sky, casting a radiance of reflected glory. The priest mounted the steps leading to the altar, — on either side of him stood heavy silver candelabra, their lighted candles giving a steady but ineffectual light in the brilliant summer atmosphere; rare embroideries were flung down as if unworthy that the man of God should tread on them; and everywhere, above, below, was a wealth of flowers, massed so as to give broad effects of color, and casting their fragrance on the air. The music resounded through the court. The peasants crowded nearer the reposoir, their sighs telling of their satisfaction in its beauty. Then the curé turned and extended his hands; the strains sank into silence; every one knelt, and as the service began, only a little, unconscious bird interrupted the sonorous Latin, as it perched on the cedar and sang with throbbing throat of that love which was from the beginning, and shall be to the end. At the foot of the altar steps stood two children, dressed and wreathed in white; at the solemn moment of the elevation of the Host, when every head was bowed almost to the ground, they alone stood erect, scattering rose-petals, well pleased with the importance of their task.

The short service ended with a prayer in their own tongue, asking a blessing on the chateau, and

then the curé came down, nearer to his people.
This was the signal for the mothers to bring
their babies to be blessed ; one after another
they gathered about his feet for him to rest the
Host lightly on the little heads, and murmur
the words of the benediction. Something in the
faith and simplicity displayed by the women, or
the look on the curé's face as he started the feeble
feet along the path he had trodden so long and
so patiently, moved Sylvia. If everything else
were denied to her, could not she draw nearer
to her husband through the influence of his religion ? A strong desire to prove her sympathy
with him on one point at least took possession
of her ; it was only honorable to try and do her
best. Touched and softened as she, an outsider,
was, surely he would feel this moment to be a
sacred one. She invested him with all the reverence and sincerity he had taught her to think
he possessed, and for a moment she hesitated to
break in on the sanctity of his thoughts ; then
she reflected that it was her duty to let no opportunity slip which might bring them ever so
little more into accord.

She turned slightly towards him, and looked
at him ; he was absorbed in the contemplation of
something which brought an eager light to his
tawny eyes, and a sensual expression to his glistening lips. Sylvia felt a cold shock at his

appearance, and then her gaze involuntarily followed his, and rested on a fresh-colored, well-made peasant woman, who was returning his glances with an air of intelligent familiarity. The young chatelaine grew sick and faint with disgust. Standing by her side, before the altar to his God, her husband could carry on a vulgar intrigue with a peasant. That there was nothing but the impulse of the moment in it made no difference to her; she did not go beyond the glances exchanged, the expression on his face — that was enough.

She slipped away unobserved to her own room, and lay there on her couch shivering with the loathsomeness of it all. What was there for her to complain of? Intangible ideas, nothing more, and yet she felt that some noisome influence had crept near her. In spite of her contempt and scorn, she whispered : " Still, he is brave ; let me think of that."

As she lay there a sudden knock at her door aroused her, and Philippe entered abruptly. There was an angry look now in his eyes, and Sylvia found it more wholesome than the one it had blotted out.

" Are you tired, my dear ? " he asked with perfunctory politeness.

" Yes, very tired," answered Sylvia.

" No wonder, with all the nonsense out there.

It seems to me that the curé adds something every year to make the whole thing more intolerable. If he only chose some pretty girls for the banner bearers, it would not be so bad."

"Or he might organize a ballet to amuse you," said Sylvia bitterly.

Philippe raised his eyebrows, and laughed. "Don't let my mother hear you say that sort of thing," he advised. "It does not matter with me, of course, for I have graduated from all these superstitious ideas: but they are very real to her. And let me say," he added, growing grave, "that it is always becoming to a woman of position to assume a soupçon of devotion."

Sylvia made no answer, and after a short pause he resumed: "I did not come here, however, to preach to you, but to tell you that something decided must be done about Justine. She is making a devil of a row with Marcel, and it must stop."

Sylvia sat upright on her sofa, a flush rising in her cheeks. "Very well, then, dismiss Marcel; it is simple enough," she said quickly.

The angry look had come again to Philippe's face, but his voice was calm, and he spoke slowly. "It would be still more simple to dismiss Justine," he said.

"That is out of the question," retorted Sylvia hotly.

He smiled. "You go a little too far, my dear; nothing is out of the question that I desire. Don't get excited, but try to take a reasonable view. Justine has made trouble."

"I will hear nothing against her — nothing, nothing," protested Sylvia. "She is all I have left of my very own, and no earthly power shall separate us."

Philippe grew white with anger.

"I have had enough of your American independence; you are my wife, and, by Heaven, you shall obey me."

Sylvia hated him less at this minute than she had for weeks. She liked his authority, although it enraged her; but as he lost his self-control she regained hers.

"Philippe," she said very gently, "I never meant to annoy you, and I beg your pardon if I have been careless of your feelings, but I do ask you to let me keep the woman by me who has been a mother to me all my life. It is not much at this time for me to have a wish that she may stay with me through the autumn — surely, it is a little thing for me to ask."

Philippe rose and went towards the door. "Of course you are like every other woman, and make a good use of your weakness; but understand this: I will have no more interference with my household from that old spy. She is always trying to find out things that are no business of hers. The next time she makes trouble will be the last under this roof."

Almost before he angrily slammed the door behind him Sylvia heard a long, shivering sob, and Justine came slowly from the dressing-room. She stood halfway across the room, her face covered with her hands.

"Let me go away, Madame; let me leave you, my lamb, before I bring more trouble on you. I heard what he said — how he spoke to you — you. Oh, my God, I cannot bear it!"

"Come here, Justine, — come here, my poor old dear. There, don't cry so hard, it hurts me to hear you. Listen to me. You and I are together for life, until death takes one of us. Who is there who loves me like you, Justine? No one."

"If you had been my own child, I could not have loved you more, my precious one. When I heard that you were to be the countess here I thought my heart would burst with joy. I had prayed for it, and see what my prayers have brought you to."

"No, Justine, be honest, and don't blame yourself, my poor dear. I chose my life with my eyes open."

She paused, for as she spoke she realized that the words were a lie. Justine broke in: —

"No, no, neither your eyes nor mine were
open. There has been falsehood everywhere.
To think that my own nephew could have lied
to me, the " —

" Hush, hush — the past is past; let us leave
it behind us, and see what we can do with the
future."

After all, Philippe was her husband. She
could not hear him accused either directly or by
inference, however stern her own judgment of
him might be.

" Good may come to us, my Justine. One
thing, too, is sure and certain; you and I are
to be together always. Nothing, nothing shall
part us."

" And you do not think me a spy, Madame? "

" You old silly soul, no, of course not. Do I
act as if I did? "

It was a new position for Sylvia, to have some
one leaning on her for comfort, and even in her
own sorrow it warmed her cold heart. She sent
Justine for tea, and demanded much petting
from her, thus calming the poor creature by letting her see how necessary she was to her mistress's comfort. But though the heavy groaning
sobs ceased, and her dark eyes became dry, a
deeper hatred of the count scarred Justine's faithful, narrow, fanatical nature from that hour on.

In the long summer days which opened like

roses, and faded in the ashes of burnt-out sun-
sets, — days of beauty, luxuriance, and poetry,
— Sylvia might have yielded to the monotony
and helplessness of her life but for two things:
the hours spent with her mother-in-law making
dainty preparations with loving fingers, talking
and hoping as women do with such a hope
ahead, and her occasional calls at La Source,
where she grew to feel like a child of the house.
Her friendship with Monsieur Regnier grew and
waxed strong. There was a bond between them
of which he was ignorant, but which was made
apparent to her by certain tones of his voice,
and flashes of his eye which called Maurice
vividly before her. She soon found that his
studies had made him unlike the people who
surrounded her. He was broader, more daring
in the views he took on all subjects, especially
on religious matters. Neither a fanatic nor a
scoffer, he looked at his relation to his Maker as
a matter which was solely his own affair. He did
not interfere with those beliefs which brought
comfort to others, and he demanded the same
treatment for himself. He was always a kind
and friendly host to the priests with whom his
daughter loved to surround herself, but he
sternly repelled any advances on their part
when it affected his position towards religion.

It is easy to imagine what a breeze of interest

Sylvia created in his lonely mental life. She came fresh and unprejudiced to give just the stimulus he needed. The benefit was mutual, for from his lips Sylvia heard those views of life and its duties which appealed most strongly to her. They would spend whole afternoons pacing up and down under the fragrant lindens, talking of the message that had come to the world from the Cross on Calvary, and what its meaning was. For the first time Sylvia began to think of Christ as an influence, a power of to-day, not as a dim vision of pain and renunciation. There are some natures who find and love Him first, pouring out their best and finest adoration at his feet, and because of Him loving those made in his image. There are others who must work up to the highest, purest love, because their teaching begins at the other end; they first love the things and creatures He made and through this love they find Him. The Alpha of the one is the Omega of the other; and step by step, beginning humbly and ignorantly, Sylvia found herself finding life not less difficult, but herself more capable of bearing it.

Monsieur Regnier was not in his right place. He recognized that other surroundings would have opened up new lines of action to him, and he might have been a power in the world; but, with that dignified acquiescence to the inevit-

able which was one of his strongest characteristics, he had accepted his lot from the start
without rebellion if without enthusiasm. There
was much quaint humor in his make-up, a certain faculty for seeing the possibility of a smile
where another would have found but tears.
Some ancestor, a devoted follower, perhaps, of
Henry IV., had transmitted to this remote descendant a drop of Huguenot blood, and it was
enough to turn him from the church of his family, although it had not had strength to darken
his natural cheerfulness with the austerity and
rigor that seem inseparable to our minds from
French Protestants. He would doubtless have
died for his faith had he lived in the days of
Catherine de Medicis and the Guises; he would
have died singing, like the brave Huguenots who
perished at Amboise, their voices ceasing, as one
by one ended his song here only to resume it
above, — but Armand Regnier would have lived
as they died, with music on his lips, and light
in his eyes. His religion gave him joy; he felt
that grief and discontent were wrongs done to
the infinite wisdom that has placed us for a time
in this world of sharp contrasts. To one looking
on from the outside, as, for instance, Madame
de La Roche did, there was a deep pathos in the
thought that from an accident merely this man
of intellect, with a capacity for action and lead-

ership, had been condemned to a life of obscurity and monotony; but he saw only the guiding hand that had led him through a childhood and youth of peril to his native land, and that had given him a kindly asylum under the roof where by rights he should have been master.

During the many years he spent there he had never by word or deed shown any envy of his younger half-brother, or any sign of bitterness. The only way in which he had ever hurt them was by his resolute adherence to his form of faith. In vain had his father, then old and feeble, tried to convince him by setting the cleverest and most subtle of churchmen to argue with him. He never denied any of their statements, or let them see that he found their answers to his questions unsatisfactory; but he set his course for himself, and, steering by the steady light of the Star of Bethlehem, he sailed straight on.

The old count used to shake his head pathetically. " I should not mind it if you were an atheist, my boy, but a Protestant — it is too bourgeois, I cannot understand it," he would say.

It may have been that no sect could have claimed Regnier: he worshiped at no temple; he had his own theories and beliefs; he lived up to them, but he never tried to convert an-

other to his manner of thinking. His idea was
that from the very beginning God had revealed
himself to man in the way most appealing to
his age and surroundings. If He could do this
with nations, why not with individuals?

But this was the only flaw in the love and
trust his family had for Armand. In all other
ways he was, if anything, too submissive to their
wishes. This was shown when he accepted the
wife his half-brother chose for him in the happy
glow of a young husband who has found unexpected happiness in marriage.

At that time Armand was forty, and had
settled himself cheerfully into his lifework as
steward of the count's property. He had his
suite of rooms, already the beginning of a noble
library, and marriage was the last thing he
wanted. But his tender heart had ached many
times as he remembered how his religious attitude had troubled his father. Here was a case
that involved personal inclination merely, and
he gave in. The six years he spent with his wife
were the only ones he ever looked back on with
regret. She had been a small-minded person,
had hurt him daily in a hundred different ways,
had made peace of mind impossible in her company; but he remembered only that he had
not loved her, had not done his best to try to
broaden and stimulate her mind, never reflect-

ing that not one harsh word had ever been uttered by him, and that she had not for one moment suspected his lack of love for her.

"She gave me Maurice, too," he used to say sometimes to himself in a reproachful mood; "but, *dame!* she gave me Berthe as well, so perhaps we are quits."

His daughter was not the trial to him that his wife had been, although it was hardly her fault that she was not; she had all the capacity for it. She ruled his household, his expenditures, and flattered herself that she ruled him, but that was his little secret, and he chuckled quietly over it; he was free. He had established 'certain laws when she first came to live nine months of the year with him, and as he had cunningly allowed her to suggest them herself after some clever leading up to the subject on his part, she adhered to them with the tenacity of her shallow nature.

In this way he was absolutely free from any interruption when in his library, or out of it, during certain hours, and thus he maintained his liberty, for he almost lived among his books, when he was not busy in his vineyards. There she did not care to follow him, but her sturdy, fat-legged children always escaped from restraining hands to follow grandpa, and when he gathered them about him at a·safe distance from

the house, he felt that he could forgive Berthe
everything in return for this pleasure. He loved
to tell them old-time tales, and watch their solemn
faces, and the slow laughter rippling over them
when the joke had had time to sink in. He could
always find something in the day's work to bring
a smile, for he had a keen sense of humor, and
this was one of his qualities that appealed most
strongly to Sylvia, who felt the need of laughter
in these sombre days.

At the chateau no one saw a joke, and sometimes she felt that she must either laugh, or cry
her heart out.

Flora had gone early in the summer; she felt
uneasy and troubled whenever she looked at the
new countess. At times she almost wished that
she had never meddled with her affairs at all,
but the wish was not a hearty one, for she could
not honestly bring herself to despise the tidy
little sum at her banker's, especially when she
remembered that, if Philippe were a man of his
word, it was only the beginning of prosperous
days. Still she was glad to get away among the
outside world. She only, with the exception of
old Justine, saw how changed Sylvia was; how
capricious she had grown, how she avoided her
husband.

There was a note of despair about her that
would suddenly disappear before a burst of high

spirits almost hysterical; to this would succeed hours, often days, of a quiet self-withdrawal from those about her. To the superficial observer these changes were inexplicable; to us, who have the key, it is easy to follow Sylvia's moods. A chance word would make her realize forcibly that she was Philippe's wife, that she was bound to him until death did them part, and she was ready to give herself to the placid river if she could only escape; but when the cloud was heaviest the vivid belief in Maurice's honor dazzled her with its brilliancy; she might have lost his love, but she had her faith in him now and always. What wonder that the contrast brought a reaction that amounted to an ecstasy while it lasted?

But day by day Sylvia's moral nature grew stronger, and she began to perceive that the feeling for Maurice she was nourishing and fostering was a sin, not against her husband only, but against herself, and that part of herself which would not die with her.

Then the struggle began. Sins of imagination are so intangible that it seems almost useless to take them seriously, and often Sylvia mocked at her own efforts to drive Maurice from her mind.

"A man who has forgotten me probably, or remembers me only as a virago, and I take my-

self to task because I love to think of him, as I
might of a statue or a picture ! What nonsense
it is ! I am growing morbid. I *will* dream of
him, and all the wonderful, poetic things he used
to say to me ; it harms no one."

But after a sunset stroll in the garden, looking through the branches of the cedar at the
glowing sky, while her heart sang but one name
and bounded at but one thought, she found it
harder than ever to meet her husband with
calm indifference. Then would come to her the
reflection that perhaps Death was waiting for
her, and that with each succeeding day she drew
nearer to him. She could not tell whether she
regarded him as friend or foe ; but the idea always brought a strange quiet with it that seemed
to muffle the sounds of daily life. Philippe paid
but little attention to his wife's caprices in these
days ; he found that she responded distantly to
any mark of endearment from him, and as these
politenesses had become rather a bore to him,
he let her severely alone.

His life for the time being was entertaining,
and he had enough money, or almost enough,
after his debts were paid, to begin some large
improvements on the estate ; besides this interest he was getting his chase into fine condition
for the autumn hunting, and making his stables
as nearly perfect as such establishments can be.

In consequence of an addition of several stalls, which were duly filled with fine horses, Sylvia found herself almost steedless, for the new and exceedingly haughty coachman demanded such an amount of time to fulfill an order, and so much red tape was necessary before he could be communicated with, that often the dinner-hour arrived before his mistress had had her drive. Sylvia was too proud, perhaps too afraid of her own temper, to appeal to Philippe, who cared for nothing so long as the stables shone like jewels, and the horses and harnesses were kept sufficiently polished; but she displayed her American independence by hiring a separate stable for her own horses in the village, and with a new coachman established over them she once more drove when and where she pleased.

This small, silent skirmish astonished and rather delighted Madame de La Roche; she had never seen a woman before capable of asserting her rights so decidedly and so noiselessly, and her son's indifference to his wife's actions annoyed her.

He, when country life became a little tiresome, would run up to Paris, "to look at some horses he had heard of," and as he generally brought one or two friends home with him the chateau began to resume its old air of bustle and gayety, which delighted the hearts in the servants' quarters at least.

Madame de La Roche grew daily fonder of Sylvia, first because there was a depth of childlike affection under the reserved exterior that showed itself but shyly and rarely ; and also because the bond of a common interest drew them together. She recognized the fact that there was not even a pretense of love between the husband and wife. This troubled her to a certain extent, for she would have gladly relived her youth's romance in their lives ; but she comforted herself by thinking that years and habit would bring them closer to one another, and she was so relieved by being freed from the degrading pressure of debt, so happy to see Philippe contenting himself in a regular, well - ordered manner, that sentimental burdens ceased to oppress her.

And so the summer slipped by, while outwardly the people in the chateau led the same life, side by side ; but inwardly each was going his or her own distinct way. It is almost alarming to reflect how small a part of us are our surroundings. What an elusive unrestrained vagabond is the self that looks through our eyes ! It would be the study of years to trace the cause of the subtle turnings and twistings in our own souls, and yet how often we hear the expression, " I know him as well as I know myself."

No one really knows any one ; and this being accepted, how was Sylvia ever to learn her new family, or they her, separated as they were by race, by all the weight of past generations, and by the responsibility of those to come ?

CHAPTER XV

WITH the opening of the hunting season a new era began at the chateau de La Roche. The touch of the freshly acquired gold was like the kiss of the Prince in the palace of the Sleeping Beauty. During the spring and summer Philippe had been pushing things, with the result that the ample stable, which for many years had given shelter to but one or two horses, now presented a brave front to the army of grooms that drilled and manœuvred under the direction of the haughty head coachman, imported from England. Rows of guest-rooms that had seen only the faint glimmer of a thief-like sunbeam which ventured to glide through the closed shutters, now basked in the full rays shed by the sun in at the wide-open casements. Galleries, silent in the past, or echoing but to the nibble of a mouse in the paneling, now rang to the busy tread of the many servants running hither and thither to the rooms of guests invited for the hunting.

Sylvia had begged off from receiving many women, so the outsiders were chiefly men, who

appeared only at dinner, talked rapidly and con-
vincingly of the day's sport, proving that if they
had missed their game it was but the fault of
the powder, and if they had been successful, it
was their superior skill. She quite lost run of
their names, they followed one another in such
quick succession. Some were handsome ; some
tall and well-made ; most of them were clever,
talking with an epigrammatic smartness not
difficult to adopt; but not one combined the
qualities owned by Maurice. Even a commonplace man would have been invested by Sylvia
with a halo of romance arising from the fact
that she had wronged him ; and Maurice was no
commonplace person.

For the first time in his life, Philippe was almost content ; almost, but not entirely so. In
the early flush of good resolve following his
marriage, he had paid some of his most pressing
debts, promising himself, and his creditors, to
continue this act of justice as he received his income. But after his return to his property, he
was like an impatient child ; he could not wait
a year to make good the damages of time, so he
plunged into all the expense incident on repair-
ing. Then the ambition seized him to renew the
traditions of his family, and to show the neighborhood as fine a pack of hounds as any his ancestors ever owned ; so the dogs were bought at

great expense, and established with the necessary piqueurs, grooms, etc., on an outlying farm.

But his expenditure was not limited to the
country. The Parisian apartment had lately
grown into a hotel, whose occupant was beginning to give Philippe a notoriety, dear to some
men, by being known as the most luxurious and
extravagant of her world.

These drains were undoubtedly heavy, but
they could have been met, if the old passion for
gambling had not resumed its powerful fascina-
tions for the count, fastening on him with fresh
strength after his short rest.

He was fully aware of its dangers ; he realized
its despotism, and he swore again and again to
abandon all play ; but it was late in the day for
him to acquire self-control. The habits of his
youth, when a slight penance could ease his conscience from all sting of remorse, no matter what
the offense had been, and the shallow skepticism
that had followed close on the heels of this early
credulity, made him an impotent prey to his own
passions. The fact that he was so soon again
heavily in debt troubled him, but he found it
easy enough to reason away any feeling of shame
caused by the reflection of the unworthy desires
that had brought him to this pass. All expense
incurred for the improvement of the estate would
make it more valuable for those who would come

after him, so what he had done in that direction was not blamable. The establishment in Paris was paid for scrupulously from his own income, so no one could reproach him about that; thus he argued casuistically to himself. But the gambling was not to be dismissed in so cavalier a fashion; the debts run up there were what we call — is it in sarcasm? — debts of honor. To meet their imperative demands he renewed his obligations to the Jews; but that could not last long; for they had learned that it was only the income of his wife's fortune which fell actually into his hands, and alarmed for the safety of the large sums already advanced, they began to dun him.

This was the reopening of an old wound; consequently more unbearable. He could not stand this sort of thing as well as he had formerly; his nerves were losing their iron consistency. Since he had reaped the actual benefits of wealth, he had become in a certain manner conservative. He was in an uncomfortable state, and felt it an injustice that Sylvia should have such huge sums lying at rest, earning leisurely interest, when he was so tormented. He thought once or twice of taking her halfway into his confidence; of telling her just enough to make her feel an impulse to help him : but some subtle instinct kept him back. He was riding home from hunting one misty evening towards the end of October when the cares, banished during the excitement of the day, thronged round him.

"It's a pleasant state of things when I dread to go home, for fear of finding some confounded message to worry me; this must stop. Why don't I speak to Sylvia? She's my wife; she belongs to me. What is there about the woman, confound her, that makes me respect her?"

It was true; she had forced him to accord her respect, if nothing else. The fact was that he did not dare to ask her for money, and as he pondered an idea struck him: he would write to her man of business in Boston telling him to advance the January interest. That was all that was required for the present; it would stop the barking mouths of those curs, and afterwards he would economize, — he would, by "the beard of his father," he said to himself with a grim smile.

The letter was posted that evening, and led to consequences far different from the ones he had looked for.

Philippe banished it as well as he could from his mind during the next fortnight, when he might expect a cable in reply to it; but in the meantime, ho, for a merry life!

One cold, cheerless afternoon in November the countess was sitting with Sylvia in her salon. Outside the leaves had fallen, and all was dull and sodden-looking, but within, the trees on the tapestry were forever green, and the strange imaginary beasts of fable-lore pictured there were eternally innocent in a tropical clime. Sylvia had chosen the older wing for herself, and her rooms were on the ground-floor on the court side, but twenty feet or more above the terrace on which the cedar stood, so that she could see into its very heart. The apartment was supposed to be the one occupied by François I. on his first visit, and Sylvia had chosen it partly from the association, and because the rooms were large and exquisitely proportioned ; also somewhat on account of the conveniences they boasted.

In good weather it was but a step across the court to the Renaissance wing, where the older countess lived, and where the family met at meals. When it rained, there were two ways of reaching it under shelter, either by going up a flight of stairs which took one through a covered passage over the entrance arch, and down again, keeping on by the kitchens and offices ; or by descending a winding stair in the wall, that went directly from Sylvia's bedroom to a tunneled way leading to the chapel in the rock. A modern housebuilder would hold up his hands in despair over such clumsy exits and entrances, but one must suffer a few inconveniences if one lives in an historic chateau.

Sylvia had grown into the old wing, with all
its memories. She had gathered her belong-
ings about her, imparting to the grim chambers
a touch of modern life, and the surroundings of
a woman who thought and read, and kept up
with the march of the day. Reviews and new
publications lay on the tables; a portfolio of
photographs from the modern masters shoul-
dered another where the older schools were represented; a package of music, just sent from
Paris, and not yet opened, lay on the piano;
but with it all the unconquerable essence of the
past dominated the atmosphere of the salon.

This afternoon, the two women were seated
with their work, talking in the snatchy way that
people fall into when they live together. Suddenly Madame de La Roche folded her knit-
ting up in a neat roll, and said: "Philippe is
very restless when he stays at home. He is
worrying me to send away Pierre."

Sylvia was too much on her guard with herself to take any active part in the occasional discussions between Philippe and his mother. It is
only really loving wives who feel the necessary
security that permits freedom of speech con-
cerning their husbands. So she said in rather
a non-committal tone, "What fault does he find
with the poor old fellow?"

As she spoke Philippe strolled into the room,

with the out-of-place manner men adopt when they find themselves cut off from their usual occupations. There was no deer hunt that day ; an unexpected interval had come between two visits ; and altogether he was ill at ease. It did not add to his amiability to bear the constant wonder in his mind if Sylvia's man of business would cable promptly. He had hoped for an answer the day before, but had been disappointed.

" What poor old fellow ? What are you talking about ? " he asked, opening a review, and running his eye over the contents.

No one answered for a moment, — Sylvia, because it was not her wish to say anything that might lead to a dispute, and his mother because she would have preferred to put off the inevitable hour of discussion to some day when Philippe would be in an easier humor. If she had drawn his attention away by speaking of some other interest, he would probably have forgotten the whole matter ; but the entire silence reached his consciousness through his desultory reading, and throwing the magazine down on the table. he repeated sharply : —

" Don't you mean to tell me who it is you are pitying ? "

" Sylvia and I were talking about Pierre, and I was telling her of your discontent with him," at last replied the countess, once more undoing her roll of work, and beginning to ply her needles. She knew from experience that the matter would have to be fought out now, and she was well aware of Philippe's tenacity regarding his own wishes.

Sylvia turned her head away, looked out at the dreary landscape, and wished that they would carry their domestic affairs somewhere else. She hated difference of opinion, and had a nervous shrinking lest she might be appealed to by one or the other.

" Discontent! That's a mild way of putting it! The fact is that he is impossible. It is absurd to think of having a well-run establishment with him for butler."

" Your father was known as one of the most particular men of his day, and he trained Pierre. *He* found him satisfactory."

" So he probably found the bonnet you wore on your wedding trip enchanting, as it undoubtedly was: but how would it look to-day?"

" Ah, Philippe, you should not speak of flesh and blood as you do of inanimate objects. Have you no gratitude for Pierre, when you remember that he saved your life when you were a baby?"

" There's always been a question in my mind as to how long we should be slaves to gratitude.

He saved my life — good ; he risked being bitten by a dog who was supposed to be mad — good again. In return he was rewarded by you and my father, he was held up to me as my pre-server ; and this little game has been played for nearly thirty years. It's time to stop it, and cry quits. I shall provide for him, give him a cottage in the village, and a pension."

Madame de La Roche could look very severe when she was roused. Her son's words stung her, and she said firmly : —

" It is not agreeable to me to take my stand as the actual owner of the chateau ; but I am driven to say with firmness that it is my wish to keep Pierre, either to the end of his, or of my, life."

Philippe looked at his mother. He knew quite well that her will equaled his when she had any object to fight for, and the faint color that had crept into her cheeks, together with her flashing eyes, warned him that he must draw back. So he came down from his high horse, and aired his grievances.

" I don't think that I'm very demanding, my dear mother ; just listen to the kind of thing his parsimony makes him do all the time. Night before last when I had those fellows at dinner, I had told Marcel to ice some champagne. It is some wine I am trying, and I wanted it that night surely. Well, round toddled the old miser,

filling the glasses with rather an unusual generosity. When I tasted the stuff, I saw at once
there had been some mistake. So I whispered
to him, ' You 've got the wrong bottle.' ' Oh,
no, Monsieur le comte, there are only very
young gentlemen here to-night, who can't tell
good wine from bad, and the other cost so much
money that I sent to the grocer's for this tisane
in its place. It is nice and cold, and no one but
Monsieur le comte can tell the difference.' I
was angry enough at that, and told him to serve
it in the servants' hall, and give us the other.
He trotted off, and in a moment changed the
glasses and poured out from another bottle of
tisane under my very nose ! Now do you blame
me, when I find fault ? "

Sylvia had been giving rather a languid attention to the conversation, until Philippe poured
out his woes about the champagne. Then the
comic side of the story struck her : the image
of her autocratic husband being forced to economize against his will brought an involuntary
smile to her lips, and unfortunately she caught
the countess's eye at the moment. The smile
became more pronounced, and suddenly they
both burst into uncontrollable laughter. The
knowledge that Philippe was being made justly
indignant by their behavior only made them the
more helpless.

" It is something to be grateful for that I have
found a way to rouse some interest in me," he
said, throwing a furious glance at his wife,
which sobered her in a second. He was going
on, when the door opened, and the cause of the
interview came into the room, bearing two blue
envelopes on a tray.

" For Monsieur le comte, and to one there is
an answer," he said.

Philippe forced himself to take them quietly,
and to open them with deliberation ; but he
could not control the angry frown that crossed
his brow as he read the first. It was from Sylvia's man of business, and the three curt words
struck him as an insult, — " Wife's signature
necessary."

He drew his hand down over his mouth, as he
stood staring at the short sentence. It was a
check, and a most unpleasing one.

Pierre, who had been watching him with the
undisguised interest of an old and somewhat
spoiled servant, interposed : " If Monsieur le
comte will read the other dispatch he can tell
if there be an answer. I don't hold with the
idle messenger waiting long in the kitchen : he
will be sure to drink his weight in good wine."

" Send him to the hall, and tell him I will see
him myself," replied Philippe, who had by this
time read the second message, — a repetition of

the almost daily demands for payment from one of the Jewish brethren, and as it was a trifle threatening in its form, he decided to reply. As he spoke to the old butler, he seated himself at Sylvia's writing-table, and pulling open a drawer, took out a sheet of note paper, with the family crest and coronet stamped in gold. But before he had time to sully the fresh page with his pen, Pierre had gently removed it.

"Monsieur le comte will pardon me. Here is a bit of paper that will do well enough for a telegraph message. I save odd sheets for that."

Without giving Philippe time to answer, he placed before him the blank side of a faire-part, the wide black edge showing what gloomy message had been its errand. Both the watching women held their breath : they knew that Pierre had risked a violent reproof, and both dreaded the outburst that they expected. But Philippe was too much engrossed in his reflections to notice the interference. He sat with his pen balanced for a short time, and then dashed off a few words ; after which he rose and left the room without speaking.

"Pierre really is aggravating. I will go and give him a lecture," said Madame de La Roche, following after her son.

Sylvia leant her head against the window with

a sigh. The short-lived laughter had left her depressed. She scorned the mind that would trouble itself over such trivialities, not giving Philippe any credit for his power of organization, and failing to find sympathy with him when he was annoyed by details. She was in the same listless attitude when he returned, and seating himself by the fire, again opened the review that he had thrown on the table. He knew that before him lay a task. The business-like brevity of that dispatch irritated him; confound the canaille who dared to send him such a message. The little episode with Pierre, too, unimportant in itself, added a sting and increased his ill humor. His eye ran down one page after another, and still he pondered as to the best way of opening the subject to his wife. At last a way presented itself to him. He rose, and lighted a cigarette; then he said in an unconcerned manner : —

" By the way, Sylvia, I wish you'd write a line to your man there in Boston, telling him that you would like the January interest advanced as soon as he conveniently can."

When he first spoke, she turned her head from the window, where she had been looking on the cedar as one looks at a friend, and her whole face took on an altered expression : it grew cold and hard.

" Is it possible that you have already spent all
the July income ? "

" Yes.   The kennels have cost a deuced lot
more than I expected ; but then it 's true that I
pushed matters, and it is the first outlay that
takes the most money.   There will be nothing
so heavy again."

" I dislike to trouble Mr. Henderson.   I
promised him that I would not make any change
in the existing arrangements unless it was something serious.   I would rather wait until January."

" It is not a question of what you may or may
not prefer.   The money is necessary to me, and
at once.   Do you understand ? "

" There is nothing complicated in the state-
ment."

" I don't suppose that you care to force me
to order you to send for it ? "

There was an insolent arrogance in his voice
that stung Sylvia ; for the first time she thought
of her conduct in giving up her entire income to
her husband as a generous action.   Up to this
moment it had seemed but the natural thing to
do.   Her eyes threw him a quick flash of scorn,
as she replied quietly : —

" If you do, I am afraid that I shall disobey."

Philippe walked to the bell-rope, and gave it
a violent pull.   He knew that he could not force

her to do as he wished, and he said to himself that he had set about the matter in the wrong way. His idea had been that it was best to play a game of bluff, and act as if he were but demanding his right; but he now saw that he must alter his tactics somewhat to gain his wife. The thought galled him. It was infuriating to feel that he must bend before a woman, but his need was so urgent that he controlled his anger for the time.

There was nothing more said until a footman answered the bell. Philippe ordered his horse at once, and when the man had left the room, he turned again to Sylvia.

" That is your final decision, then ? "

" It is," she answered, her head bent over the white wool in her hands.

The noise made by the violent slam given to the door told her that she was alone. Alone, indeed ! The very hand that should have been the first to protect her was the one to pilfer her. Every soul is to a large extent isolated; but Sylvia's position was peculiarly solitary. She felt absolutely sure of no one. She had no specific suspicions against her husband, but her woman's instinct told her that he was not open with her.

A tormenting thought, that had often been with her of late, came into her mind, — the dread that if she died, Maurice would never know that she had been deceived; that he would always think of her as a woman of paltry ambition and violent temper. A vague wonder came to her, if she should be able after this life to vindicate herself in his eyes? But it glided away, leaving the same chill fear behind.

She had not moved since Philippe left her; but sat watching with heedless eyes a steely blue cloud, burdened with hail, that was passing up the valley. The stones falling from it bounded on the hard ground, while the trees swayed and complained in the rough wind, that showed them scant ceremony, and played rude games with the reluctant, fallen leaves, urging them to assume an air of gayety, whirling and dancing about, which their sad-colored habits denied.

The biting cold brought by the shower struck through the small leaded panes of glass. Sylvia shivered and went to the fire. As she stood there the cloud passed over, and a ray of low sunlight struggled into the room through the boughs of the cedar. A sudden idea came to her. She rang the bell and ordered her close carriage at once. She would see Monsieur Regnier before night: a talk with him always did her good, and — she blushed faintly as she thought, " I shall see *his* picture, too."

It was dusk by the time she reached La

Source, and the warm glow of the library fire was doubly grateful after the chill left in the air by the recent hailstorm. Monsieur Regnier was sitting before it, the shaded light of his reading-lamp on the table by his side leaving the rest of the long room in obscurity. As Sylvia walked in unannounced, she saw the doubtful expression in his face change to a look of welcome ; he rose and came towards her with both hands out.

" I could not see, but I am sure that it is my little chatelaine," he said. " This is very good of you. I am all alone, you know, and I am in need of sympathy this evening."

" Let me take off my hat and gloves," said Sylvia, laying them aside. " When I come here I like to make believe that it is home, and that I am going to stay. There, I will keep my furs round me, for I am chilly."

She took a chair that he drew near the fire for her ; turning it a little, so as to see Maurice's picture, which was under the lamp, as if his father had been looking at it.

Monsieur Regnier took up two letters. " I have been much stirred by my afternoon's mail," he began ; " I will read you what my boy wrote me." He sat quite still for a moment, running his eye over the page ; then he read : —

TLEMCEN, November 12, 1869.

MY DEAR FATHER, — I am scratching off this line to follow my Wednesday's letter, because I am afraid —

His voice, which had trembled at first, died quite away. He shook his head impatiently, and handed the letter to Sylvia. "There! you will have to read it yourself; I 'm an old fool," he said brokenly.

She took it eagerly, and bending her head went on to herself : —

— because I am afraid you may hear a garbled account of a little brush I had this afternoon with some natives, and will be anxious. Some of these devils had captured a Sister of Mercy, a woman who spends her life trying to help mankind, in marked contrast to the mass of her sex, and I got permission to go to her rescue. I was on fire to begin with, thinking of her possible fate, and when I came to close quarters with the beggars I grew mad with the fighting fever, and felt like a bull-dog in the ring. I believe I even growled, I was so imbued with the spirit of one! My men acted like trumps. They were bull-doggy, too, and long before I had any idea that we were going to be victorious, the dirty curs of Arabs turned

tail, and left me with a good deal of the feeling
one has going downstairs in the dark, when he
thinks there is another step, and there is n't. I
must confess to being disappointed that it was
all over. We came back with our prize, and
now I am going to bed. I hope that I am too
tired to dream of dear old La Source. I am
there in dreams half the night, generally. It is
your fault for being such a father that it is impossible not to love you and home too much.

Embrace my sister for me, and give my love
to her children. •

I clasp your hand, my dear father, and am
your dutiful son, Maurice.

Monsieur Regnier had watched Sylvia as she
read, and at any other time would have felt
some surprise at seeing the waves of emotion
that swept across her face; but he was so stirred
himself that it seemed only natural to him.
When he saw that she had read the last word,
he handed her the second letter, saying : —

" He may treat it as a joke, but his superior
officers don't."

Tlemcen, November 12, 1869.

Monsieur, — It is my pleasure as well as my
duty to inform you of the gallant behavior of
your son, Captain Maurice Regnier, to-day in a
sharp encounter with a large force of natives.

The expedition was undertaken by him at his own request, from a sentiment of humanity which does him credit. He cut his way through fearful odds, and saved a Sister of Mercy from a fate worse than death. It would have made you young again to hear our men cheer him on his return. He is the idol of the regiment, not only for this, but for a dozen exploits almost its equal. The foregoing sentences I write as his commanding officer; the following ones as his friend, and I fear they may pain you. He is a changed man since his return to us from his furlough a year ago. He has something on his mind, — something that has made him hard and bitter. He takes every chance to risk his life; he seeks every privation. One would think he wished to die, provided the end were glorious. Has he had any disappointment? Is he in debt? Seek it out at once. Find out the cause, and remove it, for the good of France, which cannot afford to lose him: for your own good: for his own life!

Permit me to congratulate you on being the father of such a son, and accept, monsieur, the most sincere expression of my regards.

ANDRÉ DE CLERMONT.

As Sylvia read the last part of this letter the color surged to her face, and died away leaving

it paler than before ; for a moment her breast
rose and fell convulsively, and then with a sob
that seemed to wrench her very soul she dropped
on her knees, burying her head on the arm of
Monsieur Regnier's chair.

"Oh, how can I bear it? how can I bear
it?" she gasped. "I love him, and I am so
powerless. It is my punishment, for I thought
myself stronger than fate ; now I see my weakness."

"My child, my dear child!" exclaimed Monsieur Regnier, alarmed by her emotion; this
woman, always so self-controlled even when her
eyes contradicted her gay words and smiling
lips, now in such an agony of self-abandonment,
frightened him. Was she going mad? What
did she know about Maurice? He laid his hand
gently on her hair and said: "Tell me all; I can
understand ; but take your own time — don't
hurry."

For a moment or two she knelt there, the
painful sobs growing fainter ; then she lifted
her head and looked at him. In spite of the
traces of tears and marks of suffering, her face
seemed years younger than the one which he
had grown to love : the subtle, illusive expression with the strange fascination had disappeared, and there was a new, child-like honesty
in her eyes.

"I never, even to myself," she began, "acknowledged that I loved Maurice; I did not want to; I dreaded the power of love; I had seen too much of its havoc; but I half promised to marry him after a week's thought. He went away, and they lied to me about him. They told me — they made me think — ah, I cannot tell you what they said, but I believed them — God forgive me! I sent him away with insults. I can see now that it was my love for him that made me so violent, so mad with rage. But I never faced it until I came here, and heard the truth from the countess. Maurice was always true. At first that was enough for me : I only cared to think of that — but now, there is another thought — I must tell you."

"Go on, my child," said Monsieur Regnier, as her voice died away. His tone encouraged her. He was beginning to understand ; the memory of Maurice's hopes at the time when he came home to obtain money for Philippe; the despairing telegram that followed quick on the heels of his departure : the gloomy mystery in which the affair had been shrouded, — all began to explain itself to the father's mind.

"This is it," she continued : "December will be here soon, and it is possible that I may not live through it. At times I hope I shall not: my life is a useless one ; if I leave a child to inherit the name, and money to build up the old place again, I shall have served my purpose in the world. But oh, I cannot, I will not die and leave Maurice with a memory of a cold, hard, ambitious woman. If I live, it is for the best that he should think of me so; but if I die, tell him the truth — dear, dear friend, take that stain away from me."

The old man was moved deeply; pity for the woman before him, heart-rending sympathy for his brave boy bearing his lot in silence, for a moment prevented him from speaking. He gently raised Sylvia, and made her sit in a large chair; she leaned back, the simple, uncomplicated expression deepening.

" I promise you, my dear," he said at length, " that Maurice shall know the truth. It is better for both; a deception can never work for good. That is not what troubles me; it is the way you must face your feeling for him. You do not speak of it as a sin — you do not seem to regard it as a wrong against Philippe."

Her face hardened.

" I have given my husband all that he married me for. He is master of my entire income; he is content."

Monsieur Regnier leant forward, and placed his hands on hers : his touch seemed to calm the burst of scorn called up by Philippe's name.

" You cannot stop there," he said impressively; " you will be, if you live, the mother of his child ; you have linked yourself in a chain that has continued for centuries ; you have no right to bring the shadow of evil on the family you have entered. It is not merely to your husband that you owe fidelity, it is to his ancestors and to his descendants. When you, a stranger of different land and creed, married a French noble, you threw away your birthright for a coronet. It was a barter, your wealth against his name. If you are a woman of honor you will fulfill your share of the contract ; you will try to satisfy yourself by serving to build up a great name, nearly extinct ; you will so live that when you die you may feel that your example and influence have counteracted the evils of inheritance, and your children will be nobler and sturdier than their forefathers."

" Must I then renounce all happiness," said Sylvia piteously, " and feel that my freedom is lost forever ?   It is fearful."

" Ah, poor little girl," said Monsieur Regnier, " that is a consideration that never presents itself beforehand.   You wanted to be a countess or a duchess ; you thought that it would mean a life just as much your own as the years behind you, only with the glitter of rank added : no one told you that your *self* was of no more consequence as an individual than that of a high-bred mare, bought by the breeder to improve his stable. This sounds brutal, but it is the truth, and I am so little philosophic that I resent it bitterly; and if I had my way every girl whose mother brings her from abroad in search of a title should be taught it. The old world is accustomed to it, and looks for nothing better as a rule; but these poor, new world children make my heart bleed with their innocent arrogance."

This was an old grievance, and he spoke strongly; she heard his words, but her past emotion prevented her from clearly understanding them: besides, a new feeling was at work. She spoke abruptly.

"Something very strange has happened to me to-day; I have found myself the real being, for the first time in my life. I seem to have gone back, and become a little girl again. I have never been real, even to my own soul. I have always hidden my true feelings until it has become a second nature. I think Dick was the only person I ever spoke frankly to until now. I have told myself that love was a curse, a blight, for so long that I thought I believed it; but since I came here, and heard about Maurice, suddenly I am another person."

She spoke half to herself, for the first time noticing a change that had been gradually taking place in her since the day when her heart had stirred, faintly but decisively, at Maurice's words of love; her emotional nature had since then grown slowly stronger, until at the first opportunity it dominated her with an imperious force. Monsieur Regnier saw that she was overexcited by what had gone before, and endeavored to calm both her and his own feelings. She did not stay long, for she wished to be alone with this new, wondrous personality which interested her deeply, and Monsieur Regnier, moved and saddened, wrapped her furs about her, and watched the lamps of her carriage as it rolled down the avenue in the November dusk. But his thoughts of her died away with the sound of the horse's rapid trot, and as he seated himself once more in his silent room, it was to his boy, his brave Maurice, who was showing a grim determination to fight down his sorrow, that his mind turned.

"And he can write me merry, jesting letters when his heart is breaking for her. May God help him, for she is more worthy of his love than most women," said the sorrowing father as he carefully smoothed the colonel's letter, which Sylvia in her burst of grief had crushed.

She, in the mean time, leaning back against the cushions, forgot her past, her future, her husband, even Maurice, and became absorbed in herself.

"I never thought of myself before," she pondered. "I have thought of what I should do, where I should be, what might happen to me, but never of *me* — Why, I am a woman; I am real: I am like those loving, tender, heroic girls I have loved and envied when I read about them, but I never dreamed of having feelings like theirs. I could be a Viola; I could be my duke's page, and find content in serving him; I would carry his messages of love — Oh, no, no, never! I would kill Olivia first! I would not let him love her. I would compel him to see through my disguise. He could not help feeling the air throb against his cheek as my heart beat, and it would bring him to my feet. O Maurice, my Maurice, are you thinking of me to-night? Do you know" — A shudder crept over her. "I am a link — only a link in a great chain. I am responsible to my husband and his house. Monsieur Regnier said so. O God, why did you send me feeling when it has become a sin? Why did no one, *no one* ever tell me what love meant? It is fate, though I thought that I had conquered it — instead I am doubly beaten."

She sat, her eyes closed, rigid in her corner. She felt that she was capable of anything, everything, for Maurice's sake, except giving him up, and that was what pride, honor, and womanliness imperatively called her to do. She

fought her battle out as bravely in the solitude
of her evening drive as Maurice had fought his
under the African sun, and like him she was
victorious for the time. Luckily the thought did
not strike her that a resolution could be kept
with comparative ease when to break it would
mean the result of an unaided effort. This was
the time for suffering; but when leagues of land
and sea no longer separated them, when once
more his voice thrilled her, and his eyes met
hers, then would come the time for resistance.

When she reached the chateau she had regained her self-control, and her nerves were
calmed, half by her will and half by the sheer
fatigue that follows any great emotion. She
went directly to her salon, and was surprised to
find Philippe waiting for her. An enormous fire
roared and blazed in the grim stone chimney, and
as he stood before it the brilliant light brought
out vividly the lines of his muscular, well-made
figure, still in riding-costume, the rich color of
his hair and skin, and the restless sparkle of his
eyes. Even Sylvia, absorbed and worse than indifferent as she was, felt an involuntary admiration of such a complete picture of physical
manhood.

He came towards her, his hands held out, his
whole manner changed since their last meeting.
He had cooled down during a hard ride, and had

come to the conclusion that he must stoop to conquer. Distasteful as the notion was to him, he set about it at once.

" I was a selfish brute to you this morning, mignonne ; and you have paid me well for it by frightening me."

As he spoke, he took her furs from her, and raised her gloved hand to his lips.

" By Jove, how cold you are ! " he exclaimed, not giving her time to reply ; " I can feel the chill through your glove. Here, sit down by this fire that I made for you myself. Where have you been so late, making me think that you were lost ? "

" I drove to La Source," she answered, holding her hands out to the fire ; she had not known before how cold she was.

" You are as white as a ghost, too," he went on, ringing the bell. " You must have some tea."

" Oh no, I don't need it ; besides, is n't it time to dress for dinner ? It must be after seven."

" Dinner may wait for you. Some tea at once, for Madame la comtesse," he added, turning to the servant at the door ; " and bring some cognac, too."

Sylvia leant back in her chair ; she was cold, cold to her heart, and very tired. She could not

think ; she only knew that it was good to feel
the warmth, and to be taken care of.   Philippe's
voice seemed to come from a great distance as
he went on talking.   He was saying something
kind — that she could distinguish : something
about how doubly precious her life was to him
now, and of the new pride that she had made him
feel.   But she could not answer for the moment ;
she could only smile languidly at him, as he bent
over her.   When the tea came he poured it out
for her himself.   It was what she needed : as
she swallowed it, the color came again to cheeks
and lips, and the fatigue disappeared.   She sat
up straight, and took in the sense of what he
was saying.

"You will promise me to be careful ? "

"Yes," she said submissively. more in reply
to her own resolves than to his appeal, — " yes,
I will do as you wish."

" That 's right," he said, rubbing his hands.

She was now mistress of her thoughts once
more, and it flashed into her mind that she had
wronged this man, her husband ; she had sinned
against him in thought and word : and she owed
it to him to atone for the disloyalty of which he
was unconscious, — not for his sake. but to right
herself in her own sight, to make herself more
worthy ; to prove to some invisible presence that
Maurice had not lowered himself by loving her.

A whole network of subtle impulses crossed and recrossed her brain.

" Now that you're looking yourself again, do you want to dress ? Or would you rather dine here ? "

" Oh, I'm quite well, thanks ; I can come to dinner. But before you go, Philippe, I want to say that I was wrong to refuse to write for the money. If you will tell me what to say, I'll send the letter this evening."

She rose as she said this, and went to the door of her own room, thus cutting short his expressions of gratitude ; but in his triumph he did not notice her aloofness. He went back to the fire, and stood staring at the flames ; he gave his moustache a twirl upwards, and a smile in which satisfaction and conceit mingled was on his lips.

" Ah," he said to himself ; " if you can't gain a woman in one way, it is pretty certain that you can in another ! "

CHAPTER XVI.

ONE evening, late in December, most of the servants of the chateau were gathered about the hearth in the large vaulted kitchen. Roaring flames rushed up the chimney, as if eager to meet and fight the wind roaring an angry challenge aloft in its turn. The light of fire and lamp fell on the brilliant battery of copper saucepans and other cooking utensils that gleamed in all their bravery on the walls. The square red tiles on the floor sent up a ruddy glow over the faces of the company. The range with all its accompanying grimness was hidden behind a huge settle, where the buxom cook rested from her labors, and the whole scene was one of social pleasure — or perhaps it is truer to say *would have been*, had not the expressions of those gathered in the generous warmth expressed a certain important gravity rather than mirth.

"You are certain it was the Paris doctor who came by the afternoon train, Jacques?" asked the cook for the twentieth time.

"When I told you again and again that I

drove him here myself, because the chief was digesting his breakfast, and would n't budge!" replied Jacques, a little tempestuously.

"That comes of thinking only an Englishman can drive a horse, and only a Scotchman can see to a garden," grumbled Pierre, the old butler; "when the truth is, that all one is good for is to stuff his belly and swear at the grooms; while the other tells you there are no grapes for your table, and sells them under your very nose, putting the money in his pocket."

A murmur of applause met this sally, neither of the aliens being present. Then a pretty chambermaid, who was darning stockings under the lamp, made herself heard.

"I know it was the Paris doctor who came, for Marcel, as usual, ordered me to unpack his valise and lay out his clothes, and then pretended he had done it himself, and got the tip — as usual, too."

"It's too bad, Jeanne," said the others; while Pierre added, "There's but one way you can get even with him, my pretty — marry him."

Jacques, the only other man present, grinned at this, but cook, laundress, chambermaid and even kitchen girl resented it loudly as being a stigma cast on their sex. As they threw epithets at him, the mildest of which was "stingy old bachelor," the door at the farther end of the room opened, and the wily Marcel appeared with two large bottles in his hands. He placed them on the table, displaying as he did so a showy ring or two, and then said, "Monsieur le comte sends you these magnums of champagne with his wishes that you drink the health of his son and heir."

A chorus of exclamations greeted this announcement.

At last, when quiet was partially restored, Pierre asked, "And the young countess? How is she?"

"As well as can be expected," said Marcel, repeating the diplomatic phrase which the doctor had used in telling his master of the great news.

"Won't you stay and have a glass with us?" asked the cook graciously, as in the capacity of hostess.

"Thank you, no," replied the great man; "it is not my brand. Good-night to you all."

Sundry sly winks and shrugs went the round of the company as he walked majestically away, but the good news prevented any ill-natured remarks, and they watched Pierre in eager silence as he carefully cut the wires of the cork, and without spilling a drop sparingly filled the glasses he had already placed on the table. He then handed one to each of the party, and standing in their midst held his own up, and said in a solemn voice : —

" I am the fourth Richer that has served in this chateau. My father, grandfather, and great-grandfather all have lived and died for their masters the Counts de La Roche. I am the last, and I leave no one to follow me, but I am none the less faithful for that. Here's health, strength, and virtue to the young master. It's not very likely I shall see him count, but until I die this old hand shall do its best to work and slave and save for him. May our Lord and the Blessed Virgin and the Saints help me."

" Amen, and Amen," cried the others, crossing themselves at the holy names, and then clinking glasses and drinking gravely.

For a moment no one spoke, all more or less moved by Pierre's little speech. Then Jacques shook his ruddy face, and said huskily: "It's an awful serious matter, having a child. I know, for my first is only ten days old. Poor Monsieur le comte."

" *Poor Monsieur le comte!* " exclaimed the cook with energy, heaving her ample proportions to an alert position. "Poor Madame la comtesse, you mean."

The other women echoed her scornful laugh, but Jacques held his own.

" No, my sympathies are all with him. In all my life I never suffered so much."

" *You* suffered ! " snorted the cook.

" Yes," he answered firmly. " I was in such a state that my mother-in-law could not make me go for the nurse ; she had to send a little boy."

" Jacques, you try my patience," said the cook ; " you had better hold your tongue and not talk about matters you know nothing of. I, who have had twins, could say a word if I would."

" Yes," chimed in the chorus of women, " you had better keep quiet, Jacques."

" Ladies," continued the groom, " you all have known, or will know, what it is to be mothers, but you can never, never, know what it is to be a father ; and for a sensitive man like me " — Here he paused, and looked round for Pierre to refill his glass ; but the butler, true to his self-imposed duty, during the discussion had slipped away with the second magnum, which he would hoard, magpie-like, for his master's benefit.

For a moment silence reigned. Each woman glanced stonily at the groom, with the exception of the laundress, the ugliest wench who ever plunged her red, mottled arms into soap suds. She giggled and looked coy.

Perhaps this sign of appreciation encouraged

Jacques, for he continued : " Yes, for a sensitive man — and all my family are sensitive, too. Now my mother-in-law has no just knowledge of the higher feelings, for when I was needing all the sympathy I could have, she pushed me off my chair, and called me a — ladies, she called me a — lout."

" Right she was, too," said madame cook energetically ; and Jacques, looking about, saw a lack of friendliness that seemed to wound his tender organization, even the laundress having a distant bearing. So he rose, wrapped his heavy scarf about him, and taking his hat said goodevening.

" I will carry the good news home to my wife," he said. " And if by chance Madame la comtesse should want a wet-nurse for the baby, perhaps some one will say a good word for my Marie."

" For *her!* " retorted the cook with fine sarcasm. " Oh no, Monsieur Jacques ; but we will recommend *you* for the position, as you seem to be so entirely at home in the whole affair."

Jacques retired abruptly amid a burst of shrill laughter, and the four women drew nearer together for a bit of gossip.

" The heir will have his pockets well lined," began the laundress. " They say the countess owns a hundred gold mines in America."

"If she owned a thousand, Marcel and the count would soon make an end of them," answered the chambermaid, setting her basket aside: and drawing close to the fire, she thriftily turned back the skirt of her dress, displaying thereby a neat petticoat, and two trim well-shod little feet. The cook instinctively drew her large list slippers under her dress, and the laundress stared in wistful admiration.

"How you hate Marcel, Jeanne," she said.

"I know him," returned she significantly. "He has every fault: he is stingy, insincere, cruel, and greedy."

"You may well say that," chimed in the cook. "What did he do last All Saints', and he pretending to be a good Catholic? Our bishop proclaimed it a fast, but the bishop in the next department did not; so what does my gentleman do but go to Monsieur le comte and tell him that he had heard of a fine horse at Blois, only to be seen that day. He gets a pocket full of money, skips over the line, eats a fine breakfast, comes home and says the horse is sold."

"Like master, like man," said Jeanne with a touch of bitterness. "I pity the poor young countess, that I do."

Pierre, who had crept in with his usual noiseless tread, heard this last remark.

" A nice one you are, to be pitying a fine lady like that," he exclaimed.

" La, you frightened me, Monsieur Pierre," returned Jeanne, forgetting her scorn for men in the presence of one.

" I wish I could frighten you all into loyalty," he said severely, looking round the little group. " It 's a sad sign of the times when the domestics discuss and pity their masters."

" Loyalty breeds loyalty, Monsieur Pierre," answered the cook solemnly. " Would n't any of us die gladly for our old mistress? and as for the young one we have yet to see what she may be. But, Pierre, you and I are past the age when we can shut our eyes to facts, and you know as well as I do that Monsieur le comte is not worthy of his name."

" Hush, woman ; is there no family pride left among you ? "

" There might be if Monsieur Maurice had been our master," said the cook with enthusiasm. " *There* is a gentleman for you. I was a slip of a girl here when he was born in the old wing," she continued, noticing with a look of scorn only Jeanne's giggle at the word " slip." " It was the same room where the new heir is now, and if ever a boy lived who was a nobleman all through it was Monsieur Maurice."

" This is treason," said Pierre angrily. " We

have no right to say what we think of our masters : you gabbling women would be better employed saying your prayers for the baby who has come to bear the name we ought all to feel proud of."

"He 'll have money enough to keep it up, won't he ? " asked Jeanne.

Pierre shook his head dolefully. " I 'm not sure any fortune can stand the extravagance of these days. They tell me that the young countess is as rich as the emperor ; but if you could see the way things go in my pantry — Dear, dear, it makes me sad. Think of finding a bottle of cognac open, hardly a glass out of it, left uncorked all night. That is what I see almost every morning. But I hope I may be spared long enough to teach the new count a little economy. And now the fire has burnt out, and it is too late to put on a fresh log. So good-night, and remember the heir in your prayers."

CHAPTER XVII.

To Sylvia the world seemed to have **receded,** and to have left her in a universe of her own, of which the baby, *her* baby, was the sun. Nothing was of any consequence to her outside the four walls of the room which held him. What did she care for emperors or dynasties in comparison with her king? Here at last was something of her very own, to love, to live for. All the exalted dreams of her past seemed to be entirely forgotten by her in her new interest; she did not even remember that she had ever longed for any greater excitement than to see the baby in his bath, or feel him in her arms. The old room with its faded tapestries was an enchanted glade to her, and the fairy prince had come whose touch was to transform it all. Every experience in her life had unfolded a new petal of her nature, and now the great mystery of motherhood had come to show glowing, radiant depths in her character.

For the first weeks she was absolutely happy. Even the daily call from Philippe failed to depress her; every perception unconnected with

her child seemed to be muffled, and incapable
of any intensity of sensation. She wished that
the daily round of little duties, each so vital
in its relation to the baby, might continue forever. A woman less absorbed, or more selfish,
would perhaps have found some sadness in the
reflection that she came first in no heart about
her; but Sylvia never noticed that only old Justine gave her as much attention as she did the
newcomer. There was pathos in the situation:
the young, beautiful woman who had given her
all to support the tottering columns of the ancient family, and who lay there beamingly happy,
not demanding any recompense for herself, only
grateful that at last God had given her some
one upon whom she could lavish the wealth of
love that had never yet found an outlet. Unsuspected capabilities of affection showed themselves, surprising herself. She wondered where
the knowledge came from that taught her how
to handle the little bundle so cleverly.

When she grew strong enough to sit before
the fire, and dress or undress the baby, what delight was hers. He was a fine specimen, and she
reveled in the deep creases, drawn with geomet-
rical precision, round the fat red arms and legs,
the sweet curve at the nape of his neck, and the
delicious hollow in the small of his back. Sylvia
used to wonder that the important Parisian nurse

did not think these points as wonderful as she did, and felt almost wounded when Justine unwarily remarked that she herself had been a prettier baby. Madame de La Roche alone satisfied the demanding mother, for according to her no child so healthy, so beautiful, so intelligent, had ever come into the world; the older woman used to feel her youth renewed, and often marveled that she was still open to such serene content as now enveloped her.

Philippe was proud and pleased. Sylvia appeared to him in a new light. As the mother of his son she had the right to an important position in his regard, and she should have it. She did not jar on him now in her helplessness as she had when, strong and independent, she had claimed her rights. To him she assumed a more becoming, a more feminine attitude, and he resolved to forget the past, and let her see the broader power over him she might acquire by a greater show of submission. It was not surprising that her quiet attitude of self-protection had annoyed him, when one considers his education, for he had never seen a woman assert herself before. Had he been in love with his wife, this would have amused him ; feeling as he did, it had only served to widen the distance between them. But now, he reflected, things would be different : they had a common interest, a mutual object in life, and if they did not pull together in future the fault should not be his. He would give up all gambling ; his former resolves went for nothing ; then he had had no stimulus to aid him, but now, for the sake of his heir, he would rival old Pierre in stinginess.

The January income arrived early in December, as Sylvia had requested, and Philippe determined with a violence which betrayed how little likely he was to keep his resolution that he would not run in debt for another franc, but struggle through the coming quarter on the small sum that remained in his hands after he had paid his debts of honor. He fortified himself by going to Sylvia's room, and watching the baby from a discreet distance while he vibrated between mother, grandmother, and nurse. As they sat there the afternoon mail was brought in by Pierre, who never failed to pay his daily respects to his young master, mingled with a few warnings to the nurse against draughts and baths. Sylvia let the letters lie unheeded while she smilingly watched the butler's clumsy attempts to attract the baby's notice.

" He has fine blue eyes like Madame la comtesse," he said, as he turned reluctantly away.

" You can't tell at his age what color his eyes will be," said the nurse haughtily ; " they may come out green, or brown, or yellow for all you know."

Sylvia tore open her envelopes. " Ah," she said, " Flora Lee-Blair is coming down to-morrow for a few days. That is very kind, for she hates the country in winter."

In his heart Philippe wished that she hated it more, so as to prevent her from coming to trouble him ; he knew what she wanted ; it was no kindness that brought her, it was because she had spent all her money. He had entirely forgotten her, and it gave him a rude and unpleasant shock to remember that in a way he was pledged to provide for her. He could not put her off ; it was embarrassing enough that she was obliged to remind him of her need, and he could not offer her a small sum, either. He saw but one way out of his difficulty : to go to Paris and play for high stakes ; if he won, well and good ; if he lost, there were his old friends the Jews. So it happened that when Flora arrived in the chill dusk of a January evening,¹ driven by anxiety to take this step, she was annoyed and disgusted to hear that her intended prey had slipped through her fingers, and that his train, taking him to Paris, had passed hers leaving it.

Sylvia was in her salon waiting for Flora with a curious, reluctant feeling : it seemed to her that the peace of the past weeks was to be disturbed ; but she determined to show her friend how grateful she was for her kindness.

She was always pursued by a sensation that she was in a way responsible for Flora's welfare ; it was for her that she had hired an apartment in Paris, and begged her to live in it and keep it in readiness for a possible visit.

As Mrs. Lee - Blair followed the servant through the stone corridors, echoing to the click of her high heels, she shivered more from gloom than cold. The drive from the station had depressed her, the country seemed so wide and empty after the crowded, brilliant Paris streets. She made an effort, however, when she came into Sylvia's presence, and the two women kissed each other with every show of affection.

" How well you look, dear girl, and how extraordinarily happy."

" Thank you, Flora. I am well, and when you see my boy you will understand why I look happy. Let me take your wrap. Are you frozen ? "

" Almost," said Flora in a preoccupied tone. She forgot that the ostensible reason for her visit was the baby, and that she ought to put on a semblance of interest. Long habit, more than nature, had made her own affairs of such paramount importance to her that only when her mind was at ease about herself could she afford to indulge in sentiment about her friends. Now she gave a dismal look over her shoulder, and crouched nearer to the fire, spreading her turquoise-covered fingers to the blaze.

"How can you bear it down here, Sylvia? Upon my word, this room seems larger to me than the Place de l'Étoile ; are you never frightened sitting alone with all those pale, weird ghosts of birds and beasts on the walls ? "

"No, I like them, and I love the space," answered Sylvia. " Dinner will be ready directly. Will you go first to your rooms ? "

"No ; I am afraid of the staircase. One never knows what may be round the corners in those winding affairs. Let me wash my hands in your room, and forgive me to-night for not dressing ; I am so tired."

Sylvia looked at her attentively. There was a new ring in her voice, something out of tune and uncharacteristic of her usual jolly, rather reckless way of speaking. This was not the time to ask questions, but the hostess resolved to find out the trouble, and remedy it if possible.

"I still dine in my own salon," she said, leading the way to her room, and lowering her voice as she approached the sacred shrine where the baby slept. " We have taken the whole suite for a nursery," she added, " and Monsieur de La Roche has gone back to his bachelor apartment in the other wing. He left no end of messages for you, and wants you to be sure and wait for his return. He will be in Paris for a few days only."

Flora made her hasty toilet, her spirits both heightened and depressed by this speech. If he wanted her to wait for him financial matters were not so bad ; but the vista of tête-à-tête dinners with the old countess, and the childish fear she felt of the grim chateau, with the gray, far-reaching night outside, made present discomfort blot out future gain. She did her best, however, and when she returned for an hour's chat with Sylvia before going to bed she was her old entertaining self.

The next morning brought clear cold sunshine. She dawdled over her dressing until the second breakfast, admired the baby enough to please even Sylvia, and somehow the day slipped by. The third morning, just as she was beginning to fear that she might go mad or die from dullness, she received the joyful news that Philippe would arrive at noon. This meant that her adored Paris was only a few hours away from her, and she decided to leave La Roche as soon as she decently could. She was sitting with Sylvia when his carriage was heard in the court. He came instantly to his wife, and Flora was impressed by an air of subdued excitement in his manner, brought into strong contrast with

Sylvia's calm reception of him. Just at that time he counted for almost nothing in her life, absorbed as she was in her child. He met Flora with a distant courtesy that he always affected before outsiders, and then asked eagerly for the baby. The nurse was summoned, and the most important member of the family was brought in. Then for the first time Flora noticed a slight uneasiness in Sylvia, a flutter, like that of a mother bird when some human eye rests on its nest where the little ones are. She did not rise from her chair, but her eye followed Philippe's movements restlessly, and her hands stirred, as if they would have snatched the child from its father's arms. He did not hold it long, and when he gave it up to the nurse, Sylvia was again herself. The whole thing was so slight that only a close observer would have noticed it; but it struck Flora forcibly, and roused a feeling of remorse in her heart.

At that moment came the sound of the first bell for breakfast, and Philippe left them, begging Mrs. Lee-Blair to wait for him to return and take her to the dining-room. A lusty cry from the baby made Sylvia rush to the nursery, and Flora was left alone to face the new and unpleasant sensation that she was to a large degree responsible for this marriage, and that it meant anything but happiness to her friend.

She tried in vain to sweep away the disagreeable conviction that she had done wrong, and it was in full possession of her when Philippe returned, and offered his arm.

As they crossed the court slowly, he said in a low tone, " There is a large sum at your banker's for you."

Something seemed to whisper to Flora: " Refuse it ; it is yours by fraud."

She hesitated, and he went on : " If you invest it properly, you will get a very pretty income from it, and, to be frank, that would be a wiser method than depending on me. Heaven only knows what may happen to me in these unsettled times."

She saw her chance now to still her conscience, and secure her future at one stroke. " Thank you," she said. " I feel now that we are quits. I have helped you, you have helped me ; that 's fair, is n't it ? " — and as they stood on the doorstep she put out her hand. He took it with a smile of relief, and held it for a moment. He was triumphant. His play had been wonderfully lucky, and in two evenings he had won enough to shake off his old man of the sea forever, he hoped.

Sylvia had in the mean time returned to her salon, thinking that Flora was still there. Finding the room vacant, she had gone to the window, and saw her husband and her friend across the court, their hands clasped. The memory of what she had seen at Trouville, and but idly noticed at the time, flashed into her mind; there, on the sands, they had shaken hands just as now. All her false feeling of calm and security left her, and she was forced to take up the old burden of suspicion of her husband. That meant, the father of her child. She must be on her guard, and seek for traces of that stained inheritance in the creature she loved the most. Was nothing perfect in this world? No affection pure, and without its flaw? As she put these questions to herself, the thought of the bond between Maurice and his father came to her mind, the mutual confidence and appreciation that riveted it, and tears arose in her eyes. They were true and noble; they deserved each other's love and admiration; the finest qualities of the strong old blood seemed to have been diverted from the main branch, and to have concentrated themselves in the unrecognized offshoot. As Sylvia stood motionless at the window, regardless of the servant arranging her breakfast, she thought more of Monsieur Regnier than of his son. The brave, wise old man seemed a tower of strength to her.

" I wonder if he would consent to be the baby's godfather," she pondered. " He could help me in so many ways; he told me that day how hard

I must work to counteract the evils of inheritance."

This idea took a deep root, and she found to her pleasure that the countess approved of her choice. Philippe shrugged his shoulders, remarked that old Regnier was not a good Catholic, and could not be expected to advance the boy's worldly interests much, but when he saw that his mother's heart was wrapped up in this choice, he submitted with a very good grace.

Now that Sylvia had begun to take up her old life, she gradually lost in his eyes the transient charms that soft silks and laces had lent her while she was still on her sofa; with her every-day clothes she seemed to him to have assumed her former irritating freedom of action; he ceased to feel at his ease in her presence. Perhaps some subtle thought-transference made him dimly sensible that she was studying him minutely, trying if possible to find some quality in him to admire, so that in later years she might say to her child, " Be like your father in that." Day by day she grew more hopeless of succeeding : her eyes saw him now with a dispassionate severity, more fatal to softer sentiments than any glow of vehemence. " If I might only respect him, I would not ask for love," she used to think.

It had been a relief to her when Flora took her rather abrupt leave the day after her inter-

view with Philippe, on her way to her own
people in England, but her instinct had been
right. The visit, short as it was, marked the
end of that interlude of perfect content and joy.
From that day the love she lavished on her child
grew in intensity, but it had lost its absolute
serenity.

Through the winter she did not see Monsieur
Regnier. At first he was confined to the house
by a heavy cold, and the doctor sent him, as
soon as he was able to travel, to the Riviera;
like many men he wrote short and unsatisfactory letters, except to Maurice, and Sylvia used
to have an uneasy feeling that she had lost him
out of her life. But this sensation disappeared
when his answer came to her request that he
should be the baby's godfather; it was short,
but showed plainly his pleasure at having been
asked. He came back to La Source in April,
and the first Sunday in May was appointed for
the christening.

The old church at the end of the village road,
with its curiously carved font, had always been
preferred by the family for occasions of this kind,
to the chapel in the rock, which seemed more
like a tomb than a place of ceremonial. The
distance was short, and the morning dawning
clear and brilliant, the party set out on foot. It
was a great day for the little hamlet; the peas-

ants dressed their houses with garlands and strewed the way with wreaths, roses, and bluets. The church bells rang a joyful carillon. Every inhabitant who could walk or be carried was in the place before the church, and those who were too old or infirm to leave their houses were propped close to the open casements, and in feeble voices blessed the young heir, who made his royal progress, gorgeous in laces, and sleeping in profound content on his pillow. The interior of the church was cool and dim after the wealth of color and light without; the altar to the Virgin was ablaze with candles, and made the only brilliant spot in the noon twilight. The old curé, arrayed in white and gold, stood by the altar, and the chateau party clustered about him, the peasants hanging round the door, as if afraid of intruding. Sylvia had learned with some amusement that she was not called upon to choose her boy's name, and listened half bewildered to the apparently endless string of appellations given to him. But it mattered little to her; and her mind soon lost count of the present in vague, hopeful dreams for the future. It was soon over, the witnesses signed their names in the sacristie, and once more they came out into the dazzling sunlight.

The children of Madame Lefevre, who had been given a holiday for this joyful occasion, each carried a satin bag filled with sugared almonds, the time-honored dragée of French christenings. The party halted on the church steps, and with shouts of joy the little Lefevres showered the candy in handfuls among the village youngsters. Then what a scrambling, scuffling, and romping ensued. Sylvia watched this scene, new to her, with much amusement; the presence of the count awed the young villagers into comparatively good behavior, and inevitable cuffs and blows were given and taken in good part. Little Maurice Lefevre evidently thought the whole proceeding a deplorable waste of good candy, and for every meagre handful that he threw among the scrambling crowd, he deposited as many sweeties in his mouth as it could well hold. Sylvia, to her delight, heard Pierre the butler commending the young gourmand in the following words: "That 's right, my little master, save some; don't throw all to the riffraff down there, and I 'll give you a big sou for what you bring back to the chateau, and you shall see them on the table at breakfast."

"Got plenty of sous at home; like bonbons best," said Maurice in a husky voice, his mouth full. This false step attracted his mother's attention, who snatched his satin bag from him, declaring in shrill tones how sure she was that he had made himself ill. Young Maurice, strong in the knowledge that he had secured more candy in ten minutes than he had ever had in his short life, submitted to this indignity, and stood sturdily licking his fat, sticky hands, getting faint and ever fainter reminiscences of past joys from the operation.

Philippe, who thoroughly enjoyed playing the good lord of the chateau on occasions like this, stood laughing and encouraging the good-natured buffeting, until the last dragée had disappeared; then, taking a leather bag from Marcel, filled with half francs, he scattered the silver in the air; it fell, a shimmering shower on the joyous young peasants, and the christening party resumed its way home amid their prolonged cheers.

This was a busy day, for custom demanded a breakfast for the entire village, and on reaching the chateau the long tables were seen spread in the court, over which a temporary awning had been erected. Everybody who was able, turned out for this festivity, and after the villagers had been left to themselves, their tongues wagged vigorously, as the middle-aged recalled the christening feast of the present count, and a few old treble voices made themselves heard as they told of incidents remembered either personally, or vicariously of the day when his father was carried about this same court,

wrapped in the same laces which now adorned
the unconscious cause of the feast. At last the
moment came when Pierre, who had superintended the repast, appeared in the dining-room
to tell his master that the revelers wished to
drink the family healths. The baby, dewy and
rosy, after a long sleep, was placed in his
mother's arms, and they all stepped out into the
court to receive their compliments.

The curé, who stood a little behind the others,
was seen to smile and nod at a remark whispered in his ear by his sacristan, after which he
stepped forward, and took his place at the head
of the principal table.

" My dear friends," he began, " I have been
asked to propose the healths, and I accept the
invitation with great pleasure. First, let us
drink long life, honest endeavor, and happiness
to the most important person present. Here 's
to Master Baby."

" Hurrah ! hurrah ! " rang out the honest
cheers, making the small hero start at first, and
nestle closer to his mother ; then, growing accustomed to the sound he opened his lips in a wide,
toothless smile, and added his tiny gurgle to the
turmoil.

After this, the names of the other members
of the family followed in quick succession, the
curé being too wise to do more than mention

them, knowing that the young feasters were
already longing for the games. As he brought
his list to a quick close, the sacristan rose, and
blushing to the tips of his wide-spreading ears,
said in a voice, unmanageable from shyness,
"There are two more healths to be drunk; the
first is to our good curé."

Again the cheers burst forth, and when silence
reigned he continued : " And the second is to
him who seems to belong to us still, as much as
when he lived here, for I 'm bound there 's not
one of us, who in the old days knew sickness, or
losses, or sorrow, without knowing at the same
time the kind heart, the good words, and the
open purse of Monsieur Regnier. He has always been our friend, my lads, and here 's to
him."

This had not been expected by the peasants,
and for a moment their slow minds did not
receive the idea readily ; but when they fully
understood, a tumult of shouts and cries broke
out ; the men tossed their hats in the air, and
the women waved their arms and screamed
shrilly. Sylvia tingled with the excitement
which is caused by a touch approaching the
heroic, and the countess put her handkerchief to
her eyes. Monsieur Regnier, more surprised
than any one present, tried to speak when the
noise ceased ; there was a tender light in his

eyes, where a tear rose slowly. His voice trembled for a moment, but he steadied it.

"Jean Meunier is right in one thing; I am your friend, but I want to confess that I never knew how much you were mine until now. You have just given me a pleasure that money cannot buy, that time cannot steal; and I thank you from my heart. I will give you one more toast only, and I want you to drink it reverently. Here's a hopeful future to the family who have for so many years lived in these old gray walls. In days long past the counts de La Roche protected and cared for the little town lying at their gate, and in war they fought side by side with the peasants. Let this feeling of mutual help continue, — go on living useful, honorable lives, and remember that next to our mother, France, you owe allegiance to your count."

Although he spoke with the fervor of enthusiasm, Monsieur Regnier's words roused but little excitement among the good people. They cheered in a perfunctory manner because it was evidently expected of them, but their hearts were in the broad field where games of all sorts awaited them, and they gladly trooped away.

Madame Lefevre, who had been pleased apparently by the compliment paid to her father, now spoke to him.

" It was all very pretty, dear papa, but what a blessed opportunity you missed. Surely that was the moment to speak to them of their souls — not of fighting."

" Either was out of place at a feast, Berthe, and I should have remembered that peasants see but one thing at a time. I must apologize," he added, turning to his friend the countess, " for striking a false note, but my boy's letters stir me so just now that I am bubbling over with patriotism."

Philippe gave a slight laugh which might have meant almost anything : to Sylvia's surprise he had behaved in a most respectful manner to Monsieur Regnier during the day, and she dreaded any word from him that might wound the brave old man. She did not appreciate the admirable deference of youth to age, taught and practiced in France with a rigor which commands admiration, and this being the first time she had seen the two men together she had prepared herself for possible friction.

Before more could be said, Berthe again broke in : " Papa, you should rest now for a little while ; you look tired."

" Yes," added Madame de La Roche. " Philippe and I must look on at the games and give the prizes. Berthe and Monsieur le curé will help us, but you and Sylvia will be all the better for a little quiet."

" You are right, as always. Come, my chatelaine from over the seas, let us go to the garden,
and make up for all the time lost through the
winter."

Sylvia went with him gladly, and side by side
they descended the broad steps leading to the
garden. After the noise and disorder of the
court, littered by the rude chairs and tables, and
the remains of the breakfast, the garden seemed
a very Eden of quiet and order. The formally
trained fruit-trees were in full bloom, and made
screens of flowers. The paths were bordered by
stunted apple-trees cut down to two feet from
the ground, and growing in garland-like branches;
with their profusion of pink and white blossoms
they made Sylvia think of a young girl's ball-
dress edged with a fragrant wreath. The foliage
of the trees was scanty as yet, and the hills on
the other side of the river could be plainly seen,
with here and there a hawthorn bush looking
like a puff of white smoke in the blue distance.

After wandering about for a while they came
back to the cedar and seated themselves. Their
talk, of a scattered sort at first, always came back
to the mainspring of Sylvia's heart, — her little
Louis, as he was to be called, after Philippe's
father. They spoke vaguely of his future, and
recalled the varied elements which mingled in his
small make-up. Sylvia told all that she knew

of her parents' characters, and they contrasted the uneventful lives of the sturdy old Boston merchants on the one side, with the glittering, exciting existences of the counts who had preceded and lived through the reign of terror.

"Find the best in him, and develop it to your utmost," said Monsieur Regnier at last. "Respect his Anglo-Saxon instincts, and trust him; don't keep him under lock and key, but give him his head; show him that you believe in him, and leave the rest with God."

This talk gave Sylvia cheer and faith, and helped her to face the future with a new, steady courage.

CHAPTER XVIII.

I⊤ was a hot blazing afternoon in July of 1870. Monsieur Regnier came swinging through his shady park, still vigorous in spite of his years, a picturesque figure in his buff linen suit, his wide hat shading his bronzed face, and the ends of his gay bandanna cravat fluttering in the breeze caused by his own rapid motion. He had been in his cornfields, and had superintended the last day's work of getting in an unusually good harvest, and now he was coming home to a bath, which would be followed by a romp with his little grandson, a calm dinner, and peaceful evening — for Berthe was in a retreat for some fancied misdemeanor. He could hear the happy laughter of the boy, who was splashing with brown bare legs in the stream behind a clump of bushes ; the house lay slumbering in the sunshine, the gay awnings all stretched, and not a breath stirring the ivy on the walls. The large Pyrenean sheep-dog who lay before the open door looked at him with one sleepy red-rimmed eye, and welcomed his master with a few slaps of his tail on the gravel.

" Poor Médor, good old fellow ; you need not try to be polite, it's too hot," said Monsieur Regnier, passing him.

As he entered the cool spacious hall the butler came forward to meet him with a telegram. He tore it open, and his genial face glowed with delight.

" That is well, Jacques ; that is well. Monsieur le capitaine will be here in an hour. Order the sorrel mare in the dog-cart to meet him at the station. Albert had better drive, for I wish to prepare things here. Send Mère Robin to me at once."

Then followed the happy planning between the old housekeeper and her master ; he suggesting this or that in a tentative manner, to be met only by scarcely veiled scorn.

" If Monsieur thought the captain would like a duck just out of the farm-yard, tough as a board, of course *she* was not the one to say no ; but it seemed a pity not to use some of a seven weeks old lamb she had just ripe for cooking ; and as pretty a little broiler as any one ever saw she had all ready for the master's dinner ; then if that lazy unfortunate of a Jacques would catch them a fat carp, *that* would not come amiss ; she had a fine melon too " — and so the dinner grew to proportions Monsieur Regnier would never have dared to hint at. Then came the

cares for Maurice's favorite wines; two bottles
of the choicest were placed in the stream to
cool; and this occasioned the calling of young
Maurice from his dabbling to be made ready
for his uncle. A merry, rosy chambermaid prepared his room, much hindered both by grandpapa and grandson, who kept running in and
out, heedless of her, with soap, cologne, a hundred little nothings, the boy giving a finishing
touch to the decorations by putting a woolly lamb
on casters in the centre of the table.

This was the first time in two years that Maurice had visited La Source, and all was in gala
dress to welcome him. As he left the train at
the little station, for him crowded with memories
of former home-comings, he looked much more
changed from the boyish soldier poet whom we
saw last at Trouville than the lapse of time war-
ranted. He had grown heavier, and in consequence seemed less tall, and more symmetrical;
the old impetuosity of manner had been replaced
by one outwardly more calm and restrained,
but those who knew him best perceived that it
covered a deeper, more significant recklessness.
Few men allow their entire lives to be ruined by
a disappointment in love, and Maurice had too
high a regard for his duty in the world where
Fate, Chance, or Providence, call it what you
will, had placed him, to shirk it in any partic-

ular. Nevertheless, worthy as he regarded his
position as one of the defenders of his country, absorbing as his hidden talent of poetizing
was to him, underneath his outer life worked the
hidden grief, altering him in many subtle ways,
— sometimes for the better, sometimes for the
worse. He had been strengthened by the first
acute suffering that he had ever undergone ; but
at the same time he had been hardened by the
shock given him by Sylvia when he was deceived
by her actions into believing her unworthy of the
love he had lavished upon her. He had become
bitter, in short, and showed it in his profession
as a soldier by proving himself a stern martinet
to his men, requiring as much risk of life and
limb from them as he himself was willing to un-
dergo ; and in his profession as a poet by a tinge
of fatalism, which made his later verses more
fascinating but less wholesome than his earlier
ones.

As he drove along the familiar road this July
afternoon, the groom found him strangely silent
and unapproachable : he remembered former
visits when the young master had scarcely given
him time to answer his eager inquiries for every
man, woman, child, and beast at La Source ;
to-day, after asking for the family, the captain
remained without speaking for the rest of the
drive. In truth he was wondering a little at

himself, and had a vague sensation of disappointment that he was undergoing a dreaded ordeal with such an absence of emotion. He had looked forward almost with horror to going home, in spite of his love for his father; he had imagined that being merely in the neighborhood of Sylvia would be distressing. He had never forgiven her; not because she had rejected him, but because she had pulled down his ideal of womanhood, never, as he believed, to be replaced. In the years since his last visit to his father he had learned a difficult and bitter lesson, and now, as the sorrel mare dashed along through the park, his heart beat no faster when the old house came into view, and even the sight of his father in the doorway brought no emotion beyond a calm pleasure.

As a rule we feel strongly on one subject only at a time; and although it was for the moment in abeyance, the thought which made the blood tingle in Maurice's veins was the knowledge that a month more might see him on the field of battle, defending France. Monsieur Regnier said not a word as his son leaped from the dog-cart, but his outstretched arms and shining eyes told of his welcome.

The silent, eloquent gesture swept away at one stroke the unreal veil of indifference which had shrouded Maurice's sensations; quick and vivid came the realization that this was the one thing in the world left him worth having, this unselfish, devoted love. An unexpected lump in his throat prevented him from speaking as he jumped to the ground. At their last meeting tears would have come readily; but after suffering as bitter as that through which Maurice had gone, tears are rarer and more painful.

Young Maurice effected a welcome diversion by breaking in on the sad silence. He pulled his tall uncle's coat, and said triumphantly, " I am in knickerbockers ! " at the same moment displaying a diminutive expanse of white duck.

" Well done ! What 's your tailor's name ? Some men in my regiment may want to employ him," said Maurice senior, glad of the chance to speak naturally.

But it seemed that he had trodden on delicate ground, for, much to the disgust of the newly breeched, his mamma had thriftily employed a seamstress for the great occasion, and the unhappy woman had pursued her task under difficulties, such as resolute kicks during the " tryings on " and scornful reflections on her sex in more calm, but yet bitter moments.

Grandpapa, who had sympathized in silence with the young hero, prevented his reply by changing the direction of his thoughts.

" Come, my boy, you must take your uncle to

his room and tell him not to be late for dinner. He does n't know yet how dreadfully afraid we are of Mère Robin when mamma is not here to protect us; and if we keep her soup waiting, we can never tell what may happen."

So with a cloud of memory brushed aside, young Maurice thrust his hands deep in his pockets, and with much care led the way up the shallow staircase to his uncle's room.

" I 'll come for you in fifteen minutes to show you down," he said. As he spoke he watched Maurice's face to see when the glory of the lamb would burst upon him; but as no remark appeared to be forthcoming, he continued: " I have given you, for always, my lamb; his name is Albert, for the coachman. I love Albert, and I am going to be a coachman when I grow up, so I can crack a whip and say *sapr-r-r-r-isti!* "

" Thank you a thousand times," said Maurice, a little unsteadily, seeing the boy shut the door, leaving him alone with a sense of relief.

Then he sat down by the table, put his head by the woolly lamb, and let a wave of sorrow sweep over him; remorse for his hard mental attitude towards his home; a regret for all the regrets that he had lost; a passion of tenderness for his father. He had allowed a woman to interfere with his love and friendship for the only person in the world to whom he meant

everything, — and what a woman! She had
proved what she was by selling herself to Philippe for his name ; she had been so wanting in
tenderness that she had found her one way of
rejecting him in an insult ; and for her, he had
spent the last years, perhaps in verity the last
years of his life, far from his father. She had
been right in one thing ; he *was* a coward! It
had been fear of her, of the suffering she might
still be able to inflict on him, that had caused him
to deprive his father of the thing he cared most
for, his companionship. His heart had grown
used to absence, and habit had made him forget
that the old cling to the young, more than the
young to the old. Now the welcome, the little
attention to details in his room, the ready affection of the boy, almost a stranger to him, which
proved how often he had been told of the absent
soldier ; above all, the shining, wistful eyes of
his father as he met him with outstretched hands,
showed him where he stood in his home. His
former greed for glory and devotion to his country appeared now to him like heathen virtues,
when he thought of the anguish one bullet might
cause if it found him out. A quarter of an hour
had not passed when he opened his door and
went into the hall, to find Maurice the younger
braced against the wall watching for him, but
he had lived long in that time.

" I was waiting, Uncle Maurice, to see if Albert felt quite well; when mamma is away grandpapa lets him come to dinner and sit in her chair; but you know he is yours now, and you may not think that is proper ? "

There was a question in the voice which quivered slightly.

" Oh, I am sure it is proper, and I want to consult you a little about Albert," answered Maurice, returning and gravely shouldering the lamb. " You know I must go away in a few days, and probably I shall be obliged to live in a tent; now I am afraid that Albert would n't like a tent."

" I should dearly; but Albert never was in such a thing; he might be scared."

" That is what I think, and I wish you would keep Albert until I come back, and call him yours; then we can decide about the future."

" Yes, yes," shouted Maurice junior, in wild joy at having his darling restored. " Give him, I 'll take him, and he may have some babies before you get back, the guinea pigs do all the time, and then you can have a baby Albert."

With this comforting remark he hugged the stiff and ungainly lamb to his heart, giving vent to his feelings by a series of high, shrill yells, which rather interfered with the sentimental turn his uncle's thoughts were beginning to take.

They found Monsieur Regnier waiting for them in the dining-room, and the party of four seated themselves, Albert having a napkin carefully pinned about his neck by the butler.

"That's the way the coachman does," explained his young owner; "he eats his soup like this, and it tastes lots better."

He illustrated by bringing his spoon directly in front of his mouth, the point aimed at it, and his chubby elbow extended before him; the result was that his chin received a double share, and he was resigned to a scrubbing from the butler and a reprimand from his grandfather only by seeing that they were both inwardly amused by his imitations.

After the boy had gone to bed Maurice and his father went out on to the terrace, and as they sat in the dim light of the stars low hanging like jewels on the velvet darkness of the sky their talk turned to grave themes. It was evident that a war was imminent: and this prospect weighed on them, and made their words few and scattered. Since Maurice's arrival Monsieur Regnier had had his bad moments also; he had been obliged to acknowledge the fact thrust before his eyes that Maurice was a boy no longer. The lines about his mouth and eyes told of youth lost forever, its spirit being killed. The former expression of enthusiasm and pleasure had been replaced by one of firmness and sombreness; the Greek beauty embodying sentient enjoyment had disappeared; and now in Maurice's face was found evidence of deep experience and struggles with life, giving him a new interest, and to his father a deep pathos.

They sat in the warm night air, the silence broken only by the bell-like notes of some distant tree-toads. Monsieur Regnier was thinking painfully, and trying to see his way clear. Maurice lighted a fresh cigarette by his nearly burnt out one, and the ruddy light as he puffed at it made his face plain for a moment. The glimpse decided his father; he spoke:—

"You will soon be leaving me, my son, and we must steel ourselves to face the worst." The old man's voice was unshaken now, although the joy of meeting had unmanned him. "If you fall, I should wish you to die at peace with all the world; are you prepared for that?"

The deep solemnity of his father's words and manner impressed Maurice.

"I think I am, with one exception," he answered. "There is one person I can never feel at peace with — one insult I can never forgive."

"I think I know who it is, — the wife of Philippe."

In the obscurity Monsieur Regnier felt rather than saw the sudden rigidity which seized

Maurice, — his very breathing seemed to have ceased; he did not answer, and his father continued.

"Last autumn, when she too was facing a possible death, she told me that if she died you were to know that she had been the victim of a cruel deception regarding you; that she could not endure the thought of an unknown future, while in your eyes she seemed to have been actuated by unworthy motives. I tell you this, on the edge of the grave in a way — and I trust you to respect the confidence."

"Thank God," said Maurice, his voice stifled, the rigidity all gone, as he bowed his head in his hands.

Monsieur Regnier touched his shoulder gently as if afraid even of so much sympathy.

In a few moments the younger man spoke again. "Tell me about her. Is she — happy?"

"I think in a way that she is: she is doing her duty, which always brings calmness, if not something better, and her child is a help to her. The countess is very fond of her."

"And he? does he treat her well?"

"Ah, my boy, we both know what Philippe is — and we both know what Sylvia is. That is my answer."

It gave Maurice a strange thrill to hear his father speak of her by her name, and added confusion to his already confused thoughts. This was a solemn, a sacramental hour for him.

"My father," he said, a profound quiet in his manner, "I will, with God's help, respect your confidence in me; I will not ask you more about her, not even if she still has any love for me. You have given me great happiness, for I can still believe in woman's purity, for she who stood to me for ideal womanhood is once more on her pedestal, and is worthy of the love with which I honored her. I must never see her again, but if I fall you will tell her — everything."

"If I survive your death, I will."

Silence fell again on them, and they spoke no more that night.

"I must never see her again," Maurice had said, and he had meant it; but destiny willed otherwise. The next day he was by the brook rigging a small boat for his nephew, while his father sat near looking at them and trying to blot the dread of the future from his mind. Each was so intent on his occupation that Sylvia's carriage rolled up the avenue unnoticed, stopped when it came to the point nearest to the little group, and Maurice was warned of the approach of newcomers only by the boy's shout of "The baby, the baby!" as he scampered over the grass. Then he looked up, and saw, coming towards him, the countess, Sylvia, and a woman

with a child in her arms. Sylvia saw him as in
a dream at first; for a moment she did not believe the evidence of her eyes. Then, when convinced, she turned swiftly to the nurse, and
clasping her child to her breast with an instinctive desire to shield herself with her most powerful armor, she faced the man whom she had
cruelly wronged, and whom she loved.

His skin, browned by the African sun, showed
no change ; but his face was tense as he lifted it
after kissing the countess's hand. She and the
children were the only unconscious ones there,
for old Justine's keen eyes saw much that lay
beneath the surface.

Monsieur Regnier greeted the countess, who
turned to him from his son, apologizing for having spoken first to Maurice, and then said with
no sign of embarrassment. "My son used to
know la Chatelaine Sylvie. so no introduction is
necessary."

They both bowed in silence, and still with
her little Louis in her arms, Sylvia took the garden chair that some one offered her, and listened
as one afar off to the talk between the others.
At first she did not heed what they were saying. Then gradually the words telling of approaching war came to her, and she realized that
Maurice was here only to say farewell to his
father before joining his regiment. She altered

the baby's position on her lap, and as she did
so she sent a swift glance at the man who had
grown so strangely familiar to her in spite of
absence, and for a moment she felt a pang of
disappointment. This stern, composed officer,
whose habits of authority had impressed themselves on him, was not the impulsive, enthusiastic boy who had lived in her memory. She
saw that he had complete mastery over himself,
whilst she dared not trust her voice to say the
simplest words.

" How long shall you be here, Maurice ? "
asked Madame de La Roche.

" I may be called away at any moment," he
answered. " I dare not leave La Source even
for an hour, for I might miss my telegram."

There was the agonizing unreality of a dream
in the situation for Sylvia ; the seconds were
slipping away ; every heart-beat marked a step
towards their separation, and nothing could be
done but sit in passive silence.

" Uncle Maurice is beautiful in his uniform,"
announced the boy in a loud tone ; " all blue
and black curly fur. I think I would rather be
a soldier than a coachman after all."

Monsieur Regnier laughed, glad of the interruption, and the countess began to question the
boy. Maurice let his look rest for one moment
on Sylvia. This was all they could claim now,

these stolen glances. The agitation of the meeting had driven the color from her face, and her features were rigid ; but all the old grace of form and movement was there, and in spite of the evident mask of impassiveness which she had assumed as a shield, Maurice caught a new expression in her eyes : they seemed deeper, more womanly, less imperious than formerly. The pride and fire that used to fascinate him in other days had given place to a tender look of comprehension and sympathy which appealed yet more strongly to him now. He vaguely noticed, remembering it afterwards, that she had lost the subtle, mocking air, and even in her silence she struck him as less complex. Manlike, he paid little attention to his own sensations ; he probably would have found it difficult to express them, in spite of his poetic temperament. For nearly two years the memory of Sylvia had been as a festering, hidden wound. Time was helping him to become used to it ; but his whole life was jarred by the underlying pain, and now he was free once more. Experience which had softened her had strengthened him, and the bitterness which had made the pain was now swept away by his father's revelation on the previous evening. He was, for the time, contented to know her worthy of the best love of which he was capable ; he was even reconciled to her marriage, and to seeing her with her child in her arms. He forgot Philippe, and remembered only the fact that good still lived in the world. And on that day he felt himself ready to face death cheerfully, having the warm glow of justified self-renunciation at his heart. Had all gone well for them in the beginning, had no falsehood separated them, they might have lived their lives in peace and happiness; but the slow ripening that experience gives might never have been theirs. Rain must fall on the peach as surely as the sun must shine on it before it is perfect.

" The baby must not be out too late, Sylvia," said the countess. She felt that they were robbers, stealing the golden moments of these last days from father and son.

" Order the carriage, Justine," said Sylvia.

They were the first words that she had uttered, and she spoke now with an effort. Her mother-in-law saw that she was pale, and fancied that she felt ill, but tactfully did not speak of it. A few more nothings were said, and then the carriage was heard. The countess rose, and taking Monsieur Regnier's arm, walked slowly across the lawn ; Justine held out her arms for the baby, and then followed, little Maurice at her side, and they were alone. Sylvia tried to speak : she wanted to say two words only —

"*Forgive me*" — but she could not. It was not pride that stopped her, it was a tightening of the throat. Still she seemed in a nightmare, unable to awake, and Maurice's eyes, reproachful and sorrowful she thought them, were crushing her to earth. The idea came to her that hell must be like this, with all the capacities for suffering and making others suffer, with no power to resist.

Maurice saw how agitated she was, and he had the key of the situation ; but he could only trust himself to say one short sentence: "We are friends ? "

" Yes," she whispered, her head bowed.

They stood silent, motionless for a moment, then she turned away, and he followed. One has seen mourners come away from a freshly filled grave with the same gestures, the same looks ; and these two, this man and this woman, had in truth just buried their past and their passions. Monsieur Regnier felt the significance of the interview. He had a double sorrow at the sight of the suffering under his eyes, and as he sat alone by the little stream after the others had all gone, he prayed with his whole being that this might indeed be the ending, and that the future might have in store no remorse, even if it promised no joy.

When the carriage reached the park limit,

Sylvia left the others, and said that she would walk home. She wished to be alone for a while before facing Philippe. A calm, full of a sadness which was not all pain, had succeeded to the racked feelings of the past hour: she was like a tired child, worn out with excitement. When she reached the garden, deserted even by the gardeners to-day, she sat down on a bench and soft tears began to flow. It was a luxury to cry, hardly knowing why. She bent her head in her hands, and sobbed gently, without violence. Some slight movement caught her attention, and lifting her head she saw Justine looking at her, her eyes like those of some dumb animal. When her mistress stirred she threw herself on her knees before her, and gave way to her distress.

" Oh, madame, oh, my lamb, mine ever since you were a baby, it cuts me to my poor old heart that you should suffer, and it is all my fault — all — all. I told you that in France things were different — that French hearts were not cold like those in your country — that honor came first — and I lied, for it is bad, bad all through here — and you suffer, my baby, my little lamb ; you, who are worth them all."

Sylvia was startled by this outbreak. Since the day when she had burst forth, having heard Philippe call her a spy, the old woman had gone

stolidly on her way, showing her devotion more
by acts than words, and her mistress had hoped
that the whole affair was forgotten in the new
interest brought by the baby. But Justine had
marked Sylvia's pallor that afternoon at La
Source. She found her in tears, and she felt with
renewed agony that she, deceived herself, had
helped to deceive the idol of her earthly love.

The countess laid her hand on the bent, heaving shoulders, and said: "My poor Justine, it
is not your fault, dear heart, it is my own if I
suffer. Every one must bear the burden of his
own failures, and you must not grieve for me.
You have been a mother to me, and I want your
love, not your tears."

Sylvia's own voice nearly gave way; the faithful sympathy touched her deeply.

Justine rose, drying her eyes. "I am forgetting my errand; Monsieur le comte is called to
Paris, and wishes to bid Madame la comtesse
good-by."

As she followed her mistress towards the
chateau her brain was at work. She saw but
one object in life worth attaining, Sylvia's happiness. Her perception, sharpened by her devotion, had found out the secret, so carefully
concealed. She had divined what lay beneath
the surface. And now there was coming a
glimmer of hope to her. The count was called

to take his place with his regiment. War was coming, battles, fighting; why should there not be a ball waiting for him? Time would show, and in the mean time the saints were good and answered prayers — sometimes.

Sylvia found Philippe ready for instant departure; he was giving orders to Pierre. The old butler was to be at the head of things, during the absence of Marcel, who accompanied his master.

The countess was listening, the light of enthusiasm in her eyes making her look like another woman. When Pierre turned away, leaving the three alone, she took Philippe's hand.

"My son, thank God for the chance He holds out to you; you have it in your own hands to add honor and glory to your name; see that you do it. Our country needs you, my boy; fight for her; give her your best; redeem your past. If you fall, leave a name that your son will reverence; a name that will spur him on to great deeds on his part."

"Yes, yes, my noble Roman matron, I will come home with my shield, or on it, I promise you; but there is no time for talk now; I must hurry. Remember, if the horses are required, try to hide my hunter; I can't hope to find one like him every day in the week. Now good-by; good-by, Sylvia — where's the boy?"

The nurse was holding the baby in the court, and Philippe, with a hasty kiss to mother, wife, and child, jumped into the dog-cart, and laying his whip over the plunging horse's back, dashed under the arch and was gone.

As the sound of the wheels died away, Sylvia thought, "It may be for the last time; I may never see him again; O my God, help me not to wish it."

The countess, who had stood fixed as a statue since her last words, turned to her son's wife, suddenly looking very old. "My dear," she said, " it may be that this is the opportunity God has given him; let us go and pray for it."

The two women, wife and mother, descended to the chapel, and each prayed after her own manner. For the moment Sylvia felt that she could forgive Philippe everything if he gave her son an inheritance of honor.

CHAPTER XIX

THE year of 1870, tragic and disastrous to France, strode on with unfaltering step. The Empire, gay, glittering, brilliant as it had been, suddenly was no more. Like a soap bubble it had floated, bounded, danced before the dazzled eyes of the people. One day it jostled against something else that was round too, but also heavy and black — a Prussian cannon ball — and instead of the beautiful spectacle the people saw nothing; the mist in their eyes came from the nation's tears. But although the Empire was no more, France remained; and from every hamlet, rough thatched cottage, nay, from the very caves in the rocks, rose her sons to defend her. Frenchmen love their country with a steady, wholesome affection. They are in love with Paris, which to them represents all the fascination which this world is capable of giving., When their queen was invested by the invading forces, and lay helpless, surrounded by enemies, anxiety changed to frenzy. A new army arose like magic along the line of the Loire, and revived the fainting hope of the nation by wresting Orleans from the Germans. From this army came an effort to relieve the capital, only seventy-five miles away, through a combined movement: a sortie from within, and an attack from without upon the same point of the ring of investment. All communication with the hapless city by land or water was cut off: only the air remained, and it proved a fickle element to the besieged. Notice of the hour at which the sortie would be made was sent out from Paris to the army of succor four days in advance, by balloon. How many hopes and fears followed its flight through the air into cloudland! Alas, it was swept by contrary winds into Norway. The sortie, made without the expected coöperation, failed miserably, and the army of the Loire, attacking too late, was broken into pieces.

The histories of that unhappy time give one the impression of reading in a nightmare. Every other paragraph begins with a useless *If*; "if" such and such things had not happened, the French would have been victorious; but such and such things *did* happen, and the Prussians made steady progress. Again did a new army arise, and yet another effort was made to free the beleaguered capital. Under the command of Chanzy, the new levies marched up from Blois along the right bank of the Loire to meet the Germans under Prince Frederic Charles. Again was there sharp fighting before Orleans, and again did the French make headway against the invaders.

These victories, and the elastic courage innate in the French character, responded vigorously to the encouragement received. The underlying romance of their nature recalled to them that France was in still greater straits when a maid came forth from the mists of obscurity and delivered her country, leaving behind her an image unequaled in history in its supernatural distinctness. Once more they rallied, and among the voices that rang the clearest with words of enthusiasm and determination was that of Maurice Regnier. In spite of his dash and energy, he had so far escaped wounds and imprisonment.

The fresh army was in a position to aid a new sortie from Paris, and all eyes in its ranks were turned skywards in search of another messenger from their capital. Without such coöperation nothing could be accomplished. The Red Prince was before them in superior numbers, and only by heroic courage and much loss had headway been made against him. While Chanzy rested for a moment on the right bank of the Loire, ready for a dash through the opposing forces if the word should be given, the Prussian was

stealthily moving a reserve division of twenty
thousand men down the opposite bank to cross
in the rear of the French and encompass him,
as at Sedan and Metz and Paris, following, as
always, the fatal coiling tactics of the boa.   The
bridge over the Loire at Blois had been cut, and
the Prussian move having been made known,
Maurice was sent to post a detachment of troops
to prevent the crossing at Amboise, twenty miles
below, towards which the division was marching.
They must be blocked at any cost.   It was a wild
wintry day, and as Maurice at the head of his
troops had ridden in the early morning across
the dreary country lying between Vendôme and
the Loire, the wind swept over the open plains
in uninterrupted brutal triumph, now and then
adding to the discomfort of the riders by veering
suddenly, bringing a storm of loose sand against
their faces.

Unconsciously Maurice had likened it, in its
fury, to the enemy against whom he was fighting
with the last desperate hope that despair sends
ahead to make the end yet more bitter.   A thousand thoughts unconnected with warfare came
into his head as he drew near the familiar place.
There, across the river, lay La Roche ; whether
Sylvia was still there he knew not ; not so far
away on the same side was his own home, and the
impossibility of stopping there for even a mo-

ment weighed on him gloomily. Although he was ignorant of it, Sylvia had remained at the chateau with the older countess ; the younger men-servants had been drafted, the women had left from fright, and the horses had been given up, so only old Pierre the butler and Justine remained with them.

Madame de La Roche had signified firmly her intention of staying in her home. " It has sheltered me for many a year, and even my presence may be some restraint if the Prussians take possession ; but you, Sylvia, had better take the boy and go to some safer place."

But Sylvia was as staunch as her mother-in-law. " We must hold it as far as we can for little Louis," she said ; and so day after day they pursued their peaceful way, the quiet of their lives broken only by the reports, distressing in their unreliability, of the war, and at times by the far-away boom of the cannon. Madame de La Roche devoted herself more than ever to the peasant women, who remained at home to care for the aged, the infirm, and the children, for the men were with the army. Sylvia took all the care of the baby, leaving Justine to help Pierre with household duties. In spite of the monotony of her days, she was more peaceful than she had been since the first weeks of her married life. Philippe was with the beleaguered forces in Paris; at last he was in a position of which she could be proud. He was suffering for his country, and in her eyes one deed of heroism blotted out years of ignoble conduct. She could talk to her boy of his father now, without feeling like a hypocrite. So she taught little Louis to say Papa, and showed him Philippe's portrait. The year-old child varied his more unintelligible remarks with liberal *papas*, to his grandmother's great delight. She, poor soul, was not Spartan where her only son was concerned, and secretly resented Sylvia's attitude, which she divined in some subtle way.

Between these two women there was mutual love and respect; but the close intimacy of their present lives showed clearly that a barrier existed, and always would exist, between them. It might have been the result either of race, creed, or temperament; perhaps a combination of all three; and there it stood, solid, impenetrable, never yielding to circumstances. But a strong bond made them cleave one to the other: their love for the child, who grew sturdy and rosy, and laughed when he heard the distant, sullen roar of the cannon, trying to imitate it.

For the second time in her life Sylvia followed in imagination the progress of two hostile forces with vital interest. Her heart beat as warmly for her adopted country as it had for her father-

land. Once more she turned with sickening
eagerness to the list of killed and wounded after
an engagement. Ah, those were moments to
make young women old — to teach unaccustomed
lips to utter real prayers. And every day the
incense of supplication arose from the inmates
of the grim old castle by the river, but with it
mingled a dark smoke, not sweet-smelling surely
to the saints — for night after night when her
day's work was completed, old Justine demanded
the death of her master and the freedom of her
mistress.

Maurice had completed his arrangements at
the farther end of the Amboise bridge, and had
given all necessary directions to the officer to be
left in command, when the westering sun warned
him that if he wished to reach headquarters that
night he must start at once. Even as it was,
the last half of his journey would be in darkness. In December, evening falls early and
suddenly upon Touraine. He was joined by a
brother officer, who was on his way from Tours
to headquarters with a handful of troops; and
having mounted their scarcely rested horses,
they began their journey up the right river bank.
The road lay over some low hills; the wind was
in their faces, and bitterly cold. The clouds,
which all day had rolled in serried ranks across
the sky, cleared towards the west, showing a

wide band of clear, pale green; when the sun reached this open space a sudden glory spread in broad, level stretching beams over the landscape, turning the dull gray of the leafless trees to dusky purple, and glittering in the windows of La Roche, which lay just opposite the riders, across the river. Without checking his steady trot, Maurice, from the instinct of long habit, let his eyes wander with half conscious admiration over the transfigured scene. As he looked he saw something which caused him to draw his breath sharply; it was a mere speck against the sullen sky, touched by the rays of the sun; not a bird — its course was too steady for that. It grew larger rapidly, increasing in size even in the brief space between seeing and speaking of it.

" Look," said Maurice.

His companion followed the direction of his gaze, and he too was moved. The two men drew rein, and halted on the upland, the patient horses hanging their heads. No word was spoken; the moment was too full of hopes and fears for speech. In the dark object, apparently motionless, but steadily growing more and more distinct, might be hanging, between heaven and earth, the last chance for France. It might bring the long expected word from Paris of another sortie; it might mean victory. So motionless sat the two officers that they might have been mistaken for carven statues, had not the tossing manes of the horses given a touch of life.

Now the balloon was so near that the hanging car could be distinguished. Blow, good wind, it has proved a friend after all!

At last Maurice spoke: " I can't make out what their course is. As they are going now they will be over the Prussians in another five minutes."

" No, they won't; they are keeping straight down the river," returned the other; " they are making for Tours."

" Look at the curve in the river, and you will see what I mean."

As Maurice spoke he pointed down to where the Loire makes a turn from right to left, " an elbow," the country folk call it; and towards this turn swept the balloon.

" They are coming down, they are trying to land!" exclaimed the officer, and the handful of men behind gave way to their intense interest.

" They will want us to fasten the cord; they must see us now. Four of you dismount, and be ready to catch the rope they will let down. Look alive, now!" commanded Maurice impatiently, as the soldiers, stiff with cold and long riding, stumbled awkwardly forward.

As he had said, a trailing rope was let down from the car: it was so near now that the heads of its occupants could be easily seen peering over the edge : lower and lower it came in a long slanting line, directly towards the soldiers ; Maurice measured its progress with his eye.

" A little farther back ! " he shouted. " For God's sake secure it ! "

The cords were not ten feet above their heads. Maurice looked up, full into the pale face and starting eyes of Philippe de La Roche. At that moment the treacherous wind veered, and with sudden, uncontrollable fury caught the balloon in its grip as if it were a feather, tossed it sideways from the uplifted hands of the men, and swept it across the river, over the enemy's forces. At first the disappointment was so keen and bitter that only the groans and oaths of the soldiers were audible. Then Maurice said, " They may even yet sweep over the Prussians, and get round to Tours : " but as he spoke a scattering fire of rifle-shots was heard from across the river. They saw the balloon sway violently, right itself, waver, and then sink rapidly behind the trees on the verge of the forest.

" All is lost," said the officer, lifting his hand and letting it fall heavily with a tragic gesture.

Maurice did not answer ; his brain was presenting a vivid series of pictures to him : he looked earnestly down at the river below. The water showed its inky blackness between huge blocks of ice, which were crashing and crowding on their seaward way; at this point where the course turned, the current whirled them across from the right to the left bank, where they shocked against the stable ice making out from shore, and rested a moment until again jostled on. He might succeed in crossing the dangerous centre of the current in safety. Beyond this death-like flood was a hope, perhaps the last, of saving France. He did not hesitate after his plan had formed itself.

" All is not lost yet," he said, rousing from his reflections, and replying to his companion's last words, which he seemed to have just heard.

" How do you know? We are helpless — everything seems to combine against us. Once let those rascals over there get hold of the poor fellows, and it is good-by to them and to hope."

" Listen to me," said Maurice, kindling. " I know one of the men in the balloon, and he is as familiar with every inch of the country about here as I am. If any one can escape, he can."

" What good will that do him if he has plans of a sortie? He may escape from them, but he can't reach us."

" I think I may reach him, though."

" How? You can't cross the bridge at Amboise; and look at the river."

" There is my hope!" exclaimed Maurice.

" You are mad, Regnier; you would be crushed between the ice before you had gone ten feet; you are too valuable a man to risk your life needlessly : I must beg you to consider the danger."

" The only danger I consider is that of failure ; we have been prudent too long in this unhappy war — now it must be neck or nothing. Come on, old fellow, and I 'll explain my plan."

As he spoke he turned his horse's head to the right, and went down a stony lane leading to the river bank. By this time only the highest branches of the trees were touched by the sun : in another fifteen minutes it would be dark. The little band followed Maurice, and clustered about him as he halted close by the stream. In the hollow they were more protected from the wind, but the air was full of the strange, swishing noise made by the floating ice. Maurice had told his companion what he intended attempting on their way down, and now there was but one more word to be spoken. He dismounted, and busied himself with unbuckling his spurs while he said, " If I never come back you will see my father for me ? "

" Of course."

" Tell him why I went, and that my last thought was of him."

The officer could not answer, but he patted Maurice gently on the shoulder. An act of heroism, even in heroic epochs, never fails to touch some underlying string which responds to it. While hearts beat warm and fast at such deeds, there is good in the world. The one moment of emotion passed, Maurice became practical again. He filled his flask from his friend's, taking first a long drink to offset the cold. He gave necessary directions about their further journey to headquarters ; he pointed out a farmhouse where his horse was to be left in case he needed him later — and all this time, in the gathering gloom, the spectral ice came crashing on ; some of the cakes lodged for a time against the projecting bank.

"I think it is dark enough now," said Maurice.

"It will be as black as midnight in ten minutes," said the other.

"Well, then, here goes ; here's a block that may carry me. Good-by, old man."

"Good-by, and — and " — The sentence was never finished ; there are times when words seem impertinent.

Stamping through the thin layer of ice formed over the shelving sand by the bank, Maurice plunged into the black water, staggering a little as the floating ice knocked against him ; the large block he had picked out was coming rather slowly on the edge of the current, but the bed of the river sank suddenly just at that point, and he was breast high in the stream before he could clutch the edge nearest him. His grasp did not stay its course, and he was carried on into deeper water; there, he managed to slide on to the rough surface; the cold penetrated to his very heart; he burnt with it, and his physical sufferings became intense, lying there, the bitter wind sweeping over him, his drenched clothing freezing rapidly; but under, and over, and round the pain rose a pæan of triumph from his soul. This was his chance, and he had had the strength to seize it. Death was naught, honor much. His innate bravery and high spirits rose with the sense of adventure. The previous years of gloom and disappointment had subdued but not killed his natural buoyancy, and in this moment of peril it rose to the surface. He half turned on his novel raft and waved a triumphant farewell to the shadowy forms on the shore. Then he began to take keen note of the direction in which he was advancing. He was still on the edge of the current farthest from the other shore; he must alter this. He began to make the motions of swimming with his feet, guiding the float always to his left. Slowly he attained the centre, and then, inch by inch, he gained the further limit, making his way carefully through the floating floes. It was hard work, but the icy chill was lessened by his exertions. At last he had steered

himself so that he was being swept directly towards a bar of sand that made out from shore ;
it was covered with a brittle coating of ice, and
in the dusk Maurice could not tell exactly what
it was ; but he saw that it was stable, and he
felt that, if he once managed to get behind it, he
could reach the land. The block bearing him
swirled through the calmer water and came with
a slight shock against the soft sand. By this
time he felt numb with cold, and his legs almost
refused to bear him when he had torn away from
the ice to which his clothes were frozen.

As he staggered along, crashing the thin covering of ice, for one moment his spirits faltered.
It was the sight of a light shining from behind a
low clump of bare, stunted willows, which caused
him to stop and wonder if his perilous journey
had been in vain. It had never occurred to
him that the Prussians would think it necessary to set a watch by the river, but the wavering
flame made him cautious. He would creep up,
and perhaps he might escape under cover of the
bushes.

But as he made this resolve the light came
towards him, and to his relief he saw it was a
torch held aloft by an old woman whose wrinkled
yellow face, and skinny, half-bare arms were
shown in its flicker. The wind carried its flame
in a long line of fire and smoke at right angles

to its support, and blew the gray hair and fluttering garments of the old peasant in a thousand ways.

As Maurice came within the radius of the blaze, she turned towards him, waving one withered arm. " Have you seen her ?" she asked. " Have you seen my little Marie, the youngest of them all ? You who rise out of the water surely have a message for me."

Maurice drew himself painfully on to the bank, and seating himself began to rub his well-nigh frozen feet. " No, mother," he said. " I have seen no one. Who is it you want ?"

" My baby, the youngest of them all. When Denis went off to fight he gave her to me : he said I must care for her, now that his wife was dead. And she came to play by the river — she slipped under the ice — and she is gone to the ocean. Listen, my boy, listen — I have lost children of my own ; I have cried over them. But they lie up yonder in the graveyard — and I could still sleep in my bed. But this little one cannot rest — she turns, turns in the water, and it is cold for the child — and I cannot sleep while she is drifting away to the sea. O my God, it is hard to bear, and my boy Denis fighting and thinking of his baby in her warm cradle, while the river is her cradle, and the ice is her coverlid."

Maurice saw that her poor mind wavered like the light of the torch, and found a moment for pity. "Never fear, good mother," he said gently. "The saints will make your baby's bed softer and warmer under the ice than you could in your own home."

"You think so?" exclaimed the woman. Her sunken eyes gleamed from beneath the loose, overhanging lids, and she laid her claw-like fingers on his arm.

"Ah," she added, drawing back; "you are a gentleman. I beg Monsieur's pardon a hundred times."

"All right," said Maurice, rising to his feet. "Will you do me a good turn, mother? I am freezing cold; can you give me some dry clothes?"

"Surely, surely," she answered, eager to serve him. "I have my boy's Sunday suit at home; come with me."

"But I do not wish to be seen, and you live in the village."

"Nay, nay, my home is in the rock, beyond the hamlet; you will be safe."

He persuaded her to extinguish her light, and then followed her from the river, through the little belt of woods, across the highway, and so to the further end of the village street. There, in the face of the cliff bordering the river road, was a low, wooden door; the old woman opened it, and Maurice followed her into a room cut out of the heart of a rock.

A few red embers threw an uncertain light on the uneven floor and rough ceiling where the marks of the implements which fashioned this rude dwelling still showed. When a lamp had been lighted Maurice saw that everything was scrupulously neat. The place was warm and dry; and the silence within after the tumult without, a relief. He paid but little attention to the bed with its gay chintz curtains, or the old carved buffet in the corner, from which his hostess drew a pile of neatly folded garments. He was mad with impatience, and her slow, fumbling movements were hard to bear. At last she pattered across the floor, and hung the wardrobe on two chairs drawn close to the fire.

" Now I will leave Monsieur to dress, while I milk Minette, for he must need something to stay his stomach," she said, casting a last look of pride at the stout, well-made clothes.

Maurice lost no time in making his hasty toilet. The absent Denis evidently made up in breadth what he lacked in height, and although not a good fit, still the young officer managed to make things go until it came to the Sunday coat. This was impossible, and he looked ruefully at his arms, the sleeves stopping halfway up. At this moment the old woman returned, a bowl of goat's milk in her tremulous hands.

" Mother," said her guest, " has n't Denis a blouse ? "

" But — yes, only Monsieur is a gentleman," she answered reluctantly.

" Well, a blouse is never amiss ; may I borrow that instead of this coat, which might be hurt? I have some rough work ahead of me to-night."

She sighed, but obeyed him, and in another moment he had settled himself comfortably into the dark blue blouse, which he fastened round his waist with his leather belt. He had caught sight of a beret, a flat cap of dark woolen, sometimes worn by the peasants. " There," he exclaimed gayly, " now I am ready for everything."

He drank the bowl of milk, adding some cognac from his flask, and then he turned to the peasant. " Tell me, mother, are the Prussians about here ? "

She eyed him curiously. " Those devils? yes," she answered, crossing herself. " They are here, there, everywhere — coming and going like ants in a hill."

" Are any at the chateau ? "

" How can I tell ? Probably yes — but I know nothing."

He put two gold pieces into her hand. " I may come back and I may not," he said. " But as long as I live you will have my gratitude."

She looked at him with admiration in her puckered face. Where is the woman too old to feel a gleam of pleasure in youth and beauty and dash? — and as he stood in the dim room Maurice represented all three, his eyes gleaming with excitement from under the cap resting on his dark hair, his muscular figure all alive with impatience. He was gone before she could find words to thank him, confusion running riot in her misty brain.

It was easy enough for him to find his way after the first moment. While he had been in the cottage he had laid his course. Having learned from his hostess that the chatelaines were still at La Roche, he thought it probable that Philippe's first move would be to hide himself in his old home. The peasant had given him some vague accounts of Prussian soldiers who had passed by the village during the day, and he knew that the country must be bristling with them. There was even a chance that some might be at the chateau; at all events he must act with caution. Avoiding equally the highway and the village road, he struck into the fields lying between them. Although not yet six o'clock it was very dark. The fierce wind tore rents in the clouds through which the stars looked with frightened eyes. The warmth of the old woman's fire, the dry clothes, and the exercise had chased away the deadly chill; he felt a pleasurable glow without and within; the excitement of his adventure, and the hopes its success held out, filled him with exultation. He knew every foot of the fields he was crossing: just where the little brook ran under its sheath of ice, and where the great walnut-trees stood. A hundred more strides would bring him to a narrow lane, which was bounded on the other side by the high stone wall which surrounded the park. Ah! here he was at the hedge marking the limit of the field, — two yards or so on one side was a gate. He felt along until his hand rested on the upper bar; then he vaulted lightly over. As he came down on the other side he grazed against an unseen body; there was a sudden movement; sparks were struck from the frozen ground by the kicks of a startled horse; an oath in German rolled out, and against the sky Maurice saw indefinitely the forms of mounted men. He had half a chance, and quick as lightning he seized it. Before the horses had ceased their plunging he had run along the hedge, crossed the lane, and with a spring had gained the top of the wall; no easy matter, but a feat that he had accom-

plished more than once in his boyhood. As he
dropped to the ground on the other side, he saw
a light shining from one of the windows in the
old wing of the chateau. He thought that it
came from his own former room, and his one
idea now was to gain admittance, so as to warn
Philippe to hide if he had gained shelter there.
The land fell away so abruptly towards the
river that the room, although on a level with
the court, was at least twenty feet above the
terrace on which Maurice soon found himself.
He must communicate with those within, but he
dared not run the risk of showing himself, for
the mounted soldiers in the lane gave evidence
of a close watch kept about the place. An old
ivy, gnarled and strong, grew against the solid
rock, forming the foundation of the east wing,
climbing nearly to the eaves. With this for a
ladder Maurice began his ascent.

The crashing, tossing trees kept all other
sounds in abeyance, and he could not tell if he
had been followed ; he must take every possible
precaution. This was not the first time that he
had gained his room by means of the ivy. As
a boy, after some frolic, undertaken from the
mere love of adventure, he had crept through
the windows in the dim morning light, tired
but triumphant, and trying to imagine himself
some hero of romance. Now there was no time

for imagination, hardly for memory. He was scarcely as light as in those bygone days, and his progress was a slow one, each branch being carefully tested before he reached the level of the window. He tore a spray of the vine, and always mindful of the eyes that might be peering through the night, he swayed it against the glass, and in its protection looked into the room. He could only see a small part, owing to the thickness of the walls; but the picture that met his gaze drove for one brief moment all thought of war, of danger, all hopes and fears from his mind. There in the brilliant firelight sat Sylvia, her child on her knee; she was " trotting him to market," and over the fury of the gale Maurice could hear the bursts of laughter when, the perilous journey made, she gathered the baby in her arms, and cuddled him, kissed him, hugged him, as if, indeed, he had been restored to her from some danger. Her cheeks were rosy, her eyes shone, and she looked as if no sorrow or care had ever laid a withering finger on her. It was a vision of home and joy, set in the midst of war and desolate hearth-stones. It was an embodiment of the Paradise that he might never realize, and the unsuspected watcher felt one sharp stab of regret. But this was a time for action, not feeling. He sank self with an imperious effort of his will, and struck sharply against the glass with the spray.

Sylvia heard the three blows; she knew it was a sign, and her whole figure stiffened, but she went on with the game as if she had noticed nothing, her white lips forcing themselves to say the familiar words, "Trot, trot to market, trot, trot to Lynn," and all the time she was thinking rapidly, "An enemy would not knock, it must be some one who needs me. Is it — oh, no — it cannot be — he." Again came the three taps, more imperatively than before.

She was alone; the countess and Justine away, Pierre in the distant kitchen. It might be her husband who appealed to her. She shrank from the thought. Then she blushed at her own cowardice, nay, worse than cowardice, for she had protested so much, and now recoiled from her clear duty. Putting little Louis on the hearth-rug, she went with a steady step to the window; she drew the heavy curtain across the embrasure between herself and the light; then with a cautious hand she undid the fastening, and opened the casement.

A voice, so close to her that she started, said, " It is Maurice Regnier; are you alone?"

" Yes."

" Let me in : I must say something to you."

She threw the window wide, holding the curtains firm so that the wind should not sway them aside. Maurice jumped in, and closed all behind him, fastening the heavy wooden shutters, before he turned ; then out of the storm and the darkness he came into a harbor of light and warmth. Sylvia looked at him, puzzled at first by his peasant's dress, and then for a moment gloriously frightened by the light which leapt unconsciously from his eyes as they rested on her, more gracious, more womanly in her bravery than even his heart had painted her. As their glances mingled, she felt herself carried along by a force more mighty than the wind without, more powerful than any ocean. She knew for the brief space of a second what part nature plays in our lives, and she exulted in its domination and her own powerlessness.

" Pa-pa, pa-pa," said little Louis, with genial welcome from the hearth.

The strange emotion had gone ; the magic had been banished by a child. Maurice was less moved : he had a nation's rescue in his keeping, he thought. This drove out other feelings for the time.

" We are safe from interruption ? " he asked hurriedly.

" Yes."

" Is Philippe here ? "

" No, no. Why do you ask ? "

" He may come at any moment. He has escaped by balloon from Paris. Hark! What was that?"

" Only the wind swaying the tapestry; go on."

As she answered, a wilder blast than the last made the faded green trees on the wall bend and sway as their originals were doing outside.

Maurice continued. " We believe that he may be the bearer of very important news, of plans for another sortie, and the safety of France may hang on this night's work."

CHAPTER XX.

While Maurice was making his way to Sylvia's room, Justine started on a two miles' walk, to a cottage where the countess was nursing a woman sick unto death. The dying peasant had been a servant in the chateau in former days, had married and settled on an outlying farm belonging to the property, and had always maintained friendly relations with the family. Her children were boys, who, with their father, were in the army, so the poor creature was left alone but for the kindly services of Madame de La Roche. Justine had gone to take her leave of Sylvia and the baby before her departure, and had carried a warm memory into the night with her. Her adored mistress had looked up with a laugh which bore Justine back to the days in New England, — one of those rare days when Sylvia had been for the time a happy, simple child. The faithful, passionate, ignorant heart glowed at the thought of the solicitude in her mistress's voice when she asked her if she were warmly dressed, and if her lantern were in good order.

"I hate to have you go alone, Justine," she had said. "It is most unfortunate that Pierre's rheumatism disables him."

To make her trip shorter, Justine had gone through the chapel, thus saving herself the tour of the buildings. She opened the low door, and stepping out, put her lantern down while she turned the large key in the lock, and then hung it about her neck. Although somewhat sheltered by the trees, she found that her walk was likely to prove a difficult one, but she advanced steadily thinking, "*She* is safe from the wind and cold; that is all I care for."

The sick woman's cottage lay in the opposite direction from the village, and nearly a third of the road was in the park. As Justine battled on her way, the wind bore to her the sound of bells from the village church. It was the angelus, the hour of prayer. Putting her lantern down she knelt beneath the stormy sky, looking up as if to pierce the clouds. The light shone full on her strong. square face, with its resolute jaw, and the lines hinting at a capacity for tremendous passions. Devoutly turned heavenward, the foreshortening of the brow and the uplifted eyes gave the expression of ecstasy Perugino so cunningly uses with his saints.

The desire prompting her prayer had grown to be a part of her very being; for nearly a year now she had demanded the freedom her mistress had wept for. At first it was with vague, unformulated phrases, but little by little she had grown bold : the war seemed to her to have been planned by Providence to rid the world of her master, and she no longer scrupled to face the fact that his death was what she begged from her saints with fervent insistence. To-night a hope was in her heart ; Sylvia had been gay and young ; in fact ever since the count had gone away a cloud had seemed lifted from his wife's spirits ; but just now, as she had wished the old servant God-speed, her voice rang with girlish lightness, and Justine took it for a sign of good. Still on her knees, her lips muttering rapidly, she felt a heavy hand on her shoulder, and her eyes met those of Philippe. She recoiled as if she had seen an evil spirit, and crossed herself.

"Don't scream," he said, "or I will strangle you. Are there any Prussians in the chateau ? "

She hesitated, looking into his pale, eager face, which had for her the fascination of a serpent. If she could only keep him away from her mistress, she thought ; if that happy smile could stay a few hours longer on the lips she loved.

" He shall not see my darling," she resolved, and, still on her knees, she lied.

" Yes, Monsieur le comte ; the chateau is full of them."

He cursed low under his breath; he was worn out with fatigue; for the last hour and more, he had been doubling and turning, pursued by the men who had seen his balloon drop; his companion was taken; he had escaped only because he knew the country so well, and his chief object had been to gain La Roche, with its secret passages, where he might find at least a temporary shelter. He might, even in the teeth of his enemies, enter his own home. He decided to try, for his present situation was too precarious to continue; the morning, at the latest, would betray him to the surrounding Prussians.

"You came out of the chapel; give me the key," he said abruptly.

"I dropped it — I have not got it," replied Justine, remembering how easily her mistress's room was reached by the stair in the wall.

"You lie, you old spy," said Philippe. "I saw you from the shrubbery; I only followed you to be farther off. Give it to me."

A lowering, determined look came into her eyes, but she did not speak. His quick ear caught the ring of horses' hoofs far away on the frozen road. He was brutalized by the sufferings he had witnessed and endured; his finer instincts were smothered. With a sudden wrench he pulled the key from her neck, where he had watched her hide it, and without another word slunk away towards the chapel door. For a moment she crouched where his violence had thrown her, one thought clear to her, — he had gone to Sylvia! The smile was to be banished from her lips, the light from her eyes. The agonized appeal once wrung from her, never forgotten by the old servant, " O God, free me ! " had remained unanswered.

Justine raised herself again to her knees; she felt the angry throb about her neck where the cord had cut in from his violent twist. She was the prey of a burst of fury, so intense as to amount to insanity. "There are no saints," she called aloud in defiance ; " if they were true saints they would not be deaf to my prayers. There are only devils in saints' shrines, and they have been laughing and jeering all this time to hear my prayers. I spurn them and all holy things. There is no God — a true God would have let him die. And now he is going to make my darling unhappy again — he never loved her — never — he wanted her money for that woman in Paris. I know him well. I know his deceits. He takes my child's gold and gives it to harlots. Would true saints permit that? No, my new master is the Devil ; I will pray to him." Half crazed by the sight of the man, hatred for whom had grown to be her master passion, dominating even her love for her mistress, she, still kneeling

on the frozen ground, continued: " O Satan, what
is my poor soul worth compared to my child's
happiness?   I give it to thee willingly, if I can
gain her joy.   A thousand years in hell is nothing
for me.   I am only a poor, ignorant old woman
— but she is a flower fit for paradise.   Keep
her fresh, unfaded.   Let her be free, let her be
happy, and I will serve thee for ever and ever.
Amen."

Who can say that the unselfishness prompting
the blasphemous prayer was not more than half
divine?   Did Satan wake while the saints slept?
she wondered, horrified and triumphant, for as
she rose from her knees the hard clatter of
horses' hoofs met her ear.   He was delivered
into her hand ; her petition was granted.

Fast against the driving wind came the horsemen ; she lifted her lantern, and its beams shone
on a Prussian officer riding ahead, with a detachment following, four abreast.   The men saw her
indistinctly ; their leader pulled up, and they
halted in line with military precision.   Satan
was prompt in his answer ; here was her opportunity.   Still shaken by her blind rage, she
obeyed the peremptory summons, " Come here."

She advanced close to the side of the mounted
officer.

" Have you seen any one escaping through this
park ? "

" Yes, Monsieur."

" A Frenchman ? "

" Yes, Monsieur."

" Where did he go ? "

" Into the chateau through the chapel door yonder."

" Who is he ? "

For the first time she hesitated ; then the word he applied to her, which had at first crushed and then exasperated her, leaped to her lips.

" He is a spy, Monsieur ; the Comte de La Roche — and a spy."

The Prussian hesitated ; it seemed to him that this good fortune was a little too fortuitous to be true. " Give me your lantern," he said.

Justine handed it to him, and he flashed the light full on her face. Its stolid, heavy expression — for the eyes had become sullen — reassured him.

" Show me the way ; but remember, if you lead me into any ambush you will be the first to suffer."

" I will tell you how to trap him : he will be in his wife's room ; guard the chapel door well yonder — but you must promise never to betray me, for if Pierre knew he would kill me."

" Don't fear ; lead on, and you shall be safe. Point out the chapel door to my men."

Without a word she took her lantern back, and strode rapidly on, pointing silently to the

door as she passed it. There was murder in her
eye as she extended her hand, but the night hid
it. The officer gave an order in German, half a
dozen soldiers halted, and as Justine led the way
along the terrace, under the moaning cedar, she
heard their blows battering on the solid oak.
Philippe, on the other side, heard them too, and
started from his temporary security. How had
they tracked him? At any rate the passage and
staircase tunneled in the wall, leading to Sylvia's
room, were cleverly concealed, and would be difficult to discover by those not in the secret. He
would hide himself there, but he must try to let
some one friendly to him know of his presence,
lest he be betrayed through ignorance. He was
sure that the chateau would be searched by his
pursuers, and he felt his courage evaporate under
the strain. He let himself out of the chapel, and
felt along the dark passage, until he reached the
winding stairs. Cautiously, stepping lightly,
pausing often, he mounted until he reached the
narrow landing. He found the latch of the door
behind the tapestry, and lifted it noiselessly;
then he heard a voice, a man's voice, — one that
he knew well, — say, " Hark ! what was that ? "
and his wife's answer came, " Only the wind."

He stood listening avidly. He heard Maurice
tell that on him hung the fortunes of France.
Behind him the Prussians were on his track, and

ho well knew that all his pursuers were not wasting their time at the chapel door; the chateau would be searched. He must form a plan and act quickly. As he hesitated, a scheme presented itself to him, clear and distinct; he lifted the tapestry, and showed himself. Sylvia started, and then suppressed the exclamation of dismay which rose to her lips. There was a pathos to her in the sight of this man; he was thin and haggard; a half-grown beard gave him a ragged appearance, not contradicted by his shabby uniform. He who had always been so fastidious about himself had risen to this state for the sake of his country. He commanded her respect, and she was grateful to be able to give it. He lost no time in greetings.

"I am pursued, but I have doubled on them. I have papers for Chanzy in my boots. Maurice, you must help me reach him."

"I will, Philippe; I can get you across the river, and my horse is just opposite; you will reach headquarters before midnight if we have any luck."

"First I must eat and drink. I am famished. Paris has not fitted me out any too well for hardships. Sylvia, get me some food."

"I will bring you something at once," she said; "but first drink this milk."

As she spoke she took up a pitcher that had

been brought in for the baby's supper, and as she poured it out, Philippe heard a confused tramp in the hall.

"No, no," he said, half losing his head; "go for wine, quick, not that stuff."

She set the pitcher down, and obediently started for the door.

"Some one is coming," she said; "hide!" and made a spring to lock it; but she was not quick enough; it was thrust abruptly open, and a Prussian officer strode in. Sylvia saw the tapestry wave as if from the sudden draught, and there, in the full light, stood Maurice alone. He was apparently unmoved, and had made no attempt to escape.

"Ha," said the Prussian, laying a heavy hand on his shoulder, and then throwing a backward glance at the group of soldiers beyond the threshold. "You have given us a good chase, Monsieur le Comte de La Roche, but I have you at last."

"He is not the man you seek, Monsieur," said Sylvia. "Cannot you see by his dress that he is a peasant? He is not Monsieur de La Roche."

The officer smiled. "You are the comtesse, I believe?"

"Yes, Monsieur."

"Then how does it happen that this young peasant is in your room?"

She came close to the officer, and put her hand on his arm.

"Believe me, Monsieur," she said earnestly, "he is not my husband whom you seek. This man is not the count."

There was a ring of truth in her voice that shook the Prussian for a moment.

"Then, Madame, we must make a search for the real count," he said.

"Find the hidden door under the tapestry," he added in German to one of his soldiers.

"I will save you that trouble, Monsieur," broke in Maurice. "I see you are too well informed for me to attempt to escape. I am the Comte de La Roche."

"No, no," said Sylvia wildly. "You must not, you shall not sacrifice " —

"My wife, cannot you give me up for France?"

She understood all that his words implied. It was not Philippe alone, it was his country that he was saving. But his sudden surrender had made the Prussian suspicious.

"You may be the man I want, and you may not be. You French are as slippery as eels. Time presses, but I can't afford to let my little count get away."

All this time the baby, who had been amusing himself in his own way, regardless of friend or foe, dug his fists into his eyes, and whimpered; then opening both arms wide, he said, looking towards Maurice, "Pa-pa, pa-pa."

"Ah, my master, you've done me a good turn," said the officer. "In this cursed land only the babies speak the truth. Come now — be off; you have wasted enough of my time."

"May I have one word with my wife?"

"No, you've had one too many already. Come on."

Maurice turned towards Sylvia, who stood rigid as a statue: she went swiftly to him in obedience to his eye's appeal. He put his arms about her, and as he pressed her to him, whispered, "Forgive me. It is for France."

But she put both arms about his neck, and lifted her face close to his: he could see the little violet glints in her eyes, and the black lashes about them.

"I will save you," she whispered back. "And this is not for France; it is to wipe out the past — the memory of that blow." As she spoke she kissed the cheek she had struck.

"Now I can meet death," said Maurice, drinking deep of her beauty, even at this moment swayed by his enduring love for her.

"That is enough," said the officer. "I am not here for play-acting, but for work. Forward! March."

He wrenched Maurice away, and Sylvia saw

him surrounded by the soldiers. Their heavy boots rang on the stone floor of the corridor. There he went, her hero, once her lover. All life was compressed into this supreme moment of ecstatic pain. She listened as if her life depended on hearing the last sound ; the heavy door into the court clanged ; the clatter of hoofs on the paved way beneath the arch rang out ; then came silence for a moment ; followed by the gallop, now loud, now faint, as the detachment rode down the avenue.

Little Louis had grown sleepy, and began to rub his face and cry. Sylvia pulled herself back as if from a great distance, and tried to realize where she was ; her mind was as yet hardly under control, as she lifted the baby to her lap, and began mechanically to undress him. He missed the accustomed kisses, and laid his chubby hand against her cheek, with a wondering look in his brown eyes. Still with her sensations stony in the reaction from the strain that she had just undergone, she went on with her work, giving the child from time to time an unmeaning caress. Just now nothing seemed real to her, neither the baby nor herself ; they were both like dream creatures. As for Philippe, she had utterly forgotten him, and started when the door behind the tapestry opened, and he peered out.

"Am I safe now? have they all gone?" he asked.

"I think so; I can't be sure," she answered.

"Ring for Pierre, and find out," he commanded impatiently. "Have you no pity for me? I am nearly starved to death."

She put little Louis in his crib, and pulled the bell-rope. Neither she nor Philippe spoke until the old man, twisted with rheumatism, hobbled in. Then she said, "Have they all gone? — is it safe for Monsieur le comte to come out?"

When Pierre saw his master he threw up his hands in astonishment. "Monsieur Philippe," he exclaimed, remembering the old times. Then recollecting himself, he added, "I beg a thousand pardons. Yes, the devils have all gone, carrying a poor peasant to Chaumont, they said."

"Then get me something to eat, quick," said Philippe, for the first time coming into the room. "Bring it in here by the fire, with a bottle of champagne — liqueurs — coffee — cigarettes. Ah, what a feast I am going to have. Do you realize, Sylvia, that I have been eating stewed rats and broiled horse?"

She shuddered, but could not answer.

He continued, his face losing its pallor in the warmth of the fire over which he crouched, and his voice becoming more genial in his growing comfort, "Have one of the other servants light a fire in my dressing-room, and set a hot bath, while my dinner is coming."

"The only other servant is Justine, and she is away, gone to the west farm to bring your mother home. I will do it myself, only — can you spare — the time — ought n't you to make haste?"

His yellowish eyes rested on her for a moment, and then glanced restlessly about. "I can't start without food — I have no strength — I might die on the way," he answered. "But the bath can wait until I dine ; I won't have you doing that sort of work."

During the pause that followed she tried to force herself to be wifely in her mental attitude towards him. He was doing his duty, and risking his life for it. Could mortal do more? And yet she found herself judging him severely because he took an interest in his dinner. She was unjust.

When she spoke again her voice was more sympathetic. "Have you made any plans for getting across the river, Philippe?"

Again he gave an unintelligible look. "Yes, plenty of them," he answered.

At this point Pierre came in, bearing a large tray. The simple dinner prepared for the ladies had only to be hurried a little for his master. Sylvia helped him draw a table to the fire, laid a cloth, and arranged the service.

"Ah, that is delicious," exclaimed Philippe, as the savory steam from the soup met his nostrils. "Here, Pierre, before I begin you may pull off my boots, and then bring me my slippers."

He held out his foot as he spoke. Sylvia looked aghast.

"The papers," she said, in a low tone.

He gave her an angry look, while Pierre did what was required of him.

She was puzzled, but not shaken yet in her belief. "I will get the slippers, Pierre," she said. "You must hurry with Monsieur le comte's dinner, for he will have to start as soon as he has eaten it."

"Yes, Madame," answered the servant, hastening away for the second course.

"You fool, can't you hold your tongue before him?" said Philippe, as the door closed.

"He is safe; I only said what he is sure to find out in a few minutes," she answered.

He gave a curious laugh. "Don't interfere with my plans as long as I don't with yours. How many husbands would be as patient as I have shown myself to-night? By Jove, how do you suppose I liked to come home after months

of absence, and find a man — an old lover, too
— in disguise, in your room?"

She turned white to her lips, but she looked
him in the face with eyes so full of outraged
dignity that his wavered. Pierre reëntered, and
nothing more was said until he had again left
them alone.

Then Sylvia spoke. " Your insult is unworthy
even of you. Show me the papers you have for
General Chanzy."

A sudden suspicion had leaped into her mind ;
she felt that she must speak so as to banish it ;
it shamed her to harbor it against her husband.

" That, my dear, is impossible," said Philippe,
carefully untwisting the wire about his champagne cork.

" Why? Where are they? What do you
mean?" she said breathlessly, resting her hands
on the table and looking across at him, stooping
so as to see into his face.

Philippe poured out a glass of the wine slowly,
not allowing the foam to rise ; then he drank it
with a sigh of satisfaction.

" The English way suits me ; a dry brand,
and serve it through the dinner after the fish
course," he said genially ; then he set the glass
down, and looked up. Sylvia's white face, so
condemning with its questioning eyes, maddened
him.

" Mind your own affairs," he burst out with violence. " You have no right to cross-examine me. All is fair in love and war, and by the Lord, both conditions existed this evening, it seems to me ! "

" You lied to Maurice and me? you had no papers ? " she asked slowly.

He shrugged his shoulders, and went on eating.

" Do you realize," she continued, " that you will be dishonored for life ? Maurice will tell at headquarters what you said."

" Maurice? He won't tell much ; he will be shot for a spy at daybreak. Idiot, to come inside the enemy's lines in disguise. I am sorry for him, but I must say such stupidity deserves death."

Was he telling the truth ? Sylvia felt that everything had stopped, except time, and as if that whirled by her so she could hear its progress. She must make one more effort.

" Philippe," she said, and her voice was pleading, " you are my husband, and my child's father. Tell me that what you just said is not true. Oh, for God's sake, do not let me believe that you betrayed the man who had risked his life to meet you, to save yourself alone."

He did not answer.

" Philippe, you have important news for

Chanzy? You are not willing to let me know of the danger you must run; you are sparing me, but I would rather know the truth. You are not really in earnest when you say you lied to Maurice?"

Hardened, brutalized as he was, he could not meet her eyes; he let his head fall forward on his chest.

"I only want one word, Philippe; for your mother's sake, for the sake of your son. Come — look at him, and then forgive me for having suspected you. Let me wake him, and place him in your arms, and teach him always to remember this night, when his father put honor first, and gave his life willingly for his country."

The shame which had bowed Philippe's head gave way to a heavy, sullen anger.

"Stop your high-flown talk; it is sickening," he said brutally. "I have done enough for my country; it is a lost cause; we are beaten. I am on my way to Monte Carlo; I am on sick-leave. Now you know the whole story, so keep quiet."

While he was speaking she had drawn away from him, gathering herself together. Then with one whispered word, "Traitor!" she swept from the room.

When she reached the end of the long gallery she paused like one dazed, and sank down on the

lowest step of the turning stone stairs. She felt
that a great calamity had come to her; something unheard of; a stain was on her, a corrod-
ing stain. There was no future; her life was
all compressed into this moment of realization.
And she had thought that she had known what
it meant to suffer. Never until now had she
imagined what shame was. As she crouched
in the obscurity she saw Pierre passing through
the hall with a freshly laden tray, and the sight
roused her. She was selfish, wicked, to give way
to her own feelings, when Maurice's life was in
danger. He must be saved. He must be saved!
But how?

Her mind worked rapidly, but she could find
no answer to the desperate question. There was
no one to advise her, no one to whom she could
turn for help. She thought of Monsieur Regnier, but he was on the other side of the river;
it would be mere loss of time to try to reach
him. Again Pierre came from her room, going
painfully towards the kitchen wing; no aid could
be sought from him, for he was too old and crip-
pled. Perhaps when Justine returned she might
suggest some plan. Even as Sylvia thought of
this, the fear struck her that it was probable
that the countess and the servant would pass
the night with the dying woman. The whole
country was sprinkled over with Prussians; their

homeward road might be intercepted, or again, they might be unwilling to leave their unfortunate charge to face death alone. She must depend on herself only, and she must act quickly. As she came to this conclusion, with a hopeless sense of its futility, she heard a sound of horses' hoofs. "They are bringing him back," she thought, and a gleam of hope flashed across the hopeless darkness. The door of the farther end opened once more, and again old Pierre came out, this time hurrying fast.

"What is it?" said Sylvia going towards him.

"Officers — Prussians — I am going to warn my master," he replied, continuing on his breathless way.

As he disappeared the great hall door was thrown open, and half a dozen men strode in. Sylvia stood under the hanging lamp, as if to welcome them; in her enemies she saw her chance to save Maurice. They spoke for a moment among themselves, and then one advanced towards her.

"You are the mistress of this place, Madame?"

She returned his bow. "I am the Countess de La Roche; I am an American," she replied. She felt that her nationality might be of some use to her.

The officer bowed again, and said, " I am afraid we must thrust ourselves upon your hospitality, Madame, for this night."

" My house is at your service, Monsieur ; in return I want your advice. A friend of mine was discovered here this evening by one of your countrymen ; he was naturally supposed to be my husband, and as he was in peasant's dress he was taken for a spy. He is no spy; but they took him to Chaumont, and — he is to be shot. How can I save him ? "

Sylvia, as she spoke, felt that every word was a lie. She was acting some strange part, too terrible to be true ; it was only grotesque.

The Prussian looked grave. " Prince Frederic Charles is at Chaumont for this one night," he said after a slight pause. " Your only hope is in him. You can prove that your friend was not here as a spy ? "

" I can," she answered.

" You had better go at once to Chaumont and plead your cause with the Prince," he continued. " I will give you a pass — you will need it. The villages are pretty well occupied."

" Thank you, Monsieur," was Sylvia's only answer, but her eyes spoke eloquently.

" I shall want something to write on," he said.

She led the way to her salon, carrying a lamp

to light them. The officer seated himself at her table, and wrote a few words on a piece of paper.

" There, Madame, that will help you to reach the Prince; more I cannot do; you must finish your task yourself. Now, with your permission, I will make the best of the few hours of comfort I may have here."

" The entire chateau is yours, Monsieur, except my room." She pointed to the door beyond which she had last seen her husband. " My baby is asleep there."

" He shall not be disturbed. Good luck, Madame."

The Prussian spoke pleasantly, but he was not sorry to be left to the enjoyment of a good night's rest.

Sylvia thanked him earnestly, and then, finding a fur cloak and a black lace mantilla in the hall, holding fast her precious paper she hurried out into the night. She hardly sent a thought back to Philippe, hidden like a thief in his own home; Pierre would save him. She did wish that she might have kissed little Louis once, that she had been able to tuck him into his crib; but even that wish was vague compared to the dominating idea, " Save Maurice." She, who had never humbled herself, would kneel to the Prince for him. She could not fail, she was strong. He should live.

Knowing a path skirting the vineyards belonging to the property, she was able to avoid going through the village, where, as she rightly conjectured, a detachment of Prussians was quartered for the night; but once beyond this boundary she was obliged to follow the main road. She bent her head, and kept steadily on against the cruel, exhausting wind, rushing down the valley as through a tunnel. A small band of horsemen passed her, bringing her heart to her mouth, but they did not notice the dark figure shrinking towards the leafless hedge. A little further along an ammunition wagon had broken down, and a group of soldiers was standing about it. She passed them, too, unchallenged. Then came the first town, a small place, but alive to-night; lights in the houses, people coming and going. This was the first test; would the words on the paper be of use here? A picket was walking back and forth across the road, the light from a window streaming out, making a wide track of yellow over the gray ground. There could be no shirking here.

Sylvia walked up to the man without a word, holding out her paper. He scanned it closely, folded it, and called a man lounging within the lighted room, who escorted her through the village, beyond the sentry at the other end. Now she could think, her mind being relieved of the

fear that her passport would prove useless. It
was a cruel privilege, for all the horrors of her
situation crowded upon her as she kept resolutely on, to save Maurice, unheeding cold and
fatigue. The brutal fact thrust itself before
her. The man she had married, her husband,
the father of her child, had deliberately sacrificed another man to save himself. A sob rose
in her throat, and she felt her eyes wet with
tears, as she thought of Maurice that evening
in her room. His dress had made him look
boyish, and the light in his eyes had banished
the expression of hardness and age which had
pained her the day she had seen him at La
Source.

"He is too young to die; too brave to be
sacrificed. Oh, my God, help me — help me
save him " —

She had no future; everything was chaos beyond this night's work. Her paper took her in
safety through the other hamlets lying between
her and Chaumont, and when at last the lights
from the castle on the hill twinkled high above
her, she felt that a lifetime had slipped by since
she left La Roche. The gate of the avenue was
guarded, but here, also, the few words did their
duty, and as in a dream she began to ascend the
long slope of the hill, a soldier by her side with
a lantern. The drawbridge was passed; the

courtyard entered; lights gleamed from every window; soldiers were coming and going; all was movement and bustle after the awful gloom of the night without. Sylvia saw her guide speak to one of the men, and they both looked at her; then they approached an officer who had just come out from one of the doors. He snatched the paper, read it hastily, and then came clanking towards her.

"You wish to see Prince Frederic Charles," he said, brusquely.

"Yes, Monsieur."

"Is your business important? He is much occupied to-night."

"It is a question of life and death, Monsieur." Sylvia spoke haughtily; the man's manner roused her.

"Step in there, and I will see what can be done," he replied, pointing to a small room under the entrance arch.

She went down the two steps leading to it. Three Prussians were seated by the fire, smoking. Two of them paid her no attention, but the third, hardly more than a boy, offered her his chair with a kindly look in his blue eyes. As she took it, bowing her thanks, she thought, "Oh, I hope no one will be gentle with me — I can't bear that; only let them be rough and rude."

Her lace fell over her face, and the cloak hid her figure. She sat in her place, unnoticed, for hours, it seemed to her, while doors opened and shut, soldiers hurried in and out, messages were delivered; and every moment the fear grew strong and the hope which had buoyed her up faded away. Maurice was here, in the same building — and he was under sentence of death — he would be shot at daybreak — Philippe had said so. In her absorption she did not shudder at the thought of her husband.

At last an officer entered, and approaching her told her to follow him to the Prince, who had agreed to see her.

"But, Madame, the interview must be a very short one," he warned her.

She bent her head, stifled by the emotions of the moment, but she followed him steadily, although nearly unconsciously. Her progress was a blank to her, and she was aware of nothing until she found herself in a small, lofty room; the windows, sunk deep in the walls and heavily barred, gave the effect of a prison; she understood vaguely that she was with the Prince, alone with him, although she had not noticed when her conductor left them. Afterwards she never was able to recall anything of the Prince's appearance, except two searching brilliant eyes, and a well-formed sinewy hand holding a pen. He was seated at a table covered with papers and maps, and at her entrance he had risen, and pointed to a chair which stood as if ready for her opposite his. Time was precious to the man of war; he looked impatiently at the silent figure before him, and then spoke a little abruptly.

"You will forgive me, Madame, if I remind you that I can only give you very little time."

Sylvia felt stifled; she undid the clasp at her throat, pushing the furs back, and drew the lace away from her throat. At first words would not come, but her eyes, heavy with pleading, her clasped hands, the swaying, beseeching attitude of her figure, above all her beauty, touched some chord in the heart of the Prince, and prepared him to listen with indulgence. Twice she opened her mouth as if to speak, and twice the lips trembled with the agony of fear; she could have faced anything for herself with unshaken courage, but it was Maurice's life which hung in the balance.

At last the words came, low, but distinct. "Monseigneur has a prisoner here, Monsieur le Capitaine Maurice Regnier; I have come to save him."

The Prince raised his eyebrows; if the question had not been so grave he would have been amused. "Regnier is the name you say, Madame?"

" Yes, Monseigneur."

He blew two shrill blasts on a whistle, and an orderly entered, to whom he gave an order. In another moment an officer came into the room, an elderly man, with a grizzled beard, and an indifferent, cold expression that seemed more ill-omened than an actively aggressive one. The Prince spoke to the newcomer in a low voice, evidently not meant for Sylvia's ears. She withdrew into one of the deep window recesses, where she could hear nothing ; but she watched them closely. The Prince's face grew grave and official. The officer spoke without gestures, and she could see no sign of any interest in his manner ; it was a matter of business, nothing more. When he had finished his account he stood motionless ; the Prince drew some figures in an absent-minded way on a bit of paper ; then he dismissed his subordinate, and looked towards the window. Sylvia came again to the table, and sat down opposite to him.

At first he did not look up, but went on making idle marks on the paper ; then with an evident effort he said : " This is a grave affair, Madame. Captain Regnier was captured within our lines in disguise ; you know what that means, of course ? "

" It means that he was taken for a spy," she answered with growing resolution ; " and I have

come to tell Monseigneur that he was not there
as a spy; he had crossed the river; he was nearly
frozen, and had left his wet clothes at a peasant's
to dry — but he was not there as a spy."

"Yet he passed himself off as the Count de
La Roche?"

As he said this, Sylvia's face grew rigid; it
might be that to save Maurice she would be
forced to betray her husband. The Prince noticed the sudden change in her expression.

"And," he continued, "he was found in your
room."

The memory of Philippe's insulting suspicion
rushed over her; if he could misjudge her, who
should know her character, what would a stranger
think? The blood surged to her cheeks, but she
remained silent.

Her confusion puzzled the Prince; it complicated matters; he went on slowly and impressively. "There is something more to be cleared
up, Madame. It is known that the real Count
de La Roche escaped from Paris by balloon,
and was traced to his chateau, where Captain
Regnier was taken; the count is strongly suspected of being the bearer of important papers,
and this Regnier was evidently in communication with him."

"But there were no papers," said Sylvia
eagerly.

The Prince bowed, with a smile which spoke volumes. She leaned towards him, her eyes looking straight at him, all alive with fire; all conventions were forgotten; it was not the Prince to whom she spoke; it was the man to whom she appealed directly.

"Oh, you must believe me — you must. My God, if there had been papers, I could have borne it better — but he only wanted to save himself, that is what makes it so terrible. If there had been any hope for France — any attempt even on his part to save her — I could have borne it — I should never have come here. Maurice would have died for his country, and I would have gloried in his death; but it was all treachery, all for private ends, that he was sacrificed."

She was superb in her excitement; the Prince looked at her with open admiration.

"I am still a little in the dark, Madame," he said. "You give me to understand that your husband was not the bearer of papers from Paris?"

"Yes, Monseigneur."

"And that Captain Regnier did not cross the Loire to communicate with him?"

She could not answer. Maurice should not be saved by a lie. The Prince gave her a searching look; her distress was so evident that it touched him.

" Why, then," he continued, "did your husband arrive in such a way, at such a time, within our lines, if he had no papers? You know, Madame, that it is not an easy matter to charter a balloon."

" Monseigneur, he was ignorant of the presence of your troops; he is invalided, and is trying to reach Monte Carlo; it was an accident that forced him to land as he did, — a bullet pierced his balloon, he was pursued, and hid in the chateau; the Prussians, on his track, entered, and found Monsieur Regnier. He believed, as Monseigneur did, that Monsieur de La Roche had important papers, and to save him took his place. Then, when I found out the mistake, I came to tell the truth to Monseigneur."

The first agitation had passed away, and the sound of her own voice reassured her; she was so strong in her knowledge, so sure that the truth must prevail now that she found herself face to face with her last chance, that her strong will reasserted itself. The man with the power of life and death in his hands sat looking at her with open admiration. He thought less of the supposed spy, condemned to a hasty death, than of the woman pleading for him, — her beauty, her courage, her energy, all appealed strongly to him. Accustomed to the study of men, he was convinced of the truth of her story. Besides, what did one French life more or less matter? Even if the case against Regnier were graver, yet it would be worth while to see that face with the glow of joy upon it which a word from him could call forth.

" Since seeing you, Madame, it is not impossible to believe that something better than duty induced this beau sabreur to risk his life crossing the Loire."

For a second she did not understand his meaning. Then, as it came to her that he, like her husband, regarded her with unworthy suspicions, the fine lines of her face became scornful. How small the minds were, capable of such low thoughts. She rose, for the moment forgetting everything but her insulted dignity, and drew her cloak about her.

" I thought that I was safe in throwing myself on the chivalry of Prince Frederic Charles."

His chivalry was touched as well as his heroism; he was too brave himself not to recognize courage in another. " And you were right. Wait, Madame," he said with respectful authority. " Sit down again, and wait. You have persuaded me that this man is no spy. What I am about to do is the action of the *Prince*, of the *man* — not of the officer. He was to have been shot at daybreak, for he would offer no explanation ; but here is his release." As he spoke, he wrote a few words rapidly on a piece of paper, and when he looked up again his eyes were kindly.

"You may take him the good news yourself."

She had won ; Maurice was free. The color rushed over her face and her bosom rose and fell. In her gratitude she could have kneeled to the man who had saved her hero ; no words came ; but she raised the Prince's hand to her lips, and her eyes spoke for her. He was touched and interested by the romance of the episode ; for a moment thoughts of warfare were banished, and he wondered what the end of it would be. In his turn he bent over her hand, and there was a sincere ring in his voice as he said, " Glück auf ! "

CHAPTER XXI

MAURICE REGNIER had been conducted to a
room high up in one of the massive towers of
the chateau, after a brief and unsatisfactory ex-
amination. He had given his own name, but had
resolutely withheld any other information. The
evidence that he was a spy was strong against
him, and his sentence was only what was to have
been expected in the unstable condition of affairs.
He was to be shot at daybreak. The officer con-
ducting the matter had been kindly enough in a
rough fashion, and had arranged to send for the
prisoner's father.

Captain Regnier's name was well known, and
gallantry is respected by gallant men in friend
or foe. The room where he was imprisoned
was but a section of the tower, and irregular in
form. Without, a covered gallery made the cir-
cuit of the building, and Maurice could hear the
measured tread of the sentinel as he made his
monotonous round. Escape was so impossible
that he had been allowed the luxury of solitude,
and there he waited alone for death. He had
not accepted the inevitable, however, without

first making every investigation for a possible escape ; but he was soon convinced that any attempt would be hopeless.

He dreaded the interview with his father more than anything. "But," he thought, "it is only what he and I have both faced all along, and neither of us looked forward to my death meaning more than a little barren personal honor ; now it means hope for France."

He had imagined Philippe's course when he found himself free ; had planned a hundred ways for him to cross the river, and tried to remember if he had told him where his horse was to be found.

Then a solemn wonder came to him : Would he ever know whether the sortie proved successful ? In a few hours death's mystery would be explained to him. By this time to-morrow the wisdom of eternity would be his — or oblivion. But that seemed too great an impossibility for him to grasp : there was no reality in the suggestion.

Over and under all these thoughts was the atmosphere of his love for Sylvia. How could the feeling die that sent the blood coursing through his veins ? No bullet could crush that out of existence.

"Poor child," he thought, drawing his hand across his eyes. "She believed that she could

save me, when she promised to — when she
kissed me." Then a wish rose in his heart that
she might die with him. " Philippe has never
been worthy of her ; but this may be the turning point in his life — he may come out all right
after all." In spite of the passing moments this
thought brought a sting ; but he crushed down
the unworthy feeling. " I should wish her to
be able to respect him — yes — love him, if she
can."

Gradually the solitude of his situation came
over him ; the stupendous isolation of dying.
His whole being seemed swallowed up in a glorious trustfulness ; words were nothing. He could
give no name to the Being he looked up to ; but
as with a flash of inward light he felt that the
love he had lavished on Sylvia, and the adoration for his country which led him to lay down
his life for it, were but symbols of higher feelings, nobler opportunities. If this world were
all, why had not some instinct pulled him irresistibly away from self-sacrifice, instead of irresistibly driving him towards it ? No prayer
was on his lip, but his mental attitude was worship. He could bear it all now ; not for himself
only, that was comparatively easy ; but for Sylvia and his father. His foot was on the threshold of eternity ; he thought that all his battles
had been fought, both with seen and unseen

foes. He felt that he had conquered self; but the supreme trial was yet to come.

Suddenly a sound disturbed him : some one was undoing the door from without, and he felt a wave of regret pass over him; for he thought that it was his father, and he longed indescribably to save him from suffering. He rose and found himself face to face with Sylvia. To her the sight of him came almost as a surprise. Until this minute she had gone on her way like a spirit; there had been no thought of self in her mind, only of what she must do. The intensity of force thrown by her into compelling everything to give way to her will had made her oblivious of her own personality. Up to the moment when she saw him, Maurice had been an idea, and she herself something elemental, working for this idea. But when she found herself face to face with him, the exalted look still about him ; when she realized how near he had been to a shameful, useless death : above all, when her long-smothered love broke into flame —then the strain was too much for her to bear, shaken as she was by the terrible emotions of the last hours.

The mere sight of Maurice seemed to promise her safety and protection, and she came swiftly towards him, her hands held out, her whole look one of triumph. Without a thought, instinctively, he put his arms about her and held her close to him. Her head rested on his shoulder; he felt a tremor run over her, then came the words, telling what he seemed to know already.

"My Maurice, I have saved you! You are mine — I am yours."

Was this the same man who, not five minutes before, had sat waiting for death? Everything faded and grew dim, except the one fact that in his arms rested Sylvia, her wonderful eyes storehouses of rapturous promise, looking deep into his own. Death, life, what were they? Shadows. Only this was real. He did not question what had brought her to him; it was enough to feel her presence.

Then the shadows deepened and became real again. This was a temptation, and his face had been turned heavenwards too recently for him to be able to shake off its influence. With infinite tenderness he drew away from her embrace, and putting his hands on her shoulders looked full into her eyes, an expression in his of wistful strength.

"I must not accept this sacrifice; you must help me to renounce you, my Sylvia. You are a wife and a mother. Not by word or look will I give you any cause for remorse hereafter."

"No, Maurice, in God's sight I am no wife. He won me by treachery away from you, my king, my hero. Love me, Maurice, love me — care for me. It is fate that brings me to you. I have always waited for you. Even as a child I adored honor, and bravery, and truth — and they mean you. Oh, do not send me away — I am so frightened. I cannot go back to him."

Tears came to her eyes, and her lips trembled; she clasped her hands, but still he held her from him.

"Sylvia, listen to me. You are, as you always were, my queen among women — my ideal. You say I am not to die; as yet I cannot understand it. I have been so near death; and as I looked forward, trying to see beyond the grave, you were with me as truly as you are now — you, my darling, and my father. Now let us think — help me, help me, for you tempt me sorely. Oh, Sylvia, I love you so, and I must give you up."

He turned away with a groan, his self-control shaken under the power of her face. She came close to him again.

"Hear me, Maurice — you do not know all. You must not believe that I come to you without a struggle. I have been brave, and true to my husband, for your sake. I knew you loved me, and I would not have you love a faulty woman. Until to-night I have been brave because you were; but now that I know what he is, my courage and strength have gone. I can struggle no longer."

She sank on a chair and bowed her head. The attitude of helplessness touched Maurice irresistibly; he came and knelt by her side.

" Tell me all; has he hurt you? If he has harmed a hair of your head I 'll kill him! "

As he spoke he took her hands in his.

" Oh, he has not hurt *me*. I could have borne that. It is *you* he has injured from the first. He lied about you to gain me in the beginning. He betrayed you to-night to save himself."

The anger in her eyes kindled an answering flame in his. His voice was very low as he said, " You say he took you from me by a lie — you say he betrayed me to-night? Think before you answer me, Sylvia, for a man's life hangs on your words."

She began to speak very slowly and deliberately. " He won me by a slanderous lie, — and still I kept my vow as his wife. I tried to turn even my thoughts away from you. Until to-night I considered myself bound to him; but then, when I found that he had deliberately sent you to your death, that he might dine — Oh, Maurice, the thought is driving me mad."

There was no deliberation now, the words came with feverish haste. " He was false all through — false — and a coward. There were no papers for Chanzy — there is no hope of a sortie — he is running away, and he lied to help himself."

Maurice had listened, growing whiter and whiter. He had crushed Sylvia's hands, still held in his, until she could have cried out with pain had she been less absorbed; then as if afraid of hurting her in his passion, he flung them from him, and turned away, a blind instinct warning him to hide his face, terrible in its rage.

Neither of them had heard Monsieur Regnier enter the room. He had been told on reaching the chateau of his son's reprieve, and tremulous with the unexpected joy had hastened to him. He had heard Sylvia's story, and his son's face shocked him when he turned from her. Maurice strode towards him, laying his hand heavily on the old man's shoulder.

"You have heard?" he said.

Monsieur Regnier bent his head.

"How soon can I leave this place? My work must not wait."

"You are free now, Maurice," answered his father; "your pardon is unconditional."

"Then you will care for Sylvia in my absence? She is mine now. I must go back to headquarters after I have killed that man."

He spoke as if no one could contradict or question his decision, but calmly spoken as it was, it conveyed a grim sense of finality that shook his listeners. Sylvia started up.

" Not that — not murder, Maurice," she said commandingly.

" And why not? " he answered sharply; " is it murder to kill a wolf? The man must die."

She came close to him, almost timidly; his heavy-contained anger was more fearful than any storm of ravings could have been.

" Maurice, my love, I have given you your life; I give you mine; but do not separate us forever by such a deed. How could I face my child if I loved his father's murderer? And God help me, nothing you ever did could keep me from loving you. If you do this deed, you kill not one but two — for now I cannot live without you — death would be better than life away from you — so I should die."

There was no answering softness in his face; it was set in lines of granite. As if he had not heard her, he repeated, " The man must die."

Sylvia looked appealingly at Monsieur Regnier. He spoke.

" There is another reason that Sylvia has overlooked why you may not have the blood of Philippe de La Roche on your hands. He has wronged you cruelly, but he and you are of the same race; I am his father's unacknowledged brother. When you recall that father, Maurice, and his many kindnesses to us, you will spare his son."

Maurice started. "There is a stain, then, on my birth?" he demanded.

"On mine," replied his father with proud humility. "I would have kept this from you, but the occasion demands a sacrifice."

The change of expression that the news had brought to Maurice's face died away, and it set itself again in the rigid lines of determination.

"The man must die," he reiterated sullenly.

The innate antagonism between them; the many insults he had received from the count; the treachery which had taken Sylvia from him, and the crowning baseness of this night's work, made a combination of deadly strength. He could not struggle against it. Monsieur Regnier took his son's hand in one of his and laid the other on his shoulder. The two men stood face to face, their eyes meeting in a look with which each seemed to read the other's soul. The patient dignity which stooped to plead, in his father's face, the clasp of the hand which seemed to promise sympathy and help, quieted Maurice. When the words came they found him able to listen.

"My boy, this night, not an hour ago, you were looking forward to death. Only you know

what thoughts came to you ; but if they were of
the life beyond, if you felt that this was not all,
had you no hopes, no fears? You bear in your
heart a great love for this woman ; she is all in
all to you ; can you expect to meet her after this
life, if you stain your hand with blood? You
might gain her for a while, but you would lose
her eternally. Is revenge, and revenge on your
own blood, sweet enough to justify this?"

Maurice buried his face in his hands. Eternity had been close to him this night ; its influence still hung about him. In the light of the
hereafter lesser things paled. For a moment
no one spoke ; then Sylvia, feeling that he was
shaken, began to move towards him, but Monsieur Regnier held her back.

" I have more to say, and it is for you both ;
you must hear me, my children, and you must
trust in the love behind the harshness. You,
Sylvia, I have taken to my heart as if you were
my own daughter ; you are not the only ones to
renounce ; and Maurice — my son — my only
son "— He held out his arms towards the
bowed head, and his eyes were full of the light
of love; his voice died away for a moment.

When he spoke again he seemed to tower
above his listeners, and his face was like the
face of an angel. He was pleading against the
love of this world, against all that makes life

beautiful; he was pleading for the life to come, and his words rang true.

"Sylvia, my child, you have a heavy burden to bear; only God and you know how heavy; but He will give you strength. Remember that this life is not all; it is only the stepping-stone to the life beyond. No one can live for himself alone. You are a link in a great family chain; if you tear yourself away you do infinite harm, not only to yourself, but to your child and his house. You have helped to give him a birth-right; you must not steal it from him for your own passion. You, and he, and Maurice will exist eternally. Each of you is responsible for all. The things of this life pass away — sorrow endureth for a night, but joy cometh with the morning. Let us each live so that when that morning dawns we can stand before the sun of righteousness, proud of our honorable wounds, borne for the sake of right. Pray for strength to give each other up. Beat down the wrong — be brave — rise to things eternal on the wings of self-surrender."

Sylvia's higher nature stirred; the months of struggle, of endeavor to conquer herself, had not been in vain. She had been weak for a while; she had lost sight of her standards under the strain she had undergone; but Monsieur Regnier recalled her from her short dream.

Even in the sudden burst of passion she had been dimly aware that sin would not be easy to her, and had rebelled against the under-stratum of her nature which almost compelled her to take the right path. Now she knew that it was the only one possible to her, and yet the idea of giving up Maurice nearly broke her heart. How could she tear herself from him, now that she had told him of her love ? As she thought of losing him out of her life she felt a reckless desire that he would kill Philippe — anything — everything, so that they might be together. Then she remembered her child, and the wild mood passed away. Once more she felt capable of all for the sake of right; she would renounce ; she would be brave. As she sent up a dumb, speechless prayer for help, Maurice lifted his head, and looked at her. Then she knew that her prayer was already answered, and that here was her help, for in his eyes she read his resignation of her, his victory over self. They had been hard tried, but they were conquerors. He stood where he was, his voice sounded muffled, and his words came slowly, as if refusing to obey his will.

" We must part ; there is no other way. But remember, Sylvia, that in life and in death I am yours and yours only : that you will be to me my star, always guiding me to the right : that the

love which might have been our ruin shall be, by
God's help, our salvation."

She came to him, and once more, for the last
time, put her arms about him.

"Good-by, my Maurice, my more than love —
my hero."

His hand trembled as he smoothed the soft
hair away from her brow, and for the last time
looked deep into her eyes; then he kissed her
once, and she felt that the consecration of their
lives to duty had begun as she turned and left
him.

They parted then with a steady resolve never
to meet again, and they were true to their vow
and each other. With their eyes fully opened
to what they renounced, they deliberately chose
the right: and their self-imposed cross, faithfully borne, gave them the wider wisdom, the
ampler sympathy, which is our inheritance from
Christ.

Little more remains to be said: passions fade
out, or are cut off, — and still life goes on. As
long as she lives Sylvia's love story will last in
her heart in the completeness of its incomplete-
ness. She left Maurice to take up her old life,
inspired by the thought that he and she had
suffered equally, renounced equally, and that
their recompense would be equal. To the countess she grew dearer each year, and became a

very daughter to Monsieur Regnier, giving and
taking a daughter's tender love. She soothed
the last moments of old Justine, who never rallied after that terrible night when she had given
her soul for her mistress. The poor creature
died unshriven by mortal priest, never having
confessed her sin. Sylvia, who did not understand her mental sufferings, did all that she could
to alleviate them, and had the comfort at the
very last to see a look of trust and joy on the
face of the dying woman as if an angel had
touched it. A long time passed before Philippe
came back to his home, broken in health and
spirit, more by his worthless life than by the
hardships of war. His presence has been Sylvia's heaviest cross, borne nobly for the sake of
right, and because of her boy from whose honest
brown eyes look out the spirits of the men who
made the name of La Roche a term of honor,
and those other sturdy ancestors of his who
helped to lay the foundations of a nation dear to
the hearts of its children, stretching from ocean
to ocean.

Maurice sleeps his last sleep in the chapel
with the old Counts of La Roche. He fell in
battle, his face to the foe, and they laid him with
his ancestors whose nobility he had inherited.
When Sylvia saw his sword placed on his coffin,
the sword he had wielded so nobly, she was able

to thank God that the man she had loved so well had gone to His presence glorified by the light of victory — victory over self. She felt that he was more wholly hers, because nothing could tarnish his memory. Eternally young, eternally brave, he is and will be to her death her hero without a blemish. She loves to sit under the protecting sweep of the old cedar, ever murmuring its mystic music, — a sleep-song for the dead soldier poet who had so loved it ; and as she touches its rugged bark, and looks through its solemn branches, there are times when the thin veil between her and the unseen world almost sways aside.

Happy ? It is not for me to say no. Is there place for unhappiness in the lives of those who are filling their days with the struggle for attainment and conquest, when we apply the words in their higher meaning ?

And had we the choice, would we dare, for a few years of pleasure in this life, give up the height, and depth, and breadth the soul may reach, through a noble sorrow nobly met?

Happy ? Let him who wore the purple, and touched the summit of earthly prosperity, answer : —

" If thou workest at that which is before thee, . . . keeping thy divine part pure as if thou shouldest be bound to give it back immediately.

— if thou holdest to this, expecting nothing, fearing nothing, but satisfied with thy present activity according to nature, and with heroic truth in every word and sound which thou utterest, thou wilt live happy. And there is no man who is able to prevent this."

www.ingramcontent.com/pod-product-compliance
Lightning Source LLC
Chambersburg PA
CBHW022010110726
47901CB00006B/1468